THE CONQUEROR

Raven reached out and her fingertips brushed his mailed forearm. "Don't go yet. Please."

And like that, deep inside of Griffyn, something that hadn't moved for a very long time suddenly shifted.

He grabbed her hand and pulled her into the night air, propelling her behind Noir, using the horse as a shield between them and the huts. His intention was clear and he barely dared breathe, waiting for her refusal. Let her pull back the slightest bit and he would step away, forget the whole thing, interpret her unsteady breathing as fear, her trembles as exhaustion.

But God, he prayed silently, *please let her move not so much as an eyelash.*

Why was his blood hammering so? Why was it hard to draw breath? He had barely touched her on two occasions, touches so innocent he could have performed them in a crowded room and barely brought a gasp. Why?

Because something about this small, courageous wisp of a woman was plunging into recesses of a desire he'd never known existed and his arousal pulsed hot and hard.

She let her breath out slowly. Her hand came up, brushed his armour and stopped.

"Raven . . ." he said, his words low-pitched.

"Aye," she whispered back, her eyes locked in his.

Without a thought for custom or destiny or anything other than the green-eyed angel before him, he bent his head to taste her trembling lips . . .

BOOK YOUR PLACE ON OUR WEBSITE AND MAKE THE READING CONNECTION!

We've created a customized website just for our very special readers, where you can get the inside scoop on everything that's going on with Zebra, Pinnacle and Kensington books.

When you come online, you'll have the exciting opportunity to:

- View covers of upcoming books

- Read sample chapters

- Learn about our future publishing schedule (listed by publication month *and author*)

- Find out when your favorite authors will be visiting a city near you

- Search for and order backlist books from our online catalog

- Check out author bios and background information

- Send e-mail to your favorite authors

- Meet the Kensington staff online

- Join us in weekly chats with authors, readers and other guests

- Get writing guidelines

- AND MUCH MORE!

**Visit our website at
http://www.kensingtonbooks.com**

THE
CONQUEROR

KRIS KENNEDY

ZEBRA BOOKS
Kensington Publishing Corp.
http://www.kensingtonbooks.com

ZEBRA BOOKS are published by

Kensington Publishing Corp.
119 West 40th Street
New York, NY 10018

All Kensington titles, imprints, and distributed lines are
available at special quantity discounts for bulk purchases for
sales promotion, premiums, fund-raising, educational, or
institutional use.

Special book excerpts or customized printings can also be created to fit specific needs. For details, write or phone the office
of the Kensington Special Sales Manager: Attn. Special Sales
Department. Kensington Publishing Corp., 119 West 40th
Street, New York, NY 10018. Phone: 1-800-221-2647.

Zebra and the Z logo Reg. U.S. Pat. & TM Off.

ISBN-13: 978-1-4201-0652-7
ISBN-10: 1-4201-0652-X

First Printing: May 2009
10 9 8 7 6 5 4 3 2 1

Printed in the United States of America

To my husband.
Through all our trials, a man who "gets it."
Who cared more if I was happy
than if I cooked or cleaned or did laundry
on days the Muse was hot.
Or the days She was cold.
Because he loves me.

No swords or swinging from chandeliers necessary.
You can be my hero.

Book One:

The Sowing

Prologue

Barfleur docks, Normandy, France
1 April 1152

"How much?"

The ship's captain looked suspiciously at the rough-hewn man before him. Rain slanted sideways on the empty Barfleur docks and it was dark, filled with echoing silence. Eerier still, though, was the way the man's dark hood was drawn forward over his head, his grey eyes glowing like banked coals.

"More'n the likes of ye can afford," the captain muttered and started to turn away.

A hand closed around his forearm. "I can afford more than the likes of you have ever dreamed of." A bag of coin was shoved into his calloused hand. "Is that sufficient?"

The captain lifted a bushy eyebrow, then dumped open the bag. Gold and copper coins spilled out, clinking loudly in the wet silence of the docks. He glanced towards the tilting, swaying sign of a pub several yards down the quay, then shoved the coins back in the bag and lashed it shut. "It'll do."

A low-pitched, mocking laugh met this.

He slid the pouch under his mantle and squinted against the glare of torchlight reflecting on the slippery docks. The man's cape blew in the misting rain; he was hard to make out as a figure of substance—he looked like black wind.

The captain fingered his grizzled beard. "How many did ye say there were of ye?"

"Thirteen."

He leaned closer, trying to discern a face amid the darkness of night and the hood the man wore. Even the man's horse, standing a few feet back, was so pitch black he could have coated a torch. "Aye. A right unlucky number, to be doing unlucky things, no doubt."

Bunched muscles lifted as the man—surely a knight— crossed his arms over his chest. "No doubt. But not as unlucky as you will be if you speak of this to anyone."

The captain touched the lump under his mantle. "Aye, well, when my mouth is spilling with good food and wet ale—and wet women," he barked in laughter, "it don't feel no need to be spilling tales."

The banked grey eyes regarded him levelly. The captain stopped laughing and cleared his throat. "Where to?"

"Half a league west of Wareham."

He froze. "What? A school of fish couldn't navigate that cove. Nay, I can't be taking the risk—"

The knight uncoiled suddenly. Without seeming to move, his hand was inside the captain's mantle, removing the pouch of money. "Someone else *will* take the risk, then. And the money."

"Now, sir, all right and all right," the captain mewed, licking his lips as he watched the bag hovering in the air between them. "I ne'er said I *won't*, just that it's unwise, my lord"— that phrase came from nowhere. What other than his manner bespoke this black, swirling shape as a lord of anything but trouble?—"and I can't be answerable for any misfortune."

He saw a gleam of teeth as the hooded figure smiled grimly. "I shall do many unwise things, captain, and not ask you to answer for any of them. At Prime, tomorrow, I shall be here with my men."

"*D'accord,*" the captain grunted, pocketing the money again with a sigh of relief.

The dark figure turned away. "And we have horses."

The captain spun too late. "Well, what the—" He stopped, realising he was alone, left to stare at empty darkness.

Chapter One

Six months later, October 1152
London, two hundred fifty miles south of Everoot's
principal castle, the Nest

The crush of people was enormous. Nobles they might be, but they were as noisome and unruly as a drunken crowd.

She wore a green gown. Woven of rare and expensive silk, it shimmered like an emerald waterfall. The bodice hugged tight, as did the sleeves, until they opened wide at her elbows and fell in graceful folds of silk. Ebony curls spilled down her back with loose sprays dancing by her cheeks. A thin circlet of silver clasped a light veil of palest green over her forehead. On the outside, she was a vision of proper breeding and improper beauty.

Inside, she was a simmering cauldron of nerves.

Guinevere de l'Ami, daughter of the illustrious Earl of Everoot, stood by the stone wall of the London apartment and clutched her empty wine cup so tightly it pressed her knuckles white. She smiled vacantly at a passing baron, who veered in her direction and smiled rather less vacantly, revealing a row of greyish teeth. Gwyn's heart sank. A young varlet carrying an ewer of wine passed next, and she leaned forward.

"May I?" she asked, smiling benevolently. Then she reached out and took the entire jug.

His unbearded chin dropped. He peered at his hand, then at her, but Gwyn was already weaving away through the crowd, pitcher tightly in hand. If anyone tried to take it from her, she'd crack him over the head with it.

Finding a small window alcove, she positioned herself beside the newest innovation, a fireplace, and tried to do two things at once: blend in with the stone wall and get smashingly drunk. Grimacing at the wine's oily flavour, she threw back a large swallow.

Fortification came in many guises.

There were few better places or, more precisely, more *grand* places, to fortify oneself with wine. This was the king's feast, hosted at the end of a grueling week of councils between the king and his mighty advisors. Men such as the wealthy Earl of Warwick and the powerful Earl of Leicester. Men with the status of her father. The few treasured loyalists amid these awful, bloody civil wars.

For sixteen years now, the English nobility had been cleaved in two. Families wrecked, friendships destroyed, legacies lost. Robbers ruled the roads and bandits sacked the villages. Underneath it all, the land had been gutted and raped. But now it was worse.

Already the news was spreading: the powerful Earl of Everoot had died. His heir, Guinevere de l'Ami, was a woman alone.

She quaffed another deep draught of wine.

The large great room of the London apartment was growing dark but, as the sun slowly set, a pale rosy hue streamed through the unshuttered window beside her, washing the room in a light reminiscent of fading roses and thinned blood.

Gwyn sloshed more wine into her cup, reflecting glumly on the sort of mind that went about creating gory metaphors of sunsets.

Losing one's beloved father not two weeks past might have such an effect, she supposed wearily.

Having one's castle besieged might better do the job. Even if one stood at a king's feast, two hundred and fifty safe, heartbreaking miles away.

She should have known.

When Marcus fitzMiles, Lord d'Endshire, spent the week following Papa's death doling out solicitude and concern like an almoner, she should have known something terrible was coming. Marcus fitzMiles was her nearest neighbour, her father's ally, and the most rapacious baron in King Stephen's war-torn realm, eating up smaller estates like pine nuts. And until Gwyn arrived in London last night, he was the only one who knew Papa had died. The only one who knew how undefended Everoot was. How undefended *Guinevere* was.

She should have known.

She lifted her chin and stared blindly across the room, eyes burning. She could not let it happen. Not so soon after Pap—. Not so soon—. Her throat worked around the tightness threatening to choke her. *Not now.*

She'd promised.

Then again, she reflected miserably, she'd made a lot of deathbed promises she simply didn't understand. But one does not bicker with a dying father when he asks you to guard a chest of love letters between him and your dead mother or when he tells you he was wrong, dreadfully wrong *(about what?)*, and begs you to "Wud. Guh. Saw." Whatever that meant. She'd knelt on the cold stone floor beside his bed and promised everything.

She swallowed thickly. Tension and fear and old, old shame flickered inside her belly like a curling red flame. She clutched her wine cup, fingers tight around its stem. *Where in perdition was the king?* Each minute gone was a minute more fitzMiles had to begin feeding on his largest platter yet, Gwyn's home.

She needed more wine. Spinning about, she plowed right into the chest of Marcus fitzMiles, Lord d'Endshire.

"Good heavens!" she screeched. A few baronial heads shifted towards the sound. Wine sloshed over the rim of her goblet.

"Lady Guinevere," Marcus said smoothly, taking the cup from her dripping hand.

"Give me that." She snatched it back.

A practiced smile inched up his mouth. He stretched his hands wide, all bemused innocence. "Indeed, you may have it, my lady."

"My thanks for returning what is already mine. Such as the Nest."

"Ahh." He inclined his head forward an inch. "You have heard."

"Heard? *Heard*?"

Marcus swept a casual glance around the room. "Indeed. Heard. As will everyone else if you do not keep your voice down."

"Keep my *voice* down? Be assured, Marcus, my voice will be raised so loudly to the king—and anyone else who will listen—that your *ears* will burn."

He raked a cool glance over her gown. "Happens you might be the one burned, Gwyn."

Her eyes narrowed into thin, blazing slits. Curled around the stem of her wine goblet, her fingers turned white. Had the cup been a man, it would have died a gruesome death. "Me? *Burned*?"

"Are you to repeat everything I say?" he queried with just enough true curiosity to send her teeth clicking together.

"Then let us have *you* repeat what *I* say, Marcus, to ensure understanding," she said in a low tone, practically snarling. *"You will never have the Nest."*

He shook his head with a small smile, as if deigning to correct a child who had erred. "Nay, my lady, you misunderstand.

I bethought your castle in need of reinforcements while you were away with so many of its knights."

"You sent your army to the Nest for my *protection*?"

"In truth, Guinevere, you yourself did seem well protected, with a score of soldiers to hand. A resplendent display, may I say, upon your entry into the city. And a wise choice, to assure any who might wonder on the strength of Everoot, with its lord so recently passed away. Nay, indeed, my lady, *you* seemed well protected." His mouth curved up in another smile. "'Twas your *castle* that was not."

Her hands balled into fists. The goblet in her hand turned upside down, spilling a stream of wine across the floor that went unheeded.

"The peasants and fools were mightily impressed by the show of force you came to the city with," he continued, then paused. "I was not."

"Which means you do not think yourself a fool, Marcus," she hissed, "but you err. I know what you intend to do and my king will hear of it."

"Recall, Gwyn, he is my king too."

That sounded distinctly like a threat. A crackle of tension jerked her head backwards an inch. Her lips barely moved as she replied, "I am certain King Stephen will listen to me."

"Perhaps he has already listened to *me*."

A buzzing started in the base of her skull. The room tilted slightly, sending the room and the contents of her belly at a distinct angle. "What do you mean? He has not agreed . . . he will not let you just take my land!"

His mouth curled up further in that disturbing smile. "Perhaps he would have me start with your hand."

In undulating pulses came the wave, washing over her so loudly she couldn't hear anything but its slow, throbbing beat. "What are you talking about?" Her words were whispered, scant.

He quirked up a brow. "Your hand. In marriage."

The goblet clattered to the ground. "Never," she whispered, backing away in horror. "Never, never, I would *never* wed you."

"Not even if your castle were . . . at stake?"

"God in Heaven."

"Of course, with my goodwill, lady, 'twould be a simple matter to see to your people's well-being." The smile dropped away, leaving his predatory eyes. "Which could be assured were my own well-being being seen to. By their lady."

"You're mad." She started backing up through the crowd. Startled faces peered down as they were brushed aside. "Whatever my father saw in you, 'twas a lie."

"He saw an ally, Gwyn. One most unwise to cross."

"I have sent my knights to fortify the Nest."

"I know. Which leaves you here. With me."

She threw her hand over her mouth, unable to believe this madness. All the blood ran from her face, racing down her body, until her knees wobbled. He watched her with hooded eyes.

Good God, he intended to wed her right here in London! He never meant to take the Nest by force, but by marriage. The siege had been a ruse to get her to do exactly what she'd done, leave her unprotected and at his mercy, never an overly large commodity in the best of times.

No, 'twasn't possible! Was he that cunning?

The answer came swiftly: most assuredly. This, and more.

She felt sick. Not again. Twelve years of self-imposed penance had wrought no change. Twelve years of denying every fickle intuition, bringing each emotion to heel, and still, in the end, they ruled her actions. Impulsive, reckless . . .

How many more people must die because of her?

Swinging about, she moved only two paces before being brought up short by the sight of King Stephen.

He was headed directly for her, the crowd parting before him in a river of samite and silk. He strode past great nobles with faint smiles and rich burgesses with polite nods, intent on her. Gwyn's knees quaked, her mind whirled.

Reaching her side, Stephen of Blois directed a faint smile towards Marcus, who had somehow positioned himself behind her. She could feel coldness emanating like a frozen river at her back, knifing through her gown and freezing her blood. Before she could do more than stare like a dolt at her king, he had her hand at his lips.

What was she doing staring straight into his eyes? She toppled down into a curtsey.

"Lady Guinevere."

"My lord King," she breathed reverently. Papa had spoken about this man for sixteen years, told of how he had taken the crown when the Old King died, how he'd held Mathilda, heir to the throne, at bay and bested the most skilled troops of England, how he had held sway over rebellious lords and money-hungry burgesses for almost two decades. Now he stood five inches away with his lips on her hand.

And Marcus at her back.

"Your gift was well-received," the king said, tapping a cluster of dried rose petals pinned to the inside of his vest. Gwyn had sent the rare, twice-blooming rose of Everoot along with her relief payment when her father had died.

She lifted eyes that had grown as round as the stopper on a flask. "'Twas well-sent, Your Grace," she stammered.

"It came with a message."

"Aye, my lord," she murmured, ducking her head again.

"Which spoke of the undying loyalty of the de l'Ami heiress."

She bowed her head further. "'Tis but a pale symbol of the devotion and constancy of your northern province, my lord."

"And a beautiful one, lady. One I will recall ere the need arises." He lifted her to her feet with a light touch on her hand. "Your father's loyalty was steadfast, and I will miss him. He was my friend."

"And so our name," she murmured.

"De l'Ami," the king mused with a faint smile. "*A friend*, and so he was."

"My father would have been honoured to hear you speak suchly. That he is gone brings me great pain, but the chance to do your will eases it, Your Grace. I am ever at your call."

The king's dark eyes regarded her bent head carefully. "I will remember that."

"My lord," Gwyn murmured. Her face was bleached white when she rose. There had been no chance to request an audience; he was already disappearing into the crowd.

She started to follow when Aubrey de Vere, one of the king's closest advisors, stepped into her path. Earl of Oxford, he was yet another with a chequered history of allegiances. Their fathers had been together on Crusade, though, and Gywn felt a small spark of hope that brightened when he grasped both her hands warmly in his.

"My lady, please accept my condolences. How sad I am to hear of your father's—"

"My lord Oxford," she interrupted, closing her hands around the edge of his palms, "I need an audience with the king. *Now*. Can you make it so?"

He squeezed her fingers back. "Surely, my lady," he said soothingly. "First thing in the morning, I'll review the king's schedule and—"

"No. I need to see him now." She pushed forward, craning to see around Oxford's huge shoulder. She pushed so insistently, in fact, that she might have completely pushed by, had he given even an inch.

"Ahh, but my lady," he said in a smooth, polished voice, designed to make her relax. It made the hair on the back of her neck stand up. "The king cannot. He has had too many demands on his time this evening."

"That is ridiculous," she snapped. "He is right there. It will only take . . ." Her voice drifted away as she became aware of two things: one, the king was nowhere in sight; he'd hurried—

or been hurried—away with astonishing speed; and two, the earl of Oxford and Marcus were holding each other's gaze over the top of her head. Oxford gave an infinitesimal nod.

Cold fear dripped down her spine. She stared without sight at the back of someone's blue gown, heart thundering in her chest. The earl lowered his gaze and bowed with a gallant flourish, his polished smile firmly in place.

"First thing in the morning, my lady, upon my word. Would you care to stay here at the king's residence, to ease your travel back in the morn? No? You needn't be startled, my lady; 'twas but a question. Well, then, in the morning."

He moved away through the crowd like a ship cutting through water. Gwyn's head spun. Shivers spidered across her skin, a web of tingling terror. This was not possible. St. Jude, this could not be happening.

Marcus's voice murmured by her ear, "You know, Gwyn, the king thinks your loyalty will hold *me* to his cause as well. Who knows but that it will? With such beauty to come home to"—he picked up a strand of her hair in his fingers—"mayhap I could find some measure of loyalty in my heart."

She stomped her heel on his boot and fled.

Only after he'd searched the crowd for her, after he'd poked his nose into every crevice and cranny for the green-eyed beauty, only then was Marcus fitzMiles forced to admit she had left. The little fool.

She thought to be rid of him so easily? Not with an earldom at stake. And more to the point, not with an estate once worth some two thousand marks annually clasped between those shapely thighs. Nay, be she a trull with eyebrows that met in the middle, the Countess d'Everoot would be worth the agony.

When Ionnes de l'Ami had died a fortnight back, a fact Marcus knew simply by virtue of being there when it happened, he swooped in immediately, deciding the raven-haired birdling in the Nest had simply become far too tempting.

And, to his surprise, found he had to bide his time. Lady Guinevere's wings may have been inexperienced but they'd never been clipped, and what she lacked in leadership, she made up for in her capacity to earn loyalty. Her knights were like attack dogs. Marcus found he had to cluck and pet them when what he wished to do was kick them from here to the Cinque Ports.

So he waited, standing at her side when her father was laid in the crypt, offered condolences which made her frown, extended administrative counsels which she shunned with an airy disdain—and which he tolerated with a smiling good grace that made his jaw ache—and waited. Biding his time.

But the waiting was over. De l'Ami was dead, d'Endshire soldiers were at her gates, and King Stephen was in disarray, unable to offer more than feeble resistance to the takeover, if indeed he offered any at all. The king had not agreed to his petition to wed Guinevere, fool that he was, but if the countess believed it, so much the better. It would be easier to convince her.

But easy or not, Guinevere would be his wife. The Everoot empire had some of the deepest roots in all England, tendrils that spread in a series of manors and forest rights from Scotland to the Irish Sea. And the Nest in Northumbria was the heart of the wold.

And in that beating heart lay a treasure far too spectacular to be imagined.

He scanned the crowd one last time. She was indeed gone.

He wanted to spit on the fragrant rushes in fury. Shouldering through the crowd, he found one of his men outside the huge wooden doors. "Find the Countess Everoot; she'll be at her home on Westcheap. Keep her there until I arrive."

The knight turned to go, but Marcus clasped his shoulder and spun him back around.

"And send for the priest," he hissed.

Chapter Two

Twenty minutes later, d'Endshire kicked open the door to the Westcheap apartment. Throwing off his cape, he stood momentarily in the flame of torchlight, then looked to the grim-faced knight who stood beside the door.

"She's gone, de Louth?" he asked.

The place was in shambles, as if a storm had moved through. Shelves were cleared of their contents, swept in wild disarray over the floor. Clothes were scattered over the rushes and benches and a toppled trestle table was upended in the shadows. Tapestries that once hung on the wall lay slashed to ribbons on the floor. But there was no woman.

De Louth nodded grimly. "She left everything behind." By way of illustration, he picked up the end of a gossamer length of yellow silk trailing down the stairs. The delicate fabric caught on his calloused hand as he held it out for inspection. Marcus barely glanced at it.

"Gone when we arrived, my lord. No woman, no servants, no guards—"

"And no chests, I'll venture?"

"Chests?"

"Coffers. Chests. Small wooden boxes."

The reply was indeed dry, but not as dry as de Louth's mouth became. He shook his head.

"She made a speedy exit but I didn't see where she left any small chests behind, other than the one at the foot of her bed. And we went through that. See for yourself." Marcus pushed by and took the stairs two at a time.

The room was in greater shambles than the downstairs. Dresses and tunics were thrown about in long, twisting heaps of colour. A candle had been knocked over and hastily extinguished, its thick tallow congealing in a warm puddle on the floor. Marcus's gaze swept to the chest. The padlock was wrenched in hideous twists of iron, the chest's curved lid flung open.

He crouched on his heels, fingering the twisted iron latch.

"Nothing?" he asked, his tone alarmingly soft. "You found *nothing*?"

De Louth swallowed. "This." He extended a small silver key, hung on a rusting linked chain. Marcus unbent his knees. "I found it on the floor, my lord. Looks like it fell when she fled."

"Christ on the Cross," Marcus murmured, almost reverently. "One of the puzzle keys." He pulled the chain from de Louth's palm, his eyes locked on the steel key, his voice soft and almost crooning. "I recall seeing this, years ago. There are three, you know." He slid the long silver chain between his fingers, smiling faintly.

"No, my lord. I didn't know."

Marcus's eyes snapped up. "Find her. Tonight. *Now*."

"My lord." De Louth choked out the words and left the room. The gossamer veil he'd held in his hand fluttered to the floor, a tawny splash of colour against the dull wood. Marcus barely spared it a glance as he trod behind his man, crushing it under his boot.

* * *

Gwyn dug her spurs hard into the horse. "I am sorry," she muttered, and then did it again.

Steam rolled from the stallion's flared nostrils as he snorted in anger and half rose on his hind legs, his monstrous hooves pawing at the air before dropping back to the earth. Great clods of damp earth flew into the air as he leapt forward in a ground-eating gallop.

Gwyn rolled wildly around on the saddle, jamming her pelvis into the pommel before righting herself again. Biting her lip to clamp down on a screech, she bent low over the horse's withers and guided him with a deft but trembling hand.

Sunset had come and gone, evening had turned into night, and she was barely two miles from London and the danger it held.

When she had arrived back at the apartments on Westcheap, no one had been present, not even Eduard and Hugh, the two young knights left behind to guard Gwyn when the others were sent north to relieve the siege. The house had been eerily quiet. She'd flown through the dark rooms, skidding on her knees to a stop in front of the huge oak chest at the base of her bed.

Gowns and smallclothes and bolts of bright fabric flew into the air as she searched frantically for one of the "promises," the small, simple but exquisitely-wrought chest her father had bequeathed to her on his deathbed. The padlocked, curved chest held letters of love her father had written to her mother when on Crusade.

She was *not* leaving it behind.

She almost screamed in frustration as she flung another handful of underlinens over her head. Through the window floated the sound of booted feet.

"Please Jésu," she begged softly, practically in tears. As if in answer, her hand alighted on a soft, bulky felt bag. She grabbed for it and tore a fingernail in half on an iron hinge.

An unintelligible shout blew through the window.

"A few more doors up," answered another.

Sweat pouring down her chest, she flung herself to her feet and grabbed the one remaining pouch of silver. The chest tumbled out of her hand and fell, spilling parchment scrolls across the floor. Gasping, she bent and swept up the box and the parchments. Tying both satchels around her waist, she clattered down the stairs to stare wild-eyed about her. Hair tumbled from its knot as she shook her head, trying to clear it.

Eduard and Hugh, the two guards left behind for Gwyn's protection, were still nowhere to be found. One thing was certain; she couldn't waste time to find two errant knights. Spinning into the stables, she saddled a sidestepping Crack, Hugh's newly acquired warhorse. He would be heartsick at finding the stallion gone.

"'Twill teach him a lesson," she huffed as she guided the sensitive, thousand-pound behemoth to a block of stone and scrambled into the saddle, throwing her leg over top. She had no time for wayward knights, less so for the niceties of riding sidesaddle. Reining around, she shot out of the stable yard less than ten minutes after returning home.

Aldersgate would be long closed, as would all the gates leading in and out of the city. She galloped towards it, slowing only when it came into sight. A hefty bribe ensured she was allowed passage through. It also ensured anyone who wanted to follow her could, but there was little she could do about that. Trotting under the gates, she had kept to a placid pace until a rise in the land and a copse of trees hid her from view. Then she'd dug her spurs into Crack and sent the wind whipping by her ears.

The autumn night was chilly and damp. Thin slivers of fog hovered a foot in the air like ghostly ribbons. Crack's churning forelegs tore through them, sending the mists spiraling away to cling around tree trunks and reeds. The only sound was the cold wind whistling by her red-tipped ears.

Crack suddenly threw himself up in the air, ploughing the earth into furrows with his hind legs, his head swinging to and fro in fury at the conflicting messages of bit and spur. Gwyn pulled harder on the reins and threw one terrified glance over her shoulder. It couldn't be. Not so soon.

Hooves. Coming up on the road behind her. At a dead gallop.

She slapped the reins against his shoulder, sending him into a frenzied, bounding leap. Hair stuck to her neck in long, sweated claws. She plucked at them furiously, gasping for breath. Twice she craned her face over her shoulder and peered through the whip-like strands of hair. Each time there was nothing, only low ribbons of fog, deepening darkness, and the thundering of hooves dim beneath the sound of her pounding heart.

A third twist in the saddle brought the awful sight: the outline of five horsemen and their monstrous stallions on the crest of a small hill. With billowing capes, swords swinging from their sides, and steam pouring off their surging mounts, they looked like spectral beasts from Hell.

She dug her heels into Crack. The boggy, pockmarked highway was dangerous in daytime but an exercise in madness at night, which is why it was with a curse but no surprise that she almost pitched over the horse's head as he went down on his knees, his hooves splayed in four different directions. A wave of mud crashed over the saddle.

She slithered off. The stallion threw his head into the air, his eyes red and wide and wild, then scrambled up and raced away into a stand of trees, leaving Gwyn on her knees in the centre of the road, muddy and bedraggled and utterly alone.

Chapter Three

"Dear Lord, save me, for 'tisn't possible to do so myself," she whispered, staggering back to her feet.

The moon was rising and she could just make out the crossed swords that heralded Marcus's device as the five soldiers advanced. One was a knight she recognized as part of Marcus's personal guard: de Louth. The others were men-at-arms clad in hauberks and steel helms. She stood, wiping mud from her chin and chest.

On they came, the soft clop of hooves turning into a sucking sound as the horses waded into the edge of the wide mud puddle that had sent Crack flying. She locked her eyes on de Louth, riding two paces before the others. Five against one.

"My lady Guinevere?"

His voice carried in an eerie echo through the darkness. They were about twenty paces away. "My lady? Lord Endshire sent us to seek you."

"You may tell him," she said in a breathless pant, swirling her skirts around her ankles as if straightening them, "that you found me in good spirits, and do thank him for his concern."

The knight paused, checking his horse momentarily. The others stopped behind him, dark mirrors. Their eyes were almost invisible under their helms, their noses covered by the trunk-shaped nasal that fell down from the steel.

De Louth cleared his throat. "He sent us to assure your safety."

"Be assured, sirrah, Lord Marcus sent you to assure his *wealth*."

De Louth touched his heels lightly to the horse's side and began moving forward again. She swallowed a ball of fear. That would never do. Hair plastered to her mud-streaked face, she lifted her chin.

"I am well safe, sir, and would appreciate being left alone to be on my way."

The men checked their progress again, exchanging glances.

"What foolishness, this, my lady?" De Louth's voice was pitched around surprise. "We have left the king's court behind where such pleasantries count for something. You are alone, un-horsed, on a deserted highway. And you think yourself safe?"

She shifted her weight and mud squished out of her slipper. "Safer than with your lord, methinks, and I will stay here until my horse returns."

The knight chuckled, a low, amused sound as the five advanced further through the fog. "Do you know, my lady, there was rumour only yester morn of one of Henri's spies inhabiting this very stretch of highway? What do you think he would do if he found one such as you upon it?"

"Mayhap the same as you? Truss me up on the back of a horse and take me where I don't want to be?" She pushed her sleeves up her arms. They slid back down to her wrists, wide, embroidered things that were more irritating at the moment than was warranted. "I have already been enlightened as to what awaits me with my lord Marcus, and prefer to take my chances with the Norman rogue."

"'Tisn't a *chance* of what the baron will do, Lady Guinevere." His steel conical helm was closer now, and mist-laden words rose out from beneath it. "'Tis quite certain, if you gainsay him."

"Only if you bring me back."

The small group fell silent, standing off in the mists. De Louth guided his men forward carefully, reining to a stop every few paces as if she were a wounded animal they were set to trap. The hooves of the huge warhorses settled in the mud, slid a few inches, then lifted again with sickening, sucking sounds.

A thick stand of trees extended on her left and right, an outcropping of forestland. Looking frantically over her shoulder, she saw only an empty road and darkness. No buildings, no people, no escape.

Wild-eyed, she scooped up a handful of rocks and retreated a pace. They came on. Backing up again, she ran smack into a tree.

"This isn't going as you planned, is it?" asked the tree.

Fear oozed down her spine. She lifted her face to behold a towering caped figure. Sheer black against the mists, his square-shouldered silhouette with trailing cape was like a mythical beast. She moved her mouth, but no sound came out. From eight inches above, his eyes were fixed on d'Endshire's men.

"Step behind me, lady."

"What?"

"Step behind me if you would be safe." Grey-blue eyes flicked down briefly and she saw the outline of a fixed jaw and straight nose before he lifted his head again. "Why do they want you?"

"Do you know who they are?" she murmured through utterly dry lips.

"I do." His voice was low, rumbling and unruffled.

She looked at the halted line of soldiers. They were staring in amazement at the sudden apparition and she felt the first inkling of reprieve. A bit of moisture seeped back into her mouth.

With one arm the apparition flung back his cape and stepped in front of her. "Why do they want you?" he prompted calmly.

"*They* don't. Lord Endshire does."

Something flickered in the gaze he dropped to her. "Marcus fitzMiles wants you?"

"Not quite. My money."

"Ahh," he said companionably, his eyes on the now-advancing line of knights. "He's never been one for surprises."

"Who dares assault my lord's betrothed?" called out de Louth. The soft hiss of swords sliding from scabbards made a steely-leather hush in the damp darkness, then there was silence.

"I'm not his betrothed!" she shouted over her saviour's arm, then lowered her voice. "He sent his men to assure me I wished to wed him."

"Mmm." Silence except for the sound of back-stepping boots and advancing hooves. "They've done a rather poor job of it."

"The army at my castle was to succeed should they fail."

"No surprises," she heard him mutter.

Then, before her mind could register movement, he swung to his right under a giant oak tree and raised the most monstrous-looking longbow she'd ever seen. He tugged one of three arrows from his belt. Sweeping the bow in an arc overhead, he pulled the string taut to his jawline and peered down the length of the weapon.

De Louth flung his arm to the side, halting his men. "We want only the lady, rogue," he called out. "You'll not be taken to the sheriff, nor accosted in any way. You have my word on that. Just give us the woman."

He barked in genuine laughter, the sound startling amidst the deadly, somber scene. "And you have my word on this: you will leave without the lady. If you try to take her, your blood will spill across the false king's highway. And you will still leave without her. Go, now."

Gwyn started. *False king's highway*?

"Not without the woman."

The apparition, who was becoming quite real, lowered a square chin and sighted along the arrow shaft. "The lady stays."

One of de Louth's men spurred his horse forward, visions of gallant knights brighter in his mind than good sense. An arrow hummed in the air and sliced through his windpipe. He slid off, spinning as he fell. Gwyn caught a glimpse of a wicked tip, bathed red, nuzzling out the other side. A flutter of bloody hands, a strangled cry, and the soldier hunched sideways, dead on the road.

The other four stared in astonishment, but the man at her side already had another arrow notched and ready for flight. Silence descended. The terms were clear: no more arrows would be launched if they left, and they were not leaving.

"Oh my," she breathed, touching his arm. "You've killed one of Marcus's men. He will not be pleased."

In the distance, de Louth dropped his foot from the stirrup and kicked the dead man onto his back.

"Endshire's pleasure has never been my concern."

She dragged her gaze up to his shadowed face. "You are either foolish or mad. Let me tell you of Marcus's pleasures. Once he was so enraged by the death of his merlin that he smeared his falconer, d'Aubry, with honey and staked him on an anthill for five days. D'Aubry did not return, at least not all of him."

He glanced at her.

"Marcus has served honey at every meal since. Warmed over," she emphasised.

A pair of muscular shoulders shrugged. "As I said, Endshire's pleasures are not my concern," he murmured, and something close to comfort pulsed through her heart.

Reaching down, de Louth tugged the arrow free from the dead man and looked at it. A glint of silver flashed across the road as the moon emerged from behind the clouds, then de Louth dropped the arrow. He slid his boot back into the stirrup.

Gwyn wrapped her cape tighter around her shoulders. "I ought to force you to leave this matter to me—or me to it—and take your leave, while your hide is still intact."

"I would not go."

"And I would not have you end up as d'Aubry the falconer."

"My hide is not a matter for Endshire to decide." He glanced down, one corner of his mouth crooked in an infinitesimal grin. "And I prefer sweeter things than honey, my lady."

She was about to smile back, could have smiled, *wanted* to, but didn't. It simply did not make sense, given the circumstances.

De Louth was straightening in his saddle, turning to his men and speaking in a low voice.

"Well," she said, squaring her shoulders, "if you're so determined to see to your death, I won't be ungrateful." Neither of them looked away from the line of sword-bearing soldiers as they continued their conference in low voices.

"Have you a weapon?" he asked.

"A rock."

"A *rock*? Do you know how to throw one?"

"Know how to throw one? Perdition! You just . . . throw it."

He grunted, and the men dropped off their horses. In the length of time it took her to inhale, her rescuer had dropped his bow, unsheathed his sword, and pushed her behind him, away from the circle of soldiers closing in on him.

All bore broadswords and some held falchions and wickedly sharp daggers. They came forward in a jagged arc. The forest hunkered on the other side.

Her liberator swung at legs and arms, desperately outnumbered, but did not appear desperate in the least. He crouched on slightly bent knees, his eyes flitting back and forth with an expert's care, moving with the grace of years of practice.

One of the soldiers stabbed forward, slicing her saviour's tunic open before he leapt back. His unmarked surcoat and tunic fell away, revealing the steel rings of a mailcoat. He wore armour. Expensive armour that was well-fitted, and carried a gleaming sword worth a small manor.

Who was this rich rogue who stalked deserted highways and

rescued demoiselles in distress, at peril to his own obviously noble neck?

Another clash of steel rang out, more flashing sparks, and another de Louth minion went down, dead on the road. Everyone backed up a few wary steps, and all was quiet except for laboured breathing and the gritty sound of boots on dirt as the men circled one another.

Sheer numbers assured Marcus's men of their victory, although their eyes flicked occasionally to their slumped comrades with a wary glance. Neither party appeared willing to abandon the fight.

"I think we've got them now," Gwyn observed between pants as she kept her body conspicuously behind her warrior's rock hard, pounding-heat body.

"You do, eh?"

She gripped several rocks so tightly. "I do."

He swept his gaze down for a second with a faint smile. Blue-grey eyes, a body packed so solid with muscle it was like a mountain, and that smile. She felt another wild spark of hope. Three against one were not favourable odds.

On the other hand, it used to be *five* against one.

Another surge of reckless hope. It forced a smile through her fear.

"You're enjoying this?" he enquired, looking back at their assailants. "There's a riot by the bridge I can take you to when we're finished here."

"This will do nicely, thank you."

He suddenly pushed her, hard, away from the circle of soldiers closing in on him. De Louth and his minions advanced in a line this time, swords grasped with two hands and swinging before their bodies. They backed her saviour up against the edge of the forest. His boots slopped through the muck.

Gwyn started flinging rocks, trying to distract them, but no one noticed. Perhaps that was because she hadn't hit anyone. Cursing herself, she scooped up another handful and pelted the men with the small, stinging missiles. One clanged against de Louth's helm.

As if it mattered. She might be what they were hunting, but she mattered naught anymore. Blood-lust had overtaken their 'rescue' mission, and she could hear their soft grunts as they parried closer and closer to their prey, taking no notice that they shoved her out of range as they did so.

Her champion backed up and stumbled. One knee hit the earth.

"Over here!" she screamed.

Three pairs of eyes snapped to her. She started running.

One soldier stumbled to his horse and spurred towards her. De Louth and the other paused, momentarily distracted. In that pause, her saviour took his chance. Dropping to his other knee, he caught up his bow and launched two arrows in rapid succession.

The second hit its mark first, embedding itself deep in de Louth's thigh. He dropped to the ground, screaming. The first hurtling arrow travelled further.

It punched through the boiled leather armour protecting the chest of the rider just as he leaned sideways to scoop up Gwyn. He jerked backwards, his hands a death grip on the reins. The horse flung its head madly, skidded to its knees, and collapsed. Gwyn tripped and fell.

From nowhere, her rescuer's hand closed around her wrist.

"Come," he rasped, pulling her roughly to her feet. At first they didn't see the dagger wrenched from the last soldier's belt and flung. There was only the soft *whoosh*. Everything dropped into slow motion. The iron blade tumbled and flashed through the air. Gwyn loosed a long, slow scream.

Her saviour shoved Gwyn one way and himself another, but the move made him vulnerable to the soldier hurtling towards him, standing over him, raising a sword. He twisted reflexively, taking the blow on his back rather than his chest, from a fisted hilt rather than a whetted blade. Still, it was a thundering impact that knocked him to his knees.

D'Endshire's mercenary straddled his body and raised his sword again for the death blow.

Gwyn went streaking through the air, without a thought and with the rather dubious weapon of a raised slipper covered in muck.

The soldier glanced over in astonishment and spun to avoid the impact, sending his sword careening harmlessly into the earth. Gwyn nailed his forehead with her slipper, then landed square on his shoulder with the even more doubtable weapon of her belly. The bluntness of the attack was offset by the fury behind it, and the two went flying.

Gwyn groaned as they landed, her lungs crushed by an armoured shoulder. The soldier rolled to his feet, clutching his head with splayed fingers. Blood poured from between them. He stared blearily at his hands, then her, then back to the sticky mess dripping between his fingers.

This time, when he lifted his head, his teeth were bared around a roar that blew her hair back from half a yard away: *"Bitch!"*

Dropping onto her prone body, he wrapped his gloved hand around her throat. "My lord is a fool for wanting a piece of you, hellion," he rasped. "I'll save him the trouble."

Slow, hard pounding. No breath, only choking. Her chest was raw, her lungs screaming. She resisted the urge to pass out, fighting for her life. Strange images passed through her mind: her beloved Windstalker chomping hay, her father at dinner, the wardrobe where she kept the spices, undone chores.

The surprisingly calm query "Did I remember to freshen the rushes?" wafted through her mind, and it was then she knew her life must be over.

The thudding pain in her head meant nothing beside the pain of knowing she would die with a pounding Ache in her heart and a hundred dirty table linens on her conscience.

Chapter Four

Fading into unconsciousness, Gwyn didn't realise the weight was gone until the warrior stood above her, sword dangling in hand, blood streaking down the side of his face.

Beside her lay the bloody-headed soldier, rather more bloodied now. His skull was split in two. Already his innards were oozing out, a pulpy mass, mixing with the mud.

Gwyn's mouth began moving but no sounds came out. In the distance, the sounds of running footsteps faded away. Her saviour spun as if to give chase, then, with a few muffled words, turned back.

"Is he dead?" she whispered, as if someone might hear her and somehow not have noticed the combat of a moment ago. As if the hacked body might still, somehow, hold life and be awakened by her words.

Dark, shadowed eyes flicked to the prone body. "Quite." He kicked the body away and stretched out a gloved hand. "Come."

"Completely?"

"All the way." He held his hand in front of her nose.

"Truly dead?"

"Nay, he's but half dead, and will haunt you for years to come. Now, come, get up."

Flat on her back, Gwyn frowned. A gnashing pain crowded

into the back of her head. "I am more afraid of being haunted if he is *fully* dead, sirrah."

This brought a moment of quiet. "Are you getting up or not?"

"Have you killed so many men, that one more means naught?"

He straightened and glanced around the deserted road. When he turned back, she could see only the gleam of his teeth as he smiled grimly. "And you, lady, have you been on so few highways that you know not the danger of riding on them alone?"

She opened her mouth, shut it again.

"Know you so little of men that you would think one such as he is not better off dead?"

Again he gestured to the man's body. His smile receded as he ran his fingers through his hair, ruffling the dark locks into damp spikes.

"Know you how weary I am, and that I wish only to be home?"

He towered above her outstretched body but she was not afraid. Certes, he'd just saved her life. Whyfore be affrightened?

Her mind catalogued the various and persuasive reasons: perhaps because he was such an imposing figure, all hard slabs of muscle and piercing eyes? Perhaps because he'd just killed four men in less time that it took to de-feather a chicken? Or perhaps because he held in his hand a sword that still dripped with raw blood.

"Get up."

"I . . . I—"

"*You*—" He reached down and grabbed her hand. "Do not listen well."

He lifted her clean off the earth, hauling her away from the body. The soldier's split head lolled to the side and a thin trickle of reddish spittle dribbled from the corner of his mouth. Dropping to one knee, her saviour lifted his chin, as if inspecting his handiwork, then crossed to the other dead men and did the same before dragging them to the side of the road.

Her saviour's next words came from the dense stand of trees, where he was depositing the still-warm bodies. "We've only a little time. D'Endshire will know as soon as de Louth reaches the gate, and then he'll be after you."

"Or *you*." She ran her hands over her dress from collar to waist, fluttering. "Happens he might enjoy finding you more, at the moment."

There were sounds of shuffling and earth moving, then he emerged with a costly steel arrow-tip in his palm. She stared in horror. It could only have been plucked from the dead man.

He picked up his sword. "As I have said, his pleasure is not my concern." Lodging the arrow-tip in his belt, he walked towards her, sliding his blade back into its sheath with a whispery sound. He retrieved his bow, lying beside the oak tree. Then he whistled.

From nowhere came the sound of a snorting horse, and a raw-boned rampager appeared from between two giant oak trees. He looked like a furry error, all slanting edges and legs. He wore a bitless bridle inlaid with silver, though, a headpiece that would cost more than a bribe for the Nottingham sheriffdom. Costly finery for an error.

The warrior made a gesture with his hand and the horse started picking his way over. She watched as he ran an affectionate hand over his horse's neck, murmuring in the tongue of the Normans to his obviously beloved mount.

Her gaze drifted aimlessly, then froze. Why, there was her slipper, huddled along the side of the road like a frightened child, half-hidden beneath the muck. She hobbled over and picked it up. By all the saints, how had she thought to save her saviour with *that*?

And what was she to do now? Her original destination, so swiftly planned as she tripped and ran down the streets of London, was St. Alban's Abbey. But the monks were twenty miles away, and unhorsed, that had become an insurmountable distance.

She put her hand to her forehead. Everything seemed sinister. The mists, the dark, rutted road, and most especially the sword-bearing stranger who was watching her now with grey-blue eyes, his body motionless. What before had been red-hot fire in her blood became ice-cold fear, and it slid down her back in knife thrusts.

"So," he said with a booming roar—at least that's how it sounded—"what am I to do with you?"

The chill plunged deeper into her spine. What did that mean: *do with her*? Hadn't she spent the whole first part of this evening assuring no man should do anything with her?

To this awful end.

She shoved her foot into her slipper. Cold, wet mud slopped out the sides. "My thanks for saving me, sir, but there is nothing you are required, nor invited, to do with me." He lifted an eyebrow. "I am truly grateful for the risks you have taken here," she added. "Not only to your person, but any reputation you might have."

He didn't appear overly concerned about that last, considering that nothing about his grey-eyed, taut-bodied regard changed. He didn't appear very pleased. She didn't have many choices. She cleared her throat.

"You wouldn't be pilgrimming towards Saint Alban's Abbey, now, would you?"

He shook his head.

"No, I didn't think so." She took a breath. There was one other option, much closer, although she did not know the way herself. But perhaps this knight did. Of course, it was not the safest option. Papa had always said Lord Aubrey of Hippingthorpe, who had estates nearby, was a man with a ridiculous name and a most dangerous temperament.

Well, Gwyn decided, pushing her foot deeper into the cold

muck filling her slipper, danger was really quite relative now, wasn't it?

She looked up at her saviour. "You wouldn't be able to direct me towards Hippingthorpe Hall, would you?"

The smallest flicker altered his gaze. "Are you to name every stop along the road to York?" he asked coldly.

She drew back, hugged her tattered cloak around her shoulders, and lifted her chin a little bit. "No. Of course not. My apologies for all the . . . troubles. May I recompense you?" She began fumbling with the bag of silver tied around her waist.

"No."

"Are you certain? Your tunic was torn, and . . . ?" She drifted off as he crossed his arms over his chest and regarded her like he might some heretofore-unknown insect.

"Well, then," she remarked brightly and turned on her heel. With great dignity, she began hiking down the highway, a lone, dark, limping figure, damp skirts clinging to her knees, which she kicked away on every alternate step.

"For certes, I stepped onto a strange path when I left the house tonight," she muttered, pushing unruly strands of muck-covered hair out of her face. "If I thought life was a thing in my control, I have been proven wrong." She fumbled to remove the heavy clump of fabric that edged its way higher and higher between her legs. "And I do not like that."

Behind her, Griffyn 'Pagan' Sauvage stood for a long time, staring down the road. A breeze crept up and blew persistently around the hem of his cape.

The last thing he needed, the very last thing in all the world, was another burden. Tonight of all nights.

Griffyn's mission was clear and uncomplicated: Prepare England for invasion. Lure the powerful, enlist the merchants, persuade the wise, and bribe the fools, but come hell or high water, clear the way, because Henri fitzEmpress, Count d'Anjou, Duke of Normandy, and rightful king of England, was poised to blow through the country like a tempest and conquer it from Sea to Wall.

Landing in secret on the English coast six months ago, Griffyn had met with dozens of war-weary lords since then, men balanced on the edge of a knife, and convinced them Henri's blade was the sharper. He had done things no other man had been able to do, and he was planning to do them one last time, tonight, in the most vital meeting of his entire mission. At a remote hunting lodge half a mile off the king's highway. One carefully-arranged meeting with the most powerful baron in Stephen's realm, the earl of Leicester, Robert Beaumont. Turn him, and they had the country.

The name of that hunting lodge? Hippingthorpe. The very place she'd asked to go.

Could she be more in the way? Literally, in his path.

The fate of two kingdoms rested on this meeting. Turn Beaumont and England would fall like chaff.

And Griffyn could finally go home.

A flash of pain eddied into his chest. Dimmed by time, it was always there, a burning ache: home. Sweetly scented hilltops, primeval forests, and heather bracketing the everlasting moors. Mountains and seas. Wild, windswept, *home*.

He did not need a distraction. Not tonight, not ever.

He watched her lone, dark, limping figure diminish in the distance for a moment longer, then cursed softly and swung away.

Chapter Five

Gwyn sniffed and peered optimistically up the highway. Then she scowled. St. Alban's did not appear to be any closer. Then again, she'd only been walking for about ten minutes.

"I suppose I'll have to sleep in a hollowed tree stump tonight, and hope no wild boars find me too tempting to resist." She wrinkled her nose. "With the way I smell, I'll attract them from all around."

She glanced up at the sky. Clouds were moving in. Her brows came down in an angry glare. "Perfect. I could have predicted a storm. Of *course* it would rain. Why not send a cloud of locusts and splay me with boils next? 'Twould be a fitting end to this wretched night."

She was trembling from head to soggy foot, chilled from the outside in. Her fingertips were numb, her knees trembling from cold and spent emotion. Lifting a hand, she wiped her nose and scrubbed at her eyes, which were beginning to leak. "No crying," she ordered in a furious whisper. "You brought this on yourself. Headstrong, foolish, wretched girl."

She kept walking, stumbling through mud puddles and over a small crest in the road. Her legs wobbled and threatened to give out fully. Part of the reason became clear when she looked down: the heel of her slipper had given out completely.

She plunked herself on the ground and wrenched it off. Accursed thing. What good was a pair of shoes if they couldn't stand up to a night of combat? Her dress was torn from collar to waist, and she clutched feebly at the shreds of silk, trying to pull them tighter, feeling colder and more alone than she ever had in her life.

"What do you think you're doing?"

The question came from above. She craned her neck back and stared into the pewter eyes of her saviour. He sat astride his raw-boned horse with an easy grace, and against the backdrop of night sky and blowing tree limbs, appeared even more the mysterious presence he'd been when he stepped out of the shadows and saved her life.

She lifted the slipper into the air. "My shoes are wet."

The grimness in his face shaded with something else. "What are you doing?" he asked again, his words a deep rumble of masculinity.

"I'm going north." Hot tears pushed against her nose.

He nodded, then paused. "That's a very general area."

She tried looking fierce. He appeared undeterred, kept staring at her with those unfathomable eyes. She began again with frigid dignity, her only defence against the panic and tears welling up inside her. "I wish only to go north and am beset with people who wish otherwise. May I not simply walk along the king's highway—"

"No."

Angry tears pricked harder.

A dark gaze slid down her cloak and up again. "You are not safe on the highway, and certainly not alone."

She could feel the tears coming, poking hotly at her nose. "That is unfortunate, because that is what and where I am. And it comforts me. Being alone is a common state. Whereas sitting in the mud is not."

He shifted on the horse and when he spoke this time, it was softer. "So come with me."

"I don't know where you're going."

He laughed, a low, pleasing sound that smoothed the edges of her fear. "You don't know where *I* am going, mistress? I am going to warmth and a bed. Whereas you are going into certain danger, if you continue on alone."

"I am well used to being alone. What I am not used to is my feet hurting as they do, or my dress sticking to me as it does, and . . . *Perdition!*"

She stared glumly across the highway. Wind rustled the reeds and grasses along the side, making a soft hissing sound. Dark clouds were rolling in, blotting out the stars. She glanced up to find him, of all things, smiling. She frowned darkly "Think you 'tis amusing?"

"Nay." He shook his head back and forth, a swipe of enigmatic darkness against the blackening skies. "I just . . . did not expect such . . . candor from a maiden."

"Oh, *that*. Well, I've had much exposure to many of the things men do so well."

He arched a brow.

"Poor governing and rich cursing," she responded to the silent enquiry with an airy nonchalance. Mud pressed against her buttocks.

"Rich cursing," he mused, his gaze travelling over her hunched figure. "And poor governance. What else, I wonder?"

"Being witless when it comes to direction and a distinct desire to not ask for help," she said in a warning tone.

It did not seem to deter him. His slate-grey eyes were warmer now, almost blue, and fairly danced with mirth. "But I am not lost, mistress."

"I am."

"Thank heavens you are with me, then."

She snorted in a very unladylike way. It was sinful really, Gwyn decided glumly, getting to her feet. Such handsome amusement in the face of her plight.

She glanced back down the road and caught sight of a hand

peeking out of the bushes. Small and white, it could have been anything at this distance. But she knew it was a hand. A dead man's hand.

It was too much. She squeezed her eyes shut as her belly rolled over. Her head lolled to the side and she stumbled sideways a step.

He slid off his horse and was at her side, steadying her.

"I am sure I can make my way if I could but find my horse," she said weakly. His hand rested on her back, his hip pressed up against hers. He pursed his lips as if about to speak, but said nothing.

She started disentangling herself; the heat from his body was too unsettling. As she pulled away, her hair tugged as it caught on the innumerable and exposed metal rings of his mail hauberk. They stared at one another through the webbed strands of dark hair, then, with a faint sigh, he bent to disentangle her. She waited patiently while he unlaced each curl and set it free.

"You could lash goods on a ship with this kind of netting," he muttered at one particularly stubborn knot.

A trickle of soothing heat ran around the edges of her heart again and she sighed. Startlingly long-lashed eyes lifted and peered through her hair. "You are fine, mistress?"

The pain in the back of her skull started travelling forward. "Absolutely fine."

He loosed the last curl and arranged it around her face in soft, knotted waves. "You might have just flown away." His breath floated past her ear as he spoke.

"W-what?"

"You could have simply flown away to escape. Your hair is as soft as a bird's feather and as black as a raven's."

She blinked vapidly. "Raven?"

"The bird?"

"Oh, *ra*vens." A wave of nausea rolled through her. Her

head whipped with a new surge of pain, and she moaned softly. "My head hurts."

"Be gentle with it."

She pressed her hands against her temples. Watery mucus flooded in her mouth. "By all the saints, I am a fool," she muttered.

"We've all been the fool one time or another, myself more so than the rest."

She couldn't respond. Her stomach was roiling and rolling, its contents burbling and burping and demanding to be freed. St. Jude, not in the middle of the king's highway!

"Oh God," she moaned softly, her head lolling to the side.

He lowered her gently to her knees. Palms splayed out in front of her, she knelt on the ground like a dog and rocked back and forth, filling the air with soft moans.

"Go ahead," he murmured, lifting the hair that had fallen in front of her face. He tucked it behind her ear, but when the curls slipped out, he swept them up and kept them in his hand.

"Oh, I can't," she cried, then did.

After, he led her to a hollowed tree trunk filled with fresh rain water and cleaned her up. He helped her wash her face and hands, cooled her head, and made her laugh twice, which was really more than she could have expected, given the circumstances.

"Well then," she said in a shaky voice, after it all was over. "I suppose we can see to the defence of the bridge now."

He stared a moment, his jaw opened slightly, revealing even, white teeth, then he started laughing. Rumbling, self-assured masculine laughter. "They wouldn't have a chance against us, Green-eyes."

She laughed weakly. "None a'tall." Then she passed out.

Chapter Six

When she came to, she was sitting on something soft. *Moss*. She ran her fingers over it, then realised she was propped against the crunchy bark of a tree. She sat up. Her saviour was crouched on the balls of his feet, watching her.

"How long?" she murmured in a broken whisper.

One of his shoulders lifted and fell. "A moment. Two."

"Good heavens." She pushed herself straight. "My apologies."

He rose and brushed his hands across his thighs. "Not required. You've had a fright, a fight, a serious knock to the head, and almost got married. 'Tis enough to send any maiden swooning."

"I didn't *swoon*," she retorted, stumbling to her feet. "I fainted, which I have ne'er done before."

"Mmmm."

She looked at him glumly. "What now?"

He clucked to the black behemoth of a horse standing a few paces away. The fur-knotted beast came and her saviour mounted with a graceful swing of his body. He leaned over and extended a broad, calloused hand. "You do not think too highly of men, Green-eyes, but your choices are limited. I will not take you against your will—"

"Then—"

"But I will not leave you."

Nothing could have stopped it. Tears began pouring from her eyes en masse, like passengers fleeing a sinking ship. She lowered her head and the tears dripped down her cheeks and off her chin. She heard a muffled curse, then felt herself being lifted into the air, slid against the warm fur of a horse, and deposited on an even warmer lap of hard muscle. She started mumbling through the cascade of tears.

"I have to g-get home."

"Where is home?"

She snuffled. "Saint Alban's."

There was the briefest pause. "You, a monk? I wouldn't have believed it."

She smiled just a little.

"Well, 'tis too far away with a storm coming and Endshire's men on the highway," he murmured. "And I have places to be. I'll take you somewhere safe and warm and dry."

"But—"

"And later, I will ensure you get to Saint Alban's."

"Your word, sirrah?" she pressed. "You've no idea how I need to be home. Have I your *most solemn word*?"

"My most solemn word, lady. I know all about needing to be home."

"I can never repay you."

"You never have to."

Fear and exhaustion corded together and pushed her over the cliff of decency and common sense. She had dim memories of gripping the only ballast available, his torn tunic, and burrowing into the granite-hewn structure that lay beneath. Through a fog she recalled pressing herself into the warm hardness of his body, unmindful of the iron rings digging into her skin. One hand went up around the strong column of his neck to steady herself, and her face rolled into his chest, where it lodged for a good two minutes. All in all, a less-than-comfortable ride. Or it *should* have been.

It was not. Although his thighs were as hard-packed with muscle as the arms that surrounded her, his lap was as welcoming and warm as a fur-laden bed. She wanted to snuggle in deeper, and only the dim knowledge of a morning to come kept her from following the impulse.

His arms wrapped on either side of her loosely as he held the reins low on Noir's withers. He clucked every so often, sometimes to her, sometimes to the horse. Noir responded by quickening his pace, she by nestling further into his body, purposefully forgetting about the dawn.

And she talked to him. She talked because the night was dark and a storm was rolling in. She talked because panic was nipping at her heels and if she stopped, she'd slip into insanity. Reason enough, but still a weak excuse to tell him all the mundane details of her life.

In fact, she realised in a dim corner of her mind, she was pouring out information like a water spout, just as if he cared. Perhaps, she reflected later, he had asked some small, leading question to still her panic, but that was a poor excuse to chatter nonstop until the man's ears were numb and his mind mush. She talked about big things and small, about how she hated dealing with merchants and how she loved marinated mushrooms.

When his replies came in the form of nods and "ummm's"— which could denote disinterest but, to judge by the look in his slate-grey eyes whenever he dropped them to her, was tolerance—she spoke haltingly of how she missed her mother, how she was sometimes irritable when she meant to be kind to her friends, her father, who was now dead too, and how she was coming to accept the fact that she was terribly, crushingly alone.

She talked herself back into a calm, then bounced atop his muscled thighs in silence. After a moment, she pushed back her hair and angled a careful glance up.

He was staring at the sky. She looked up too, but clouds scuttling across the sky were of little interest, so she looked back at him, her gaze travelling over a face that was turning out to have fine, noble lines and a most disconcerting handsomeness. Not that she cared, of course. Still, one could not help but notice, for goodness sake.

Without warning he dropped his gaze. "What is your name, mistress?"

She stiffened. The unguarded Countess d'Everoot had already proven to be a mighty temptation. Sooth, just six months ago the Duchess of Aquitaine had to flee from *three* matrimonial-minded abduction attempts on her travels home following her divorce from the King of France.

Still, Gwyn decided, angling her saviour a sideways glance, this one had rescued her, at serious risk to himself. He did not look the kidnapper, and while he felt dangerous, it was of a different sort than any she had a name for. Certainly no danger to her life or limb.

"Guinevere," she finally said.

If he noted the absence of any identifying tags, such as her home or parentage, he did not show it. "Pleased to meet you."

She laughed. "Yes, rather. And yours?"

It was his turn to pause. "I'm known as Pagan."

She looked at him a moment, but he didn't say anything more. So she lifted a shoulder and let it fall. "If God chose to answer my prayer with a pagan, so be it. Who am I to argue?"

He glanced down, smiling. "I think you would argue with God Himself, did it suit you, mistress."

The smile, though, not his words, captured Gwyn's attention. The faint sign of amusement deepened the curved lines beside his mouth, making him even more handsome and slightly less imposing, which, truly, was difficult to do in any other way. His body was encased in mail from shoulders to knees. Moonlight glinted off his close-cropped black hair whenever the tree cover opened for a moment. His face was fixed in rigid tightness, but the tension did not detract a whit from bloodlines that had crafted a noble face, its handsomeness almost taunting. Only a scar that lashed from temple to jaw marred the surface, that and a day's growth of beard.

Yes, it would be difficult to describe him as anything but 'imposing.' And kind. And sacrificing. And heart-stoppingly handsome.

She ripped her gaze away.

After that, she didn't remember much for the rest of their ride. When she tried to recall it later, it was too fuzzy, too laden with emotion. She had only dim memories.

Griffyn's were rather more vivid.

If she'd been expected, he could have protected himself.

He'd been riding to the most important meeting of his entire sojourn in England, thoughts lost in dreary dreams of the future, when he'd heard the sounds of arguing. A woman's voice, sing-song with fright, but the words were defiant. Brave and hopeless. The spirit that prompted them was worthy of a battle she could never give, and so he'd ridden out. He must have been bored. Or out of his mind.

She was unlike anything he'd ever known before, and he was totally unprepared.

He was not a child, for heaven's sake. At twenty-six years of age, with seventeen years of exile under his belt, in disguise and courting death, he was a spy for his king. The things he'd done in the execution of those duties were undoubtedly more challenging than managing one lost waif, no matter how beautiful or spirited or . . . well, simply no matter anything.

And yet, here she was, on the back of his horse. Distracting him.

He'd never been distracted before.

He suddenly realised she'd been talking.

". . . and I couldn't think when I saw them there, Marcus's men. All I knew is that I was doomed."

He looked down at the top of her dark, tousled head. "You didn't appear to think all hope was lost, mistress, the way you stood in the middle of the road and ordered them on their way."

"I was angry," she explained. "That's all that was: bravado, and anger. But I knew I was dead. More sure of it than tomorrow's sunrise. Then you came. You saved me."

He shifted on Noir. His mission had nothing to do with saving anyone from anything. This was about settling old scores, about taking back what was his. It was about conquest. The last thing he needed was an indebted woman, particularly one whose trembling body was pressed up against his, her slender, pale arm thrown around his neck.

"I'm no saviour, mistress," he gruffed.

She cocked her head up. Green-eyes peered at him sidewise. Definitely, he did not need this.

"You just saved *me*," she pointed out.

"We saved each other, then," he allowed gruffly.

"You would not have needed any saving if it weren't for me, Pagan," she persisted.

A corner of his mouth twitched. "'Tis so."

"Then I'm indebted."

He lowered his gaze slowly. "Guinevere, 'tis best if you don't see me as the saviour of anything."

Her body was moving slightly now, not so rock-hard and rigid as it had been. This was encouraging, and disturbing, for it was leading his mind in directions he had no desire to go. A female body warm and pressed against him, swaying with every step Noir took. Into him. He glared at the tips of Noir's furry ears and took a long, controlled breath.

A sudden shift of her weight brought his attention back down. She'd bent forward and cupped her forehead in her palms. He tugged Noir to a halt. "Your head hurts."

"Only when I breathe," she whispered.

He swung a leg over Noir's rump, and dismounted, then rummaged through one of his saddlebags.

The dark, comforting space below Gwyn's down-turned head was suddenly invaded by a pungent odour as he nudged a silver flask in front of her face. "Saints assoil me, knight," she complained, lifting her head. "What in perdition is that?"

He lifted his eyebrows, then pushed the flask closer. "Say 'tis medicine and you'll be closer than many others who call it by another."

Gracing him with a suspicious slant of her eyes, she sniffed again. "It smells like something my dog would cough up."

He laughed. "You're priceless."

"No one has placed a bid as yet."

"Their loss. Drink."

Levelling a doubtful gaze at her would-be leech, she tilted back her head and drank. The liquid ran hot through her throat, raking its way down in a fiery blast.

Griffyn watched as she tipped sideways, her hair flying as she sputtered and slipped halfway off the saddle. His hands flashed out and closed around her hips. The flat bones shifted under his thumbs. One long, slender thigh dangled beside his ribs. His fingers pressed into curving, soft roundness and for a heartbeat, all his world contracted to become womanly flesh and desire. He watched her heart-shaped face as she lifted it, wiping her dripping chin as she moved, rasping and astonished. A waterfall of black hair swung behind, fluttering over her face before settling around her shoulders. He let her slide to the ground.

Her neck was arched back the slightest bit, her eyes wide. Unsteady came her breath, he could feel it on his cheek, his jaw. Erotic. Her bodice lifted and fell, revealing tempting curves and satiny skin with each unsteady inhalation. He drew in a slow breath and removed his hand.

Bedraggled she was, but Griffyn knew women as well as he

knew war, and beneath the dirt staining her skin was the face of a goddess. Her body, an expanse of silk and rose he'd seen full well before covering her in his cape, proved the splendor went on, over rounded breasts and down a curving spine.

"What was that?" she sputtered, her voice still raspy from the fiery drink.

He grinned slowly. "You tell me."

She glanced at the bottle, back at him, and a smile spread over her face, turning the delicate features into a breathtaking vision of loveliness. *"Good."*

Dirt-stained, disheveled, homeless lass, she was. She was also the funniest, most surprising female he'd happened upon in many a year.

And he was in danger of losing himself underneath the vision of himself as saviour to the homeless lass.

"I'm glad you liked it," he said, then lifted her into the saddle again, this time ignoring the way her hips felt under his hands *(perfect)*. He remounted behind her.

"So, are you in orders?" he enquired, more from a desire to focus his mind away from her body than from any true curiosity, "or was there some other reason for going to the Abbey?"

She laughed. "It was just . . . a way out. A way out of the city . . . away from Marcus . . ." She trailed off.

"Just away, is it then?" he said in a low, comforting rumble.

"Aye," she admitted in a small voice. His thigh shifted under hers.

"Umm."

She was relaxing further. Aside from the clues provided by reasonable, tear-free conversation, he could feel the weight of her increase against his arm as she leaned back. He flexed his arm the smallest bit to support her.

She chatted on, her words becoming a tinkling, background music. He was surprised it did not aggravate him. Reaching up, he unclasped the pin holding his cape and slung the heavy woollen material around her shoulders, covering her bedraggled dress, which was beginning to tempt his mind in directions he had no desire to go. Her cape he slid off and threw over Noir's rump, a tattered, bloody mess.

". . . which is why," she was saying, her forehead wrinkling, "for me to cry in the face of brewing storm clouds tonight is such a plaguesome mystery. I mean, I do *not* cry. And so, 'tis most odd."

"Perhaps you were not crying about the storm."

Those impossibly green eyes turned slowly up to him. Rolling in fat tears that did not, as she had predicted, overflow, the emotion brimming in them was anguished enough to speak. So it was not necessary for her to say what she said next, because he knew it already.

"No, I believe I was crying about something else altogether."

Good God, he could lose himself right here, on the back of his horse.

And that was unacceptable.

Recall your mission, he counseled himself grimly.

And not the one for Henri fitzEmpress. A more private, well-simmered vengeance, seventeen years in the making: Destroy the House of de l'Ami.

Chapter Seven

They sat at the edge of a small clearing. Lurking around its edges was the deep, dark forest, with its sharp-edged black trees and small scurryings in the undereaves. In the middle of the clearing squatted five or six daub-and-wattle huts. And in front of the ragged half-circle they created roared an enormous bonfire.

Gwyn sighed in relief, then considered it more closely. That was a great deal of wood and peat to be burning so wastefully. Some dim recollection coalesced in her mind. She looked to Pagan.

"What is the bonfire for?"

"All Hallows' Eve."

The night when the portal from the Other World to this world were opened, the only night in the year. Magic flowed, spirits dwelt.

The smokey greyness of his eyes was unreadable in the darkness. "Warm and safe and dry," he reminded her.

"If you say."

"If you behave."

Her eyebrows went down. "Behave?"

"Don't talk too much. Can you manage that?"

She dropped her head to the side. "Of course."

"Good. And a ride to your Abbey tomorrow."

"You?"

He swung off Noir just as the door to the largest hut swung wide. A thick band of yellow firelight spilled out over the muddy earth.

"No. Them."

Two figures appeared in the doorway, one behind the other. Large, broad-shouldered figures who seemed to be holding blunt-edged weapons of some sort. Aloft.

Pagan said something in the guttural Saxon tongue and that's all there was to it. The men lowered their weapons and came out with welcoming gestures. Gwyn could understand nothing of their Saxon-held conversation, but it was clear Pagan was not worried.

She rested her hands on Noir's furry, warm withers, patting his neck while listening to the murmurs of the men's conversation, watching Pagan. He stood unaffectedly, a day's growth of stubble roughening his face. He put his foot up on a log. The leather of his knee-high black boot rose up his calf, dully reflecting the firelight. One mailed forearm rested on his bent knee as he nodded and laughed at something one of the men said.

Gwyn found herself smiling too, and her belly did a little flip when he turned his dark gaze back to her. He said something to the men, then started over, his stride long and confident.

They walked together into the warm hut. Eight or so souls stood and sat in the small open space at the centre. It was crowded, but not uncomfortably so. Over the firepit near the centre hung a black cauldron, and inside the contents bubbled and burped. To the right, behind a half-wall, Gwyn could hear a cow shuffling in the hay.

All the faces were staring at her. She smiled. They didn't exactly smile in return, but neither did they brandish swords. They were dirty faces, unkempt, but they did not appear hostile, nor like they wanted anything from her, and for the moment, that was sufficient.

One of the women, the blunt-nosed, square-shouldered matron, came forward and, with a nod, indicated Gwyn should sit at the table. A bowl of hot stew was plunked down in front of her. Small flecks of colour swirled in the dark brown broth, carrots and onions. Alongside lay a chunk of day-old rye bread.

"My thanks," she exhaled in true, great gratitude.

Pagan nodded to her. "I'll leave you here, then, mistress."

"Oh!" she exclaimed, startled, then tried to hide it. How embarrassing. Certes, he had more important things to do. She had no claim on him. "Of course."

"Tomorrow morn, Clid there," he said, gesturing to one of the square-shouldered men who had greeted them, "will be your escort to Saint Alban's."

She swung her leg over the bench. He was already backing towards the door. "I cannot express my thanks, Pagan. I owe you more than I can ever repay. You saved my life."

He shrugged. "Your virtue, more's the like. I don't think your life was in any danger, mistress."

"Oh, truth, sir, 'twas. For I'd have killed myself before I married Marcus fitzMiles."

He paused, gauntleted hand on the door jam, and grinned over his shoulder, just like a friend would do. "Me too."

She pushed to her feet then, feeling reckless and unruly and everything she hadn't let herself feel for a dozen years. Crossing to the door, she kept her eyes on the dirt floor and fumbled with the bag of silver tied round her waist, shocked at how weepy she felt.

"Lady, please." A touch of impatience sharpened the masculine rumble of his words. He turned and walked out.

"I am simply looking for a way to recompense you," she explained helplessly to his back.

The length of his mail-clad body stilled, then he turned and strode back to within inches of her. He swept up the hair by her ear with the edge of a warm, calloused hand, and leaned in. "Smile."

Something hot flashed through her body. "Sir?"

"Smile for me."

He could have said anything. In that husky voice, his long fingers brushing back her hair, his breath warm on her skin, he could have said he was a traitor to the king and she would have smiled. And when she did, slowly, hesitantly, a corner of his own mouth crooked up in reply.

"I have been recompensed," he murmured.

Something hot and cold and shivery came down like a rainstorm through her body. Every breath she tried to take came rushing back out again. She could hardly listen to his next words, with his muscular body pulsing heat onto hers, his lips just by her ear, whispering words that were all of sense, nothing of the animal arousal he'd just awakened in her.

"Take care here, Raven. Don't talk too much. Don't ask too many questions. Hide that silly pouch of silver and whatever you've got in the other one."

He ran his index finger briefly along her jaw. It was a careless gesture, but it made the hot-cold chills explode like fire through her blood. She reached out and her fingertips brushed his mailed forearm.

"Don't go. Yet. Please."

And like that, deep inside of Griffyn, something that hadn't moved for a very long time suddenly shifted.

He grabbed her hand and pulled her outside, propelling her behind Noir, using the horse as a shield between them and the huts. His intention was clear, and he barely dared breathe, waiting for her refusal. Let her pull back the slightest bit and he would step away, forget the whole thing, interpret her unsteady breathing as fear, her trembles as exhaustion.

But God, he prayed silently, *please let her move not so much as an eyelash.*

Why was his blood hammering so? Why was it hard to draw breath? He had barely touched her on two occasions, touches so innocent he could have performed them in a crowded room and barely brought a gasp. Why?

Because something about this small, courageous wisp of a woman was plunging into recesses of a desire he'd never known existed, and his arousal pulsed hot and hard and inassuagable inside him, all from the feel of a curving spine and the sight of a delicate, dirt-stained face.

Without a thought for custom or destiny or anything other than the green-eyed angel pressed against his horse and panting, he bent his head to taste the trembling lips. Sliding his thumb slowly down her neck, he brushed his lips over hers.

Her small intake of breath, like velvet on air, made him stiffen into a thick, hard rod. Catching hold of his breath, he pressed the tip of his tongue against the seam of her lips, pushing them open ever so slightly.

Gwyn threw her head back, stunned by the bolt of wet heat that blasted through her body. A slow-moving shudder rippled behind, quivering between her thighs, lashing pleasure through her blood. His tongue slid in further, coaxing her to open for him, taking long, slow sweeps of her, mining an unknown passion that was pulsing heat between her legs. She dimly realised she was embracing him, had her arms around his neck and was pulling him down. Ever gallant, he responded, cupping her face with one hard, gloved hand. He locked his other hand around her hip and tugged, coaxing her closer, his thumb pressed against the rounded flesh of her abdomen, coming dangerously and head-spinningly close to the place where hot, wet heat flashed inside her womb.

"Oh, Pagan." The wasted whimper slid out of her, a moan, a ministration, a murmur of something she didn't even know how to dream about.

Without thinking, which was *no* part of what she was doing, she pushed her body into his. Breasts, belly, hips, everything arched up into him. An invitation.

In a single, confident move, he dragged her up off the

ground, tight against him, so her toes scraped the earth, his mouth hungry on hers. He pushed the flat of his hand against her belly and slid up her ribs until his thumb rested just under the swell of her breast.

She threw her head to the side, crying out. She had no idea what she might have done next if Noir hadn't shifted just then, away from the pressure.

Griffyn did, though. He knew exactly what he would have done to her, starting with her parted lips straight down to her curling toes. But when Noir shifted, that woke him up. His hand shot out and grabbed the reins.

He dragged his head up a bare inch and found her eyes almost closed. Only a thin glitter of green was visible. The rest of her face was suffused with incipient passion: red, parted lips, panting chest, flushed cheeks.

A breath of air never tasted before.

He let her go as if burned, released her onto obviously wobbly feet, his breath ragged, his very blood burning. Had he just almost ravished a noblewoman as if she were a strumpet, backed her up against his horse and gone to lift her skirts? Had he truly abandoned his mission on the eve of its execution? What had he become? A distractible man? A desirous man? A fool?

Never before, and never, *ever* again.

Groin pounding, heart thundering, he wiped his palm over his mouth. "That was wrong of me, Guinevere," he muttered. "I was foolish, and I am sorry."

She kept her eyes downcast. "You were not the only fool."

"I have never—" He wiped his hand over his entire face this time. "I was wrong. Please forgive me."

She touched the back of her hand to her lips. "You've never what?" she asked in a small voice.

"Pressed myself on . . . an unwilling . . ." He scratched his head briskly. "I am sorry."

She drew herself straighter and met his eye. "I was not

unwilling." Small tangled curls idled over her brow. She brushed them back. "'Tis true we've both done things tonight we've ne'er done before." She paused. "For instance, you saved my life."

"Aye." A small explosion of released tension took the form of a laugh. "Never done that before."

"So we can allow a few . . ."

"Allowances," he finished.

She smiled, that enchanting, faerie-like smile which made him forget he had no heart. He was uneasy to realise he was quite willing to stand here all night in order to make her do it again. Smile, that is. Smile, and moan, and part her lips and then her thighs . . .

"And now, you must go." She said what he should have done ten minutes ago.

"Aye," he said, but didn't move.

"You have things to do. As do I." Each word broke like a tiny ice chip. "So, please," she glaciated. "Go."

He planted a swift kiss on her lips, then swung into the saddle and reined into the woods without looking back once.

Gwyn watched for a long time, her breath fast and un- steady. Each breath birthed a small smokey puff in front of her mouth. She stood there so long the echo of Noir's hooves merged with the sound of her own furiously beating heart, then silence.

She was treading a very dangerous path tonight. All Hal- lows' Eve, indeed. Doorways that lay closed every other night of the year were flung wide open. And she had just walked through one.

Such beliefs were nonsense, of course, even though she'd grown up with them, tutored by her childhood friends, the Scottish villagers and servants. But they were old pagan be- liefs, not of the Church—.

She stopped walking. Oh, Lord. *Pagan.*

She trudged back to the hut, her belly hot and flipping,

which was absurd and ridiculous and most certainly immoral. It was also reckless, to be so focused on one errant knight when her beloved home was at risk. Recklessness, her besetting sin. Wayward, disobedient.

A wretched disappointment.

She tugged Pagan's cloak tighter around her shoulders, grateful for its warmth, then spun sharply. If she was wearing his cloak, that meant he had none. She peered into the trees, but he was gone. Long gone. Far gone. Never to be seen again.

She blinked away the sharp bite of tears the frigid temperatures must have brought to her eyes. Time to attend to what mattered. Pagan had his mission, she had hers: get word to the king. Only Gwyn could save Everoot now. It was all in her hands.

In fact, she considered glumly, perhaps the whole *debacle* was a gift from God. A chance to do proper penance for one very old, very awful sin.

And to do that, she needed to be somewhere, *any*where, other than this village with its milk cows and single swaybacked plough horse.

I'll never see him again, echoed inside her head as she pushed open the thin wooden door to the hut. She was surprised by the thought, considering she'd already forgotten him.

But she was aghast at the emotion that followed: despair.

The door swung wide and the villagers looked up.

"I need a horse," she said.

Chapter Eight

Griffyn looked up as the sharp, cautionary whistle dusted down through the dark night air. He whistled back, three trills and one long sustained note. Silence, then high on the hill, the manor gates creaked open, wood pressed hard against ancient wood. Hippingthorpe Hall was admitting its guest.

It was a moody autumn night, stuffy. The atmosphere was thick and murmuring. Overhead the sky was clear, blooming with bright, glittering stars, but in the west, clouds huddled ominously. A gust of wind galloped across the plains, dragging a lock of hair over Griffyn's forehead. He brushed it back impatiently.

His heart still pounded, his loins still ached, but he would never have brought Guinevere here, not if she'd begged him. Hipping was a dangerous fool, and no one knew he'd already changed sides, secretly forsworn his oath to King Stephen and joined Henri's cause.

Some would call that traitorous. Griffyn even might have, in different circumstances, but he chose to call it prudence. Above all, it was a secret. No one knew Hipping had changed sides, but change he had, and he was an opportunistic turncoat. An heiress loyal to Stephen might be in true peril.

Griffyn rode over the narrow bridge spanning the moat and

ducked his head as he passed beneath the murderous wooden spikes of the portcullis gate hanging tautly overhead. If they lowered it now, he'd be skewered, skull on down. Helmed faces peered grimly at him from the narrow windows of the gatehouse, attended by crossbow quarrels aimed even more grimly, and directly, at his throat.

He rode Noir about halfway into the centre of the dark, silent bailey and, swinging his leg over, dropped to the cobbled ground. Hipping's burly figure appeared at the top of the stairwell, backlit by the torches burning on the walls behind him.

"Welcome, Pagan," he growled, grabbing Griffyn's wrist in greeting. "We thought mayhap you'd changed your mind. Out doing dark, clandestine things, no doubt."

Griffyn smiled faintly. "No doubt."

Hipping threw his head back and guffawed, still pumping Griffyn's arm. "Just as I like it." His forearm spanned the same width as a sapling and his chest was half again as wide as a wagon wheel. Bushy grey and black hair hung down past his shoulders, and he had a wolf cape thrown over his shoulders. Glittering, shrewd eyes held Griffyn's. "But your special guest is frothing at the mouth."

Griffyn lifted an eyebrow. "I've never seen Robert Beaumont froth from anywhere."

"You've not been looking hard enough, my boy!" roared Hipping in laughter. "From across the Channel, 'tis hard to see, I admit. From where I sit, I see every twitter and shake of the great ones."

Hipping hurried him inside the building. They paused at the top of a set of stairs leading down to the great hall. The air was stale and frigid. A few tapestries hanging limply on the walls looked like they contributed much of the mouldy odour to the room. It was dimly lit, but he could see that it was emptied of all retainers.

Hipping stomped down a long corridor and pushed back a tapestry to his right, gesturing Griffyn inside.

Robert Beaumont, Earl of Leicester, rose. A brazier sat near the rough-hewn table that dominated the centre of the room, and there were several fat candles plunged into puddles of their own wax on the tabletop, but otherwise the room was set in darkness. A jug of ale huddled in the centre of the table, and two wooden cups cast flickering shadows on the oak tabletop. One sat half-emptied before the earl.

The middle-aged Beaumont stepped around the table and grasped Griffyn's wrist warmly.

Griffyn bent his head. "My lord. A pleasure."

"No, the pleasure is all mine," said the most powerful earl in the kingdom. After a very deliberate pause, he added, "My lord."

Griffyn went still.

"Is it good to be back in your homeland, Pagan? It's been a long time."

Griffyn inhaled slowly and rubbed his palms together, looking down at them. Then he lifted his head. "I didn't know you knew."

Beaumont spread his hands. "How could I not? You've his eyes."

"Ahh."

The earl glanced at Hipping, who'd paused at the door to speak to a servant, then lowered his voice. "Your father would ne'er have guessed it, Pagan."

"Guessed what?"

"That you would be the hound to flush out England for the fitzEmpress. He might have been proud."

A side of Griffyn's mouth twisted into a bitter smile. "He might have brutalized a convent before he said any such thing."

The earl's intelligent gaze held him. "Your father was once a great man, Pagan. Earl d'Everoot. Lord of the most powerful honor in the realm, captain of great men, advisor to kings."

"That is one way to recall him."

Beaumont nodded slowly, letting the statement settle into

quiet, before he sat, motioning for Griffyn to join him. He lifted a jug of Hippingtun brew and started pouring. "Your father built the earldom of Everoot into something more powerful than anyone could have dreamed, Pagan. Then he changed. Or rather, something changed him."

"Aye. Greed."

Beaumont shook his head. "Neither your father or de l'Ami ever said much about it, but I always suspected."

Griffyn's heart started tapping out a faster beat. "Suspected what?"

"No two men come back from Crusade like they did, Griffyn. Ionnes of Kent, a poor knight with nothing but a new name— *de l'Ami*—becomes rich beyond his dreams, blood-brother to one of the highest peers of the realm, Christian Sauvage, Earl d'Everoot. Your own father's power expanding like a hurricane, they two as close as hounds, then—" Beaumont clapped his hands together. "Extinguished. The friendship gone, Christian Sauvage gone, Ionnes de l'Ami becomes the new earl of Everoot. Pah, something stinks. There's something there."

"What?" he asked in a carefully measured voice.

Beaumont ran his fingers over his short, greying beard. "Something your father and Ionnes de l'Ami brought back from the Holy Lands."

"And what would that be?"

Beaumont's reply was spoken so softly it barely disturbed the candle flame sitting on the table in front of him: *"Treasures."*

Like a river freezing over, Griffyn's blood went cold. "A treasure? What treasure?"

"Treasure?" Beaumont's eyebrows arched up. "I said treasure*s*, Pagan. Plural. The plunder from Crusade is legendary. And your father and Ionnes de l'Ami brought some of it back. Rumour says 'tis hidden in the vaults of the Nest."

Griffyn's muscles relaxed in a hot wash. Beaumont did not know. *No one* knew, for all the rumours that flew about among the initiated. And Robert Beaumont, be he Earl of Leicester or

King of Jerusalem, was *not* one of those. 'Twas all guesses, as people were wont to do when money or mystery was involved.

Silent guesses, usually. Aloud, few dared whisper their speculations. Aloud, none ever mentioned a hallowed treasure over a thousand years old. And be it aloud or in their dreams, not one of them knew Griffyn was its Guardian.

Except Ionnes de l'Ami.

He'd been their family's closest confidant, dearest friend, fellow Crusader and brother-in-arms to Christian Sauvage, Griffyn's father. Then, with one, vicious swipe, he'd betrayed them all and broken Griffyn's heart. Greed had destroyed Christian Sauvage, then crept up on little spider legs and stole Ionnes de l'Ami too.

Oath-breaker. Thief.

Griffyn's hand went to the small, heavy iron key hung around his neck since his father had died, an instinctive movement.

"Everoot is all the treasure that matters to me, my lord," he said tightly.

The earl's perceptive eyes held his a moment, then said, "So be it," just as Hipping stepped into the room.

"Have you all you need, my lord?"

"Indeed," replied Beaumont. "Leave us to it."

Hipping nodded. "I will see to the gates." He paused. "There's something in the air tonight. My watchmen sent word there's many more men than is wont on the highway, and some are riding off it. FitzMiles is in one of his raging rampages. The king's councils are breaking up. All Hallows' Eve. There's something most odd in the air tonight." He grinned and rubbed his hands together. "I hope 'tis something either brutish or beautiful. Or both." He exploded in laughter and barreled down the corridor.

"'Tis time, Pagan," Beaumont said, but Griffyn was watching Hipping. "Convince me to have my men and castles waiting."

Griffyn nodded but his gaze lingered a minute, watching Hipping go. Hipping was like a trained bear. On most occasions, he'd follow your bidding, but never, ever turn your back.

No, he'd never have brought Guinevere here.

"Hippingthorpe's hunting lodge is near here?" she asked incredulously.

"'Bout half an hour's hard walk down the river path," gruffed the man Pagan had called Clid. He was obviously the patriarch, and Gwyn dealt with him.

Behind his bearded head, an equally bearded man threw another log on the fire, then sat on the bench. Everyone was sitting, listening to the conversation. As if they could do much else—the room was as wide as a birthing-stall, and half was in fact a stall. A cow's slow chewing provided rhythmic background, and chickens scratched through the hay.

"Aye," Clid said. Or grunted. "A couple miles north o' here." He slurped up a bit more brown broth, then eyed her doubtfully. "But why wouldn't Pagan have taken ye there straight off, iffen that's where he wanted ye?"

But Gwyn wasn't listening. Hope had sparked inside her, and she was mindless of any more mundane considerations, such as how she'd get there or whether it was wise. "What fortune! But, no," she said, and slumped again. "'Tis no use to me empty. I need lords. Or at least hardy men with horses." She looked at Clid. "Men loyal to the king."

He smiled, his rotted front tooth prominent. "Not many of them here in the Midlands, o' course."

"No," she agreed, and stared glumly into the firepit.

"But Hipple's lodge ain't what ye'd call 'empty.'"

She lifted her eyebrows.

"Hipping hisself rode in afore dawn, along with his accursed knights." Clid ripped another chunk of bread free with his teeth and worked it between his jaws. "Burning and raping and takin', and yer king doin' nothing to stop 'em."

Gwyn's heart leapt. "Hipping is there?"

"Oh, aye, he's there. And he's not alone."

She beamed. "Who else?"

"Leicester."

Her eyebrows crumpled together in confusion. "Robert Beaumont?"

"Aye."

"The Earl of Leicester is at Hippingthorpe's hunting lodge?"

"Aye."

Earl Robert Beaumont, most powerful peer of the realm, was riding to the remote hunting lodge of a minor baron? Hadn't he been in attendance at the king's feast—was it truly only a few hours ago? No, she realised. He'd been strangely absent.

"Robert Beaumont, Lord of Pacy-sur-Eure and Breteuil?" she added for clarification.

Clid scowled. "He might be Guardian of the Lord's pearly gates by now, I s'pose, the way his royal lordship throws around titles. What I know is that he's at Hipping's lodge. Arrived a few hours ago."

She frowned. Why on earth had she not seen him or any of his retinue on the king's highway?

"There's back ways to everywhere," said Clid, shrewdly reading her thoughts.

She considered this. It would be a dark and dangerous ride, what with the boars and wolves, and Hipping known as a wolf himself, but he was currently loyal to the king, and right now, nothing mattered more.

She looked into the chieftain's eyes. "I must get there."

He exchanged a few eyebrow-wagging glances with the men, then shook his head. "That's a danger for us, missy. Best that the great ones don't know we're here. They've forgotten us, and I'd have it stay that way."

"They'll never see you," she promised. "We can share a horse, and you can leave me miles from the lodge."

"That's where ye are now, missy. Miles and miles."

"But sir—"

"Every time the great ones remember we're here, it costs us. There's not much ye can offer us to make it worth that."

Gwyn grabbed one of the felt bags around her waist, fumbled with its knot, and dumped the pouch open on the table. Gold and silver coins tumbled across the scarred wood, clinking loudly in the suddenly hushed room. They gleamed brightly in the dim hut. She looked up into Clid's amazed eyes. "Please. I have to get there. Tonight. 'Tis my home at stake."

He ran his fingers through his grey-and-white beard. "Where's home?"

"In the north. Besieged."

He looked at her distrustfully. Behind him, the fire spat and crackled, then blazed brightly as a fresh log caught. "Pagan didna say anything about that."

"Be that as it may, you can see that I need to be on my way."

"Ah, well, and maybe not. Yer father will tend to it."

Her throat constricted. "I haven't a father. I've myself and a dozen knights, and ever so many villagers and their children and if I can't stop Lord d'Endshire—"

Clid grunted. "Marcus fitzMiles?"

"—then it will fall, my men will die, and I will be wed to—" She stopped short and stared wide-eyed into the firepit, blinking hard.

They sat in silence for a long time. Gwyn became aware Clid was fingering the pile of coins on the table. Sifting it through his fingers, letting it clink back down. She looked over. He was watching her, a brooding expression on his face.

"Beseigin' and burnin' and weddin'," he muttered. "What kind o' place would Marcus fitzMiles think was worth all that effort?"

"Any place he could get his hands on," she quipped, but swallowed the taste of something unpleasant. Fear.

Clid didn't change his look, except perhaps to become more guarded. "Why don't ye tell me yer name, missy?"

She lifted her chin. "My name is mine own, sir, and I would keep it so. Truth: we will all be safer that way."

She could see a slow smile emerging from beneath his beard and it wasn't a pleasant thing. "But since I donna know ye, lassie, I can hardly be trustin' ye, now can I?"

A low rumble of nasty laughter rumbled through the room. The men exchanged glances. Something cold flowed down her spine as Clid turned back to her. "That's a powerful lot o' gold for a lone missy to be carrying about—"

"Have it all." She cupped the pile and pushed it towards him.

"—and it makes me think ye might be worth more than whatever that pile there adds up to, so I'll ask ye one more time: what's yer name, and where's this castle of yers that fitzMiles wants so bad?"

Gwyn's mind sped through half a dozen responses, from pleading to fainting to snatching the knife from his belt and slitting his throat, but before he finished his sentence, she decided. Lie.

"I have to use the outhouse."

Admittedly, a weak defence, but it amused him, and that was sufficient. He erupted into laughter. Bits of food sprayed over the table. Pleasant. All he had to do was think her a fool and she had her chance. A slim one, but a chance.

"Go, go." He waved his hand in the air. "Elfrida, go with her. Show her the way to the 'outhouse.'" The manly troupe exploded into more uproarious laughter.

Gwyn smiled as if she had no notion of what lay in store. The square-shouldered matriarch Elfrida shuffled forward, glared at Gwyn, and snapped the door open. They walked a few yards behind the huts, the woman trudging beside her. Gwyn's mind raced. Elfrida The Matriarch might lumber along like an ox, but she wasn't letting Gwyn get more than a hands-breadth away, and that would never do. The forest lay about thirty steps further on, a creek bed gurgling at its edge. Four huts sat to their right, dark and silent except for the sounds of farm animals shuffling inside. Gwyn caught a glimpse of the plough horse.

They stopped and the woman pointed generally in the direction of 'over there.'

"Anywhere near them saplings. Ye'll smell it. I'll be standing here," Elfrida grumbled.

"Yes, I think I smell it already." Gwyn smiled. "But, ma'am, I hate to ask . . ." She dropped her voice. "I'm in need of . . . I'm afraid I've just come on my . . . monthly flux."

The woman's face shifted slightly. Her eyebrows went up, then down. "Oh, all right." She turned and shouted "Elfwing!" for what seemed like an eternity, but no one came.

Gwyn smiled encouragingly. "I can't really go back inside like . . . this."

She pulled aside the cloak and displayed her skirts for viewing. In the darkness it was hard to detect colour, but not shade, and there was clearly a huge, dark stain right in the middle of her skirts. Cloaked as Gwyn had been, the woman didn't realise the entire dress was in much the same state, nor that the stain was not Gwyn's own blood, nor that much of it was not blood at all, but mud and muck flung up in her various pursuits of the night.

Elfrida backed up. "I'll have ye a rag. I'll be right back." She pointed again, this time the other direction. "We girls go over there, near the forest edge, this time o' the month." She started off. "Don't try anything," she warned, looking back over her shoulder.

Gwyn smiled in a friendly way and waved her hand in the air, indicating the general vastness and emptiness of her surroundings. "What could I try, and where would I try it?"

Elfrida grunted and walked off.

Gwyn started running.

Chapter Nine

She reached Hipping Hall and was escorted inside at knife point. A lowered blade, once they knew who she was, but it was not sheathed entirely, which Gwyn found distinctly odd. She was a noblewoman in obvious distress, torn from stem to stern and shod less well than a rouncy. What on earth could be imperiled by *her* bedraggled presence?

"Lady Guinevere," Hippingthorpe himself greeted her, holding her hand and pressing his lips to the back.

Gwyn smiled warmly, ignoring a shudder inside at his touch. He might be slightly revolting, and he might have a spotted past in the loyalty department, but he was her writ to the king, and she would have done almost anything to secure his goodwill.

"Whom do I thank for this unexpected visit, my lady? Where is your father?" He looked around as if he expected Ionnes de l'Ami to appear from behind an oaken post.

"He's . . . not here."

"Ahh." Hipping turned back to her, his glittering eyes hard. "Of course not. In nigh on twenty years, your father has ne'er passed within a mile nor passed a single hour with me. And yet, here you are, his only daughter. I can barely countenance that he sent you on some sordid mission on his refined behalf." He laughed uproariously. "Always too good for the likes of the lower barons, eh? And *everyone* marks lower than the Lord d'Everoot."

Gwyn fought to keep the smile tipped upward on her face. "Nay, my lord. My father respected all the king's men. But, since you mention it, I am on one, small, middling mission."

His eyebrows went up just as his gaze happened down. His bushy brows shot straight to his overgrown hairline. "Lady, what has happened?" He pulled back her cape and had full view of her stained, torn, tattered gown. "God's teeth, what is this?"

"This is Marcus fitzMiles."

Hipping looked at her, his hand still holding one side of the cape aloft. "God's bones! Endshire? He attacked you?" She nodded, feeling light-headed with relief. Hipping was a barely tamed nobleman, but noble he was, and he would help her. "What demon possessed him to attack you? Your father will have his head."

"Yes, well. My father is dead."

Hipping dropped the cape. "Ionnes de l'Ami is dead?"

"Aye. Pap—the Lord Earl passed away a fortnight past, God rest his soul. I just gave news to the king and his council last eve. As you can see," she smiled bitterly, "fitzMiles didn't grieve long."

"No, but well," Hipping replied absently, his gaze growing distant. He stared into space a moment, then snapped his fingers, calling for a servant and a bath.

Gwyn's knees almost buckled with relief. Hipping himself bustled her up the stairs to one of the rooms on the second floor. It was clean, with a small bedframe, a straw-filled mattress, and a narrow window.

"Thank-you," she exhaled. "'Tis perfect."

He turned to her. "Now tell me, what is this mission of yours? How can I help?"

"I must get word to the king. Marcus led me to believe King Stephen had approved of a match between him and the

House of Everoot, but I believe my king would ne'er countenance such a union."

"No," Hipping agreed. "No, he would not countenance a union of the de l'Ami heiress with any lesser baron, would he?"

Gwyn felt a flicker of concern. She smiled cheerily. "Word of your assistance will rate highly with the king, my lord. I will ensure it."

"Will you, now? How kind." He took her hand and sat her on the bed, then backed up a few steps. "Tell me, Lady Guinevere, how are you holding up under all the strain?"

"Oh, well, my lord," she laughed awkwardly, fumbling over his abrupt solicitude. "Such things are always hard, but we . . . well, I am doing well."

"Aye, but your father must have left some important and burdensome things to you, as his heir." He eyes dropped to the single bag left hanging around her girdle.

Gwyn followed his gaze. "Just some letters of Papa's," she said brightly.

His eyes ratcheted back up like a drawbridge. "Really?"

"Aye." Her hand went to the bag, her fingers curving around it, instinctively protecting it from view. "Lord Everoot's private missives to my mother the countess while he was away."

Hipping digested this. "Away on Crusade."

She hesitated. "Aye."

"Are you certain there are only *letters* inside?"

"Meaning?"

"No . . . objects."

"Objects?"

"Of unknown origin. Of . . . Holy Lands origin."

"Of course not," she snapped.

He held up his hands. "As you say, lady. I ask only because there are rumours of treasure connected to Everoot, but Endshire found nothing."

Her blood flowed chill. "Endshire? Found nothing?

Where?" She pushed up off the mattress and said gravely, "I think Lord Endshire's loyalty is in question, Lord Hipping."

"Really?" he drawled, powerful amusement twisting the word into a taunt. He leaned back against the wall and crossed his arms over his chest. "How about you let me see these letters of your Papa's?"

She smiled bitterly, realising the time for pleas to the heart had passed, if indeed it had ever been to hand. This was about power.

Drawing her cloak around her shoulders, she lifted her chin into the haughtiest pose she knew how. "Lord Hipping. I am cold and wet and torn like baggage. If you wish to negotiate with me, I would be warm and dry throughout it."

He considered her for a long moment. "Very well, Lady Gwyn. I will send up food and a bath." His eyes settled on the bag again. "As soon as we read through those letters."

He left, and as he closed the door, she heard the key turn in the lock.

"Your rooms are ready. And again, congratulations, my lord."

Griffyn nodded for what he hoped was the last time tonight. It was late, the hall was dark, lit only by firelight, and Robert Beaumont had already gone up to his own chambers, flush with success, negotiations complete. Henri fitzEmpress had his essential ally.

"But won't you stay up for one more drink?" Hipping asked one more time.

Griffyn shook his head. "I'm weary, and have a long ride tomorrow." Fatigue was no mere pretext. He'd secured the allegiance of one of the most vital allies Henri fitzEmpress would ever need, and all he felt was tired. Weary with spying, with war, with all the machinations of the world. He needed another lost waif to lift his spirits, he decided, stifling a yawn, but they were hard to find.

Something crashed on the floor above them. He and Hipping jerked their heads backwards and stared at the ceiling. It sounded like something heavy hit the floor hard, perhaps a washing pot. Hipping looked over with a convivial smile.

"My betrothed."

"Ahh."

"Just arrived."

"Ahh. Congratulations."

Hipping paused. "She's still adjusting."

"Mmm. Your wash pot may not."

Hipping laughed out of proportion to the inane jest. "Aye. I shan't bother her with my attentions again tonight. The priest has been sent for; tomorrow shall be soon enough."

Griffyn felt a strange ripple of unease. *Not required*, he told himself. *None of my business. Leave it be.*

He was shown to his room by a washed-out looking servant. The room was plain, small, and smelled of rot and mould. Which was not the problem. Small cracks in the wooden walls allowed wind to inch in, making it quite cold despite the brazier burning. But that was not the problem either. It was looking for a chamberpot that ruined everything.

Finding none in his room, and knowing the full tankard of the infamous Hippletun brew he'd imbibed would soon be needing release, he went in search of a chamberpot, a privy, or a servant to direct him towards either.

What he came across was a violent pounding coming from a chamber door at the far end of the corridor.

He stopped and stared. The wind?

Another spurt of wild hammering, then silence. No. That was not the wind.

'Tis neither any of your business, he cautioned himself. Enough time and energy had already been expended tonight on things that were none of his business.

He backtracked to the stairwell and found a servant who directed him to the guest privy outside. The rising winds almost blew the door off the privy. He manhandled it closed a few times, then, admitting defeat, let it bang maddeningly open and shut, thudding against the wall on each crest of wind as he completed his business. He tromped back inside, rubbing his eyes. Sleep. All he needed was a few hours' sleep.

He reached the upper landing. It was dark despite a torch slung in an iron ring hanging on the wall. Instead of turning left to his room, though, he paused and looked to his right.

Silence. Only the muted moaning of the winds. No cries for help, no frantic hammering. He stomped down the corridor anyway, uncertain why.

"Because I'm a fool," he muttered out loud.

He stopped in front of the doorway. Oddly, there was a key resting in its lock. He put his hand on it, paused, then turned it, feeling the fool. More silence. Nothing to be seen or heard.

"Of course not," he said to the emptiness. "Because there's nothing here."

The door crashed open and Guinevere fell into his arms.

Chapter Ten

They fell into a clump against the far wall, Griffyn propelled backwards by her headlong rush. He struggled to his knees and clamped his hand over her mouth, which she'd opened to scream.

"I cannot believe it," he announced, removing his hand when he saw she was not going to loose the shriek.

"Oh, thank the Lord," she cried in a whisper. "Pagan! How came you here? No, no, not now. I cannot believe you came, but we must get out of here—"

"We? What are you *doing* here?"

"—for I've only a little while until he comes for me."

"Comes for you?" he shouted back in a whisper. "What are you talking about? I left you with Clid, a safe refuge, and now you're *here*?" He stared at her a moment. Realisation dawned. "His betrothed."

"I am *not*!"

He rubbed the heel of his hand across his forehead, muttering, "I can't believe it. How incredibly unlikely. Abducted, twice in one night."

She scowled. "Astonishing. I can barely bestill my wonder. I left the village—"

"*Why?* It was warm and dry—"

"Yes, yes." She brushed off his kept promises with an urgent whisper. "But not safe."

"Aye, well, I can see how being here suits you so much the better."

She touched his arm lightly, but the subtle contact felt more forceful than that, a flash of feminine verve. "You were *mad* to leave me there," she whispered vehemently. "But there is no time for that now. I came because I had to. I know of Hipping's reputation, of course, and the trouble he's caused my lord king. But I did not know he was a . . . a *brigand*." Her lips twisted, and Griffyn wondered if Hipping's lips had touched hers. The thought, against all reason, brought a flood of anger surging through his blood. "He is holding me against my will."

"For what?" he asked suspiciously.

She paused for half a heartbeat. "It doesn't matter. Politics."

The evasion seemed unnecessary, and would have caught his attention if he hadn't had his attention captured by so many other things, such as the bewildering verity that he was kneeling on the floor of a minor nobleman's corridor with a woman he'd already rescued once tonight and left miles from here not three hours ago. And she needed more rescuing yet.

Then again, abductions were commonplace enough. Kidnappings, forced betrothals. An unprotected woman on the road was fair game.

And all of a sudden, Griffyn's largest concern was not expanding Henri fitzEmpress's frontiers, it was the raven-haired, flushing-cheeked demoiselle in front of him. Her tousled hair and wild eyes made him worry, but it was her incredible, indomitable spirit that turned his tides.

"I hate to be a burden yet again . . ."

He grabbed her arm. "Let's go."

He leaned in and took a quick survey of her room—much nicer than his—then grabbed a lantern sitting on the table. Lowering its flame to almost nothing, he propelled her down the stairs.

Keeping close to the shadows, they made their way straight out the front door and through the rising winds to the stables without being seen or heard. No one could have heard an approaching army over the winds, and no one was about to witness this abduction.

Griffyn pulled open the stable door. A powerful gust wrenched it out of his hands and flung it wide, slamming it against the wall. Muttering under his breath, he shuttled them inside and hauled it shut behind them.

The roaring quieted. There were the dim sounds of animals crunching hay and shuffling. It was warm, with tighter seams between the planks of wood than of his guest bedchamber, he noticed grimly in passing. He began fumbling around in the darkness, feeling about on the ledge by the doorway for a flint.

Her shadowy figure moved down the row of stalls. "Where's my horse?"

He set the lantern on a small ledge. Light spread further into the dark stable. "What horse?"

"I had a horse."

"What?"

"A horse, a horse. I came here on a horse."

His looked at her suspiciously. "Where did you get a horse?"

She shrugged. "From the village."

"They gave you a horse?" he said in flat disbelief. The purchase of a single plough horse would require the village's annual intake, which was nigh on nil, for a few decades.

"They didn't exactly *give* me the horse."

"You took the horse."

She gave him an evil look. "Yes. I took the horse. I didn't kill a man, so you need not look at me like that. I planned to ensure Old Barney was returned, but now, well." She stopped.

"Well, that's that," he muttered, stalking to Noir, whose seventeen-hand measurement at the withers made him stand taller than any other horse in the stables. He nickered at the sound of Griffyn's voice.

"What's what?" She hurried after him, tugging hair away from her face.

He led Noir out of his stall and grabbed the saddle. She came to the horse's head and reached out to pet him.

"I wouldn't," Griffyn said grimly. He threw the saddle blanket over Noir's sloping back, then placed the saddle atop, just at the horse's withers. He slid the saddle and blanket back an inch, smoothing the fur. "He doesn't like . . . people."

"He seems to like you."

"Yes, well, I'm not a person. To him." He flipped the cinch off the saddle and let it drop. Reaching under Noir's belly, he grabbed the buckle and pulled.

"Oh."

They didn't say anything else. Griffyn dourly finished his saddling, then bid her to the huge oaken stable door.

"I'll open it, you hold it. Keep it from slamming."

She nodded. He nudged it slightly ajar. The winds flung it wide and smashed it gleefully against the wall. She almost fell down trying to hold it back.

He glared at her.

"I'm sorry," she whispered fiercely, wrestling with it. Griffyn reached over her shoulder and pushed it shut. "Think you I wish to be discovered any more than you?"

"I have no idea what you wish for." He threw her up in front of the saddle and climbed up himself. "I would have thought a warm, dry place, but apparently not. You prefer storms and abduction. Sit close as you can, no, lean back against me, and here, I'll wrap my cloak around us both. No one will come out to examine us too closely, and the winds should make a mockery of any clear shape or form. I came, now I'm leaving, and let us hope they will see it like that. But if they do come out," he added more slowly, looking down into her wide, bright green eyes, "don't scream when I kill them."

She blinked. "Give me a blade. Truly," she insisted when he just looked at her. "I am in earnest. You saw me with a rock. Imagine me with a blade."

"I'm terrified," he muttered, but unsheathed the blade wrapped at his thigh and slipped it to her, then pulled his hood up. "Now slide down as far as you can, sit as close as you can, and silence, if ever you can."

"Pah," she snorted from her dark, cloaked nest.

Griffyn lifted his head and, pressing his heels against Noir's flanks, rode slowly through the bailey and under the inner gates, which were still raised, a good omen. This porter had not been alerted he was staying the night. Perhaps the outer guards were as ignorant.

No one even appeared to notice he was passing until he reached the guards at the outer bailey, and they waved him through with barely a glance.

He rode under the straining portcullis gate, the wicked wooden talons hanging half a foot above his head, and like that, they were outside in the king's woods, he with a mission to accomplish and a heady woman huddled beneath his cape.

Chapter Eleven

Noir barely made a sound on the soft dirt path. His hooves trod through the damp, flat leaves. Overhead, the moon slid back and forth behind ragged clouds and cast shadows between the branches. In the darkness of the forest, small rustlings disturbed the underbrush and in the distance a larger animal, to judge by the sound, exploded a few sticks under paw. Overhead an owl winged by, disturbed by their intrusion, his hooting a haunting sound in a darkened wood.

Walking at the horse's head, Griffyn was trying to understand the astonishing turn his night had taken, from unexpected battle to the unexpected cargo now riding his horse.

He scowled at a low-lying tree limb and sidestepped the path into a puddle of mud that would have reached to his shins if he hadn't leapt back in time.

Said cargo, he admitted grudgingly, was an amiable enough companion. More so. Much more so. She was nothing he could have expected. Fleeing one of the most bloodthirsty barons in Stephen's England, she had not cowered. She'd not fainted. She had not screamed or pitched or whined. She had stood at his side, fearless as any warrior, and smiled.

Smiled, for God's sake.

Which is why he was doing it, he supposed.

He scowled.

The longer he walked, the colder he got, the more he ruminated on how this night had come to such an unforeseen conclusion, the more convinced he became of one fact. He tugged Noir to a halt and turned to confront his more-than-amiable, maddening cargo.

"You had no intention of staying," he announced grimly.

Her heart-shaped face crumpled in confusion. "Staying where?"

"They could have been monks chanting Paternosters and you would have left at the first chance."

Her face cleared. "Trust in this, Pagan, the men you left me with were *not* monks—"

"You couldn't stop talking, could you?"

"What?"

"What did you say to them?"

She blushed. "I barely said a word about anything, but when they saw the coin—"

"I knew it. But I don't think you left because it was unsafe. I think you left because you didn't want to be there. And you never do things you don't wish to do."

Her jaw dropped. "That is simply not true!"

"Tell me the last thing you did that you wished otherwise."

"I—I—I, why right now!" she sputtered, flinging her arm out. "Behold, here I sit on your beast of a horse and let you hold the reins, guiding me ever deeper into the king's chase, with never a notion of whither I go, nor whence I might return. Might I prefer to be safely ensconced in a bed? Mayhap to sleep? Pah. Think you I chose this night, Pagan, I shall learn you a different tale."

He started walking again, grimly satisfied. "Of course you chose it."

He could feel her glare penetrating through the back of his head. "Then so did you."

He didn't reply. She was silent, too, for perhaps a moment,

then her voice chirped up again, light and airy in the deep, dark wood.

"At least give me the reins."

He laughed. He didn't mean to, or want to, but there it was.

"Truly, Pagan. I have a way with horses."

He looked over his shoulder. "Aye. Losing them."

She smiled wanly.

He lifted his eyebrows. "Are you planning on losing mine?"

"Are you planning on dropping me off at another den of iniquity?" she retorted pleasantly.

He laughed again and hopped over a log. "They weren't so much iniquitous."

"True. They were vain, covetous, and self-serving. Let me think what that harkens to mind. Oh, aye: Men."

His smile faded. "I won't begrudge you your opinion, Raven." He ducked his head to avoid another tree limb, and they walked awhile in companionable silence. "I personally wasn't speaking so much of your woman-ness, but your . . ." he waved his hand vaguely in the air.

Gwyn's eyes narrowed. "My what? What's this?" She mimicked his hand wave.

"Your . . ." He pursed his lips, thinking. "Fickleness."

"Fickleness? *Fickle*ness? You think I've been fickle?"

He looked wary. "I'm just saying someone should keep a better eye on you—"

She slid off the horse and landed with a thud. "A better eye? On *me*?" She stalked forward, finger in the air. "Happens you might try being herded into marriage with someone whose very presence on the earth offends you, with warts and foul breath—"

"Endshire doesn't have warts."

"Oh, as if you'd know. He has them on his soul. Have *you* ever been chased through the streets of London and up the king's highway? Have *you* ever been told to ride in a litter 'for your protection' so you don't have your own horse to escape upon?

"Have *you* ever—" She was moving closer in a fury, every "you" punctuated by a jab toward his chest, until her fingertip hovered an inch away from his body. "—had your own inclinations but been thwarted by those who are simply stronger than you, and so they will *always prevail*. Because of *these*," she said as she jabbed a furious finger toward his sword, "and *those*." She reached out to pinch the muscles of his arm.

It was a mistake. The moment her hand closed around the bunched strength of his upper arm, encased in steel and leather, she felt his heat and power throbbing onto her, and almost fainted.

"Aye. I have," he said in a deceptively quiet voice. "There is always someone stronger than thee. And what of me, mistress?" His gaze turned hard, his tone cold. "What of the things I have left behind tonight? How am I to figure in your mad accounting?"

He wrenched his arm away, breaking her stunned grip, then it was she in *his* grip, she propelled backwards, she leaned up against Noir. And she remembered far too well what had happened last she'd stood near the horse.

"Well," she whispered. "Quite well, Pagan. You have been nothing but . . . my saviour."

He was still a moment, his face a taut mask of impassive regard, then he flung his fingers open.

"Foolish," he muttered. He raked his fingers through his hair, tousling the dark spikes. "And less patient than I ought. You've been through a lot tonight."

"Well," she agreed with a shaky laugh. "I've certainly been through a lot of men."

He stared a moment, his hard face given the gift of surprise, then threw back his head and laughed so deeply the woods rang with it. He laughed so hard and so well she forgot all about being afraid, aware mostly that her arm felt cold without his fingers on it. She felt unruly and reckless and peculiar, washed out and energized all at the same time, as if she'd been breathing too fast.

Emotional storms were like that, she supposed, although her recall was dim. It had been a long time since she'd given rein to her emotions, and her life the last twelve years had been much more tranquil as a result. Better. Truly. Who could say otherwise? Doing as she was told, stifling those pesky urges and intuitions that ruined everything, 'twas for the best. Truly. All was well.

Except for the fact that no matter how well she behaved now, nothing could bring Mamma back. Or Roger. And now Papa was dead too.

Willfulness had its price. But why did so many others have to pay?

The familiar free-falling sensation began again, and she slipped down into the Ache, that yawning chasm of despair that had cracked open twelve years earlier on the day her brother, much-loved heir to the Everoot earldom, was killed. By Gwyn.

Mamma died three months later, her heart broken in two. Papa kept on, of course. As a shell.

Gwyn's body started closing in on itself, as it always did when the memories came. Her shoulders crumpled, her throat tightened. *Oh, Mamma. I miss you so. It was a terrible accident. I told Papa that ever so many times.*

"Here."

Pagan's voice jerked her out of the awful reverie. She flung her head up to find him watching her, the flask extended. She shook her head, dispelling the dark thoughts, and reached out. "You feel blessedly uncomplicated."

"You mean the drink does."

She recoiled as the now-familiar fire threaded its way down her throat, then lifted the flask in mock toast. "Aye. To simple drinks."

"And complicated women."

"Oh, my," she laughed softly. "I don't know that they're worth all that much, in the end."

The smokey greyness of his eyes was unreadable in the darkness. "And what would you know of it?"

"Of complicated women?"

"Of the men who toast them."

"Oh." She blinked. "Nothing."

"I didn't think so."

There didn't seem to be any more else to say on the subject, or else far too much, and she was feeling much too . . . unruly, to trust herself to do either. Instead, she took another long, scorching swallow. When it had settled into her belly in a nice, hot wash, she asked the question she'd been wanting to ask since they'd left Hippingthorpe Hall.

"What were you doing there, Pagan?"

"Where?"

Unruly, indeed. Or drunk. The look on his face should have warned her off. "Hipping's hunting lodge."

A slow smile curved up his mouth, but it was dark and dangerous. "You don't want to ask me that."

"No," she said, her voice dropping until it was barely a whisper. "It doesn't seem particularly sensible, does it?"

"I would advise against it."

"Sirrah," she said weakly, "I would advise against nigh on everything we each of us have done tonight."

There was a long pause. "Ah, well, but you haven't had it all yet, Raven."

The masculine rumble was all confident, sensual threat. Peering up into eyes that shifted from blue to grey to smokey black, Gwyn had the sense she was falling. Her head was spinning, her fingers cold, her face hot. She presumed it was fear. It ought to have been fear. It mimicked fear, teasing her skin into ripples and making her heart hammer.

But it wasn't fear at all.

"Where are you taking me, Pagan?" she asked.

He paused for the briefest moment. "I know of an inn."

"And I know of an Abbey," she said weakly. Did it sound as desperate as she felt? "An inn doesn't seem particularly . . . sensible either, does it?"

He dropped his gaze to the cleavage she'd been struggling to cover with the shreds of her tattered dress. As if physically pushed, her hand fell away. "I may be running a bit shy of sense at the moment," he admitted in a low voice.

Pause, a heartbeat, then she said, "I believe I am entirely bereft."

"Bien," he murmured in the low kind of masculine rumble that could be threat or promise, but was definitely pulsing wetness between her thighs. Heat radiated off his body and whispered of wanting. It undulated in waves over the cape, through her dress, onto her skin. Pulse, heat, *come closer,* pulse.

His shoulders stretched huge and blocked the moonlight washing through the woods. Dark hair, dark eyes. He stood with his legs slightly apart, his boots planted in the earth. Around his hips was strapped a belt hung with a sword and a veritable arsenal of blades. A faint, musky odour clung to him, of soft leather, of wood smoke and forest. Pewter-grey eyes steeped in mystery long-lived and danger about to burst, she stared into them and knew within the length of his rock-hewn body was a force she'd never reckoned with before.

He was danger and she had most certainly, most tremendously, fallen.

She lifted her fingers to trace his jaw, then rolled her hand over and brushed the knuckles of her fingers against his lips. He watched, motionless, then the hot stroke of his tongue slid between her fingers.

"Oh," she murmured on a hot exhale.

He caught up her hand, eyes still locked on hers, and stroked his tongue over the centre of her palm. Her knees buckled.

He caught her up and when Gwyn knew she should have

been screaming and pushing him away, God save her if she wasn't opening beneath him, letting his tongue spread possessively into her mouth, letting him suckle her lips, explore every inch of her, crash in on her with a wave of passion so intense she forgot she was standing, breathing, living, doing anything but being kissed. Engulfed. Possessed.

She wrapped her arms around his shoulders and hung on, her mouth open for him, meeting every passionate lash of his tongue with one of her own, until there was no difference between breathing and kissing, no space between them; they were all a single length of hot touching desire.

It was an unyielding assault. Gwyn knew nothing but that her life was forever changed. The hard heat from his thighs burned against hers, loosing a firestorm of wet heat that slid down her belly and pooled between her legs. She entwined fingers in his hair, her mouth open, welcoming each lash of his wicked tongue. With breathtaking skill, he locked his hands around her hips and gently, inexorably, rocked her hips into his.

Throbbing, perfect, painful wanting washed through her. "Oh, no, Pagan," she whispered, not meaning the *no*, only meaning *she hadn't known*. She'd never known there was anything like this man.

Griffyn heard his name and didn't heed the *no*. Her body was moving in a subtle, instinctive rhythm and told him which cue to attend. He plundered her willing depth, plunging his fingers deep into her hair and dragging her head back, lashing her harder and deeper, coaxing her body to bend back for him, which she did, trembling, ready, until their bodies touched from chest to knee, and it surged desire through him, hot and savage.

Reckless with passion, he kissed down the side of her neck and as he did, he pushed his hand up under her skirts, sliding his calloused fingertips up the back of her silky warm thigh. Then, God save him, she bent her knee in response to his touch, and the move pressed the hot cradle of her into his erection.

A tremor of bone-jarring desire crashed down on him, stunning him. He hadn't expected this. She was nothing but an accident. A brief chivalrous impulse amid a lifetime of blood and swords and hatred. *She was nothing.*

Nothing, mayhap, but he wanted her so badly it hurt. He felt like the unseen shelf his life had rested upon was being kicked out from under him. Silk and hot skin, feminine heat and panting desire, funny, intelligent, and brave beyond imagining, whispering his name, needing *him.*

Why did that matter so much?

The question cartwheeled so loudly through his mind, it bounded into the realm of consciousness and brought him to his senses. Using every shattered fragment of self-control he'd cultivated through years of long-checked vengeance and knocking knights off their horses, Griffyn loosed his hands from her hot body and took a step back.

"I can't seem to stop doing that," he muttered.

She swayed at the abrupt release and stumbled, righting herself by way of a desperate grab at a well-placed tree limb. He made a conciliatory move forward but the look of horror on her face brought him up short. Her hand grabbed the dark wood, clutching it as if she were on a sinking ship.

A waterfall of black hair fluttered by her face before falling over her slender shoulders. Loose sprays framed her face. One was caught in her mouth. In the shaft of moonlight splashing between the tree limbs, she looked like a nymph, a magical sprite, achingly beautiful and completely unnecessary.

"I should not have done that," he muttered as gently as his lust-ravaged body would allow. His blood was thundering, his groin pounding with an ache he could barely withstand. "Again."

"No," she agreed.

Planting his hand on Noir's withers, he dropped his head. He'd lost his mind, his reason, and his sense of honour, all within a few hours of meeting the woman, and the costs were escalating, up to and including capture and death if Marcus d'Endshire or Aubrey Hippingthorpe discovered his where-abouts.

The path they now used, and the fortress to which it led, was hidden, but not so well hidden that a few soldiers nosing in the bushes couldn't stumble upon it. Not so well forgotten that a few questions to an aging villager could not point them to a crumbling stone fortress steeped in Saxon lore and ancient blood.

And now he was taking her there, to his lair of rebel spies. Like a fool. Like a dimwitted drunkard. Like a man in love, his brains addled by too much affection and too vivid images of bedtime romps. Which he was not. None of these.

So why was he doing it?

Because of the smile.

He dragged the heel of his palm across his forehead. His erection was still throbbing, his heart still hammering inside his chest, the remnants of a desire so potent he could taste it. Hot honey. She would taste like that. She *had*.

He rubbed his hand across the back of his neck. "I am sorry, Guinevere. You needn't fear me in such a way ever again."

"I'm not afrai—"

"Can you walk?" he asked coldly.

She drew back. "Quite well, thank-you."

He looked at her doubtfully. At the moment, balance seemed a credible accomplishment. Her hair lifted in the winds that surged amid the tree trunks, and her torso angled distinctly sideways. Her face was intent and childlike as she tried to smooth the wrinkles from her once-fine gown, and the whole scene sending a wave of such lust and unexpected tenderness washing through him that he felt weak.

This was madness. Enchanted she was, aye, like a demon, and he was furious for being cast in her spell. He reached for the anger like a drowning man.

"So what is it to be, mistress?" he asked curtly.

Chapter Twelve

Gwyn continued brushing off her dress, her mind reeling. His question made the world tilt. Said in that husky, masculine rumble, hard-edged and taut with restraint, it didn't speak of what he *had* done, it bored straight into her soul and whispered of what he was going to do.

What she would have let him do.

She stuffed her fingers in the folds of her dress and stared at the ground. Churning belly or no, she wasn't so far gone to misunderstand that being wrapped in his arms was more dangerous than encountering sword-wielding foes on deserted highways. All they could do was assail her body. Pagan was reaching in deeper than that, channeling straight into the recesses of her soul and tapping the Ache.

She need fear much more than ravishment.

She swallowed thickly. She must keep her distance from him. The night was more spirit-filled than she could have imagined, and they were impish, mischievous, meddling things. King's feasts and mysterious knights, besieged castles and sword fights. And kisses. Searing, passionate kisses that stoked straight down into her soul.

Far, *far* away.

"What is *what* to be?" she snapped, sounding as irritated as he.

A slow smile spread across his features. It was dark and dangerous. "I've mentioned an inn."

"And I've mentioned an Abbey."

"And do you insist, we shall wander the forest towards the monks' retreat, encountering more danger as the night progresses, growing stupider as each hour passes."

She drew herself up and filled her lungs with air. "Speak for yourself, sirrah."

He shot her a dark look. "I am."

The air left, deflating her. "Oh."

"But this is not the time for a wolf's head to be roaming the forests. Nor is the middle of a tempest," he added ominously. His words were snatched by winds that were lifting into occasional gusts around them. Cold-edged, powerful gusts that smelled of rain. "Or, we can go to the inn, wash your wounds, tend your head, get some food and rest, and awaken with fresher minds and smoother tempers."

"Your temper has not been so rough," she said meekly, twisting a bit of torn fabric in her hands.

"I was not speaking of me."

"Oh."

"So what shall it be?"

She looked at him skeptically. "I don't know of any inns in these parts."

He sighed, a defeated sound. "I do."

She stood in damp indecision, hope and suspicion strangling each other. *He would help her . . . he had just killed four men . . . she was not alone . . . in her defence . . . he was tunneling into a reservoir of dangerous emotions . . . his eyes . . .*

She stared at a wet leaf pasted overtop her slipper. He was crouched on his heels beside the horse's leg and brushed dried clumps of mud from the fetlock. Black boots rode up the length of his corded calves, and the tightly packed muscles of his thighs bunched beneath the chausses he wore. Against the purple-green forest, he was an outline of dark danger. And her only hope.

"We will go to your inn."

Griffyn blew out a silent gust of relief, but looked askance when she strode to Noir and tried to mount without assistance. Her hand clasped over the horse's withers, her foot fumbling for leverage on a downed tree. It was slippery with moss, but when he approached, she scowled so fiercely over her shoulder that he stepped back and crossed his arms to watch. The horse was almost seventeen hands high and towered above her like a small castle. He was also being remarkably patient.

Griffyn's jaw tightened when she slipped. "Lady?"

"The world is not what I thought it to be," she muttered, as if he'd asked a question to which that would be a fitting reply, and scrambled up Noir's side.

Her head disappeared for a few moments in the trees and when she emerged, she had two or three sticks protruding at odd angles from her curls. Matted leaves lay flat on her shoulders, with one particularly wet clump lodged in the cleavage of her dress. She removed it with scornful dignity, her eyes fixed straight ahead.

He shook his head, took up the reins and clucked to Noir.

They walked in silence for a long time before either of them broke it. Not surprisingly, he noted crossly, 'twas she.

"Where are you taking me?"

He barely glanced over his shoulder. "I told you, Guinevere: an inn."

She offered him an arched brow, which he saw even through his sidewise attention. "And I told you, *Pagan*: I know of no inns along this stretch of highway."

"Perhaps," he admitted, "'tis a bit off the highway."

"A long bit, by the look of it. We've been riding for half an hour."

"You've been riding, and it's been nearer an hour."

She raised her eyebrow another notch. "You may have your beast back."

"We're almost there."

"Where?"

"Duck," he said, and without looking back to see if she had, he did, bending his head beneath a low-lying tree branch. When he lifted it, they were in the centre of a clearing.

An old, disused path meandered away into the ferns at the far side. In its centre rose the battered remnants of a single building, huge and hulking, its wood and wicker walls half torn away. Only the stone portions stood, and even they were crumbling.

Gutted by fire and looters, most of it was only a half-shell now. Towards the back of the edifice, three gloomy stories rose, squatting sullenly over the crippled forebuilding. In a few windows yellow candlelight glowed, looking like gaps where the eerie maw had already lost its teeth. In the dark night, the battered structure looked sinister and imposing and almost alive.

He heard a sharp intake of breath from behind. His stallion threw his head in the air and sidestepped.

"Easy, Noir," he murmured.

She was staring. "I thought you said you were taking us to an inn."

"'*Tis* an inn." He gestured with his hands for her to slide off into them.

"That," she insisted in a squeaky voice, pointing, "is not an inn."

"An inn houses travellers, no?"

She started to nod, then stopped. Her head fell to the side as she studied him. "No. I mean, yes."

"Well, then," he said, as if that settled the matter.

Extending his hands, he held them up again. She gave him a disdainful glance and, untying the bulky pouch she had tied around Noir's saddle, she disappeared over the far side of the destrier. Noir kicked out with his hind hoof, barely missing her. From under the stallion's belly, he watched her small slippers stumble to the front of the horse, where he met her with a cool glance.

"You're determined to lose or injure every body part before the night is through, is that it?"

"Humph," she snorted.

Injury to her body was the least of Gwyn's worries at the moment. Much more worrisome was the thudding inside whenever Pagan looked at her. It harkened back to the Ache. Only this, while it lodged in the same places—heart, womb— did not lie on top like a smothering rag. It was different.

Dangerous.

"Humph," she said again, and crossed her arms over her chest.

Every muscle in her body was sore. The autumn winds had thoroughly chilled her damp fingers and toes. Her clothes were beginning to dry in mud-caked wrinkles, and she was so addled by his kiss she could barely think straight. She stared at the façade of the building, pretending he wasn't staring at her profile. "So, where is the innkeep?"

Just as she spoke, a man came hurrying out to them. Pagan lengthened his stride to meet him halfway across the clearing and she watched as they spoke swiftly, unable to hear the hushed conversation. The man reached out and took Noir's reins, then disappeared into a far building.

A moment later, a pair of men rushed out of the crumbling building and into the stables. They raced out on horses a moment later and, lifting their hands to Pagan as they galloped by, disappearing into the woods.

Pagan returned, his face set in grim lines. "Come."

"The innkeep?" she queried in an innocently sweet tone.

He did not look amused.

"And the servants, I suppose?" She smiled brightly, nodding to where the men had ridden away under the eaves of the forest.

He turned on his heel and walked towards the crumbling building.

Her gaze bored into the broad expanse of his retreating back with evil intent, but he did not seem to feel her enmity. Nor did he seem to care she was still standing there. He neither turned nor slowed.

Sighing, she followed him, tracing an erratic line through the high, mist-strewn grasses on one heeled and one unheeled slipper. "Methinks they must hurt for business, set so far from the highway," she huffed in a loud and irritable voice.

"They've patrons enough," was his curt reply.

She sniffed. "How fortunate."

She continued on, arms wrapped around her body, fingers clutching the satchel with her father's love letters in them. She dared not think any further back than the past half hour. What could she do about any of it just now?

She began threading her fingers through her tangled hair as they tramped through the long, wet grasses, but her fingers shook. Everything was warped, and even the earth beneath her felt wobbly.

As for Pagan, he had turned from an engaging, mysterious saviour into a dangerous, sensuous rake, then into a close-lipped beast of a man in about as long as it would take to fill a bathtub. And now she was at a remote inn with him. Wonderful. What joys still awaited her this evening?

It started to rain.

Chapter Thirteen

It came down in torrents, as if the heavens had grown weary of their load and decided to leave it to the earthbound creatures to manage. A bright flash of lightning seared the heavens and a few moments later thunder fell through the crack, rolling and pitching as it came. Hard darts of rain slanted from the sky, driving wet pellets into their eyes and between the folds of their clothing. They entered the building with water streaming from their fingertips.

Pushing back her hood, Gwyn heard voices spilling through the walls, but saw no one. Laughter and jocular voices rose momentarily from a far room, then fell away again. The place was clean, she decided, with wide, open spaces. Even the stairs were broad, not close and curving like the Nest. Odd that no travellers were in sight, but it seemed well-tended enough to serve for the night.

From out of the shadows peered a small, feminine face. For the only human in sight, it was strange indeed to have her gaze at them from the shadows, as if she didn't want to be seen. She smiled at Gwyn, who returned the gesture, feeling odd. Then her face turned to Pagan. "My lo—"

"We need a bath," he said firmly, propelling Gwen up the

stairs in front of him. "The innkeeper's wife," he said when she angled her head around in mute enquiry.

They climbed the rest of the way in silence, passing through a darkness alleviated by a series of torches set in iron cressets bolted to the walls. The light was soft and welcoming, if the shadows a bit eerie. Her silhouette was short and squat, then long and jagged, but always, plastered on the wall above her head, Pagan's shadow was the darkest thing about.

"My room," he said at her back, gesturing to a door at their right.

She stopped short. "And where am I to stay?"

"These are the only rooms."

She chose to neither reply nor move, waiting instead until his thigh brushed against hers as he strode ahead and pushed open the door.

Someone had prepared for his return, and Gwyn couldn't stifle a relieved sigh when she poked her head through the doorway. The rooms were small and clean, holding an antechamber and, in the distance, a bedchamber set mostly in darkness. The doorframe was low, so low Pagan had to stoop as he entered. Wicker walls reflected a golden glow from the fire burning in a brazier, and dark red tapestries, worn but clean, covered two walls.

Through a small doorway hung with another faded tapestry she spied a bed piled with a mountainous covering of furs. She sighed again, feeling a tiny bit of hard-packed tension ebb from her shoulders. She swung her neck in a small circle, stretching it.

"First, a bath," he said.

Her shoulders hunched back up. *"What?"*

A knock came at the door. Pagan opened it and in came a short succession of servants bearing a round, fat tub and steaming buckets. How did he arrange such a thing so quickly? In no time a bath was ready and the room empty again but for her and Pagan.

She stared at the tub, her back to him. She was not going to look at him. No, because she knew as surely as her head hurt he'd be staring at her with that steely-eyed stare, or, worse yet, smiling that small, heart-shattering grin. And then the thudding would begin.

She heard his bootsteps start towards the door. "Sir, might I . . . ?" she said. His boots stopped moving. "You mentioned a messenger?" she said directly to the wall.

"I will arrange for it."

She half-turned her head. "But . . . all the way out here?"

"The innkeeper's son serves as a courier at times. He will take your message."

"Oh." Steam from the tub rose against a backdrop of red tapestries. She could feel his presence behind her, standing motionless, watching her. She sucked her lip in between her teeth.

"Guinevere."

"What?" she mumbled.

"Get in."

The edge of the sloshing, steaming tub warranted all her attention. She could barely rip her gaze from it. "You . . . you . . ."

"Are leaving." The door squeaked open. "But I'll be back."

She jerked her head around, but he was already gone.

Several moments later, a tap came on the door and she opened it to find the feminine face who had smiled at her from the shadows downstairs smiling at her once again. She spoke in a voice so quiet Gwyn had to duck her head closer to hear.

"He said you're to tell me your message."

Gwyn smiled gratefully. "I thank your son for carrying it."

The woman blinked. "My son?"

"Oh, I am sorry." Gwyn's cheeks flushed hot. "I was told

the innkeeper's son would carry my message, and I thought you were his . . . well, I am sorry."

"No, no," the woman replied hastily. "No need, my lady. 'Tis my son, indeed. My son who will carry your message."

"Well, then, I am in luck," Gwyn said slowly. "Please, come in."

They sat at the table. It was an odd feeling, to be tucked in this remote inn, no one knowing where she was. The windows were shuttered and it was dark outside, so she could tell nothing about the world outside her room either. The only thing she knew for certes was that the storm was getting worse and the innkeeper's wife didn't know she had a son.

She directed the missive to Cantebrigge, to her friend Mary and her husband John, lord of a small but strategically important manor, where Gwyn had planned to stop on her return trip, before all the madness began. It was unlikely, but possible, that King Stephen had indeed sold her to fitzMiles, and with Everoot at stake, she was not taking chances. She would not send a message directly to the king, revealing where she was. She needed a conduit. John of Cantebrigge was favoured by King Stephen, and would know what to do.

She spoke slowly, carefully crafting her words to tell of her need yet reveal nothing of import should the message, or messenger, fall into unwanted hands.

"Dearest John: Lord d'Endshire plans to wed me against my will," she said slowly, "and set upon me when I was without assistance." She looked at the candle flickering on the table. Its flame was small but bright. "By God's Grace, I was saved by a miracle, but am with the knowledge that our lord king has allowed this debauched thing, although I cannot fathom it. Would that you send him my plea for mercy and an audience. My greater need, at present, is to be succored at Saint Alban's, whence I have escaped. Take the back paths, and speak to no one, John. Everoot may depend upon it."

The maid repeated it word for word, then withdrew. Gwyn

glanced at the bath. All she could do now was wait, hope her friends in Cantebrigge would believe the message was truly from her. And that was a large hope.

In these lawless times, no one depended on anything but death and King Stephen's taxes. A message such as hers, with its urgency and need for secrecy, with no seal from the true sender, could be interpreted as either plea or ruse. John of Cantebrigge might well think it a trick.

She had momentarily debated handing over the only thing in her possession with the identifying de l'Ami device on it, but swiftly decided against it.

Everoot had, as did few other places in the realm, such as Chester and Durham, privileges to minting rights. A great deal of coin was melted and stamped at the Nest upon a time, but in the lawless days of rape and plunder that marked Stephen's reign, there was little work to be done, and even less profit to be made. The privilege had become a burden.

Even so, while no longer minting coin for the realm, the Everoot minting tools had created the most precise, indelible, unforgettable stamp in the land—a budding rose. Its lines were etched like a sunrise, clear and precise. When others chose boars and hawks and bears, her father had taken an emblem that was dear to his wife's heart—the twice-blooming rose of Everoot.

It was distinctive. It was rare. It would be recognised anywhere, and it adorned the steel-plated, curving lid of Papa's box.

She shifted and her foot touched the felt bag. She bent over and touched it, almost as if it were a talisman, then sat straight again.

What purpose would it serve, to have sent the thing along? They would believe the message or not, but she was certain her friend John of Cantebrigge would not wait upon a charm or seal before coming to her aid.

And she could not give it up, not even for a moment.

She picked up the bulky bag and pulled out the chest. It was a beautiful thing. It had a strange attraction about it—made one *desire* to touch it—but beyond its simple, almost unearthly beauty, it was precious because, in the last moment of his life, Papa had thought this the most important thing to bequeath to her, the small chest that held love letters between him and Gwyn's mother while he was away on Crusade. Strange.

But then, she decided for the hundredth time, *he had loved Mamma so much.*

And Gwyn had seen to her death as much as if she'd plunged a blade through her heart.

Her heart twisted. She'd spent the last decade of her life trying to make it up to him, to no avail. Of course, killing one's brother and mother did have unintended consequences. Such as one's father hating one.

She ran her hand over the chest and tipped up the lid. Her parents' letters lay inside. She touched them reverently, as always, then pushed her hand down, feeling along the bottom. She felt a little further.

Oh, Lord. Coldness washed through her limbs.

It was gone.

Her heart skidded a little. In addition to the chest, Papa had given her two little keys, one gold, one steel. His frenzied insistence on safeguarding these items had been mystifying, since neither key opened a single lock throughout the entire castle. Gwyn knew: she'd tried them in every lock in the castle since then. But promise she had, on her knees, at his deathbed.

Now the steel one was missing.

She picked up the scrolls with trembling fingers and looked inside. No key. She sat back, her blood chugging, mind racing. Yes, that must have been it. When she'd dropped the chest back in London, the key had fallen out.

But whyfore feel so awful? They were remnants of the past,

of no value. But they'd mattered to Papa, and so it felt like another minute, irreparable hurt.

Her hand went instinctively to her skirts, touching the hard length of metal concealed inside a pouch sewn to the inside of her skirts. At least the little golden key was safe.

What could it matter that she had lost the steel one?

She pushed sharply to her feet. The chair tipped backwards. She plunged the chest back into its pouch, then knelt beside the tub. Warm steam rose up to engulf her cold, damp fingertips. She began disrobing.

She glanced at the bag again. Papa had been a lettered man— uncommon in a warrior—and Gwyn's mother had learned from him. Stranger still, Gwyn thought with an unsettling pricking just on the fringe of her awareness, that Papa would so vehemently deny the skill to her. But so it was, and the letters remained unread. Surely she could have asked William of the Five Strands, her aging, cantankerous, beloved seneschal, to cipher them, but Gwyn felt strongly that they were private, for her eyes alone.

She had looked through the missives, of course, ran her gaze over the ink and her fingertips over the scraps of soft vellum and crinkled, aging parchment, but she couldn't read a word of the spidery ink-lines. One day, she would learn to read.

And then, maybe, she could fathom the mystery of what lay *underneath* the letters, in the locked compartment with the steel lid that not even fire could unseal.

Chapter Fourteen

Griffyn stalked down the stairs to the main hall of the building, which was not an inn and had never been an inn. What it had been was a fortress for Saxon sentries some ninety years ago, on the eve of William the Bastard's invasion. It had not passed its usefulness either. Men still stood amid its walls and plotted the overthrow of empires. Men like Griffyn and his band of knights bred in the killing fields of Normandy.

When Griffyn had given Noir over to the soldier who had hurried out upon their arrival, he had also sent word for the men to convene in the feasting hall within the half hour.

Twelve men and a woman sat around two huge, rough-hewn wooden tables and lounged against the wicker walls, their calloused hands wrapped around tepid mugs of ale. A brazier burned hot coals in the centre and on each of the two tables sat three or four candles, affixed in a puddle of wax to keep them upright. Twelve men gathered in relative darkness, steeped in danger and peril for their lord.

Griffyn told them what had happened in swift, clipped words. First the meeting and agreement with Beaumont, the most important item by far, but he soon discovered it paled in contrast. Much more interesting was the tale of near-abduction, sword fight, and subsequent rescue. Twice.

He received a series of skeptical looks, more than a few guffaws, and too many curses to count when he relayed an account of the battle with d'Endshire's men.

"So, they're dead?" queried one Norman knight, Damelran.

Griffyn brought his gaze from the fire in a slow arc. "Not all of them. De Louth escaped."

"There's a piece of comfort," the knight quipped as he lifted his mug for another swallow.

Griffyn leveled him a flinty look. "Glad to be of service." He observed the smirks around the room, half-shrouded in shadows, and half-lit by flame, and scowled. "What would any of the rest of you have done? She was alone and in danger."

The chorus of hooting and laughter that followed his declaration drowned him into silence for a good two minutes. He looked around glumly. All were men he trusted with his life. None were men he trusted with this kind of information. They would only turn it into something it was not, and have a lot of annoying fun with it. It was already happening.

Men clapped each other on the back and lifted their mugs in unamusing and inaccurate toasts. Alexander, his second-in-command, watched him silently, the only one not joining in the revelry. Griffyn met his gaze and shrugged. Alex shook his head and took a swig of ale. The rest of the room stayed in different spirits.

Hervé Fairess, an Angevin knight with a wicked sense of humour, was fighting so hard to contain his laughter his eyes were crinkled up and his red cheeks puffed out. The 'innkeeper' and his 'wife,' in fact a Norman knight and a young widow sympathetic to any army who would crush the king who'd killed her husband, had no such compunctions. They sat in the shadows and laughed until they cried, hanging on one another as if they were drowning. Griffyn sent a fierce scowl around the room. No one paid it any mind.

He cleared his throat. The room stuttered into silence in five seconds.

"As I said, she was in danger."

"Not so much danger as we're to be in when d'Endshire comes looking for a ghostly knight who appeared out of nowhere and whisked his betrothed away," observed Hervé Fairess.

"I agree." Alex's voice came low and calm from the back of the room.

Griffyn shook his head. "We leave this inn at dawn, England in two days' time. We'll be in Normandy the next morn, and will not be here to be bothered by Endshire. And," he added on an impatient gust of air, "she *wasn't* his betrothed."

This started another small quake in the room. Alex spoke over the ensuing laughter. "She may not have been, Pagan, but what does it matter? She's in our camp now. What if she discovers who we are, or what we're about?"

"She won't. She'll wake up tomorrow to find an empty inn, and be on her way." He looked around the room and shook his head, despairing of them. "All we have to do is get through one night with a woman in our midst. Cannot we manage a simple thing like that?" he asked plaintively.

When they started laughing again, he shook his head in disgust and went to the back of the fire-lit room, where Alex sat at a table.

He dropped onto the bench opposite. "Do you have anything more to say?" he asked curtly.

"Oh, aye."

"Thought so," he muttered.

He splashed the contents of a pitcher of ale into a wooden mug Alex pushed his way, then leaned back, resting his spine against the wall. He unbuckled his hauberk at the shoulder and the heavy mail flap fell forward onto his chest. He put a boot up on the bench, slung one forearm over his knee, and stared into the fire.

The sound of cold, wet raindrops pattered on the windows and walls. The fire burned hot, and the room smelled faintly of drying leather and old straw and smoke. Firelight flickered and the low murmurs of his men grew quieter as they dropped off to sleep.

Griffyn took a long swallow of the tepid ale, then wiped his mouth with the back of his hand and looked at Alex, an eyebrow cocked in silent query.

Alex answered in kind, lifting his brows, then his gaze, to the ceiling.

Griffyn shrugged. "I don't know how to be any clearer. I will see her off in the morn, and we'll be finished with her."

Alex wiped his finger over a wet ring of liquid left by the pitcher of ale. "Finished, is it?"

"This is not the first time I have met a woman, Alex. Nor," he added crossly, "the first time I have enacted my knightly vows. Some I know might do well to adopt a similar stance."

Alex rubbed his fingertips together, drying the wetness. "Is that what this is? Your knightly vows?" Griffyn lifted his eyebrows again. Alex lifted his higher. "Is that what you were doing up there, Pagan? Being knightly?"

"This is ridiculous," he announced.

"Vows?"

He exhaled noisily and ran his fingers through his hair.

"Why is she here?" Alex said. "You have more important things to do. Anything that distracts, intrudes." The firelight bounced shadows on the far wall. "Why is she here?" he asked again, his voice low. "I mean, truly, Griffyn. What is going on?"

Griffyn shifted his gaze over. "What is it," he asked so flatly it wasn't a question anymore. "What are you worried about, Alex? You know me."

They were quiet, the only sound the crackling fire. "I know you, Griffyn. I do not know her."

He spun the mug between his fingers and held his silence.

Alex waited a moment, then went on. "You have a destiny, Griffyn. You are of the bloodline, the Guardian. The Heir." He looked at Griffyn's implacable face and shook his head. "'Tis neither my place to convince nor instruct you."

"Oh, aye? Then why do we go over this same matter time and again?"

Alex's face hardened. "*Because there is treasure to be guarded.* Or do you not believe?"

Griffyn leaned forward, across the table. "I'll tell you what I believe, Alex," he said in a low, swift voice. "I believe greed and fear exist, and that is what motivates men. Holiness does not, or rarely. Goodness makes them attack. Legends of hidden treasure excite them like nothing else. *I do not want it.*" He threw himself back on the bench and pushed his fingers through his hair. "I do not want what it makes men become."

He stared across the room. His men were dim bundled shapes stretched out in front of the fire. Rain slammed against the shutters.

"In you flows a thousand years of blood, Griffyn," Alex replied quietly. "'Tis too weighty a thing to ignore. Your life is not your own."

Griffyn's fingers tightened on the mug. "My choices are."

"You're the Guardian, Griffyn," Alex insisted in an urgent, low voice. "You must accept that."

Griffyn looked over. "And you are a Watcher, Alex. Not my father."

Alex's face hardened. "Aye. I am a Watcher. I protect you. I do my duty."

Griffyn's face creaked into a smile. "Call it duty if you will, Alex; we all of us make choices."

"And yours has been to reject this destiny since the day your father died. Do you think that will make it go away?"

"No," Griffyn said dully. "Nothing will."

Nothing would ever make the awful truth of whom he was destined to become go away. The treasure in Everoot's vaults had a long legacy of destruction. Powerful enough to inspire quests and madness, holy enough to bring kings crashing to their knees, it had simply crushed his father and Ionnes de l'Ami under the weight of its want.

Its existence was barely breathed aloud in the secret councils of those who suspected, but the rumours persisted. *In Egypt. The Languedoc. Jerusalem!* No one knew for certain it even existed, let alone where it was.

No one supposed it was in a remote English donjon, stripped of any glory and even the light of day.

And Griffyn was its Guardian.

He stared at the curling burl lines of the wooden table, not seeing wood, but his father's raging, wild face. He wanted to be nothing like Christian Sauvage. And, in his heart, he knew he could be nothing other.

Brutal, sinful, wasted and wrecked by greed. *That* was his destiny.

"Griffyn," Alex's soft voice intruded.

He snapped his gaze up and stared at his lifelong companion. Alex reached out and clamped his hand over Griffyn's clenched one, which was fisted on the tabletop.

"I don't know why you think it matters what we want, friend," Alex said, almost sadly. "You are what you have been bred to be. Charlemagne's heir. You carry the burden: Guardian of the Grail Hallows. And for good or for ill, Griffyn, our hope lies in you."

He tore his hand free. "Call me Pagan when she is about."

He grabbed his mug and walked out.

Chapter Fifteen

Ahh, had God created anything more perfect than a bath? Anything better than warm, scented steam rising from hot water, lapping at your chest and chin? Better than the feeling of being clean again?

Gwyn decided not. She leaned her head back against the tub and closed her eyes. The room was Pagan's, without a doubt. It had his musky odour of maleness. The realisation that this was pleasing brought her eyes open again.

Why was she *not* frightened, lying in a tub in a strange man's boarding room? The night was like some strangely stretched version of reality that warped and shifted as she walked through it. Dowered. Saturated. Weeping with it.

But there was something about Pagan, something that seemed honourable, however his physical presence brought to mind granite cliffs. However his behaviour, prior to and following their strange passion-dance, sent her mind into dizzying spirals that spurned sense. In fact, he seemed—

He seemed to be coming up the stairs, if the sound of thumping boots reckoned rightly.

She scrambled naked out of the tub, dripping wet, and darted her gaze around the room. Her clothes, filthy, mangled, muddy, were near the door. If she ran for them, she'd be caught. *What was she to wear?*

Griffyn kicked the door open and stepped into the chamber with two flagons of ale atop a tray. Twenty minutes of grooming Noir had finally combed out the agitated remnants of his own tangled emotions following the conversation with Alex, and as he walked back through the lashing winds and rain, he'd realised all he wanted was to sit with Guinevere. Just sit with her. Forget about the world for awhile. Mayhap make her laugh.

He balanced the tray and peered around until he found her. Out of the tub, standing by the small table, avoiding his eye and fingering the edge of a red . . . a red . . .

"What is that?"

Her wet head lifted, revealing a chagrined smile. "I had nothing else to wear."

He cocked his head to the side. "And so you chose . . . ahhh," he exhaled in understanding. The empty spot on the wall where one of his tapestries had hung explained the outlandish tunic draped around her.

He briefly ran his gaze along her body, then turned to the table and set down the tray of ale. Aye. Much better to be here, with her beauty, than downstairs, alone with the grinding memories.

He kicked the door shut behind him. "Come." He gestured to the table.

Her bare feet padded over the planks of wood. She sat on the bench he had pulled out. She looked at him a moment, her elfin face bright, scrubbed clean. He set the tray on the table. She stared at his hands.

"Did I take your bathwater?"

He quirked an eyebrow. "Am I that dirty? Your message has gone off."

"And you've my undying thanks. For too many things to count."

He stood squarely in the centre of the room and stared into the brazier fire, deciding it was better by far *not* to look at her. Her hair was drying in a curling mass of dark silk, tossed over her shoulder. The crimson tapestry had slipped off one shoulder.

A light tap came on the door. He waved Gwyn into the bedchamber and opened it. Maude stood with a tray of food in her outstretched arms.

"Food, my lord," she whispered, as if it were a most secretive package.

He smiled faintly and took the proffered offerings. "Come," he called to the dark opening of the bedchamber, laying the tray on the table. "Eat."

It took all of five seconds for her to arrive at the edge of the table, curling her toes and nearly drooling. He watched as she descended on the simple fare with a gusto uncommon among soldiers on campaign, wondering idly if she would gnaw through the wooden plates once all the food was gone.

"Good," she mumbled through a mouth filled with bread crust and cheese.

"Umm." He splashed more ale into her mug and thumped it down in front of her.

Nodding her thanks, she sloshed a solid third of it down her gullet before coming up for air. He shook his head, bemused.

Becoming aware of his scrutiny, she lifted her head from the feeding trough to look at him. He stared back.

"Aren't you going to sit?" she asked.

He dropped onto the small bench opposite her, tilted the bench back, and crossed his arms over his chest.

Dark green eyes travelled the length of his torso, then back to his face. "And eat?"

He obediently picked up a hunk of cheese and popped it into his mouth.

Her lips curved into a smile. "You are quite biddable."

"Oh, quite."

"Always?"

"More so than you, I'll wager."

The laugh that greeted this was utterly marvelous. Her face was dissolved in gentle laughter, and the dark tresses pulled back over her shoulders revealed delicate features of shoulder and neck. His gaze travelled down, drawn to a nasty bruise discolouring her exposed skin.

The bench thumped forward. "You're hurt." He ran a finger over the bruise on her shoulder, a soldier's swift appraisal. A ripple of goosebumps sped under his hand. He froze.

She was blushing a pale shade of pink. Dark, wet hair hung in tangled locks across the scarlet linen and her white shoulder, creating a startling contrast in colours. The combination of such an ethereal face and the sudden, innocent desire dawning there made him snatch his hand back as if burned.

"I'll tend it when you're done," he said roughly.

She ducked her head and muttered some inaudible reply. She could have said Stephen's army was marching for the inn and he wouldn't have heard. Such a hard, hot pounding hadn't surged through him in many a year. It was so powerful and close at hand he felt short of breath.

"What did you say?" he asked, dimly aware she'd been speaking.

The query brought her head up, which he did not want at all. It would be better if she kept her head wrapped in a poultice all night long. No, he amended, glancing at the body concealed beneath a thin layer of linen and nothing else, her entire body should be swathed in woollen, wrapped from hairline to toes.

"I said, I did not expect such a thing as all this from my night," she murmured. "Did you?"

He groaned audibly. This would never do. She could be swathed in sacks and buried under a haystack and it would not help. Already the image of her stretched out and sighing beneath him, black hair streaming over the pillows, was more vivid than the whole past year of his life.

"Nay, I never expected such a thing as you."

She smiled faintly. "Fools, I think we agreed."

"Without sense."

"Entirely."

He drew back, leveled his tone. "I would have you regain yours, Raven, ere something happens you'll be sorry for."

"Sorry?" She shook her head, her smile fading. "I think not. I have regrets, 'tis true—"

"So do I, and I would not have this night become one of them."

She looked around, at the worn furniture, the glow of the brazier coals, water dripping down the stone pathways in the walls in narrow, silent rivulets. "I am convinced we too often measure regret against the ways of the world."

"There are worse things."

"Even so, that would not protect me tonight. The things of the world are far away right now. I can scarce recall them to mind."

"I can," he said firmly. "You like mushrooms, but hate eel. You think yourself foolish, but wish for a certain blue gown. You can afford neither the dye or cloth, so never buy a bolt of a lesser fabric. Your steward—William of the Five Strands, no?—does not see to the fish traps as he ought. The harvest was never fully brought in this year, and may never be again. Too many have died. Once, you had a dream of the window in your mother's bedroom being fitted with stained glass, like a chapel, for she's an angel to you now, and it would bring her closer to home."

Gwyn's lower jaw started to fall open as he worked his way through her panicked ramblings from the beginning of their ride, partially verbatim, partly paraphrased, but dead on in content. By the time he reached "an angel to you now," she was staring open-mouthed.

"Pagan! I did not even know you were listening!"

"Oh, I was listening," he murmured in a steel-edged voice, his restraint drawn to snapping. "And you ought listen to *me* right now, little bird: *Be careful.*"

"Sensible, you mean."

"Most assuredly."

She paused, and he had a momentary thought he might escape unscathed. That she would do the prudent thing, save him from this rampaging desire. But her next words smashed the thin hope, taking him with it like water over a falls.

"Sense is only one way to know a thing, Pagan," she whispered. "I'm sure we could find another."

In a single move he was up, around the table, his arms around her waist, pulling her to her feet. He swept her hair off from her face. The half-dried curls picked up coppery glints from the firelight and her hair glowed in a black-fire curtain of silk around the delicate, sense-damaging beauty of her face. Their lips were inches apart; he could feel each shaky breath she dragged into her lungs.

"God forgive me," he muttered, then plunged in after his words.

Their mouths locked, hard and greedy. He claimed her with no gentleness; the moment was betide and he moved in with unchecked assurance. Her hair was like silk, and her skin hot. Her lips were parted wide beneath him, her tongue meeting him with every stroke. He gathered fistfuls of her hair, gripping the dark silk with savage passion, and cupped them at the nape of her neck. When she dropped her head back and moaned into his mouth, it almost broke him.

Gwyn knew nothing but that her life was changed forever. Wide-open and demanding, his hands engulfed her ribs. He bent her backwards and plied her mouth wide, hunting deep in the recesses of her mouth, dragging free shuddering sensations she'd never dreamed of before, pulsing, hot, greedy urges.

He pushed her backwards with gentle, insistent hands and,

when her buttocks pressed against the table, he stepped between her knees. Flexing the muscles in his thighs, he lifted her off the ground and pressed her onto the table, his hands and mouth like a well-informed thief intent on its plunder.

His body was a wall of heat and muscle, the tapestry a thin veil he would heed only so long. His powerful thighs were between her knees, muscles pressing forward. His hands were everywhere, coaxing her body into moves she'd never imagined before, bending back, reaching up, her hips sliding in an unconscious rhythm. Firm, thick fingers cupped her head and lifted her half off the table to his mouth, until her torso was stretched against his and she could feel his hammering heart. His arousal was hard and pushing ever closer to the place that quivered and wept moist desire. Invading her.

"Do you know what I want to do to you?" he rasped against her lips. She was nodding, knowing nothing, certain of everything.

His hand slid up her ribs and closed around her breast. Gwyn's world slewed sideways. He was a magician, he knew exactly what he was doing to her, working her with expert caresses, making her cry out in longing and hope for some unknown release. Never before had she felt heat where she felt it now, sizzling through her blood, throbbing between her legs. He moulded his hands against the tapestry like it was her skin, seducing her, loosing little rivers of hot wanting that pulsed up and down her spine, laying claim with such breathtaking skill her body bucked of its own accord.

When her body shuddered, Griffyn almost took possession of her right there. Spread her thighs apart with his knee and plunged himself into her wetness. The hot place between her thighs stroked against his erection, pushing, prodding, dangerous, perfect pleasure. Tongue, lips, sucking, teasing, the woman was *good* and he ached to slide her legs apart and make her fill the room with howls of pleasure. Her hands were around his neck, her thighs quivering on the tabletop, her body arching backwards into his invasion. She was ready.

A pounding erupted at the door. *Bham, bham, bham!*

Someone was hammering at the door.

He ripped his mouth away. "Leave us," he growled, but the door was flung open before the words were out.

"Pagan!" Alex ran in shouting. "There's news!"

Griffyn spun, planting his body in front of Raven's, his hand going reflexively for a non-existent sword.

Alex put his heels to wood. "Pagan?" he said more quietly, and hesitantly. His gaze avoided lifting over Griffyn's shoulder. "There's news."

Griffyn nodded, but his words were soft-spoken and lethal. "Go. Now."

"My lord." Alex bent his head and retreated out of the door.

Gwyn sat up. They were frozen in their positions for half a minute, then he felt her shift behind him.

"I should just shrivel up and die now, really," she said quietly.

He turned around. Poor idea. She was barely human, all hot desire and imagination. Quivering body, dark hair spilling over the table, tapestry beginning to part and reveal silky inner thighs, debauched she would be if she did but inhale again.

He spun on his heel and crossed to the opposite end of the room. Outside the storm had descended with riotous enthusiasm. Propping the heels of his hands on the wall, he dropped his head and stared at the floor, trying to calm his breathing.

A rustling drew his attention back to the table. He shifted his gaze to peer under the length of his outstretched arm. She was sliding off the table. Her feet hit the ground with a small thump.

"I believe 'tis my turn to say I am sorry," she said.

He looked away and shook his head. "Nay. 'Tis I, again, who am at fault." His muffled words rose up from between his outstretched arms.

"No." He heard her coming, the soft padding of her feet, the slight whisper of the ridiculous tapestry trailing behind her. He spotted a blotch of red fabric out of the corner of his eye. "You told me," she insisted. "You warned me."

He took one hand off the wall and rubbed it along his jaw. He drew a deep, centering breath. "And *I* knew you were not one to listen. I should have left."

Her hand touched his arm briefly, then dropped away. "I knew what was happening." Her face flushed pink. "I mean, I did not *know*, but I . . . I am sorry. I will be . . . good."

Feeling slightly relieved that they were talking again rather than wrapped in a lust-pounding embrace, he pulled back from the wall and looked at her skeptically. "Does that mean obedient?"

A smile pressed against the corners of her lips. He could see the dented dimple beginning to peek out again. *God*, to have a woman like this.

"I expect it does not, but we may hold out hope," she observed dryly.

He chuckled low in his throat, feeling strangely weary after this battle of seduction. "Mistress, if ever you become docile, may God have mercy on all our souls."

"He will surely spare a pagan."

"He will surely damn me for what I was about to do."

"But I would not."

God's truth, she was perfection. Brave spirit, intelligent eyes, body of a seductress, she was funny and sweet and like nothing he'd ever known before.

Not for him.

He turned and strode out the door.

Gwyn watched him disappear with long, self-assured strides, leaving her heart hammering in her chest so swiftly she worried for her health. She fell asleep with a smile on her face and no Ache in her heart for the first time in twelve years.

Chapter Sixteen

Alexander was waiting when he emerged into the narrow corridor. Griffyn said nothing as he pulled the door shut and started down the hallway. Alex fell into step beside him.

"How long were you at the door?"

"I wasn't at the door. I was downstairs, intent on matters holy."

Griffyn gave him a sideways glance as they thumped down the stairs. "Holy? Sounds serious. I wouldn't have expected it of you, Alex."

"I've been known."

"To what?"

"Do what we all do—seek redemption. Or vengeance," Alex added as they swung into the gathering hall.

His men sat in a small circle in front of a brazier, trying to keep themselves warm in the dampness permeating the room. Outside the storm battered against the walls. The wind screamed, then went silent, losing its voice momentarily. On the table, a candle flame flickered wildly, pulling upwards towards the ceiling, then squatting low and fat around the wick, huddling close for its own warmth.

Griffyn pulled a blanket over his shoulders and sat on a

bench amid the circle of shadowy men. They all looked back at him, oddly quiet. Griffyn scanned their faces.

"Redemption or vengeance." He turned to Alex. "Why do I have the feeling you are expecting one or the other from me tonight?"

"There's news."

"What?"

"Ionnes de l'Ami is dead."

He lifted a mug and splashed ale into it. The only sign he'd even heard was his knuckles tightening into whiteness around the handle.

"When?"

"A fortnight ago. They've been trying to keep it quiet."

"Who's 'they'?" he asked in a tone devoid of emotion. The foul traitor, the focus of his silent enmity for these seventeen years, dead? The man who had betrayed his father, forsworn his oath, stolen Griffyn's home, broken his heart, *dead*? And not by Griffyn's hand?

"His heir."

"Heir? The son died years ago."

"There's a daughter."

Griffyn stared into the flames. "I forget. What's her name?"

"Guinevere."

He entered the bedchamber long after the moon had risen and watched as she slept. Her hair drifted across his pillows like some dark, exotic silk. Her face lay half pressed against his pillows, her stunning body stretched beneath the blankets.

De l'Ami spawn.

God was cruel. Ionnes de l'Ami had been too many things to count. The worst of enemies and closest of friends. He had once saved Griffyn's father's life, deep in the depths of Palestine. He'd been the man whom Griffyn once called 'Uncle' and thought threw the very stars into the sky.

Griffyn collapsed onto a bench by the bed and leaned forward, forearms on his thighs, watching Gwyn but not seeing her.

He had been young back then, fewer than eight years to weigh against the centuries-old destiny awaiting him, back when de l'Ami had been 'Uncle' and the summers had been long. The laughing, grey-haired bear, Ionnes de l'Ami had known Griffyn's destiny, cared for him more than his own father did. Taught him some of his earliest lessons: how to wield a sword, the right way to carve a duck, the importance of laughing at oneself.

Oath-breaker.

Liar.

Betrayer.

His hand went to the key around his neck. *Your inheritance. I am sorry*, Griffyn's father had whispered, then died. About time, too. Past time.

His father's half-mad ravings those last few years had been awful, and unbelievable. His violence more awful and unbelievable yet.

Griffyn no longer had time for the rages of old men, deformed by greed and cunning too long practiced. Everoot was his inheritance, and this little iron weight around his neck was surely not the key to the castle. That rested in his name and sword arm. And he was finished with people standing in his way.

He felt like pounding the wall. He smashed his fingers through his hair and sat forward, grinding his elbows into the tops of his knees. What, then? Ionnes de l'Ami was dead, so he was to wreak his vengeance on a woman who was two at the time of the betrayal?

To what end? he asked himself bleakly. Stake her up by the fingernails and she still wouldn't be the one who'd hurt him.

He stared down at his fists.

Every truth he'd ever believed, every person he'd ever

trusted, every lesson he'd ever learned, had turned out to be false. How could she ever be the exception?

Everyone got infected with the sickness of soul. Everyone who knew of the hallowed treasure in Everoot's vaults got corrupted, deformed. Ruined.

Which brought him sharply around to Marcus fitzMiles. Endshire was sniffing around Everoot's skirts, was he? If men at their best were greedy and corrupt, Marcus was a worm in the muck. Let him try to batter the Nest—she had defences Marcus hadn't dreamed of.

Griffyn sat back and crossed his arms over his chest, his eyes narrowed in on the candle flame. The old King Henri had put Marcus's father, Miles, into a baronage because the wily royal dog saw the virtue of keeping his enemies close to hand. It was a prudent move. Not prudent enough, though.

First father, then son, had taken several vows to honour the old king's daughter Mathilda as successor, as had the rest of the English nobility. Then, when it suited his purposes, Marcus had turned to King Stephen. As had the rest. And, when it further suited his purposes, he set himself to imprison beautiful women and stock his own coffers forthwith.

Henri fitzEmpress would be coming to take back the land of traitors exactly like d'Endshire. Griffyn suddenly decided he'd ask to ride in the van the day the army rode north and set fire to fitzMiles's keep.

His gaze drifted back down to the sleeping beauty in his bed. When had he last laughed from the depth of his gut? When last had his blood pounded and spun his head from pure, perfect passion? When had he last been surprised, intrigued, impressed by a woman? Not in all the bloody long days of his life.

He would burn d'Endshire to the ground.

Half an hour later, as he watched with a half-drawn lid, his thoughts far from his bedside vigil, her eyelids fluttered open.

Chapter Seventeen

It was the crash of thunder that awakened her. Gwyn dragged her eyes open. A pale, uncanny light illuminated the room. Not yet dawn, but that was all she knew for certes. Such an awakening could be hours away, or a moment. Or never. The darkness was secretive and alarming.

Where was she?

She lifted her hands into the air. They were pale, shadowy things in the firelit chamber. Moving her head to the left showed more darkness.

"Where am I?" she whispered.

"Safe," came the murmured reply. She looked to her right. A dark hulk slumped on a bench against the wall, but his eyes glinted firelight as he watched her. Everything rushed back.

The Nest besieged, Marcus's absurd, dangerous proposal, the attack on the highway, her saviour, Saxons and Hipping, dream-like wandering through hidden paths. What a mysterious night, clogged with phantasms and caped heroes. And searing kisses, straight to the centre of her soul.

This last thought swept the cobwebs away entirely. Pushing aside the heavy weight of furs, she swung her legs out.

Her sore muscles had stiffened while she slept, and the

sudden movement sent them screaming in protest. She dropped back to the pillows with a small cry.

Griffyn watched from the bench without moving. "Lie back," he ordered in a quiet voice.

She nodded obediently. The soft, rough sound of hair moving against linen accompanied her nod. An arc of hair puffed above her head on the pillow, fine strands of black silk that reflected the glimmering candlelight in the room. Her eyes were red-rimmed, her cheeks puffy and creased red from the pillow. A rather large bump on her head had swelled to noteworthy proportions already, but Griffyn's experience with battle injuries told him it would be fine. Her hand fluttered towards her head and found the nub.

She sat up again, but more slowly this time. "My head?"

"Was knocked right well, but you'll be fine."

Gwyn nodded doubtfully. She examined the room, then turned her gaze back to him. "I can never repay you, Pagan."

"I don't want anything from you," he said woodenly and pushed to his feet.

Gwyn perched back on her elbows and watched him, unable, even had she wanted, to take her eyes off his striding, vaguely predatory form as it paced the room. There was something different about him, altered from before her sleep, something that not only made her think of rocky cliffs, but about being dashed against them. She slid back under the covers.

He suddenly paused in his restless march and pinned his grey gaze on her. "So, who are you, lass, and how came you to be alone on the king's highway?"

"I told you: Lord Endshire is too eager a suitor."

"And you were going to the Abbey to await rescue?"

She paused. "I have already been rescued."

"What do you think Endshire wanted with you?"

"My money, for certes," she said tartly.

"Have you so very much?"

"Not anymore."

He kept watching her with the leonine regard, and some perverse part of herself felt both afraid and aroused. "You squandered it?" he suggested dryly. "Marcus will weep when he hears the news."

"The wars weep with it."

He turned away. "They weep with blood, mistress." He crossed to the brazier to stir the coals. His face was backlit by the orange glow, and the planes of his face deepened, so he looked sculpted from some smooth stone, hard and impenetrable. Yet thus far, he'd been nothing but gentle.

Almost.

Gwyn felt a small sliver of unease and slipped further under the covers, peering at him down the slope of her nose. "They do indeed. With blood and money and the wails of women whose husbands have died."

He looked over his quite broad shoulder. "Have you lost a husband?"

"None would be satisfied with me."

He looked back at the coals. "A father, perhaps?"

She sat up a little straighter. "Aye. How do you know that?"

He didn't answer.

"You men may keep your wars," she said sharply, urged on by some grating force inside. "My father fought far too many in the Outremer, and thought them rousing things."

"My father was in the Holy Lands, too, when the Holy City fell."

She smiled bitterly. "So, you, too, think war a glorious thing. Whereas they are an awful business, and I care for them naught."

"Happens you might care if they were to take your home from you," he said coldly.

"As Marcus tried, you mean? Trust in me, Pagan, I need no war to hoist men's ambitions on me or mine. That is a burden women bear in the most peaceful of times."

He put his palms, outstretched, over the glowing coals. "And yet, here you are, and not with fitzMiles." He swung away from the fire and crossed the room, bringing a jug of wine with him. Pouring it into two mugs set on a narrow table under the window, he came to the side of the bed and extended one. "One for the ladies, I suppose."

She laughed, feeling pleased at his little toast. It must have been an errant mood that had poked at him these last few minutes, like brambleweed. She relaxed back into the pillows and took the proffered drink. "One for rogue knights and frightened women, more's the like. We put up a good fight, did we not, you and I?"

"Aye," he said, dropping onto a bench near the wall. "Never have I seen a shoe propelled with such ferocity before, and hope never to again."

She laughed and fingered the rim of the mug. "At least not if 'tis coming at *you*."

"Indeed. I shall watch closely to see that your slippers are securely attached to your feet ere I anger you ever again."

She lifted the cup. "My thanks."

"I want you to stop thanking me."

"That was the last. I promise."

He stretched out his boots and wrapped his cloak around his shoulders. In the shadows his face was mysterious, dark hollows under his cheekbones, his eyes hooded and deep. The cloak was drawn over his long, taut body, his knee-high boots crossed at the ankles.

Gwyn drank deeply, then lowered the mug and considered it suspiciously. "I ought to drink a more watered wine than this."

He lifted his brows.

"I became rather . . . addled when I drank your posset earlier."

He smiled, a small mark of amusement that seemed to creep out despite his best intentions. And still it was heart-stopping in its sensuality. "That was no posset, mistress, and you've nothing to fear from this potion."

She sipped again. "'Tis good."

It was quiet for a few moments, and she peered beneath her lashes at his shadowed figure. Even motionless he filled the room.

He wore simple grey braies and a loose-fitting chainse without belt. The collar opened in a V, exposing a chest dusted with dark hairs and plated with muscle. The strong column of his neck descended to wide shoulders and a rock-hewn body, taut with sinew that came only from long years of wielding a sword and wearing heavy knightly attire. She was unable to drop her eyes further, but knew the rest of him would pulsate with the same presence. Even small movements, such as picking up a strand of her hair and bringing it to his lips, as he had last night, revealed sliding muscles and the easy grace of a well-honed predator.

Her heart started a small thundering. Alchemy. The rest of the world receded and there was only Pagan's dark eyes and this feeling in her blood. She looked away but the feeling still hummed through her body from head to toe, long and flat and sweeping.

Home was a long way away, and she was glad.

He was watching her. In the dimness she could not tell what flickered in his eyes as she met his gaze again, but a quivering cord of heat began to unravel through her body.

"And what of you, Pagan? What are *you* doing here?"

"Sitting with you."

She smiled. "I mean at this inn."

"Sitting with you."

She drew a deep breath and let it out. "What were you doing on the highway last night, alone, at such an hour?"

"You would rather I had been with someone?"

She laughed. "No, I think not. So." She eyed him with a considering look. "You will not answer me. You are used to wielding power. Only those who are can sidestep questions with such ease. And, my compliments," she added, nodding her head, "for you do so as deftly as you wield a sword."

"Ask away, mistress."

She paused, quite certain that whatever he had been doing on the king's highway, or at Hipping's lodge, not only had nothing to do with her, it would be something not open for discussion. There was no point in fishing for information. "How came you to carry a flask of drink with you?"

His brows arched halfway up his forehead. "*That's* your question?"

"I know I will get nothing else from you, and at the moment, I find it does not matter in the least."

She looked around the room. Outside the storm was raging. Every so often a monstrous gust of wind broke free and stormed the building, reducing the walls to a quivering mass of woven reeds and crumbling stone. Even inside the air was damp, but with the shutters closed, the fire burning, and Pagan watching her, she was warm and comfortable. "So what I want to know is why you would carry around a flask of the very drink that could calm a panicked woman."

The lines around his mouth deepened into a grin. "It soothes men too, Raven."

"See?" she exhaled, throwing up her free hand in mock exasperation. "I will get nothing but what you wish to share, so I will ask nothing more."

He picked up the jug of wine. When he cocked a brow in mute question, she replied by extending her empty cup.

He leaned forward and tipped the flagon forward, sloshing wine in. She nodded her thanks and retreated to the pillows. Outside the storm kicked and screamed, throwing itself against the stone walls, trying to get in.

"Highways or halls, mistress," he murmured in his deep, masculine rumble, "there are always things to be seen and heard, when one is watchful and listening."

She eyed him sideways. So, he was answering. Of a sort. "And is that what you were doing? Watching and listening?"

"A bit."

"In times like these—"

"In times like these," he said, cutting her off, "pretty ladies shouldn't ride out on highways alone. They might meet dangerous men."

She slipped back into the warmth of the furs. "You have already pointed out you are not one."

He reached out again, this time retrieving a chunk of bread from the wooden platter set on the window ledge. Popping the bread in his mouth, he chewed, his gaze held on her. A sort of grimness had descended on him again.

"Not to you," he finally said.

"Lucky me."

"I'll say," was his dry rejoinder.

"Then to whom?"

He laughed and shook his head. "You're unstoppable."

She set the cup of wine on the furs covering her knees and tried to balance it. "Most find it simpler to surrender."

"I am not most."

The cup tipped over and she grabbed it just in time. No, she decided, sliding her eyes surreptitiously along his body, he was not 'most,' nor 'many,' nor anything but 'one.' Something about him pulsed with passion and verve and it was seeping into her bones, making her life sit like a yawning chasm of despair beneath. She had a sudden flash of insight, seeing her life before and after him as it always had been, aching and dry, like a week-old fish.

A streak of white light illuminated the room, then thunder descended in a mighty, crashing boom. Gwyn jumped half out of bed. Strange eerie moans keened their laments around the eaves of the building. A blast of furious wind set its shoulder to the side of the structure and pushed. The ends of her hair lifted in a ghostly breath of damp air that surged through the cracks in the walls. The shutters lurched and creaked, ballooning out in a thin wooden bubble, then sucking in, as if some giant god were blowing full a pig's bladder for children's play. Then, with a mighty crash, the shutters flung wide and crashed against the walls. She jumped fully and clutched the covers to her chest.

"Rest easy," came Pagan's low, steady voice.

He moved through the room like a strange dancer, hidden in darkness, then appearing in jerky moves as flashes of lightning split the sky. After each flash of blinding light came another detonation of thunder; the storm had settled in over the abandoned inn.

Winds whipped at Pagan's chainse as he crossed the room, moulding it to his body. When he reached the window, he spent half a moment staring out. No oil parchment covered the opening; only the slatted wooden covering protected the inhabitants. Gwyn watched as lightning lit up the planes of his face, her mind spinning. Good Lord, she was not who she'd thought herself to be. All she wanted was for him to kiss her again.

"I used to ride in such storms," she announced, staring at his back.

He angled his chin to the side, giving her his profile. "Ride? In a storm like this?"

She smiled. "Perhaps not quite like this. And aye, I rode. My horse. Windstalker."

"A goodly name," he replied, and pulled the shutters closed. With a flick of his wrist, he lowered the small iron rung, locking them in place. Casting his enigmatic eyes over the dark humps scattered throughout the room, he reached for a hemp towel slung over the bench and hooked it over the edges of the window. It fell down as extra covering, lifting and falling as winds buffeted the walls.

"You've a good horse too," she said. "Noir."

"The best," he agreed quietly. "I had another, though, when I was young."

"The ones when we were young are always the best." She

pushed herself straight against the pillows. "I got Wind when I was eight. Not all grown, mind you, but a foal, mine to raise. Papa said I was too young, but Mamma convinced him. She understood how I felt. She always underst—" She stopped short and swallowed. "I spent every moment with Wind. I remember nothing else of that year or the next—only Wind."

"Mine was Rebel."

She smiled encouragingly. "Your horse."

He nodded, the tension in his jawline receding somewhat. "There was little else for me, either, for a time."

She laughed, nodding, understanding. "Wind is in his prime. Twelve years old and in the stables." When that earned a smile from him, she returned the gesture, pleased to have made the grimness recede. "I ride him every chance I get. He is my best companion. And you, do you still ride your Rebel?"

A spasm of something passed over his face. "He died before he reached a year. In a fire. The stables burned."

Her face dropped. "I am sorry. When?"

"I was eight."

"Eight," she echoed, falling silent. A grievous loss, or so it seemed. That one so steeped in strength and power could feel the loss of a treasured horse so deeply, after all these years, said much about him. About what she could trust in him.

How was it, she wondered, that after one night, one revealing conversation, she knew more about this man than she'd known about her brother or her father or any of her friends in all their years together?

"I will sorely miss Wind when he is gone," she said quietly. "Such things cannot be mended."

"No, they cannot," he agreed, his voice low-pitched and rough as wood smoke.

She tucked her lower lip between her teeth and pondered the covers. A minute passed, then another. It was a deep, steady silence, like the man, and she did not feel the need to fill it with idle chatter.

Then he leaned forward, his forearms resting on his thighs. His grey eyes seemed to burn through the darkness, and he said in a soft, rough voice, "Tell me something else, Raven."

"What?"

"Tell me something else of your home. I have been gone from mine so long, it would be good to hear of one that is loved."

His face was barely visible in the light from the brazier. Through the hemp towel over the window, only muted flashes of light seeped through the coarse weave, and she could see only the cup balanced between the fingertips of his hands, his dark head bent and watching her.

He was flaming, barely restrained, and the feeling of destiny burned down to her toes: things would happen with this man. He was riding the churning tide of a Fate he himself was carving, like an ancient Grecian god. His very being breathed ruthless, reckless chance.

He filled the Ache.

A slow, thick wave of certainty flowed over her. She sat up in the bed and wiped hair away from her face. "I once talked my father's scribe into walking me a goodly length of Hadrian's Wall. It was a long trek, and we were tired when we were done."

A faint smile lifted his lips. "Along the Scottish border. You are a persuasive woman."

"Girl. I was ten."

He smiled more broadly and lifted his cup in a toast.

"Papa was very angry when I returned."

"No doubt. Which was?"

"Three days later."

He started laughing. It was low, barely audible beneath the thunder and lashing rain, but it was there, rumbling under the storm and seeping into her blood.

If making him laugh brought her such deep-rooted pleasure, what would it be like to make him love?

She almost fell out of bed at the thought.

"What other borders have you walked, Raven, when your heart feels earthbound?"

Her head fell back on the cushions, tears pressing hungrily against her nose. He didn't understand. He couldn't understand. *No one* understood.

"Talk to me, Raven."

And so she did. She talked because the night was dark and she didn't know where she was. She talked because she needed a reprieve, however brief and however gained, from the yawning Ache, and in this man was the only place she'd ever found it, mad as that was.

She talked because he needed her to, and to succor *his* ache was a taste she'd never sipped on before.

And these storm-tossed revelations were nothing like what she'd told him before, when they'd ridden in the woods. Those things had told something of her, but they swam on the surface of her life, bobbing on daily events, the things that could have mattered, but did not.

The things she told him in the storm-veiled darkness were sunk so deep inside she felt like she was mining her very soul.

She told him about Windstalker and their midnight rides. About how she used to walk the ramparts in thunderstorms when everyone else was abed. About how she struggled alone against the force of the loneliness and sometimes thought herself losing. She talked about the difficulty of running her castle, of being hen-mother and war-lord, of how she'd stared into the abyss of her life and batted her eyes, how she almost succumbed to despair when her father had died.

She never mentioned her castle's name, and she never told him hers, but she told him everything that made her who she was, everything from five years of age until just a moment ago: the aloneness, the lost mother, the misting nights, the wishing-it-could-be-other moments, the Ache.

Good God, she wasn't speaking of *that*, was she?

"I understand."

Chapter Eighteen

Griffyn spoke from where he sat in the dark corner of the room, but he felt light, buoyant, snared. The image of this woman walking on a deserted battlement, dark hair flying, as lightning streaked across the sky, was simply too beguiling. She had passed her breath over the room and it was transformed. He didn't know it was dark, he didn't know he was captured. He only knew her.

She looked through the shadows at him. Time slowed to the pace of the tears spilling down her cheeks. The bench felt solid beneath him, yet it was as if he were floating.

"Raven."

A gulp of watery laughter bounced across the room. "That is a poorly given name. If I could have—" she said, choking softly on the emotion, "I would have flown away so many times. You've no idea."

"But you didn't."

"Only because I've no wings."

"You didn't, and you wouldn't have."

She nodded, collecting herself with little tearful gasps, her breath coming in short, jerky inhalations. "I love my home so much it hurts," she said, clutching her fist to her chest. "But all those things I did . . ." Her voice trailed off, then lifted again on a hush. "All the things I've ever done in my life, were wishing for only this one thing."

A hammering started in Griffyn's chest. "What?"

"This thing right now . . . with you."

As if in a dream, he rose. "And I, you, Guinevere." Kneeling beside the bed, he took her hand and lifted it to his mouth.

For a brief second Gwyn held to herself, exquisitely aware. Her choice was to move away or step forward. Embrace it or squander the hope it held.

God forbid. How long had she been waiting for some such alchemy as this man was?

Her whole life.

She reached out and touched his cheek. "I don't care what your name is or what you've done. The world is far away right now, and I would that it kept its distance for this one night."

It was nothing for him to crush her to him, to bend his head and lay claim with a raw, enveloping kiss that left her witless. Putting a knee on the bed, he pushed the furs away, and bent low over her, his dark head intent, moving with breathtaking skill down her body she'd barely known existed, until his long, carved body was stretched out above her, hot and hard and wanting her. She was hyperventilating, the room spinning around. A wet pulse began deep in her womb. Right where the Ache pulsed.

She would follow this man into Hades.

Later, she would deny the blasphemous thought. At the moment, though, she put her arm around his neck and drew him down. His mouth closed over hers, claiming her, his tongue hunting in the recesses of her mouth for the breathy gasps and moans that shuddered free. He was sweeping her senseless, making her arch her head back, press her breasts into his chest, cling to his neck.

He slid a wicked hand under her waist and lifted her hips into his. Hot, sizzling spurts of fire burgeoned in her womb. More. She wanted more.

He was demon-fire, danger to her soul, and she reveled in it.

Griffyn knew it, too. When she bent her knee, when she begged for more in wet whispers against his chin, when she let him lift her hips, he knew something unforeseen had happened. She was falling into his blood, his bones, his very being. The breath locked in his throat, unable to fathom the crashing awareness drowning him. A well-dammed river of tenderness—*years of work*—was beginning to overflow.

Stop now, or never.

She whispered in his ear and called him saviour.

Never.

He tore off his shirt and braies with one hand while the other roamed her body. She moved against him wherever he touched, her body a wave of desire under his command. He knew what her body wanted and gloried in knowing it, in making her half-lidded eyes close in ecstasy, in releasing the breathy, pleading pants from her lips, in knowing he could bring her lush, curving body shuddering right to the edge.

His hands spread out around her breasts. His thumbs flicked over the russet nubs until she cried out and arched backwards into his arms. He took one breast fully in his mouth, sucking, his tongue flicking across her nipple.

Her breath shot out in a gasp, and Griffyn pushed her gently back onto the bed, feeling drunk on the sight of her body spread out beneath him: high cheekbones lit by firelight, tangled ebony hair spilling all around her face. Her eyes were just barely opened, a glint of green behind the lids, her rosy, kiss-swollen lips parted.

He slid his hands over her hips, down to her trembling thighs. Pushing them ever so slightly apart, he slid his fingers up her inner thigh, until he hovered against the pink folds dripping with slippery juices. His hand was determined and sure, gliding across the wetness that trickled along the line of her folds. One gentle brush against the sensitive flesh brought the desired moan. His confident fingers searched and, as her body shuddered, he found the small spot at her apex and flicked it gently, lifting his head to watch.

Her head jolted back and her hips bucked into the air. Her tongue clung to the edge of her mouth, as if holding on for life. Her breath drifted out, heavy with moans. Slowly one eyelid opened and a green eye locked on his.

"What are you doing to me?" she whispered, her voice pale and ragged.

A corner of his mouth curved up. "Making you mine." He slipped one finger fully within her pulsing wetness and she flung her head to the side. Her hips arched up instinctively.

"You are ready," he whispered with hoarse satisfaction. Rising and putting his weight on one knee, he spread apart her legs with his other.

Her hips came up against him, moving in a natural rhythm that surged lust through him so fierce he had to stop, hold himself still and look at the wall, counting backwards.

"Please." Her soft voice almost drove him over the edge.

"You've ridden horses your whole life, lady?" he asked raggedly, positioning himself between her thighs.

She nodded, interlacing her fingers around his neck.

"Then mayhap 'twill be without any pain, this first," he growled against her ear. The idea of being the first man to delve her depths but bring no pain was a powerful, head-spinning notion.

Gwyn felt soft hardness, velvety hot flesh push against her thighs, move up between her legs. She arched backwards as cords of heat whipped through her body. His hardness strained against her, then he slid the tip of his manhood along her seam, wetting his erection. She threw her head back, banging the wooden post she'd somehow slithered close to, and whispered the only thing she could: *"Pagan. Aye."*

He nudged her legs apart even further and pushed the tip of his hardness into sensitive flesh already throbbing in spasms of pleasure. She cried out in breathy words, indistinct, uneven, and fully charged. *More.* He clenched his jaw for restraint. Then she lifted her hips.

Slowly he entered her, one smooth, effortless plunge that brought her nails raking down his back. He pressed in further but felt no barrier, only her wet warmth, urging him on. He moved inside her again, holding back, filling her in long, slow strokes so she could grow used to the feel of him. It was exquisite torture. Wet and tight, her flesh was hot, swelling, sweet womanly depths. The muscles of his back and legs were taut with restraint. Another slight push forward made her sigh, a breathy, wanton thing. The small, aching whimper pounded lust through his blood. He growled and shifted his hips, nudging in further.

"Oh, *that* feels good." Her voice came up like a sigh, and she lifted her hips, widening his entryway.

With a ragged groan, he lifted himself into her with a long, unstoppable thrust. Needing to fill her, to feel her hot slippery pulsing along the entire length of him. Dropping his head, he bent his elbows on either side of her, muscles flexed and gleaming with sweat, and lowered his head to her breasts. Their hips met in another long, slow thrust.

"Jésu, woman," he exhaled in a ragged voice.

"Don't stop," she whimpered.

As if he would ever stop again.

The desperate passion built with furious swiftness. Her neck was arched back, the top of her head pressed against the pillow, her mouth wide and panting, her hips pounding against his in the reckless rhythm. Shifting his weight to one elbow, he put his other hand beneath her knee and bent, lifting it into the air.

"Oh, Pagan."

Her flesh shuddered and rippled around him. Growling, he lifted himself higher into her. Thrust, slide, hold. Thrust deeper, slide longer. Push.

"Oh. Pagan."

He felt it begin. The sudden freeze of her glorious body, the tightening of her fingers in his hair, the senseless, jagged whimpers, caught short as if on a sob. Her passion-drugged eyes slid open and locked on his.

"Tell me, Raven, does it please you?"

She shuddered over the edge. Her head jerked backwards as her body exploded in thudding tremors that undulated along his shaft, and he lost himself too. Hard, hot spasms of orgasm surged through him. He propped himself on his elbows and their bodies hammered together for plunge after plunge of hot, wild thrusts. She was calling his name, crying. Something never before felt, picked Griffyn up. It sent him hurtling through walls of denial, toppling old convictions of aloneness, crushing his commitment to mistrust, and sending him spiraling head-long into some heretofore unknown sentiment. He did not dare name it.

She just held his face in her hands and cried into his mouth. "Aye, aye, aye."

It took a long time for their hearts to slow again. He held her the whole time, and when she quieted, he lifted himself and lay down beside her. She turned towards him, satiny inner thighs curved around his, still quivering. Her mouth planted hot, aimless kisses along his neck and jaw.

He closed his eyes and ran his palm over her hot hair, murmuring nothing. Finally her whisperings quieted.

They lay this way for a long while, their bodies spent and sweaty, entangled and enflamed, and tried to catch their breath while their minds tried to register the import of what had just happened.

A few minutes later Griffyn pushed himself up on one elbow. He looked down at her, searching her eyes for a reaction. But they were closed, her lips parted in a faint smile as she slept.

Chapter Nineteen

Before dawn, Griffyn was striding through the clearing in front of the Saxon fortress, surrounded by men preparing to mount up. The light was sullen and grey, and the clouds hunkered low, creating a sopping wet blanket that leaked fat drops of rain on the helms and tunic-clad bodies walking in circles and beating their hands on their thighs to keep warm.

Griffyn walked through the centre of the group, with a word here and there to his men, talking quietly and clapping arms. A red-eared, white-furred cat followed him, winding between his legs as he strode through mud puddles.

"Ruadgh." He muttered the cat's Celtic name in faint irritation when he and the feline got entangled in one particularly muddy leap. She smiled up at him, her blue eyes closing slightly, her tail stuttering back and forth in feathery twitches. She rubbed up against his boot-clad leg, leaving a silky thatch of fur on his breeches. He sighed and ran a hand over her arching back.

"Nuisance," observed a gruff voice.

Griffyn turned.

"She's a devil-cat." Hervé Fairess expanded on his opinion crossly, then reached down to run his calloused palm over her back. She purred happily, rolled over, and sunk her claws into his hand.

"Arrgghh!" He leapt back, clasping his hand to his chest, and glowered at the creature. "Devil-thing," he growled.

Griffyn smiled and ducked his head beneath Hervé's horse's neck, heading towards Alex.

"All is ready? Well-good. I will join you at the Wareham docks within a day."

Alex shot a brief glance at the upper window of the building. "After Saint Alban's?" Griffyn nodded silently. "Is that wise?"

Drawing in a half-formed breath, Griffyn pursed his lips and looked at the sky. "Quite possibly, no."

Alex looked at him sharply. "Does she know who you are?"

Griffyn slowly arched a brow. "Do *you* know who I am?"

Alex ignored the oblique threat. "Because you know what could happen if she revealed who—or where—you are, correct?"

Certainly he knew. Death. Dismemberment. All sorts of nasty things.

Griffyn scowled, primarily because these very real considerations were not what had stayed his tongue with Guinevere. In fact, cold, vengeful satisfaction had counseled *revealing* his identity. Something much more tender had persuaded him to hold his tongue.

"Pagan, all I am saying is that if this goes badly, it could go very, very badly."

"I am not seeking counsel on it, Alex."

Alex lifted the flap of his hauberk and looped it into place over his shoulder. "As you will. My lord."

Griffyn nodded. "I'll meet up with you before the horses are loaded on the ship."

Alex pulled the mail basinet up over his head. Its metal links sat heavily on his blond hair, framing the incredulous look now on his face. "You'll ride to Saint Alban's Abbey, drop your cargo, and be at the Wareham docks the same day as we, who leave straight away for the docks now?"

"Aye."

Alex shook his head and called to Hervé Fairess.

"What is it?" he asked, hiking up his hose as he came.

Alex gestured to Griffyn. "Pagan is going to Saint Alban's."

Fairess glanced at the inn. "The girl? Aye, well, she can't stay here. I've done a few fool things myself for the ladies."

"And we're waiting here for him," Alex continued. "The others will go on."

Griffyn shook his head. "No. You *all* go on."

"No," Alex retorted, copying Griffyn's tone and urgency. "Hervé and I will wait here."

"Alex's idea has some merit, my lord. If I may."

Griffyn ran the palm of his hand over his face. "Or even if you mayn't."

Hervé had an expression of determination on his wet, red face. "You've never asked me to bind my tongue before, Pagan."

"And if I were to start now?"

"I 'spect it'd be a little late," Hervé reflected uncomfortably. He hiked up his breeches again. "But as I was sayin', you're the one to say what's this and that, and I always said you should be—"

"My thanks."

"—but if you're thinking of going anywhere alone, *especially* the docks, that's bad thinking, if I may say so."

Griffyn rubbed his hand over the shadow beard on his chin and cheeks. Hervé never meant insubordination, but he always, somehow, did it.

"That's what I said," Alex said, seconding the notion. "If this goes badly—"

"If this goes badly," Hervé cut in, looking at Griffyn with such intensity the only thing he wasn't doing was wagging a finger, "the last person we need captured is *yourself*. Us, they'll ransom off, if they even bother capturing us. You?" He shook his head sagely, his lips pursed, and ran his finger across his neck in a swiping motion.

Griffyn exploded in laughter. "I'm not a child, these aren't bedtime stories, and you're not going to frighten me."

"'Tisn't your fear I'm speaking to, Pagan. 'Tis mine, and the men's. It's unwise to be risking your head. And," he added significantly, "the fitzEmpress will surely have *ours* if anything happens to *yours*."

Alex crossed his arms over his chest. "He's right."

"He may well be right," Griffyn said firmly, "but you will simply have to manage Henri's moods. If I die, I suggest telling him the news after he's had a few cups of wine and been with the Lady Eleanor."

Hervé frowned. "Now, sir, 'tisn't a laughing matter."

"Indeed it is not. And therefore, I will not endanger either of you, so important to me, for something I alone have taken on. This is not your burden. You go with the men. I need you there."

"We need *you* there," Alex countered.

"And so I shall be. Within a day. Now go."

They didn't look happy, but their protests subsided. The rest of the group, after a final consultation on plans and back-up plans, mounted their horses and reined into the woods. Alex and Hervé sat on their horses, one like a willow tree, the other like stump of petrified wood, in the centre of the clearing. Griffyn looked pointedly over his shoulder.

They reined around and plodded under the dripping eaves of the forest, then paused just beneath a low-lying branch. A shower of rain dribbled down on them. Hervé glanced up dismally.

"I know what Pagan said, but—" Alex began.

"—we wait," Hervé finished.

Alex nodded. "He'll come this way no matter what, on his

return." He looked over his shoulder. "She's trouble. I feel it in my bones."

Hervé glanced back at the inn too. "What harm is there, Alex? She's just a woman."

"She's more than that."

"How much more?"

Alex shook his head. "I don't know."

Turning away, they slowly dissolved into the brown and green dampness.

Griffyn walked back to the inn, aware of a truly novel thing: without warning or bidding, the rage of seventeen years was slipping away.

Ionnes de l'Ami had become as greedy and single-minded as Christian Sauvage—simply look to the hand he'd laid on the world. Forsworn an oath, stolen a castle, betrayed a blood brother.

Surely then, Gwyn, too, knew the desperation of watching your father warp before your eyes.

Like ice that has melted to just the right degree, everything started flowing. And that was, he admitted, surprisingly welcome. Rage had fanned his actions for too many years to count, driving him onwards, making him friend of kings and counts, but also making him unnatural. Mayhap it was coming time to focus his energies elsewhere.

Soon they would retake the country and he would go home. To the Nest. Mayhap, seeing as the woman abovestairs would be there too, would one day be his wife, he might settle his bones into this new thing: family.

It need not be as it had been for these last seventeen years, as it had ended for his father. It might, possibly, be like what he'd had a glimpse of last night. There was only one way to find out.

Chapter Twenty

The sun was westering by the time they reached St. Alban's Abbey. Gwyn rode behind Griffyn, constantly aware of his bulk before her. They sat silently just inside the covering of trees, a few dozen, hidden paces from the abbey walls.

A handful of monks were arrayed out front, milling nervously and talking in animated conversation Gwyn could not overhear. Hands gestured, people pointed. She pressed her cheek against Pagan's back and sat quietly, absorbing his heat and solidity.

He reached around silently and held her wrist. She knew this for what it was: a parting. Not that it should matter, she chastised herself savagely. She neither knew who he was nor whence he came, but somewhere deep inside her she knew *what* he was, and that meant good-bye.

It *should* mean her head being separated from her shoulders. She ought to be grateful. She felt like dying.

One of the monkish voices rose above the others clustered outside the Abbey. "They come!"

From over the far crest of a hill, a handful of riders approached. They wore silk tunics diagonally split with colours, red and gold.

"Lord John," called out one of the monks, his dark robes floating over the soggy earth as he hurried to greet them.

"Why, that's John!" Gwyn exclaimed quietly, peering over Pagan's shoulder. "The one I sent the message to, just last night. How on earth did he get here so quickly?"

John of Cantebrigge flung one foot over the saddle and by-passed the monks, heading straight for the abbot, who was lingering inside the gates. He tore his helm off as he went, and pulled the churchman aside, bringing both closer to where Gwyn and Pagan stood in the shadowy eaves. The men spoke quietly and in rapid voices.

"I ne'er thought you would make it," said the abbot, Robert de Gorham.

John of Cantebrigge looked at the abbot hard. "So my messenger arrived?"

"Barely an hour ago." The abbot lifted his hand and waved the others inside. A trail of monks and armoured men started inside the abbey walls. "We ought go in, my lord. 'Tis a dangerous place—"

"With Endshire about," John of Cantebrigge finished grimly. He wiped his arm across his sweaty face. "I was returning to home from the London council—praise God, or who knows when I'd have been found—when a rider caught up with me, giving word that Lady Guinevere was making her way here."

"But how?" exclaimed the abbot. His dark Benedictine habit shrouded his frail figure, and with the onrushing night darkening the skies, he looked like an enrobed spider with pink cheeks. And a shiny, tonsured head.

John shook his head. "I know not. I did not know the messenger. He wore no emblem, carried no seal, gave no information, and disappeared before my men could apprehend or question him. Unheard of, that. I thought," he added grimly, "it might be a trap."

"None that I know of. But the countess is not here."

"Christ," snapped John of Cantebrigge.

"My lord!" The abbot's voice rose an octave on his emphasis.

"My apologies to you and your God. But where in Christ's name *is* she?"

"My *lord*!" The abbot's voice dropped an octave on this reprimand. John sighed.

"I have been doing penance for many years, my lord abbot. A few more won't hurt me. You can lash me inside, but right now I'm more concerned with Lady Guinevere. You've heard nothing? Seen nothing?"

"Nothing."

John said something unintelligible, then: "I'll send out my men out to scour these woods. Perhaps she's lost."

"But how then did she ever send word?" enquired the abbot.

John shook his head as they turned and walked back towards the abbey.

Gwyn had been sinking further and further into Pagan's back during the conversation, as if hiding, which was the oddest thing, for had not this been her destination for the entire day and previous night? And was that not her very own friend, come to save her?

Why then did it feel so like being hunted?

"You'd best go, Raven."

"Aye," she agreed tonelessly. She slid off the horse. He hopped down beside her. "And you?" she asked fiercely. "What will happen to you? Where do you go now?"

He didn't say anything. She held back a shameful sob. The world was tilting, sending every thought into the tangled nest of her emotions. She stepped backwards, towards the abbey, out of the trees, into the solid, sunsetting world.

"Pagan—"

He reached out, his fingertips reaching out into the sunset, and she held her breath, hoping somehow he could change what had to be. But he didn't. His fingers ran along her cheek, then dropped back into the shadows. His blue-grey gaze travelled slowly over her face, as if he were memorising her.

Nothing mattered but that look in his eyes. Not John, not the abbot, not the king nor his wars nor Papa from the grave. Nothing but that look in Pagan's eyes.

Someone shouted. She jerked. His gaze tore from hers. Another shout. Her name. Someone was calling her name. She'd been seen.

Pagan melted back into the trees. Gwyn looked over her shoulder. One of John's men was calling and running for his horse.

She spun desperately. Pagan's perfect, dark shadow was disappearing into the dimness of the wood.

Another shout rose up from outside the abbey gates. She twisted around again,. There were John of Cantebrigge's men, then she saw the others. A whole host of others, with crossed red swords on their tunics and a sable-black pennant, riding under the Abbey gates.

Marcus d'Endshire.

Her heart stopped beating. She reeled backwards. Something hard thumped against her thigh. She looked down wildly. Papa's heirloom chest. Shivers spread outward over her skin like cracks on an ice-bound lake. If she went in with that, Marcus would take it. The letters, and whatever lay beneath.

The knight from the abbey was galloping towards her.

She made a choice. Her only choice. Reckless, intuitive, dangerous.

She slipped back under the eaves, heart hammering. "I don't even know you," she whispered, more to her self than his.

Griffyn heard her murmur and ripped his gaze from Marcus's men to her lovely, frightened face. "You know me, Raven."

She wrenched the lumpy felt sack from around her waist and shoved it into his hands. "Take this."

His fingers closed reflexively around the bag. "What is it?"

"Family heirlooms. For God's sake, *take it*!"

Her whispers were short, staccato bursts of sound. Griffyn felt himself standing at a crossroads. Guinevere obviously thought it wasn't safe inside the abbey, and deep inside, he knew it too. But neither was Everoot safe, if she was not there to keep it until he returned. So he let her go.

Her face was white and frightened under the shadows under the wet trees. Her dark hair slid forward over her shoulders as she reached out to him.

"You will find me?" she whispered.

He grabbed her hand and held it to his chest. "I will," he said, thinking she'd never been so beautiful as she was just then, disheveled and desperate and needing him.

"Promise," she insisted, tears filling her eyes.

"On my life," he vowed hoarsely.

The tears started spilling down her cheeks. "On mine, Pagan. Promise on mine."

He grabbed her face between his palms and crushed her lips under his in a harsh, possessive kiss. "On our lives."

Releasing her, he pointed to the abbey gates, which were slowly rolling open. He swung up on Noir. "Go."

Gwyn turned towards the abbey, barely able to see through her tears. She pushed under a low-hanging branch and looked over her shoulder. "You promised," she whispered.

There was a shout from the abbey. Two men were coming through the open gates. Pagan melted into the shadows. She barely caught an outline of black-edged cape astride a dancing stallion. A lifted hand. And he was gone.

Chapter Twenty-One

Gwyn made her way clumsily, stumbling through growing darkness, over rutted dirt and tufts of dried grass of the outer abbey gardens. The shiny chestnut rump of the last horse of Marcus's entourage had just disappeared through the gate when the knight on the galloping horse reached her.

Gwyn sighed as she was, once again, hoisted onto a horse by a strange man. He hurried her through the outer gate, which was pulled shut behind them, and trotted past the orchards and the maze of buildings that crowded inside the protective wall of the abbey fortress. Chapter house, cloister, slype—a wide, roofed corridor connecting the cloister with the cemetery—barn, friars' dining hall. They finally arrived at the abbot's lodgings on the west side of the abbey church.

She was bustled up to the abbot's dormir, where she was met by John of Cantebrigge himself, who was pacing in front of the brazier. The abbot turned, stunned, frozen in the act of holding out a sheaf of parchment to Marcus fitzMiles, who was taking off his gloves.

They all gaped at her. The extended papers ruffled unheeded to the floor. She tried to look at John, but it was Marcus's glittering gaze that held her.

"Good. You are safe," he observed coldly.

"Aye," she snapped, regaining her voice and moving into the room, "though by none of your efforts."

John hurried to her side, and, giving her a brief hug, held her upper arms between his hands and looked her over carefully, his eyes missing nothing. "Gwyn," he murmured, "Are you all right?"

"I am." It was tempting to relax into his concern, but instead she nodded briskly and looked over his shoulder at Marcus. She mustn't appear weak. "Why is Lord Marcus here?"

The abbot of the wealthy and prestigious abbey, glided over to her. "Lady Guinevere," he said, taking her hand. "We were worried greatly. Praise God you are safely returned to us."

"My lord abbot, I would praise God if I were returned to *you*, but why, I ask again, am I returned to *him*?" She nodded at Marcus. The abbot looked enraged.

Marcus smiled, the picture of calm, solicitous concern. "Lady Guinevere, you have ever been prone to fits of exuberance. 'Tis one of your charms. But with your father's passing, and none to guard you, I am growing concerned that you may do yourself harm."

He moved to her side, took her hand and kissed it.

A small, binding thread of good sense made her hold her tongue until he was close enough to be the only one to hear the whispered venom of her words. "Marcus," she hissed as he bent over her hand, "I will surely do *you* harm before this night is out. I suggest you worry more on that."

He unbent. "But I do worry for you, my lady, as do we all." He gestured to the others.

A small, pricking fear snaked up Gwen's spine. Her friend John was looking at her as he would a small child who'd nearly been crushed beneath a horse's onrushing hooves. The abbot was looking at her as if she she'd been the one guiding the horse. He nodded his tonsured head pretentiously.

"You speak truly, my lord Endshire," he droned. "And well

do we appreciate your concern. Without you, we might ne'er have known to watch for the lady."

"*You* sent word that I was missing?" she cried, looking back at Marcus.

He bent his head in a humble nod. "I thought perhaps you might come here, after you left London so swiftly last night."

"I left swiftly," Gwyn gasped, unable to believe this mummery he was performing, "because you threatened to wed me against my will!"

"I did but explore the possibility with you, my lady. That you took offence was not my intention, nor my desire."

"Your desire? You *explored* it? Why, you threatened me!"

"I explained to you the value of such a union."

"You sent troops to the Nest—"

"For your defence."

"—and said if I did not wed you—"

"Then you at least would have some protection from the forces arraying against you," he finished smoothly. "My men are there for the defence of Everoot. These are dangerous times, Gwyn," he went on, his face becoming more serious as he dropped the use of her title and affected intimate concern, "and with your father so recently dead, there are those who conspire against the House of Everoot."

"Indeed! With you among the worst!"

She turned to John, but his look of concern had deepened into one of unease. She spun to the abbot, but his hands were pushed up the sleeves of his robe and he was nodding his shiny head pompously. Gwyn wanted to fly into a rage.

"My lady," John interjected quietly. He took up her hand again, kindness and worry in his look. "You need to be cleaned up."

She stared numbly at the far wall, reality hitting her. They did not believe her. They thought 'twas as Marcus had said—either that, or it was more convenient to believe such. They thought she had fled like a small, impetuous child, unable to know her own mind nor to think clearly. They thought her . . . incapable.

She turned numbly and let John's gentle hand guide her to the door.

"Where did you get the cloak, my lady?"

Marcus's voice slid up her back like a cold hand. Her foot paused on its way to the ground, then she hurried forwards, pulling on John's arm, trying to get out of the room before Marcus could ask his dangerous question again.

"My lady, where did you get the woollen cloak?"

"John," she turned pleadingly to her old friend, "perhaps I *am* a bit turned in my head." She swallowed the bilious rancor that accompanied pretending to be witless, and peered into his concerned eyes. "It has been a harrowing night, and I would rest now."

"Stay, lady," Marcus ordered quietly. "I would speak with you a while longer."

"John," she pleaded, trying to keep the desperation out of her voice.

Marcus laid a hand on her arm. "Wait."

Gwyn threw him off with a jerk. She was dangerously close to flying into that rage, and it would be the worst possible thing. Assaulting Marcus with bared teeth would hardly prove her a reasonable, capable adult.

She and Marcus stared at one another, eyes glittering, shoulders squared.

"My lady," interjected the abbot into the silent showdown. "Lord Endshire has not only brought word that you were in danger, for which you should give thanks rather than a critique of our Lord's grace." Here he frowned firmly. "But he also brings word that our lord king is considering giving your wardship to Lord Endshire, to ensure protection for you and your estates."

Her mouth dropped open. "My king would not do that!" she cried. She wheeled to John. "Stephen made a promise to

Papa! He promised he would not . . . he would not—" She tossed a helpless look over her shoulder at Marcus. "*Give* me to anyone without my consent!"

"King Stephen has other subjects than you, Lady Guinevere," Marcus observed.

The abbot sniffed. "This childish selfishness bodes ill."

Marcus glanced at the abbot, then took a sip of wine before continuing as if the churchman had not spoken. "Subjects who must be kept happy, as must you, of course." He smiled. "I will do my best."

This was not happening. She could barely control herself. Her hands clenched into fists and her face flushed hot.

"And so," Marcus was saying, "our king felt the need to protect his interests. Namely, Everoot."

"You mean *Endshire*," she spat back. "You threatened him. You threatened my king."

"Lady Guinevere," the abbot reprimanded.

"He did," she said, suddenly calm. "You sold your loyalty for a wardship."

Marcus bowed slightly. "You shall be worth it, my lady."

"It is not decided yet, is it?" she demanded, spinning to John.

He shook his head sadly, but the abbot interrupted. "By your actions," he proclaimed, "'twill be determined if such a thing is necessary." Here he sniffed, as if doubting they would see much to convince them otherwise. "To mine own mind, 'tis becoming more and more clear that such governance is indeed required."

Her ears started ringing, and the world slipped a little into grey. She leaned on John's arm, trying to still the dizziness and panic flooding through her body.

"Gwyn," John murmured encouragingly. It came softly through the ringing. "Mayhap you ought stay and speak with Lord Marcus."

She ran her tongue over dry lips. He would ask questions she could not answer. Questions of where she'd gotten the cloak, of where she'd spent her night. With whom. Every answer revealed would doom Pagan. Every answer denied would seal Everoot's fate.

"Aye, John. I will stay."

Marcus smiled.

John left and the abbot glided behind a tapestry leading to another room, leaving them alone. The only sound was the abbot's robes shurrushing over the flagstone floor in the distance, then silence. Marcus gestured to an elaborate chair by the hotly glowing brazier.

"Gwyn, sit."

She debated arguing the point, and then admitted it would be pointless, fruitless, and idiotic. She sat down.

"We were all so worried."

"Do stop, Marcus," she snapped. "They have all gone, and there's no one else to fool."

He laughed. "You've a temper that will be the death of you one day."

"Or *you*," she quipped sourly.

His laughter slowly faded. He put one hand on the arm of her chair and bent down. "Where did you get the cloak?"

She turned her head to the side, away from him. "What does it matter?"

He braced his other hand on the other side of the chair, so she was sitting between his outstretched arms. He bent at the hip and leaned nearer her face. "Where did you get the cloak?"

"'Tis mine."

"Not bloody likely," he whispered very close to her lips.

She swallowed. "Marcus, how is this helpful?"

His lips pressed together so tightly they turned white. His usually aristocratic, aquiline face turned quite red.

"'Tisn't," he agreed. His breath skidded by her face, and the acrid, choking scent of wet leather and iron filled her nostrils. "What would be helpful, is for you to answer my questions."

Gwyn started slipping off the chair, the sweat of her fear was building so thickly.

"I cannot see how my clothes are of any interest to a man," she said, hiding the tremor in her voice as she retreated to the only style of communication that would work with Marcus: self-assured irreverence. He had no patience for weakness, no respect for fragility, and without one or the other from him this night, she was in dire trouble. "Still," she went on, affecting idle disinterest, "I can send you my dressmaker to consult, seeing you are so enamoured of her work."

He leaned back a bit and looked the torn and tattered gown up and down. "If she dresses you like that, I've no interest whatsoever."

Gwyn had a wild vision of Marcus fitzMiles, Lord d'End-shire, one of the most cunning lords of the realm, dressed up in a woman's tunic and headdress, capering about a maypole. The mad humour of it almost sent her into hysterics. She shoved her tongue inside the range of her teeth and clamped down hard.

"I know the cloak is not yours, Gwyn. That is why it matters." He ran the side of his finger along the lump inside her cheek where her tongue was pressed. "Humour me."

She gave a wild laugh. "I cannot imagine how to begin doing that."

"You do it with every breath, lady."

The abbot flowed back into the room like a river of muddy water and looked at them askance. Marcus pushed away from the chair and paced to the far wall just as John returned, followed soon after by two servants. One carried a tray of wine and some foodstuffs, the other carried furs for Gwyn.

The abbot propelled Marcus to the desk on the other side of the room and was speaking in low tones, his tonsured head bent over the sheaf of parchment that had fluttered to the floor upon her arrival.

Marcus was looking directly at her.

Chapter Twenty-Two

She sat, huddled in a chair, bundled in furs and sipping warmed wine. Almost an hour had passed, and around her the abbot and John and Marcus were still rehashing the latest news that had gripped the war-torn country.

"Stephen has confirmation that the rumour of fitzEmpress's spy is true. He fears he may have infiltrated some noble houses during the London council meetings."

Marcus and the abbot listened to John relay the king's concerns, Marcus with a yawn, the abbot with a worried frown.

"I had hopes he'd already been killed," fretted the abbot. "We've had no confirmation from anyone on the matter, but we've lost no more lords to the Angevin's cause."

"Yet," concluded Marcus. "'Twould be unwise of them to announce their defection while in London. We shall hear what word comes in a few weeks' time, when they are safe behind castle walls and the harvest is brought in."

John shook his head and leaned the heel of his hand against the wall, hitting the hilt of his sword on the stone. It clanged and he caught it with his free hand unconsciously, his pleasant, ruddy face serious. "We can't simply wait him out, Marcus. Time is on his side. If the spy is here, we must flush him out ere we find Henri fitzEmpress camping on our shores come spring."

"Winter, I would venture," Marcus suggested calmly. He sat on a bench with his legs pushed out in front of him. "One or two more nobles to his cause, and Henri will not wait for the marriage bed to dry afore he comes for England. And Pagan Sauvage is a convincing man."

Gwyn rose out of her seat like she was yanked on wires. "Pagan?"

Every head turned to her. Marcus went still.

His gaze, fixed on the far wall, shifted slowly over. He stared at her a moment, then smiled, a slow, terrible smile. He pushed to his feet.

"Ready your men, Cantebrigge. She came from the south woods."

He and John were already striding out the door, talking rapidly of horses and pathways.

"No!" Gwyn cried, running after. "No! *You can't!*"

They paused long enough for Marcus to lean back and run a finger by her cheek, whispering, "I knew it" in her ear. Then he strode away with the abbot quick on his heels. She started forward again, but John put a restraining hand on her arm.

"Gwyn!" He gave her a small, impatient shake. "What is wrong with you? This is the spy we've been hunting. Due to him, your king may lose his crown!"

"He saved my life!"

John's pleasant, kind face screwed up in an expression of disgust. "Do you know who he is, this Pagan of yours?" he demanded furiously.

"N-no."

He made an impatient move with his hand. "Pagan is Griffyn *Sauvage*, Guinevere," he fairly hissed. "Christian Sauvage's *son. Heir to Everoot.*" Her face went cold and white. "Pagan's father and your father were once friends. The best of friends. They shared everything. Women, wine, wars.

They went everywhere together. Everywhere," he repeated significantly.

Something dim started coalescing in her mind. Something frightening. "The Holy Lands," she whispered.

John looked at her sharply. "Aye. And Marcus's father was there too, my lady. The three of them. Do not forget that."

She felt nauseous. "What?"

"Did your father not tell you anything? Marcus was your father's page, years back—"

"What?"

"—long before you were born. He was forced on your father by Miles, Marcus's father. Griffyn Sauvage was supposed to go to your father as squire too, but something happened. I do not know how, or why, or anything of the tangle, but something binds these three families together, something unholy. Sauvage, fitzMiles, and the de l'Amis."

"Marcus knows Pagan?" she asked weakly.

"Marcus knew his father, and aye, he knows the son. And Marcus has as much reason to hate him as the de l'Amis do."

Hate, she thought numbly. *I am supposed to hate him.* "What are you saying?"

"What I am saying, Gwyn, is that if you gainsay Marcus one more time, you are doomed. Everoot will go to him in wardship, and so will you. And then he will take you to wife."

Her hand went to her mouth, fear rushing through her like a raging, frothing wave of madness. The movement seemed to anger John.

"Was your night with Pagan worth so much you would barter Everoot for it?" he demanded savagely. "Why did you not mention anything of your rescuer?" His face paled. "God save us, Gwynnie. You didn't know, did you?"

She shook her head wildly, denying it, all the while, inside, crying, *Yes, yes, I knew he was not what he seemed, and that should have been enough.*

She held her hands to her face. Her fingertips were freezing on her cheeks. She could barely concentrate on John's face. It was weaving and slipping in and out of focus.

"I've no time to tell you stories, Gwyn. If you would have Everoot be yours, then it must *be yours*. Above all else. Do you understand me?" He looked at her oddly. "Did you father not even teach you so much as that?"

She reached out instinctively for John's arm, reaching for anything stable in her wildly shifting world. Papa knew Pagan. Papa hated him. There was something unholy binding these families.

John touched her grasping hand and softened briefly, back to the gentle, companionable John she'd known for years. The one who could explain this madness to her.

Only he didn't.

One of his men appeared at the end of the shadowy corridor and beckoned. "I must go," John said. He turned her, gently this time, by her shoulders and led her back to the room, pausing before the door on his way out. "'Tis best this way."

He shut the door.

Gwyn stared at the wall. The silence of the room was deafening, hurt her ears. She looked down at her hands, upturned and opened on her lap. They were the same hands as a day ago, a week, but they were not hers. She looked dumbly around the room, seeing familiar objects—a desk, cupboard, table—but now so hideously warped they seemed revolting.

Two things her father had left her, the only two things she ever treasured—Everoot and the box of letters. She'd given one to a pagan she'd loved for a day. The other would be lost if she tried to save him.

Thrusting back the chair, she ran to the door, flung it open, and plowed smack into one of Marcus's knights. It was de Louth. Good God, she was surrounded by nightmares.

"Get . . . *off* . . . me!" she shouted, fighting the hands that were suddenly wrapped around her.

De Louth's voice was quiet but firm as he caught her up

and deposited her back in the room. "Be calm, my lady." She thought she saw a small flicker of emotion cross his face, then it was gone. Limping, he took up a post by the only door in the windowless room, and stood with an expressionless face.

"He said you're to stay here."

Griffyn rode hard for London. He rode on the back paths, galloping past tree trunks and over downed logs, silent but for Noir's thundering hooves. He was blasting past the treacherous woods near the Saxon outpost when they found him, spilling swords and fury across another moonlit night.

Ten men were too much for one, and he was dragged off in chains. In their wrath, they missed capturing his horse, Noir, who cantered away under the eaves with a small bundle tied around his saddle. Later, Hervé slipped out of the forest shadows and took the horse. He and Alex silently tracked the company to the walls of London, then rode like demons to the Gloucester port where the others waited.

Griffyn was thrown into the Tower of London, beaten daily, threatened with beheading, and lashed on his back within an inch of his life. Only Henri's intercession, bartering him for a highborn hostage taken on their last campaign, won him his freedom six weeks later.

Throughout his imprisonment, the only thing that kept madness at bay were thoughts of Raven. Of her laugh, which was almost scent here in the filth and grime. The look in her eyes when he'd promised to find her. The thought that the world might, indeed, be filled with light, and not the darkness of his father's awful desires and unbreakable oaths. That he could go home again. That he had a home to go to, and Gwyn was waiting for him.

The horrors of his rat-infested prison were not so vivid as these lucid dreams, and it was the hope of her that sustained him.

Then he overheard two guards talking a week before his release, when his body had been beaten too many times to count, and his dreams shattered like a million shards of ice.

Voices tinged with a Norman accent, mixed with Saxon roughness, lent a strange, rustic, lyrical quality to the rough talk of the wardens outside his cell one evening.

"Aye, well, and what do ye expect? A woman gave him up," said one gruff voice in reply to some unheard comment, then grunted. "We ought to begin hiring wenches as spies. I've said it before. Men can't keep their cods and their brains working at once, and the women is a good bit cheaper to pay into the bargain."

This was greeted by a coarse laugh. "Aye, well, there you're right. I wouldn't mind a bit of spying bein' done on me, if I had one as savory as they say this one was. But 'twasn't a wench, Dunnar. 'Twas her ladyship."

Griffyn dragged one swollen eye open and stared at the slit of light coming under the door.

"Aye, I heard she was tupped right well," said the first, grunting again, "and 'twouldn't have been given up mor'n what she already did."

More coarse laughter.

"'Twas the lady, all right," said the second. "Word is the king's going to increase her lands, her bein' the heiress 'n all."

"Pah," came the spat reply, "as if Everoot's not a big enough thing for herself to manage."

Griffyn went still.

The other laughed in reply. "And ye're thinkin' ye might do wi' some'a the rewards?"

"And why not?" the Grunt retorted indignantly. "Ack, I know 'twouldn't be right, but I do mor'n those rich earls and whatnot. Pah," he spat again. "I'd like to compare what she done to the years of shit-hauling I been doin' down here these past years."

The voices started to fade away. Griffyn rolled to his knees and braced his hand against the wall. It couldn't be.

"I could do wi' a bit of som'in' meself," said the first guard with another coarse laugh, "but I'd ruther a piece of the lady than a piece of the land, iffen ye know what I mean."

The other spat a series of curses and their voices started to fade further. A squeal of rusted iron indicated they'd reached the outer door and would soon be gone. Griffyn dragged himself as far as his chains would allow and stood, swaying on his feet. He leaned one palm against the fetid wall and bent his head, listening.

"Naw, the Countess Everoot stumbles 'cross a spy, gets rightly tupped as her first reward, then turns him over and gets an increase in the lands so's now they reach halfway to York. Bloody nobility. Can't trust 'em so far as ye can spit."

Griffyn staggered backwards, his head filled with a hot, hard roar. The agony of realisation dropped him to his knees. He slid down the wet wall, his knees bending under him, the back of his head against the hard, wet stone.

Sometime over that one storm-tossed night, he had imagined, for just a moment, he had found love. Instead it was betrayal, the ever-present truth.

He banged his head backwards against the stone, fighting the almost overwhelming urge to bellow his rage and fury. Traitor, deceiver, betrayer.

Spawn.

No one ever changed. It was in the blood.

His heart was splitting and hardening all at once, so it was a splintered mass of frozen shards by the time he was ransomed seven days later.

Interlude:

A Fallow Year

Winter through Summer, 1153
All of England

The armies of Henri fitzEmpress marched across the parched earth of England and laid it to waste. Castle, garrison, village, homestead; everything was decimated.

King Stephen fought on, along with his combative, petulant son, Prince Eustace. Some said the king was goaded by those who feared Henri fitzEmpress's wrath, or perhaps the obligation to tread, weary now, a path long chosen. The prince had more at stake: a kingdom.

But for most, the truth was plain to see. The civil wars would end as soon as Henri fitzEmpress was crowned king.

Still, a few loyal outposts held their castles, kept their garrisons manned. Kept their faith. They would die, of course. By sword or starvation, they would die or be subsumed.

The fitzEmpress captains went out before the main army like locusts upon a field. They ate their way through the countryside, and everything fell before them. The good and the bad, the chaff and the wheat, and no one kept count anymore.

And then, in August, the news went out: Prince Eustace, heir to the throne, was dead.

August 1153
The Nest, Northumbria, England

"It's all gone, my lady. The entire harvest. Wheat and rye, both crops, withered."

Gwyn looked up at her William, her balding, beloved seneschal, who sat opposite her at the table. He brushed all five strands back over the slope of his head and frowned at the parchment scroll he held aloft, the report just received from the eastern manors. He was simply repeating what he'd already said, thrice already.

Gwyn nodded wearily and looked out the window. No breeze came through the wide, fourth-story window, only hot, dry air and the small voice of a child playing some game.

"Sell the harps," she said flatly.

"My lady! They were your mother's!"

"Have Gilbert prepare the wagon. To Ipsile-upon-Tyne," she said, referring to one of Everoot's chartered towns. "Take it to Agardly the goldsmythe. His serjeantry includes providing travel for Everoot's goods, and he knows every minstrel from the River Clyde to the Thames. They'll fetch a middling price."

She heard the parchment ruffle to the table. "Enough for wheat for the year," William murmured, "if they both sell."

She nodded. And that was it. There was nothing else to sell.

The child's voice faded away, but Gwyn kept staring out the window, ashamed by the realisation that this worry was not the thing that assailed her heart the deepest. The deepest cut came from the knowledge that she had betrayed Pagan a year ago.

A bribe to the prison guards a week after her return to Everoot had resulted in half the money being returned in clipped coins and no news of him. "Dead," said her messenger. "Surely dead."

The news almost killed her. Which was as it should be, an eye for an eye, a life for a life.

Forget.

She gripped the edge of the table in front of her. God alone knew how she'd tried to banish the memories of that night almost a year ago when the world was dowered with magic and a pagan invaded her soul, but her dreams were wayward. They awakened her each morn, pulsing wet heat between her thighs and knifing pain through the centre of her heart.

Please God, give me some penance to do that will settle all these debts.

"Or let me die," she whispered.

William looked over. "My lady?"

She shook her head. It was all death and destruction this hot, swirling summer. Henri fitzEmpress's armies had invaded in the winter, as Marcus predicted, and ravaged the countryside, cutting a deliberately vicious swath through the south and west, collecting submissions as they went.

South, west, and east, the world she knew was falling to bloody pieces on the sword of an army that was slowly, inexorably, moving north. Towards Everoot.

And she could do nothing. Animals had to be fed, fish had to be caught, and crops had to be tended, even though most of the hardiest men had been sent to fortify the king's armies.

It was left to the women and young to reap the harvest, to prepare and store it for the coming winter. Which was promising to be a long one. The dog days of July had come and bitten hard. They might kill as many as the wars. Dust rose up at the mere thought of a walk, and the wheat shivered dry husks onto the heads of those trying to bring the awful harvest in.

It could be worse, she reminded herself firmly. She could be going through all this while wed to Marcus fitzMiles. Or warded to him. She'd rather sell pasties at the fair than be bound to Marcus.

But the king's chivalrous and long-standing promise to her father had held firm a year back, despite Marcus's awful threats. Or perhaps because of them. Pride was a powerful goad even for her gallant king.

However it came, though, Everoot was still in Guinevere's hands, unless and until it dripped between her fingers like melting ice. The summer drought was burning through the earldom's already-meager resources. Even Mamma's harps would be but a bucket of water against the inferno.

"And there's word of the Welsh matter," William said, his dour tone even more gloomy than usual. "Another steward has gone a'missing on the Welsh manor by Ipsile."

The estates on the Welsh Marches were infamous for running off stewards. Or killing them off. And no one knew why. Gwyn dragged her head up through the heat. "Dead?" she asked wearily.

"No. Just gone."

She rose, pushing away the parchment rolls and wax tablets scattered across the broad table. "That's all for now, William. I'll find another steward . . . later."

The office chamber was set deep in the castle walls, where no fresh air or light came in, but in the dog days of summer, it was cool and refreshing. Reluctantly, she pushed herself into a corridor damp with hot moisture; even the stones were sweating from the heat. Her steward hurried behind.

"Proceed with your plan to replace the fish traps on the upper river, William. You are right: they've been vandalised and catch nothing but reeds."

She went limply through the heat, to the north-facing solar where her women waited for her to join them.

She chatted for awhile, then let her sewing drop to her lap and stared across what was to be a nursery, devoid of children, where she took one precious hour from each day to embroider and chat with the women. It was the only time she could spare.

Today, the murmur of their voices was laced like thin strands of silver through the hot, heavy summer air. They sat on benches, heads bent, busily chattering, their fingers darting over their sewing. Every so often a colourful veil or hair ribbon would lift—red, green, sapphire—and a pair of bright eyes would peer out to smile at some joke, before dipping down to work again.

Her entourage had grown rather alarmingly over the past six months, but what could she do? When the daughters of valued vassals and southern nobles needed a safe place to flee to, was she to turn them away?

Nay, 'twas only in the far north, on Everoot lands, that a safe refuge existed. The word had gone out: Guinevere de l'Ami was one of the faithful.

But it was not only the noble-bred who required a safe haven, she discovered as the famine-month of July began claiming its victims last month—more than usual with the men away at war. Girls of the village needed a haven too, their need no less for their humble station. And what was she to do with them? Let them die?

Most assuredly not. It was not all sacrifice, she reflected, casting a hopeful, anxious eye on the bright tunics and shining plaits of hair. The girls brightened her days and in these troubled times, no price was too high for that.

She rubbed her slick neck, then leaned against the backing of her chair and closed her eyes. Despite the draining heat, she let the light from the open window drift across her thighs. The sounds of chattering faded to a golden background buzz.

"Milady?"

She dragged one lid open. Her small page, Duncan, another refugee from the wars, was standing in the doorway. Looming behind him was a dark shape, unrecognisable. She opened both eyes.

Duncan stepped aside, revealing a dust-ridden, grim-faced messenger who moved into the archway and filled it with somber leather and dirt. He swung a wary glance around the room. When all he encountered was bright colours and soft, feminine laughter, an almost hungry glance passed over his face. He turned back. "My lady?"

She rose, her sewing slipping unheeded to the ground. "Sir?"

"I would speak with you."

A jagged chill, odd in the summer heat, trickled over the knobs of her spine. "Girls," she said without looking away from him, "'tis time for your afternoon walk."

A chorus of groans and gripes met this, but they rose obediently and streamed out through a far door. When they were gone, a silence stretched out for a few precious seconds.

"My lady, I have news."

"You are come from King Stephen," Gwyn said, her voice flat and toneless.

When he nodded, she couldn't deny the rush of tears that swelled in her eyes. God's truth, what could he say that could hurt her now?

"The king will lose the war."

She shook her head. Denial, weariness, she did not know which. All these years of war and wanting and waste, for what? "Cannot we send more troops?" she asked in rote, like a lesson learned. "More men, more money?"

"What money?" He smiled grimly and moved further into the sunlit room, a dark, weather-beaten figure strapped in leather and despair. "What men? What troops? All are turning to the fitzEmpress. They think their plight will be better in his hands than our lord king's."

"They are fools," she spat, running the back of her hand along her trembling lips.

"'Tis said the king's son is dead."

She took an involuntary step back and dropped into her chair.

"I've something for you." He covered the ground between them in two strides and dropped to his knees in front of her.

Digging under his tunic, he caught at something, then brought out his fisted hand, which he held before her nose.

"What is it?"

His hand fell open, and on the calloused, dirt-stained palm lay a scattering of dried rose petals, their crimson colour still bright, even in death. Gwyn's mouth fell open, her words hushed. "'Tis my bloom. The Conqueror." She gingerly touched one of the dried petals.

"Aye. And His Grace now asks that you recall your vow to him, as he has recalled it to you."

"'Twas ever to be his at need," she murmured, staring at the broken flower. She recalled the councils in London, her meeting with the king overshadowed by her heartbroken tryst with Pagan. How long ago had that been? A hundred years? How much had she aged? A thousand?

"The need is great, my lady, and the time is now."

She dragged her gaze back up. "What would he have of me?"

"Safekeeping for the prince."

"You said—you said he was dead."

"I said some say that. But 'tis not so. Not yet."

"Yet?"

"He is ill, mayhap deathly so. He needs tending, else he'll surely die."

"God in Heaven, where is he?"

"Here."

She leapt to her feet, almost knocking the kneeling herald over. "Perdition, you have the prince *here*?"

He straightened and smiled faintly, a ghostly gesture on his somber visage. But the deep lines of laughter that readily absorbed this smile implied a past filled with happier times, when perhaps such expressions of joy were not so unfamiliar. Gwyn had a fleeting wonder about whom he'd shared such laughter with, and where that woman was now.

"I recall your father well, my lady. He was ever loyal to the king, and just now, you reminded me of him."

"Just now, I would have him here more than all the ginger in Jerusalem," she said solemnly. "Where is the prince?"

"Wrapped in a shroud and thrown over the back of my horse as if a sack of wheat."

"How many are you?" she asked swiftly, walking towards the door. The messenger was fast behind, reaching above to hold the door open for her, then stepping through into the cool, shadowy hall. They hurried down the winding stairs, speaking in whispers as they went.

"Just three. The lord prince, my attendant, and myself."

"And you are?"

"Adam of Gloucester."

She hurried around the final twist in the stairs. "Who else knows of this?"

"None but I. And you."

They reached the bottom. The great hall stretched out beyond. Servants were at various tasks, passing in and out. She could hear the faint giggles of a gaggle of girls from a distant room; the women had not made it out of the castle yet. Two off-duty knights sat playing a game of chess at a table. A group of young squires sat whittling at another table, released for the moment from their unending tasks as aspiring knights. Everywhere she looked were people, sweat-stained and half-dizzy, who had retreated into the cool castle air to escape the sweltering heat of mid-day. Only those who had to be outside were.

"No one knows but you, Adam?"

"And you," he reminded in a low voice, his gaze following hers over the pockets of people, people with eyes and ears. And tongues.

"Come." She grabbed his sleeve and tugged him back into the shadows.

They hurried through a long passageway that ran past the kitchens. Someone's high-pitched voice rang out, saying something about wishing for a harp. They must be in one of the offices where she'd stored the beautiful, be-stringed things the harpers used to play at the wondrous feasts once held at the Nest. None were held now, and Gwyn told herself selling the harps was a negligible loss.

Some said the times were too grim and uncertain for such revelry, but it hadn't been the uncertain times; it had been the uncertain money that brought silence to the hall. Dinners and suppers were now punctuated by knives and scattered, short-lived laughter, and the long, soundless nights were disrupted only by dried grasses rustling in faint breezes and women wailing for their lost men.

"This way."

She pointed to a doorway that led out to the detached kitchens and they emerged into the greedy summer heat. Sun burned hot on Gwyn's head, as if she'd stuck it into the fire grate. She was soaked in sweat within two steps. She could feel it trickling down the back of her neck and sliding between her breasts. It was hard to breathe.

They moved doggedly through the wall of heat to the base of the keep, where stood a pair of horses, their back hooves cocked sleepily, and a wiry man with bristly hair stood glaring suspiciously about him.

"William, 'tis my lady Guinevere," Adam announced quietly.

The wiry man with a thatch of grimy, curling grey-brown hair bowed his head briefly. "We've ridden hard to reach you, my lady." He glanced at his captain. "Does she know?"

Adam nodded, ignoring the man's rudeness. Gwyn did too; her eyes kept slipping to the shape bundled at the back of the saddle on one of the horses.

"Well, he's fading fast in this heat," Adam's attendant said bluntly. "He needs someplace cool, and a lot o' tending, my lady."

She wrenched her gaze back to them.

"And privacy. Above all," Adam finished, watching her intently.

"I could put him in my chambers, but . . ." she began.

"But?"

All she could muster was a weak grin, and the labour it took to recognise the pale shadow of humour was not worth the effort in this heat. Neither man responded to it. "People are in and out of there like 'tis the hall itself, and ordering it off-limits will raise a few eyebrows."

"And mayhap loose a few tongues. Where else?" prompted the knight.

"The storage rooms?" his attendant suggested.

Gwyn started. "My lord prince, in the *cellars*?"

"'Tis as safe a place as any, I'll warrant. Unless you've got a few of Henri's men already stowed down there in chains and whatnot?" He ran his tongue along his chipped teeth and stared at her. She turned helplessly to Adam.

"The cellars," he said firmly.

She looked at the grey-shrouded lump hanging off the horse. "The cellars, then. And may my lord king have mercy on me."

"He'll have mercy well enough if the prince lives, my lady," quipped the attendant. "If he dies, well . . ." He cocked a brow as they led the horses away from the main entrance to the keep. "You could have set him about anywheres and 'twouldn't be enough to still the king's fury."

She guided them to a little-used entrance on the northern, least-used side of the castle. There were no outbuildings, no gardens or exercise yards, and little reason for anyone to wander back here. There were only the cool shadows that edged out from the base of the buttressed tower they now stood beneath, and Gwyn hoped to God anyone seeking shade would be more inclined to the great hall than this barely-used bit of turf.

A thick wall of ivy hung down over the castle walls. She wrestled a swath of it aside to reveal a short, hidden series of steps leading down to a small covered entryway and a huge oak door at the bottom, strapped with iron hinges. Fumbling with the ring of keys tied to the girdle around her waist, she took up a mottled iron one and thrust it into the lock.

The door pulled open noiselessly, emitting a billowing cloud of darkness and a faint stench. She pinched her nose while Adam propped open the door with three rocks. She stood aside as the two men hauled their princely cargo from the horse and struggled him inside.

Once they disappeared into the darkness, she heaved the rocks away, ripped one of her nails to the quick in the process, cursed to rival a seaman, and let the door slam shut behind her.

It was dark. A full, eye-taunting darkness that brought another curse, this one fainter, to her lips. Echoes bounced down the corridor in mocking whispers.

"Do you know where we are?" Adam enquired, his voice drifting from out of the darkness to her left.

She nibbled on the edge of her finger, gathering her bearings. They must be at the far end of a disused passageway that snaked past cells and small chambers, rooms once used for storing siege supplies, wine and foods and an arsenal of weapons. Now the entire place was empty, save for small animal scuttlings and a slow drip that could be heard in the distance.

"Come."

She tiptoed sightless down the rank, damp corridor, heart in her throat. She kept her hand on the tunnel wall, trailing her fingertips across foul pockets of slime and sludge, but if she removed her hand from the wall, she'd walk smack into it. She could see nothing; the pitch of the darkness was so black it practically oozed.

Every so often the stone dropped away and her fingers would suddenly trail over empty space, an opening of some sort. A cold draft would sweep by her face, coming from some dark, untold depths deep in the castle bowels. Gwyn hurried past the openings, hastening the men with raspy whispers and a beckoning hand that they couldn't possibly see.

"Slower, my lady," came a soft command from behind. She had a hard time complying; the walls were starting to close in around her. All the imaginary beasts from her youth came rushing back, winging about her head with ghostly growls.

Good heavens, how had she ever *played* down here, sneaking about with Jerv and the others? Were they crazed? Papa never wanted her down here, and now she knew why. 'Twas haunted.

They were approaching a sort of subterranean crossroads, where several passageways met up. From up ahead came some faint illumination; just ahead lay the regular storage rooms beneath the castle.

She turned and hushed them. The men stopped where they were. She could see the ghostly grey burden thrown over Adam of Gloucester's shoulder. Glimmering eyes peered back at her, almost the only light in this dark, fathomless place.

The tunnel they had travelled through ended abruptly and met up with another one, running straight to her left. The sound of the river running was louder here; an underground river ran below the cellars here, then dipped away beside it to flow towards some unknown end.

Ahead lay a low archway which came out into a corridor with the storage chambers. Staples such as grain, wines, and armour were usually collected in the rooms here. But now most were empty. She'd not sent a servant down here for many weeks. Whyfore? To guard the empty armoury? Perhaps to fetch an unfilled barrel of wine?

But even so, not one of these empty, unused chambers was safe for the prince. They had no doors, no protection. If a *dog* came by, it would all be over.

Only one other option remained.

Gwyn grabbed a lantern off a shelf in the corridor to the storage rooms and turned to her right.

Down a short hallway, so short it looked more like a small recess in the stone, with a cutout stone bench nearby, stood a door. A huge door. Almost invisible at the end of this dark, go-nowhere cubby, it looked like it was meant to be hidden. And it was guarded by a padlock the size of her fist, the shape of a dragon's head.

Usually Gwyn shivered and hurried by. But now she went directly towards it. With chilled, trembling fingers, her lantern held high, she ripped off the pocket stitched to the inside of her skirts and pulled out little golden key.

Heart beating fast, she thrust it in into the dragon's mouth. Dust rose up as if steam were pouring from its steely nostrils. She twisted and something clicked. The key turned smoothly, the padlock sprang free. The dragon's jaw dropped open.

So. It did open something.

"Come," she called softly to Adam.

Inside, it was just a simple storage chamber, like all the rest. Rock walls, slightly mouldy, echoing and cold. Why had she been so reticent to enter?

Why was it guarded by such a ferocious lock?

They quickly set up a place for the prince in the shadowed recesses of the chamber, Gwyn fussing over straw piles and how his feet were arranged.

Suddenly, his long, mailed arm came swinging up. She almost screamed. His hand closed weakly around her wrist.

"Who are you?" the prince croaked. His eyes were barely slitted open.

"My lord prince," she answered, her voice shaking. "I am the lady of Everoot. You've been brought here for safekeep—"

"Save me," he groaned. The parched inside of his mouth crackled. His hand fell away. His eyes closed.

A swift chill started by her ears and raced downwards. Adam met her gaze and said nothing. She began fussing helplessly at the pile of dirty rushes laid beneath the prince, then sat back on her heels. She would have to bring clean linens and medicines and someone to administer them.

She had to bring everything or he would die.

"My lady?"

She looked up to find Adam's level gaze trained on her. Inhaling deeply to steady herself, she said, "You've come a long way for your king, with a perilous package, Adam of Gloucester. He will be grateful."

He dropped an inscrutable glance to the felled prince. His eyes were troubled. "'Tis nothing compared to what you are being asked to do." He extended his hand.

She took it. When she rose, though, he did not release her, but clasped her fingers tighter. "I say you do not know what you are being asked to do, but 'tis said you are a loyal lady, and you will do it anyhow, with a service beyond reproach and deserving of great honour."

She was startled. "What do you mean? I know what I am being asked to do: save my lord prince, and thereby the kingdom."

He released her hand and bowed his head briefly. "My lady. The best way out?"

She gestured her head back to the storage cellars. Barely visible through twenty yards of darkness was a stairwell, leading up into the shadows above. "That way."

"To where does it lead?" The attendant stood behind Adam, chewing on a piece of food recovered from his teeth. He stared impassively at Gwyn.

"The lord's chambers." She paused. "My chambers."

They followed her up the towering staircase in silence. Three flights they climbed before reaching a small landing, then up another series of stone steps. By now William the attendant was grumbling in the background. They finally reached the top and climbed aboard a small landing, cut deep in the rock. An arched door was before them, carved into the stone, dark and silent. They stopped.

"Let me see if the way is clear," she whispered, and twisted the latch. The door swung outwards, crowding them out to the far edge of the landing. If one of them stepped wrong, 'twould be a long time before he landed, some four stories below, perhaps bouncing off the curving staircase along the way.

"My lady, if you'd hurry," suggested William in a tight voice, eyeing the black descent, his boot dangerously close to the edge.

"Think you I am dawdling?" she snapped.

"Nay, not a'tall," he vowed heartily, still peering behind him. Adam watched her in silence.

Gwyn stared at the back of a tapestry that shielded the entryway on the interior side. It hung on one wall in the lord's bedchamber, and was the most exquisite piece of hand-dyed silk imaginable, stitched through with scenes of foxes and wolves and greening hills, and a distant stream of smoke, as if home was over the hills. Something in it had tugged at her when she first saw it at a fair two years ago, when there was money in the coffers and hope for her future. She'd bought it on an impulse. It had seemed like a message, beckoning her, fortokening all the pleasures of home and hearth awaited her, if only she would climb the ridge.

Now it just looked like a limp layer of cloth between her and the rampaging world.

By the time she had gotten the three of them back down to the hall and the squire outside to round up the horses, she was bathed in sweat again. Her hands twisted around themselves as she waited with Adam at the edge of the hall.

"You've royal permission to do as you see fit, my lady," Adam said quietly.

She nodded.

"'Tis a most burdensome honour you're taking on."

"I gave my word. Everoot holds to its word. Papa would have taken the burden." She swallowed thickly. "Roger would have. My brother, Roger. Prince Eustace was his friend. If my brother were running the estate, if he were aliv—" She pressed her lips together rather than let the heavy press of on-rushing tears pour out. "They would have done a great deal more. I can do no less."

"Still, some would rather not," Adam said quietly.

"Some prefer to enjoy the fruits of other's labour, and consider themselves well fed," she said firmly.

He ran his hand over his hair-roughened chin. "Aye. But sometimes, my lady, we don't recognise the spice until after we've eaten. One must be most careful what is on one's plate."

She lifted her eyebrows. "Now you're speaking in riddles, Adam of Gloucester."

The thoughtful look passed. "I don't mean to. Be careful, be safe and be well, my lady."

She walked with him to the door. A few eyes strayed to the pair, but no one really wanted to know what the grim-faced soldier had to say. If anything of import had occurred, they would know of it soon enough. He was just one of many messengers who hied themselves north to tell what news from the wars in the south, or to beg money to start another one. More often than not nowadays, no news was good news.

By the time Adam sat astride his horse again, the wiry, impudent squire at his side, the gatehouse had already been alerted to their departure. Gates to both baileys were raised, the drawbridges dropped. Gwyn stood midway up the keep staircase in the shimmering waves of heat. Adam edged his mount close and reached up a hand.

Surprised, she touched the tip of her fingers to his, smiling down at the kind, grim man who'd brought her such a doubtful treasure. He leaned sideways in his saddle and she crouched down to him, the heat from the sun burning hot on her back.

"Be careful what is on your plate, my lady."

A chill felt its way up under her dress. He dipped his head in a brief nod, then reined away. They cantered under the arched gateway and disappeared in a cloud of dust and shimmering heat.

Gwyn unbent her knees. She felt as if she was about to faint, and shook herself. She was giddy from the heat, that was all. And there was some small consolation, she realised bleakly: for the first time in ten months, she hadn't thought of Pagan.

An hour of peace from the restless, passionate memories, from the awful, agonized regret of the choices she could never unmake.

That made three people she'd killed.

Where the moisture came from, she did not know, but her eyes filled up with tears, and she stumbled sightless back into the castle.

Book Two:

The Reaping

Chapter One

The day before Michaelmas, 28 September 1153
Northern England, Ipsile-upon-Tyne

The conspirators met in an alley. The huge harvest moon had already crested and slunk down past the tops of the buildings. It filled the alley with dark, slanting shadows.

"How much?" asked the first, who had requested the meeting. He was lean and muscular, taller than average. Other than his build, identifying features were hard to make out. The only distinguishing aspect of him was a small but brilliantly vivid tattoo inked on his left chest, evident for a brief second when he reached inside his tunic to yank out a bag of coin.

"You don't waste time," said the other, looking back to his would-be customer's eyes.

"I have no time to waste. I want the key. How much?"

"Why do you want it?"

The tattooed man took a step forward and said in a low voice, "I'm willing to pay. A lot. That is all that need interest you. Do you have it?"

He nodded coolly. "I'll ask again: why do you want it?"

The tattooed man reversed his step and crossed his arms over his chest. "I know the rightful owner. He'll want it back."

He glanced down at the bulging pouch of money in the man's right hand. "Mayhap I'd get a better price from him directly, than you. Did he send you here?"

The tattooed man moved forward with the grace of a leopard. He wrapped his mailed hand around the other man's neck and crashed him against the town wall rounding behind them. *"Where the hell is it?"*

"I don't have it here—"

"You said you had it," he said in a dangerously quiet tone. "Are now you saying you do not?"

The man with the key thrust his fingers up, inside the band of strangulation around his neck. He jerked free, furious and gasping. "*God's bones,* I have it, but not here—"

"Fool."

Without looking back, the tattooed man turned and strode away into the darkness.

The man with the key gasped for breath a few more moments, alone in the grimy alley. Then he pushed off the stone wall. Briefly, he dipped his hand into his pocket, felt the small steel key resting coldly inside, and continued out.

Next customer. This one had been mad. He would go straight to the source this time.

Chapter Two

The day after Michaelmas, 30 September 1153
Outside the Nest, Northumbria, England

A cool puff of autumn air exhaled across the battle camp. For months now, it had been only hot, dry air—the drought-like conditions of the summer had not abated with the onset of autumn and the harvest—so the sudden coolness drew everyone's attention. Griffyn barely noticed. He was staring at the dark, turreted battlements of the Nest.

Home. Somehow, through eighteen years of anarchy and a shattered heart, God had seen him home.

Camped before his own castle walls with an army, of course. He smiled grimly. Not the homecoming he'd planned, but in truth, the one he'd always known must be.

The soaring walls were exactly as he recalled. The forest eaves, two leagues away, were as beckoning at twenty-eight as they had been at eight. He leaned his shoulder against an oak tree with sweeping branches and watched the darkness unfold.

Alex came striding up the hill as darkness fell fully and stood next to him on the small rise of land. They were the only two upright figures in all the warm, dark land.

The village was darkened humps on the plains below.

Small fires burned here and there throughout the army camp, but the men had pushed away from them as soon as the food was cooked, and now lay sprawled in dark bundles. The unexpected autumn breeze cooled the night, but it was still too warm to huddle with anything that didn't moan beneath their battle-hardened bodies.

Suddenly Griffyn straightened. A single shape appeared on the battlements, motionless. Another weary wind blew up, gathered from the forests behind. It lifted the fabric of the figure's gown in a long, billowing sweep.

A woman.

She stood a moment longer, then took a step and stumbled on the ramparts. Righting herself, she disappeared over the inner side.

"She's gone," said Alex quietly.

Griffyn passed him a look in silence. Aye, gone. Down a set of steps or perhaps flung herself off the battlement walkway in a fit of despair. The thought did not amuse. He planned to see to her punishment himself.

He wasn't certain if she'd seen him, but he hoped so. Hoped she had seen him and known the moment of despair. Hoped she felt as wrecked as he had when he'd learned his home was lost forever to his once-beloved foster-father, Ionnes de l'Ami, eighteen years ago. As wrecked as he'd been when he learned he'd been betrayed by the daughter, too.

He turned to Alex, refocusing with effort. "When did you get back?"

"Just. I rode a day's ride south. The news of a royal army coming to cut off our rear guard was but a rumour."

Griffyn turned back to the castle. "Good."

They were quiet a few moments, then Alex said, "We should attack the west side. I know you plan otherwise, but—"

"No."

"Pagan, the wall is weak, and will fall like chaff."

"It's my home," he murmured. Alex fell silent.

They stood like this until pre-dawn greyed the edges of the horizon. The camp stirred. A cold meal, then the men took their positions. Griffyn mounted Noir as the first streak of pink scratched across the sky, ripping open the dark night still domed overhead.

A dawn breeze pushed free of the wood behind them and rustled the dry grasses at their feet. The sounds of the horsemen heading off were muted. Noir stamped his hoof and pulled on the reins.

Griffyn pulled his helm down over his face. "Let's get this over with."

Gwyn heard them before she saw them, even though she stood with her marshal and captain of the guard, Fulk, atop the easternmost tower, waiting for war to swoop down on them. The sound was like wind rushing through trees down a mountainside.

There was no hope in outlasting a siege, and so, after consulting Fulk and her heart, she'd agreed to send out a fighting force. Too few were holding on, too few cared to. If King Stephen lost this castle in the north, the world would be like leeches hung from his heart from here on out. His son, the prince, lay dying in her cellars. She had no choice. Everoot must fight.

The gates swung open and her knights and men-at-arms marched out, even as the invading force appeared atop the far rise. She squinted to see. They paused, and their leader cantered to the front of the vanguard. A huge, raw-boned black horse, billowing mane, prancing, high-stepping, arching its spirited neck.

Her eyes opened slowly. A raw-boned black charger?

The helmed figure in front of the hordes lifted his hand, then swept it down. His cavalry kicked into action, thundering

down the hill, spewing clods of dirt and brown grass in their
riotous wake.

Gwyn's throat squeezed tight. The roar of hooves drowned
out her hammering heart, and the sun glinting off their bright
shields, pressed tears into her eyes. Helmed faces and armoured bodies charged down the hill, lances pointed and lowered for death—they were not people, they were weapons.

Then, without warning, they pulled up. The riders sat back
and hauled on the reins. Their snorting chargers reared up
on their powerful hind legs, and like that, forty rows of onrushing knights skidded to a furious, rock-throwing stop.

What trickery, this?

Her army, primarily on foot and arrayed in uneven lines not
even half again as strong, drew to a halt as well. The two lines
stood perfectly still, like statues. An unexpectedly cool breeze
blew through the valley. Everyone froze in the sudden, re-
markable silence.

"He's givin' us a chance to surrender," Fulk observed
grimly, "afore the bloodshed begins."

"Who is he?" she demanded, squinting at the sunlit valley.
"Who dares—"

Her throat squeezed shut. God in Heaven.

Pagan.

She flung her hand over her mouth in horror.

Who else *but him*, sitting astride his great black destrier at
the crest of a hill, his helm removed, giving her one last
chance? One last chance to surrender . . . to him. Whom else?
Griffyn Sauvage, her ghost of passion.

He was looking directly at her.

She almost laughed at the madness of it all.

Saint Jude save me, she prayed, her heart pounding giddy
blood from earlobe to ankle. She smoothed her skirts with a
trembling hand. "Call them back."

Fulk spun and looked at her. "My lady?"

"Call them back." She pointed over the wall. "Do you know who that is?"

He nodded. "Aye. Sauvage."

Her hand fell. "You know him," she said flatly. "You know Griffyn Sauvage."

Fulk shrugged. "I was with your father for many years, Lady Gwyn. Afore yerself was born."

"So, you know there's history there. Between our families."

He averted his gaze. "A bit of it."

"A bit of it," she echoed. "Tell me, Fulk," she demanded. "How do you think we stand, with Griffyn Sauvage and his army out there?"

Fulk looked over the battlement walls again, then shrugged. But the twitch of something in his eye gave him away. He knew how things stood. They could fight. And they would lose.

Gwyn was already planning for the future. She would open the gates. That was better than having him batter them down. A pitched battle would only give him more cause to run through the castle like a firestorm, laying claim to everything. And he must not be allowed to discover the prince. So she would open the gates. Feign surrender.

Feign, she cautioned herself. Pretend. Do not truly do it. Do not succumb to all those things succumbed to before: his passion and decency and the way he made her feel like there was hope.

Was *this* not the weight of her penance, finally bearing down?

Had she thought it would be easy?

"I will not have our men die needlessly," she said to Fulk. "And I see no wisdom in angering Sauvage any more than. . . ." Her voice trailed off. More than what? How could he hate her more than he already must? "Call them back. Open the gates. Surrender the castle."

Fulk nodded grimly. "Aye, my lady." He strode off, shouting for his commanders.

Gwyn watched him go, her heart tumbling and fluttering, her blood moving fast and cold through her body. Inside, her mind was screaming: *He's supposed to be dead!*

And her heart was chanting: *He's alive, he's alive, he's alive.*

Chapter Three

Griffyn rode under the gate with his sword drawn but hanging by his side. His gaze travelled swiftly over the crowded bailey. Surely Godwin the marshal, or Hamish the blacksmythe might have survived the years.

Then he snorted, dismissing the glimmer of childlike excitement. Only the strong survived, and eventually they died too. How many times must he be taught that affection was perilous and pointless?

He peered up at the dark, turreted battlements of the Nest, set against a backdrop of brilliant blue skies. It almost hurt his eyes to keep them open. Home. He was home again.

It was utterly quiet. Hushed villagers and householders thronged the edges, making a colorful, if tattered, pathway. Most bowed their heads as he passed, some bent their knees. He heard the whispers.

"Sauvage . . ."

" . . . remember his father . . ."

" . . . like a legend, upon our time . . ."

"Thanks be to God."

Dozens of hands were raised in greeting. Linen caps removed, rough country curtsies offered. In welcome.

It ought to be a balm.

Flicking on the reins, he urged Noir up the small incline to the inner bailey. His men rode behind, their cobalt-blue cloaks flung back to reveal steel-ringed mail coats and long swords. A suddenly cool breeze blew through the bailey, carrying the scent of decaying leaves and wet bark and the salty hint of the sea.

How many times had he ridden home as a boy on the scent of that breeze, satiated after a day of hunting or hawking or simply riding, hungry and dreaming great dreams, before everything had changed?

And yet this, his moment of triumph, his homecoming, felt utterly hollow. Where was the elation, the joy? After all this time, after all the warring, and the years of coming home, the fierce satisfaction he'd felt even imagining this moment was absent. The only thing that moved him was the thought, *"Where is she?"*

They neared the centre of the bailey, hooves clacking over cobbles.

"My lord earl," murmured a balding man who appeared near his boot.

Griffyn checked Noir and looked down. "Who are you?"

"William of York, my lord. I am the earl's . . . I am . . . I was the seneschal."

"William of York," repeated Griffyn. He felt so strange. His heart was beating, but far away. His words sounded warped, as if they were being turned in the air like cream through a butter churn. *Of the Five Strands*, she had called him back at the inn, and he had laughed.

"Lord Griffyn, my lady Guinevere wishes to bid you and your men welcome to the Nest."

His eyes flicked down again. "Where?"

"My lord—"

"Where is your lady?"

"My lord—" the steward sputtered.

"Where is Guinevere?"

A musical voice called out, "I'm here."

His head snapped up and everything that had been grey and distorted became clear as an untouched lake. The world took on almost painful clarity. He scanned the vanquished people before him, then his gaze locked on her. His heart started beating again, strong and loud.

"I bid you and your men welcome to my home."

He swung off Noir, threw the reins to his squire Edmund, and started over. Every step felt like it stretched furlongs. Her hair was as black as he recalled, bounding in riotous ringlets around her face. It was the first thing he noticed. That and the fact that her voice still rang like a bird song over a frozen lake, and it made him think of faerie dust.

He stopped in front of her, feeling his breath strong and hot.

"My lord. Welcome."

Something hovered at his shoulder. He ignored it. The bailey was utterly silent. Even the breeze went still, and nothing moved except a dog, cracking a bone. Griffyn heard the snaps like ice breaking on a lake. He flicked his gaze over. The dog looked up and whined, then got to his feet and slunk away. Everyone held their breath, waiting for his vengeance to spill its fury.

"Welcome, is it?" he repeated quietly. "Your army was a welcome?"

"I did not know 'twas you," she said softly enough, but her green eyes stayed on him with a fierceness that could burn holes through linen. He suddenly noticed how his cloak was bright against her frayed and dull fabrics. The Sauvage brooch alone gleamed more brightly than anything she wore, in large part, he realised, because she wore no jewels at all.

A breeze lifted a few stray stands of long, black hair to flutter in the air between their bodies. For a twelvemonth her face had haunted his dreams, and now here she was, in the flesh.

"You know now," he said coldly.

"I know more important things than even that, my lord." Her bitter words were bitten off with great precision. "I know these wars must end. I know my men have barely eaten in a fortnight, while yours have lived off the fields and barns of dozens of poor villagers along the way to *this* killing field. I know my army is small and yours huge. I know your *horse* probably ate better than my kitchen staff this past week—"

"You don't know anything."

"I know that we may lose—"

"You don't know anything."

"—and lose and lose again, and you will *still* never have won."

"You don't know anything," he said again, his tone cold and level. "You don't know what horrors my army has prevented—"

"How heroic."

"—and you surely do not know what my horse is fed, Guinevere."

They both paused. "Oats."

One side of his mouth lifted humourlessly. "You think me a simple matter."

"I think you awful. And—"

He threw down his gauntlet and splayed his fingers tightly around her chin. "And *what*?"

"Dead," she whispered, her voice trembling, which made him feel savage and satisfied. "I—I thought you were dead."

"You did what you could to ensure it, did you not?"

She hitched on a breath. "And how many deaths have *you* ensured, with your sword and your count who simply *must* be made a king?"

His fingers tightened, pressing into the soft flesh of her chin. "Your family was destined to be my bane," he said in a voice so low it barely carried through the air. "I intend to return the favour. Awful? You think me awful? You've no idea."

"Not here. Not now," interrupted a voice at his back. Alex.

Griffyn snapped back into the present. Every eye in the bailey was on him, their new lord, losing his temper and his mind over this witch of a woman.

He flung his hand down and took a deep, shaky breath, knowing how close he'd come. He could have killed her. If she'd said another word, if Alex had not stepped forward, he might have kept closing his hand tighter and tighter around her slender, poisonous throat.

He spun away.

"Take her to the solar," he snarled, and obviously someone did, because a few moments later, his heart still thudding savagely in his chest, his mind still fuzzed with fury, he was meeting with his seneschal and top officials, sending them inside to meet with the de l'Ami administrative staff, and commanding his soldiers to inspect the garrison, make the men swear allegiance or be turned out.

They scurried to do his bidding, and chaos erupted around him. Griffyn grabbed Noir's reins and stalked to the stables himself, trying to forget, to focus on the victory. Forget about his father. Forget the rage. The lost years. The woman he thought he could love. Forget, forget, forget.

Alex was overseeing the round-up and interrogation of the de l'Ami soldiers. They were staunch in their loyalty to Guinevere, as expected, but more was revealed in what was *not* said.

Stout men, but their pointed features bespoke hunger only just kept at bay. Men who were steadfast, but weary of their lands being ravaged by an endless war. Soldiers accustomed to battle and the strange vagaries of it, including honourable surrender when in the alternative lay waste and ruin.

To a man they pledged themselves to Griffyn Sauvage as lord of Everoot, and most did so willingly.

"This one," gestured Hervé Fairess, the Angevin. "He's trouble. And that one," he grumbled, pointing.

Alex shifted his gaze to a young knight with close-cropped blond hair, who stood scowling at the gryphon-clad knights. His strength was apparent in the press of muscle against his tunic, but he did not appear foolish. He appeared loyal, if his regular glances towards the third-floor solar where Lady Guinevere was being held proved anything. Loyal, not stupid. And it would be stupid to make trouble now.

"We'd best let Pagan know," Hervé gruffed.

"Pagan will know without us telling him anything," Alex said mildly, but inside, a deep disquiet was starting to unfold.

He had watched the collapse of Griffyn's legendary self-control a few moments ago in shock. Griffyn had not been trained in violence and ruthlessness to no effect, but he *never* revealed the depths of his fury. A father who had let greed ruin him, a legacy stolen, killing, killing for lost honour and for fallen kings, Griffyn's life had been fated from before his conception. But he had never let his emotions boil over. Except for that one night a year back.

And just a moment ago.

Griffyn might be coming dangerously close to the edge of a rage that had been contained for eighteen years, honed with a staggering discipline. All the grueling self-denial, all the months and years of blood and purpose, had been in the service of this single moment: the Earl of Everoot was home again.

And something was terribly wrong.

Chapter Four

Gwyn stood in the third-storey solar, staring at the knight who'd escorted her as he prepared to leave the room. He pointed to a tray of food and pitcher of wine.

"For your comfort, my lady."

She sourly suggested that if it were truly for her comfort, perhaps she could be better placed in her own chambers.

He met this with an impassive look. "You'd rather not be there just now, my lady. Lord Griffyn is . . . converting them."

Ah yes, she thought as he bowed out of the room, converting them . . . or taking possession. Whichever way 'twas phrased, it was the same. He was taking over, stripping the keep of any sign of the de l'Ami presence. Except her. She would be brought out when it was all complete, the final resistance brought low.

"They are all alike," she snapped aloud, and almost screamed when Duncan, her young page, lifted his face up over the side of her bed.

"Duncan!" she whispered furiously. "What are you doing here?"

"Milady," he whispered back, creeping out with the stealth required if they were stalking deer. "I needed to see you."

She hurried to his side and knelt, running her fingers over

the back of his head, down his back, up his thin arms, feeling for injuries. "Monsters. Why would they do harm to a little boy, after I've opened the gates? I shall expect nothing but brutality forevermore from men—"

"Milady!" he said plaintively, wiggling free. "I'm not injured. I've come to *help*."

She sat back on her heels. "Help? Help, Duncan?" She felt like crying. "How on earth could you help?"

His pinched little face was less pinched than it had been three months ago, when he'd arrived at the gates of Everoot, a refugee from the wars, he and his little sister, running for their lives. And here he was now, earnestly looking at her, thinking he—he, a ten-year-old boy—could help, while the world fell apart around her.

"I can watch out for whoever you've got in the cellars, milady."

Gwyn's mouth slowly fell open. "What did you say?"

He looked embarrassed. "I seen you go down there, milady, three times a day or more. Once, I saw ye with a tray o' food, and after that, I followed ye."

"Why?"

"I thought ye might need some help one day, seein' as how no one else seemed to know what was going on. And ye always look so sad when ye come back up again. I thought ye oughtn't be so very alone in it."

That brought tears right to the edge of her eyes. She leaned forward and hugged him tight, then sat back and said in a soft, but bright voice, "Well, now, Duncan, you may have a very good idea there. Can you be quiet?"

"As a mouse."

"And follow direction?"

He dragged his wrist under his nose, wiping it. "Better'n a monk."

She gently propelled his arm back down. "You may be right." She handed him a strip of linen. He stared at it. She pointed to his nose. He rolled his eyes and wiped. "And being alone, Duncan? You could not come up and down from there. You'd have to stay there until—" She broke off. "Until I say so. It may be weeks. Months."

"Lady Gwyn, I'll miss every fair that ever was, if ye need me to."

She put her hand on his shoulder and nodded gravely. "So be it, Duncan. To the cellars. Here is the key." She yanked the pouch off her skirts and handed over the little golden key. "You'll know which chamber he is in, for 'tis it has a terrifying padlock on it. I'll be down as soon as I can, to check that all is well and retrieve the key.

"Now," she said, rising and looking at the door. "Let us give the guard a few minutes to get fully away, and you can go straight to the cellars."

"Aye, milady." He paused. "Did you see him, milady?"

"Did I see whom?" She began pacing the room. She pulled her long braid over her shoulder and began trying to reweave it, something to occupy her time. Her fingers got tangled in the knots. It was hopeless. If not enclosed in its tight silken case, her hair inevitably came unbound like a spring uncoiling. And this morning there'd been no time for silk wraps.

"Him."

Gwyn let the tangled curls, grimed and weighted with dirt and smoke, drop to her shoulders. She looked at Duncan bleakly. "Who?"

"Sau-*vage*!" Duncan said, elongating the 'vage' into one long, lazy syllable.

"Pagan?" She plopped down on the bed. Oh St. Jude, even the sound of his name brought back a bluster of heated churning. She stared at Duncan wretchedly. "Aye. I've seen him."

"So did I," Duncan whispered back. "He's *enormous*."

"Aye," she agreed, looking away.

"As big as a mountain." Duncan paused. "Are we to be safe?"

Gwyn exhaled slowly. Safe? That all depended on what

you meant by safe. Safe from death, aye. She recalled too clearly how she'd found a gentle pagan saviour on a deserted highway, a warrior who pulled back the hair from her eyes as she vomited, a man who made her laugh when she'd rather have cried and who laid a healing poultice on her skin when she was unconscious in his bed.

Aye, Duncan and all the children would be safe. But Guinevere? Ah well, that was another matter entirely.

No, she would never be safe from the man who had set her body on fire and stilled the maddening Ache by drumming another one even deeper in her heart, a man who now stood between her and raising the battered body of the king's son to the crown of England.

She smiled into Duncan's earnest, worried face. "Everything will be fine, Duncan. Trust me."

"I do!" he burst out happily.

A few moments later, she opened the door, looked both ways, then gestured to him. Down the stairs he hurried, and was gone.

Gwyn walked to the window and peered down to the bailey. She could see no violence. No loyal servants were being dragged to the gates or the cellars. No de l'Ami knights were being lined up in the field or marched across the draw. In fact, she realised, craning her neck, there was no line of soldiers marching out of the castle at all, a trail that would mark those who were unwilling to swear allegiance to the new lord.

How odd.

"Guinevere."

She spun. There he stood, his tall figure outlined in the doorway. Gwyn was alone with him and the sound of her wildly thundering heart.

Chapter Five

Despite anger, fear, fury and hate, she couldn't deny the ripple that danced through her body when she saw his leather-clad body on the landing. Sunlight filtering through the slitted windows glinted off his dark hair and the stubble of his chin. The shadows angled his face into long, lean lines of raw sensuality.

Please God, she prayed, *not again.*

He pushed the door closed behind him. "You've run my castle well," he said in his deep, masculine rumble. Taunting her.

She composed her face into the most noxious glare she knew. "*Your* castle?"

"'Tis most certainly not yours anymore."

She dug her nails into her palms, fisted by her thighs. "You ensured that."

"Aye. Much as you ensured forty lashes on my back and weeks of a rat-infested prison I wouldn't wish on my father."

His father?

Gwyn's skirts whispered over the rushes as she walked to the edge of the room. She ran her hand across the window ledge.

"Prison?" she asked with airy nonchalance, her back to him. She even managed an unconcerned sniff. "You were captured, then, were you? They never said directly, but I am glad to hear the king's men were successful."

"They weren't." Pagan's grim voice blew across the room. "I have his castle. And his vassal."

She turned to face him. "Why didn't you tell me your name last year?"

"Why didn't you tell me yours?"

She paused coldly. "Well, it seems that our names did not matter at all."

He smiled. "If you can show me what else does matter, I'll have Henri apply to the Pope to canonise you." He took a step forward, she a step back. "'Twas a *name* that ensured I lost these lands some eighteen years ago, and my *name* that assured me of a hearty welcome in the Tower a year back." Each phrase was followed by another step in her direction. "'Tis my name which has kept me sane, and my name that has given me my lands back."

"It looked to me to be your sword."

"You, Guinevere, show a keen mind. Happens I will keep it close, and use it."

"Your sword or my mind?" she snapped.

He stopped the length of a long stride away and smiled into her furious glare. "Both."

Tyber, her aging dog, slowly rose to his creaky paws and walked out the door. Traitor.

"Your lord knows little of what he must do to win this country back," she said coldly.

Another slow smile slid across his features. "He knows enough to send men into all the rebel castles, to wed the women and silence the rebellion."

"Really?" She drew the word out, as if unwilling to fully release it.

"Aye. And 'twould behoove you to recall this, too." He lowered his voice to a conspiratorial whisper. "You have been betrayed by your Stephen, not Henri."

She covered her heart reflexively. "King Stephen ruled by right!"

"He ruled by might, and rather poorly too. You keep house up here in the north, and perhaps know little of the state of the realm, but I will tell you: 'tis *terra guerra*, a land of war."

"Are you *mad*?" she snapped, biting the words like ice chips. "You think I do not know my country is ravaged— by men like you."

He shook his head. "Every baron and knight knows the way to end the civil warring is to have Henri take the throne. 'Tis no secret, simply a matter of time. The Pope would not even crown Prince Eustace, not that it matters now that he's dead."

Gwyn felt the blood drain from her face, but he didn't seem to notice. "Stephen is kind and chivalrous," she managed to say through gritted teeth.

"He is a fool, gallant though he may be. And he stole the crown, my lady, do not forget that. He vowed to honour Mathilda's queenship, then took it whilst she was not looking. How fits that with your notions of chivalry?"

"Better than my notion of you right now."

He smiled, a dangerous curve of flesh.

Something hot and longing moved through her chest, right over her heart. She wanted him. Wanted that smile, directed at her, for her.

And how could that ever be? Lord Griffyn abovestairs, Prince Eustace below? The family her father had hated, the enemy her king had made her oath-bound to oppose. She could see the awful future shimmering right before her eyes, like a reflection in a pond.

Breaking her gaze, she retreated to the window. "I weary of these games. What do you want to know?"

"The defence. How many?"

"Some twelve in the garrison, mayhap two hundred from

the surrounding villages and town." Her voice caught in her throat. "Ignoring those who died."

His voice was a low stroke through her pain. "They will not be forgotten."

"By you?" She laughed bitterly.

"By *you*." She lifted her head, surprised to find him so close again. So close she could hear him breathing. "Perhaps you would be surprised by how much respect I show towards loyalty."

His square chin jutted out a bit, prompting a sensual consideration she squashed flat. His handsome arrogance was *not* to be one of the surprises.

"What else do you want to know?" she asked in a cold, clipped tone.

"The seneschal."

"That is my William. Of the Five Strands."

He crossed his arms over his chest. "I recall you speaking of him. You were right."

She looked halfway over her shoulder. "About what?"

"Five is about all I noted."

She bit her lip to quiet the unconscionable twitch of her lips and looked down at the ground. *Feign surrender*, she counseled herself angrily. *Do not actually do it.*

"And his leaning?" Griffyn asked.

"Towards me, no doubt." She paused. "Have you a thought for him, though, he is well endowed with a capacity for numbers, and bides his calling well."

"I've no need of him. What of your knights—how many?"

"One score at the moment."

"And what can I expect?"

She smiled thinly. "Resistance, to a man."

His smile was rather broad. "To a man, you say?"

"What?"

"They are loyal to a man, you say?"

Her smile faltered. "Do you know otherwise?"

"I know they pledged their fealty to me." He paused. "To a man."

Her mouth fell wide. A fly could have buzzed in and out with nary a tense moment. "Jeravius? *Fulk?*"

"A tall, muscular fellow with a glint in his eye? Likes architecture, stone?"

"Jeravius," she breathed.

"And your marshal?"

Her shoulders slumped. "Fulk."

He considered her from head to toe. "They said 'twas for your safety I received their pledge."

"My safety? For *my* safety?"

"They seemed to think 'twas in danger," he mused, his eyes now travelling over the room's threadbare furnishings.

"And I'm sure you were not troubled to put their minds at ease."

His gaze swung back. "What makes you think you are *not* in danger?"

An involuntary shudder of fear shot through her but an angry glare, meant to burn away his arrogance, fell well short of the mark.

"Am I?" she managed to say.

"What did I tell you before?"

"When, before?"

"London. The inn."

She looked at him sharply. "That was no inn."

His eyes grazed down to travel over her bodice, down her skirts, then back up. "What did I tell you, Guinevere?"

She took a full minute to swallow. Good Lord, he had told her a hundred wicked, carnal things.

"You . . . you said many things." She gestured distractedly to his belt. "But then you were not standing with a sword at your side."

His hands moved. He unbuckled the belt around his waist. It clattered to the ground, taking with it the sword, dagger, and falchion notched in the banded leather. And there, standing still as still as could be and without a weapon on him, danger shimmered off him in waves.

"Now, again, Guinevere: what did I tell you?"

She felt a shower of heat rain down her belly. Her gaze was pinned on the arsenal of blades flung across the floor. "You said I had naught to fear from you."

"And so it is."

"And my men?" she asked, stepping backwards and tripping over the hem of her skirt. She righted herself and backed up until her spine was against the wall. "They must believe there is much to fear. What did you say to Jerv and Fulk?"

"I did but tell them what it meant to have my home back. And what I would do to those who opposed me."

"Good Lord, Pagan. You might just as well have popped their eyes out and been done with it."

"They were a bit wide-eyed."

Her eyebrows flattened. "They are good men, loyal, and do think the world of me. If you made a threat to them—"

He took a step closer, his body radiating heat. Chills shimmered over her body like a fever. Then he slammed a palm against the wall beside her head. She jerked to attention. "I made no threats, lady." He put his other hand on the wall, so she stood between his outstretched arms. "I shall tell you what I told them: The castle is mine, you are mine, as is everything within. If you sport with me, you will get burned."

"You dare threaten *me*?"

He looked at her coldly, his eyes glittering. "You have seen nothing of what I dare, lady, nor what I have lost. You are a sheaf of wheat. And I have not threatened you," he corrected in a low voice. "I have explained my position."

"Too good, my lord," she said in a cold, clear voice. "Now hear mine: I did not wield a blade in battle, so have not yet fought. Do you think to squash me like a bug, be forewarned:

I sting, and carry a venom the likes of which you've not seen in Normandy these long years."

She ducked beneath his arm and stumbled away. A sheaf of wheat? That was what London had meant? She suddenly felt as if she'd had too much to drink and wanted to retch.

He was watching her, his eyes unreadable. "I have not forgotten the pests of England, lady. They have been in my mind for some long time."

"You mean my father," she spat.

"I mean your father. And you."

"Me?" she practically shrieked. "Me? What of *you*?"

"Me?" The look on his face was almost comical. "What?"

She threw her hands in the air. "Oh, mayhap, the *army you drove before you*?"

"To regain my home, lady," he returned in a low voice. "For my home, I would drive a chariot of hell."

"That I well believe," she spat. "For you and yours, you would do all the things we none of us should do, and the rest may rot in hell. Know this, Pagan," she vowed, her words trembling with too many emotions to name, "you cannot threaten me, nor cow me. And I do not bend."

A predatory smile edged up his lips. "You bent once. For me."

She almost died of shame. Choking on a horrified gasp, she drew her herself up. "You met me for one night, Pagan. Do not confuse that with knowing me."

His upper lip almost curled in derision. "I know you."

"You know nothing. You are a child playing at being a man. Warriors all, fighting for lands your women and children do not want, leaving a legacy of scorched earth and fatherless children behind. Listen, Pagan, whilst I explain *my* position: I do not intend to grovel at your heels, begging for any small mercy that might allow me to lift my skirts when I cross the muck in the stable yard. *This is my home too*."

"'Twould be a mercy indeed to lift your skirts elsewise, when you're in a fury like this."

"Then, my lord, expect to see me in such a fury every night henceforth, and beg that you show me no mercy."

Pagan was on the move, striding through the filtered sunlight of the room, until he towered above her. His voice reached down and jerked her head up. His jaw was locked, his eyes ice-grey, the animal rage in him barely constrained, and then she knew true fear.

"Ponder this, de l'Ami spawn," he rasped. "My mercy is the only thing that can save you now." Her face was inches from his, his chest even closer, throbbing heat onto her like a blanket. "Cross me and you'll be pleading for mercy and then some come the morn. As will every other soul inhabiting this castle."

He spun on his heel, grabbed his blades, and was gone, the door crashing shut behind him. She stood in the middle of the room, reeling. Good God, everyone in the castle? Settle her bones into his reign? With the heir to the throne belowstairs?

And what would happen if he ever discovered *that* piece of the loyalty he so avowed? She had a brief vision of her neck in a noose, swinging from a barren tree branch.

"My lady?" said a voice from the hall a long time later. The door inched open a notch and an unfamiliar brown-mopped head poked in. "My lord wishes to have the keys to the castle," he said hesitantly, nodding towards the huge iron key ring affixed to her girdle. She looked down helplessly. "And he would see you in the hall come Vespers."

"What of my prayers?" she asked in a shaky voice, thinking that now, of all times, she needed a visit to her confessor.

A worried look met this, as if the boy read her mind. "My lady, if you please, he's said he'll see to that himself."

She fell back to the bed, her hand at her pounding chest.

Chapter Six

Griffyn barreled down the winding staircase like a bull in a headlong rush. Buckling his belt as he went, he landed on the bottom step and crashed into the busy great hall. Servants and soldiers and varlets hurried here and there, dodging between the trestle tables, tapestries, and benches scattered everywhere as the new cleared out the old.

Raashid, a middle-aged Muslim, long in Griffyn's employ as estate steward, was in conference with the balding seneschal William in a far corner. Sauvage knights were trolling in and out, grabbing food from passing trays and eyeing the women who scurried to and fro. Chaotic and disconnected as they were, all occupants in the great hall sputtered to a halt as Griffyn plowed into the mayhem.

"And the streams have gone dry, but even so, earlier this summer we . . ." William of the Five Strand's tinny voice drifted off from his accounting of the demesne manor's income. He turned and stared at the new, apparently enraged, lord of Everoot.

Griffyn looked at Raashid, met his eye, and angled his head towards William of the Five Strands in silent query. Raashid smiled and nodded, and Griffyn turned away, confident the Muslim could manage one aging steward, however reticent he was to say anything terribly relevant about the estates they had just conquered. Raashid had more years of experience under his robe than a whore had customers and an almost terrifying knack for numbers. He accompanied Griffyn everywhere, no one knew where he came from, and neither Griffyn nor Raashid ever said.

Raashid nodded and turned back to William with a wide smile on his handsome, dark face. "Suppose you tell me of the estate's monetary reserves, rather than its fish runs, Master William?"

Griffyn started for the door, intending to find Alex, and almost trod into Edmund, his earnest squire, who'd already watered and walked Noir, and was now banging along at Griffyn's heels. He paused and put a hand on the boy's shoulder.

"Lady Guinevere is your task, Edmund." The boy nodded eagerly. The perils of youth. "She is not to stay secreted in that room," he explained grimly. "She comes down to sign the betrothal papers. She comes down for the meal. If she wishes, she may plan it. If she wishes, she may mortar the herbs herself, but she will come down. See to it, Edmund."

"My lord," Edmund nodded. "And should she want confession?" he added, because everyone usually did, upon a surrender. Even at thirteen Edmund knew that. There was always so much guilt to absolve. "Because," the boy was saying, "the chapel priest is down in the village, and—"

"I'll take care of that. Make sure she's down here by Vespers."

"Aye, my lord."

He started to turn away, then stopped. "Lady Guinevere has the keys to the castle."

"Aye, my lord."

"Get them."

"Aye, my lord."

* * *

Alex stood in the bailey, in the gusts of hot sun, long after the others had gone inside, letting heat blow over him like the wind. Waiting.

Sweat beaded on his neck, under his arms. He could feel it burning onto his skin, but he was used to that. Years of it, upon a time. Hot winds, parched, angry earth, denying anything green or fertile to the greedy hordes of Crusading hooves galloping over it.

He approved. Deny them everything. Men were too small to contain greatness. Even Griffyn so far had balked at reaching out for his destiny. Only then would he be truly great.

Sun baked the back of Alex's neck. He unbuckled his mail hauberk and slowly dragged it over his head, bending his neck to the side. His muscles were long and strong, sculpted from years of wielding not just a sword but lance and bow and knife. But now, today, in this heat, at this homecoming, he felt beleaguered, his armour as heavy as lead. He dragged the weight of it over his head. Sharp metal links caught at the thick quilted gambeson underneath.

"Alexander," said a gravelly voice.

He dragged the armour off the rest of the way and let it drop to the ground. Then he turned.

There he was, the stone block of flesh from decades past, Fulk. Alex and he went back far too many years to count, long before the chasm of civil war tore apart England. Fulk was once his mentor. Fulk was a Watcher too.

A false one. He'd forsworn his oath eighteen years ago, done something no Watcher had ever done before, abandoned the Heir, Griffyn's father. He'd stayed with the de l'Amis.

More proof, as if it were needful, that the de l'Amis brought nothing but ruin.

"So," rumbled Fulk. His eyes were shadowed. "'Tis yerself."

"And yours."

Fulk glanced around. They were not the only ones in the

bailey, but they were alone in this little corner. He looked back. "You're with him still."

"I am," Alex agreed. "Although you are no longer with your man."

"He's no longer around to be with."

"No. So you are with her."

"I'm with Lady Guinevere, if that's who ye mean by 'her'." Fulk stood motionless, his belt emptied of anything resembling a blade. But Alex knew Fulk did not need a weapon to do damage. A lot of it.

Fulk said gruffly, "Took ye awhile to get here."

"We were delayed by eighteen years of a civil war. Thanks be to your master and his ilk."

"Aye, well."

The response could have been comprehension or contempt, but it was all Fulk gave.

"Where are they?" Alex said suddenly.

Fulk looked confused. "Where are what?"

"The keys."

A sour smile rippled across Fulk's face, all traces of confusion swept away under his complete comprehension. "The keys are not ours, Alex. I thought I taught ye that."

Alex continued as if he hadn't spoken. "Griffyn has only one. The iron one. I assume the rest were given to de l'Ami, before he betrayed us."

"And why do ye think he did that, Alex? Why do ye think Christian Sauvage gave away two of the three keys that open the gate to the treasure of the Hallows?"

"I don't know. Madness?"

Fulk shook his head. "I don't think he was mad."

Alex laughed shortly. "You weren't with him there at the end. Christian Sauvage was raving. He was terrified to die."

"De l'Ami wasn't looking any too rathe to meet his Maker, either, Alex. They done some awful things, and no one knows it better than ye and I. But I don't think madness made Sauvage give away the keys."

"Well, I cannot think of any other reason."

Fulk scowled. "Ye wouldn't."

"Blessed Mother, Fulk, *we are Watchers*. Did you forget? We have a duty to the Heir." Alex took a step closer, his voice growing louder. "Why did you leave Sauvage? Why did you abandon us?"

Fulk let the words settle into the dust coating the cobble-stones, then shook his head and wiped his open palm over the top of his sweat-stained head. "Alex, my lad," he said sadly, "I didn't abandon ye—"

Alex jerked his head, as if deflecting a blow. "I'm not your lad," he said coldly.

Fulk sighed. "So be it. I need to see Griffyn."

"No."

Fulk's bushy eyebrows went up. *"No?"* He laughed. "Ye're not the door warden, Alex. He's not yers to say yea or nay about—"

"He's mine to protect. And I say no."

"About what?"

They both spun. Alex was surprised, not to see Griffyn standing a few paces off, but to realise his own heart was hammering like he'd just run a footrace.

"No about what?" Griffyn said again, but even though he was speaking to Alex, his eyes were on Fulk.

Fulk immediately bent his head. "My lord. We've missed ye."

Griffyn gave an abrupt burst of laughter. "Is that so? I would never have known. My father wouldn't have either."

Fulk stood his ground. "Sir, we've to live by our con-sciences. Ye by yers, me by mine. I had to decide. 'Twas yer father who placed me with de l'Ami. I was his to command, and he sent me to de l'Ami, saying if anything happened to his dearest friend Ionnes, 'twould be too big a blow for him to survive."

"Something did happen to Ionnes de l'Ami," Griffyn pointed out coldly. "The same thing that happened to my father. *Greed*."

Fulk wiped his hand across the back of his neck. "I won't deny anything ye're saying, my lord. What I *will* say is that yer father wasn't the only Guardian. And neither are ye."

Something like a spasm of shock passed over Griffyn's face. "Guinevere."

Alex stepped angrily forward. "De l'Ami *stole* the Nest, Fulk, he didn't become an Heir. And neither did *she*."

"The Hallows were here, and not a Sauvage in sight to protect 'em," Fulk pointed out mildly.

"It's the blood that makes a Guardian, not possession of the treasure. Ours is an age-old duty, Fulk. Twists of fate do not change it."

"There aren't no twists of fate here, Alex. Christian Sauvage knew 'zactly what he was doin' when he left England without it."

Alex shook his head angrily. "It matters naught, Fulk. This bloodline goes back five hundred years, the treasure a thousand and more. If the treasure is out of our sight for a few years, even a generation, what matters that? Our duty does not change. Watchers guard the bloodline. We're meant for the *Heir*. Charlemagne's heir."

Fulk shrugged. "Someone will always be in possession of the treasure. And that person needs guardin' too. Usually it's the Heir. Never been different afore."

"But when it is, people have to make choices."

"And live by 'em."

Alex stepped up into his face. "Are you regretting yours, Fulk?"

"Never," retorted the leather-strapped mountain. "How 'bout yerself?" He pushed his bearded face right back into Alex's. "Have ye been regrettin' the choice that took ye so far away from it? Wondering if it was safe, were ye? Dreamin' of *it*, rather than women, were ye?"

Alex's fist shot out.

"Enough!" Griffyn shouted, shouldering between them. Alex and Fulk stumbled backwards, glowering at one another. "You see? You see what it does?" He looked at Alex, disgusted. "And you would have me cleave to this thing? Look to the hand it laid on my father, on de l'Ami, even the two of you."

"Not me, my lord," Fulk said quietly.

Griffyn swung his head around. "No. Just that, when given the choice, you chose to break faith and stay close to the treasure, rather than your charge, my father."

Fulk met his gaze. "I'd tell ye why."

"Then do."

"Lady Gwynnie."

Griffyn lifted an eyebrow.

"She's the why. She was two. I couldn't even imagine the trials laid out before her. Her brother was alive, but there was something awful about what was happening to de l'Ami, and the civil wars kept getting worse. Men like Marcus and his father Miles were about, running free, marauding the land, getting granted estates. Wanting Guinevere." He put a hand over his hauberk to tug it straight, but for all the world, it looked like he was putting his fist over his heart, like a pledge. "She's my why. I'd do it again."

Griffyn's palm was still on Alex's chest, holding him back. Alex tore free and backed up a few unsteady paces. Griffyn lifted his eyebrows. Alex flung up his hands, looking down and away. "I'm fine."

"Are you *done*?"

He nodded. The sun was still blazing onto his body, burning him up. "Aye. I'm done."

Griffyn waited a moment, then turned to Fulk. "Guinevere. Does she know?"

"No. She knows nothing. Nothing about the Grail Hallows,

nothing about yer fathers 'cept they hated one another. She knows nothing about ye either, my lord, yer destiny. Nothing about the travails of every soul who's ever guarded the treasure, the same treasure she's been guarding all these years in ignorance."

Fulk bent one side of his mouth in the façade of a smile. "And I must say, that seems a bit unfair. And mighty dangerous."

Chapter Seven

Gwyn tiptoed down the curving staircase to the lord's chambers with her heart in her throat. She encountered no one. No guard had been placed at the lord's chambers; Pagan must have thought his threat sufficient bulwark against disobedience.

He has much to learn, she thought sourly.

Her determination did not eclipse her fear, though, and when she reached the landing and one long, terrified glance across its vast five foot space assured her no one was near, she broke into a cold sweat of relief. Her subsequent journey through the lord's antechamber—so recently her *own* antechamber—induced a health-endangering thundering of her heart no leech could have quieted.

When she finally pushed open the door to the inner chamber and found the room empty, she sighed so deeply a cat curled on the bed meowed disconsolately, roused from a warm nap.

"Mores the pity such a one as you doesn't know his wrath," she muttered as she stalked by. Pagan had a cat?

Indeed he did, perhaps the most orange-eared, fur-endowed, long-clawed creature ever assembled. It peered at her through blue, angular eyes, then yawned and stretched out a paw, as if welcoming her. Gwyn resisted the urge to stroke the feathery head and turned instead to one particular woven tapestry that had not—praise God—been ripped down along with the rest.

In fact, the room vibrated barrenness. The shield that had hung above the bed, encrusted with the image of a gauntleted hand gripping a rose, and the blood of Englishmen shorn of their greatness when Stephen came to power, was gone. The stone was brighter where it had hung for eighteen years, revealing the unseen wear that had occurred everywhere else.

The long, narrow table by the window was gone, as was the wardrobe where she folded her underlinens. Her face flushed hot. Had he taken that too? Good Lord, who had unpacked it?

She pushed aside the heavy tapestry and felt for the handle of the hidden door, then descended into the dark.

Wet cobbles toyed with her footing but a firm hand on the walls let her descend without incident. The castle underworld was dark and cloying, yet damp, and quiet as death.

She hurried to the chamber. The padlock hung open, the dragon's mouth in a silent roar. She called out softly, and the door cracked open. Duncan's pale little face looked at her, illuminated by the thick, stubby candle he held. She stepped inside and glanced down. The prince's body lay motionless on the straw.

"How does he?"

"I cannot say for sure, milady, but I've got him tucked so deeply in blankets and furs so he'll break a sweat if he tries to sneeze. But, milady," the boy's voice dropped into a whisper. The echoes came off the wet stone, bouncing moist worry back to her ears. "He's well far gone."

"Well," she said lightly, lifting the hem of her skirts, "he will simply have to hang on. We have."

"Aye, but we're not knocked into pieces by fevers and bad humours. I fear he cannot hang on much longer. He's closer to death than life, and there's a fact."

She dropped to her knees beside the prostrate form of her

prince. A fact, was it? A fact that the uncrowned king might die on her watch come some night soon? A fact that the pillaging boy-king fitzEmpress could sweep o'er *her* isle with nary a flame of resistance? Not while she was in stead at the Nest. Not while blood pulsed through *her* heart. Not if she were truly her father's daughter.

Not if she wanted this last chance to make up for past sins.

"Has he spoken?" Her lifted head shone in a wedge of light cast by the candle burning from Duncan's hand.

"Not so's it'd make any sense, my lady," he replied, worried eyes on the would-be king. "None but to groan and reach for the heavens, as if He could see anyone down here." A black look condemned the stone roof, but the gaoler lay even further above, his bootheels likely clacking even now over her father's once-hallowed halls, ordering *jongleurs* to work their magick and pretty harps to play their spell in preparation for the victory feast.

While in the cellars lurked his undoing.

Gwyn placed Eustace's head back on the rushes and took back the key from Duncan. Against every fibre of her being, she knew what she was bound to do. Surely King Stephen was aware Griffyn had taken back his home. The king would send word, instructions. She must hold on until then.

"Keep him well, and warm." A look at her young servant brought a sigh to her lips. "And yourself as well, Duncan."

"Ah, well, sure's anythin', I'm well warm," he avowed, icicles forming on his nose with each exhalation. Tears welled up in her eyes: could anyone have more loyal, valorous men, be they the cowherd's son stowed beneath a castle floor?

She patted Duncan's shoulder, promised more blankets, and rubbed her hands together for warmth. Stephen may soon be ruling at the privilege of Henri, as some said would be the case come another month, but Eustace would rule at the call of his barons one day, lords who would rise up en masse when he stepped into the glorious light of day.

Until then, Gwyn thought, her head falling, *he needs rest.*

She turned and glided up the stairs, the darkness only a faint hindrance now, since she was not looking where she went anyhow. Her mind was turning on paths far distant from the shadowy cellar.

Mindless, she reached the top landing and flipped the door latch up. It swung open. She pushed aside the tapestry with a flick of her head.

The door swung shut behind her, the tapestry fell flat against the wall and, after bending over to free a skirt hem caught in her boot, she looked up into the eyes of Griffyn Sauvage.

Chapter Eight

"Good Lord!" she cried, falling back with her hand at her chest. "What are you doing here?"

He took a step into the room, a long stride that seemed to bring him right beside her, although he was still standing some ten feet away. He was divested of most of his armour by now. The soft shirt that lay beneath mail hauberk and padded gambeson clung to his muscular body. His hair was longer than it had been last year. Slightly damp from a bathe or dunk in the horse trough, it was plastered across his forehead and down the column of his strong neck. She backed up a step. He took one forward.

"I think I'll ask you that same question."

"I was just . . . looking about." She fingered the edge of the tapestry that hid the passageway to the donjons, then snatched her hand away.

His gaze flicked to the tapestry before sliding over her body slowly, as if digesting something of uncertain flavour. "What did you find?"

"Nothing," she said in a bright, cheerful tone. "I know I should not be in here. I'll leave now—"

He kicked the door shut behind him. "Stay."

"I should go."

"You should do what I tell you."

She felt weakly behind her for some support: a table, a wall, a weapon. "Did you tell me *not* to come in here?"

He smiled, a predatory, slow grin that sucked the moisture from her mouth. "Not yet."

"If you told me to do so now, be assured I would do it with a right good will."

"Oh, I am." He ran his fingers along his jaw, drawing Gwyn's eye to the square outline of his chin, and his mouth, which seemed intent on making her squirm as it continued its tormenting smile.

"Well, then, I'll just—"

"Stay."

She scrambled backwards again. She would be climbing out the window in a trice. He glanced to the right again, his gaze travelling over the tapestry. Her heart hammered. Given a moment more, he might move towards it.

"Did your lackeys find my chemises to their liking?"

His gaze swung back blankly. "What?"

"My wardrobe." She gestured to the space it used to occupy. "'Tis gone."

"'Twas yours?"

"Whose else?" She wandered to the other side of the room, making a path away from the tapestry.

"Your father's," he suggested.

The old familiar pinch of pain tightened. "He loved that old wardrobe. Did you notice the way it was carved? Legend says 'twas the Conqueror's, but Papa always scoffed at that. He just liked the skill of the craftsman." She laughed a little, unsteadily. "But why am I telling you about my father? You know everything, is that not so? Enough to hate him for a hundred years."

"I could hate him for a very long time," he agreed quietly.

"Well, how pleasant for us."

"But I don't hate the wardrobe, Gwyn. If you want it, I'll bring it back."

"I cannot fathom how that would matter in the least." She paced to another corner of the room, leading him ever away from the linen draped innocently over the wall. "I suppose you've arranged for the meal?"

"You could have come down and done that yourself," he said. Well, true, she could have, but she'd been busy in the cellars. "You've not been sequestered."

"And why not?"

He opened his hands. "To what end?"

Indeed. She lowered her buttocks to the ledge in front of the window and almost started crying. "Truth, Pagan, I don't—"

"My name is Griffyn."

She drew up, her tears stalled by this. "Last year, 'twas Pagan for me. And your men call you that."

"Not my wife."

"Oh."

He watched her for what felt like a very long time, then said, "There are worse things than missing your father when he dies, Gwyn."

This time the tears did push forth, burning the rims of her eyes. "Really? What?"

He lifted his hands a little, tilted up. "Not."

She blew out an unsteady breath. "Well. I had not considered that." They were quiet for a moment. "There's no seed, Griffyn."

He blinked. "Seed?"

"No seed. Barely enough for to sow this winter, and for certes not enough for the spring. We might make it through the winter. We might not." He was watching her with a quiet regard, listening closely. "There's nothing left to sell. Everoot has naught. I hope you did not come north expecting treasure or riches," she added with a watery laugh. "The wars have been too long, the summer too dry. The leavings up north are barely worth it."

"Those 'leavings,' lady, are my ancestral home," he said, his voice dropping into a low, vibrating tone that would have warned off a bull. "I was born here."

Their eyes locked. Griffyn watched her face shade through more emotions than a single moment ought contain. Then she took a deep breath. "Well," she murmured. "I see we are at odds once again."

"Aye."

She threw up her hands. "When have we ever not been?"

Griffyn swung away, looking for wine. But the room was empty, save for the one, gold stitched tapestry that had caught his eye and had stayed his command when everything else was ordered stripped from the room. Everything, including the wardrobe with her . . . smallclothes. He felt a grin threatening but, glancing at her flushed, down-turned face, Griffyn decided to hold it in check.

Harder still was to make sense of the rapid and powerful changes of emotion whenever he was within five feet of the woman. He swept his gaze over the room, irked. 'Twas not his yet, nor hers anymore. It sat in a state of suspended transition, holding nothing but memories. Nothing but wretched memories. Not even a jug of wine.

He went to the door, wrenched it open, and shouted to an attendant.

Mayhap they'd expected his command, or else the kitchen staff was better trained than any he'd seen—or perchance they feared his temper—for in under a minute a tentative knock came on the door. Griffyn whipped it open, nodded grimly to the young page who stood with a tray and a flagon of wine, and growled when he was asked in a muted voice "if the lady wouldn't be needing a cup too?"

The jug went on the windowsill, the wooden cup in his hand. A generous splash of ruby liquid gurgled into the cup, which he pushed into Guinevere's palm. Then he lifted the jug to his lips and downed a goodly portion, his throat working hard to swallow the drink as he had been forced to swallow so many things ere this day. But never again.

When he finally aimed another glance at de l'Ami's daughter, she too was making use of the fuel, funneling a stream of wine down her throat with such skill he lifted his brows.

"You did not drink so adeptly when I saw you last."

The cup clattered to the floor. A line of red stained the edge of her lips and angled her mouth into a pale pink smile.

"I did not have so much cause to drink, then." She closed her mouth, the smile-stain remaining, and sat on the edge of the bed, her hands crossed primly in her lap.

"You had some cause," he remarked dryly.

"Well, mayhap I did at that." She sniffed and looked out the window. "But I'd never had the kind of fire-water you were offering that night, sir, and would do well to never sport with it again."

He looked at her delicate profile and the rampaging curls that glinted burnished fire and danced down her curving spine, and recalled the way his hands had moved across that same spine, slid over her hips and down, some twelvemonth ago.

"I liked the things you did with it," he said gruffly.

And with those simple words, he started it inside of Gwyn. A hot flush spread through her body. She rose shakily from the bed. "Faith, my lord, with your permission, I would go now."

He threw back his head and laughed so hard the servants scuttling through the hall a floor below halted in their circuits and exchanged frightened glances. "You've grown quite docile of a sudden, Guinevere."

"I was trying to be . . . easier on your mood."

He lifted both brows in mute query.

"I have decided 'tis wisest for us to get along, and I will do my part."

He half-smiled. "Which means?"

She held her breath a moment. "I will be compliant."

He laughed again, an easy sound, and the boiling tension

in her belly lessened somewhat. "Guinevere. I have seen you with a rock in your hand, a retort on your lips, and a foolish notion in your head, but I have *never* seen you compliant."

She crossed her arms over her chest. "Some find me endowed with a capacious gift for good humour, my lord."

"Where are they?" He reached out one muscular arm for the wine jug. "I will learn them their folly."

She dragged her gaze from his flexed forearm. "And what will we say of yours? I have seen you in a foul enough humour."

He considered her a moment. "You are right, my lady. We can be at one another's throats, or we can learn to get along. I prefer the latter."

She stretched out her hands, palms up. "There, you see. We've had our first agreement."

"And neither one of us shattered from the effort."

"Or exploded in rage."

"Or ran screaming from the room."

Her lips twitched. "I cannot imagine you doing that."

"I was speaking of you, Guinevere."

"Oh."

And somehow, there they were, *smiling* at each other. "'Tis a good omen."

His slate-grey eyes flicked around the room. "We shall see."

Chapter Nine

The betrothal was brief, almost anticlimactic.

Seeing her mother's dress, thinking of her muddled deathbed promises to her father, and above all knowing what was to come with Griffyn Sauvage after what had *so completely* already been, Gwyn was so weighted with sodden, confusing emotions, she could barely wring out the required words.

"I will take you as my husband," she murmured, head down, taking *verba de futuro*, vows of the future, binding them in a legal and spiritual betrothal.

It was different for Griffyn.

The priest's Latin-infused drone barely penetrated his consciousness. Raven-haired, green-eyed, crimson-lipped, Guinevere fairly pulsed with fire as she drifted down the corridor to meet him inside the chapel. The walls seemed to expand when she entered the small stone edifice, her head held high, a small filigree of silver around the high-piled ebony curls atop her head. Distinctly impious thoughts filled his mind. Quick-witted, hot-spirited, intelligent and funny, she was more than he'd ever expected in a wife, and about as far different from his mother as he could have imagined.

No, he decided as they unbent their knees, she was different from any woman—any *person*—he'd known.

If only she hadn't betrayed him.

* * *

The great hall fairly bounced with frivolity, Griffyn noted, all of which his pretty betrothed observed with a down-turned mouth. The tables on the floor were disassembled soon after the three-hour betrothal *cum* victory feast ended, and the vast space of the great hall became a stage for the evening revelries.

He had arranged for *jongleurs* and wrestlers to perform, which they did to the claps and cheers of an inebriated and inordinately relieved crowd—better to have such violence staged. Laughter and stories bounced from rafter to rafter, rising to the slats in the thirty-foot-high ceiling. Griffyn sat back, satisfied.

In fact, he decided, turning his glance to Gwyn, the night was so filled with good humour he was surprised she didn't strangle every de l'Ami soul whose throat had loosed a chuckle in the last three hours. But she hadn't. Yet.

On a platform extended above the great hall sat a band of musicians, pouring out music that, as the night progressed, more and more bodies swayed to.

The Countess Everoot's decidedly did not. She sat as stiff as a rail, her arms cleaved to her sides. The most movement Griffyn could wring from her rigid body was to lift a wine goblet in toast to their betrothal, and that was only by virtue of breathing on her neck as he did so.

He turned to the room at large, focusing in on a table where prominent de l'Ami knights sat, quiet amid the festive riot. A slender but athletically built young man sat in the middle. Jeravius, if he recalled correctly. He'd noticed him in the bailey, when the de l'Ami soldiers were being rounded up. He'd caught Griffyn's attention, the careful way he'd passed his hand over the battered curtain wall, as if it were an old, beloved pet.

Tonight, Jeravius had been intent on Guinevere, keeping his gaze on her through the smoke and festivities, leaning his shoulders forwards or back when either soldier or wrestler blocked his view.

That Guinevere sat with the kind of rigid stance a plank of wood would have admired did little to ease the knight's watchful scrutiny, and therefore little to mitigate any threat to Griffyn's command.

He rose, hoping to be inconspicuous. He may as well have herded a flock of sheep through the hall. Every head jerked to him, the music faltered, and two of his knights, engaged in mock combat, flicked their eyes to him, their contest forgotten.

His gaze drifted over the room, then he ducked his head in a nod, freeing the party to resume its furious swirl. Dancers danced, musicians piped, fires roared, and Griffyn walked down the dais steps to where Jeravius sat.

"'Tis a goodly scene," he observed, standing beside the table of de l'Ami knights as his eyes scanned the surroundings.

"Aye," Jeravius responded carefully, getting to his feet. "My lord."

"Lady Guinevere has lost much this day," he said, glancing idly around the room before looking back.

Jeravius's eyes were waiting for him. "She is a good woman, my lord, and deserves only happiness."

"Which I have in my power, and inclination, to give her." He looked over the crowd. "Think you I will be met with much resistance?"

From the corner of his eye, he saw Jeravius's blond head move in a slow shake. "Not from me, my lord."

"*Bien.* I'll do my part, you do yours."

"Rest assured, my lord."

Still, Griffyn took note of the belligerent thrust of his chin. He rubbed his cheek thoughtfully, then said in a casual tone, "I've need of a stout man to help oversee the rebuilding of the defences. 'Tis no small job."

He could almost feel the young man's eagerness pressing

forward. He waited, and Jeravius finally burst out with, "If you will, my lord, I would speak freely about the Nest."

"Please."

"The eastern wall is tunneled under ferociously, and tilts like a fish trap in winter. And for ten years now, the west wall has been tumbling into disrepair—I can't believe you didn't start your assault there. As far as the keep goes, well—"

He trailed off, his face paling, but Griffyn nodded. "That is just the sort of enthusiasm I need."

"My lord?"

"As I said, I am in need of a man. To learn from the masons I am bringing in, to assist in command of the labourers in the work. Happens I might just have found him."

Jerv took a step forward and almost tripped over the bench that was there. "Are you in earnest, my lord?"

"For certes. How long have you been a lover of stone?"

"Some long time," Jerv answered eagerly. "I suppose when I turned seven and my father took me to Westminster, then I knew for certes. But I could ne'er . . . . I am a knight. My father paid well for me to earn that station, to be fostered and tutored by Lord Ionnes. I am a soldier, my lord, meant for other things than architecture. Good things," he added, a trifle vehemently.

Griffyn nodded. "My uncle also found great pleasure in the labour of designing and repairing castles. He was the architect for the French king and the Duke of Normandy in building several castles. They've come to be regarded as masterful works, strong in defence but pleasing to the eye. He built the castle at Côte sur Seine."

Jerv's eyes widened. "Côte sur Seine?" he repeated. "'Tis said to be a wonder."

"I think so," Griffyn said simply. "Would you like to meet with the mason, when he arrives?" he asked, waiting for the buoyant enthusiasm he sensed in the young knight to burst forth. It may not be tonight, nor come another week, but it would come, and when it did, he would tap it and shape it so it would never threaten his home again.

A boyish grin spread across Jeravius's face. "If 'tis your will, my lord, I should like it more than anything." He thrust out his hand.

Griffyn reached out and clasped it. Their hands encircled each other's forearm, wary, appraising, but with the glimmer of something new: respect.

"Lady Gwyn will be mightily pleased to see the repair begun, my lord," Jeravius added. "She has oft spoken of it, but with so little money, and so few to hand. . . ." He shrugged.

"And those hands otherwise occupied, it has been put off."

"Time and again, my lord. For good cause, of course," he added hurriedly, and cast a wary glance towards the dais.

Griffyn's head cocked to the side to take in Guinevere's stiff pose. My, but she was having fun. Her spine was stretched straight, her eyes glaring blankly across the room. She could have been in the front row of the chapel at midnight for all the expression she showed.

The only hint of connection to the room around her was her hand, idly stroking the sleek head of Griffyn's aged hound, Renegade. The old dog had edged away from Edmund and sat down by a sweeter scent.

"But then, there have been so many good causes," Jeravius said, "and my lady after them all."

The words were so softly spoken, Griffyn thought perhaps he was not meant to hear. He looked over to find an affectionate, devoted smile on Jeravius's face. Why, he loved her. They all did. Exactly as she had said.

Jeravius was turning back to him, arranging his face into the semblance of neutrality. Griffyn nodded back, allowing the young knight the privilege of his disdain. Soon enough he'd have Jeravius and all the others, even the glowering Fulk, as closely bound to him as a sword to its scabbard.

And, if needed, with a more deadly clasp, too.

Chapter Ten

Gwyn had viewed the whole encounter, from Griffyn's nonchalant approach, to the ensuing conversation, to Jerv's animated leap from the bench and the clasping of wrists.

Another conquest, she thought sourly. The stiff, echoing room she had envisioned was not to be. Revelers were everywhere, householders, villagers, knights and soldiers all sat with Pagan's men and exchanged polite words. No, more than "polite." The room felt distinctly . . . jovial.

Had they forgotten 'twas but a moonrise ago they had been at war with these men? Apparently so, for they talked happily with Pagan's men, sharing ale and laughs, and secrets most likely too. She scowled.

Pagan stood in quiet conversation with Jerv, but still drew looks from around the room. He wore a close-cut tunic which revealed wide shoulders and a body plated with hard muscle and sinew. The bejeweled brooch at his shoulder flashed green and red fire, and her unwilling eye was drawn to the way the dark hose hugged his muscular thighs. Firelight highlighted the slants of his cheekbones and a wide, square chin, and from this distance, the scar was a small slash across the noble lines of his face. He was every inch the triumphant warrior. Which made her his plunder.

When his unreadable grey eyes shifted to her, she was aghast to note that even when he did not plan to, the man sent waves of seduction and sexual prowess out before him like the prow of a ship. He was dressed as befitted his victorious claim to the castle, the lands, and the lady, and he simply took her breath away.

Her fingers, grown strangely cold, fluttered at her throat. Her world was changed from this night on, and it would be by his hand.

His hands. His lips, his mouth.

Gwen ripped her attention away from the ungodly list her mind was detailing and tried to still any sign of fear.

If his smug smile was any indicator, she had failed. Miserably.

The whole thing turned her face further downwards, her mouth into a scowl, her nose to hover above the rim of her wine cup, which was now weaving unsteadily from the tips of her fingers as she beckoned for more. When it arrived, she took a deep draught.

"Careful, wife. I'd rather have you upright, at least for awhile yet."

Griffyn's words came close by her ear. She angled a sour look up. He was standing beside her chair, his thigh a few inches from her nose. "Beg pardon?"

"I would rather you be upright. For awhile."

He was grinning from ear to ear. Oh, but he was a crafty one. He'd won his home back, took a wife, and was on his way to planting a thick wedge of devotion between her and her knights.

All of her father's curses came back into her mind, vibrant and particularly applicable to the scoundrel standing so close she could mend a rent in his breeches, should she *ever* be so inclined.

"You must be pleased with your accomplishments," she observed sourly.

"I would be if my pretty betrothed did but smile at me."
Down went the corners of her mouth. He sighed. "Wine does
not agree with you."

"Defeat does not agree with me."

"Nay," he said, his eyes roaming over her face. "What can
I do to ease it?"

She pretended to ponder this. "Leave?"

He laughed, evidently willing to entertain her bad humour
for the moment. And what did it cost him, she wondered
gloomily. Nothing but a few seeds of patience probably well-
sown in the armies of the fitzEmpress over the last eighteen
years. *Let her prattle on,* he must be thinking, *in the end she
will be mine.*

"What did you say to him?" she asked abruptly.

"Whom?"

"Jerv."

His dark grey eyes held hers. "He's a liking for castles and
how they're built."

"How did you know that?"

He shrugged.

She scowled. "I could have told you that. *I* knew a long
time ago. When he was twelve, he told me his first dream of
building a castle."

"Umm."

"For years now," she insisted, as if she had to prove Jerv
was more hers than his.

He nodded calmly, infuriatingly. "How wonderful."

A fissure of fury steamed through a crack in her hard-
fought composure. "Yes, isn't it?"

He looked at her in silence.

"I've known him since I was a child. Since we were five."
She sounded like an idiot, and couldn't stop. Why was she
going on in this childish way, as if Jerv were something to
be fought over?

"Ahh."

"And he's loved such things, castles and architecture, since he was twelve."

"Seven."

This hauled her up short. "What?"

"Since he was seven."

"Seven?"

A nod of the dark head, then more silence. She downed a rather large quaff of wine. This would make what . . . three cups? Mayhap four. Who cared. She was absolutely aghast at this piece of information. Since he was *seven*? It had taken her years of knowing Jerv to discover this hidden love, and Pagan had extracted it in what . . . ten minutes?

"He told me of it when we were twelve," she muttered, more to herself than him.

"Ahh."

They were quiet a moment while the full impact of his smooth, wordless reply hit her. She turned with narrowed eyes. "You think you are so clever."

"I do?"

A wary, slightly drunken tilt of her head greeted this. He was a menace. Pure, unadulterated evil. And he was *stealing* her men. "You do not know so verily much."

"Nothing at all," he agreed, then stepped around her chair to take his seat beside her. She swiveled her rump in the chair to examine him better. Thief.

She hiccoughed. Their eyes met, and she hiccupped again. A slow smile drifted over his face, and his eyes did a downward spiral across her gown. A flutter of heat quickened inside her groin, and she set the rim of the cup to her teeth to stop herself from—'twas awful—smiling back.

"De l'Ami," he said, rolling her name over his tongue as if he were tasting it. A small shiver raced down her spine. "*A friend*. 'Tis an odd name for your father."

"King Stephen gave him the name," she retorted, swallowing another huge draught of wine.

"Stephen did not give him the name." He reached over, took the cup from her hand and placed it on the table. "My father did. In Palestine."

The wash of chills curled up her backbone. "But, no," she protested weakly. Was everything she'd once thought settled to be churned up by this man? "I was under the impression . . . my lord king gave him the name. King Stephen found Papa to be loyal and constant."

The smile Pagan sent down was slow and terrifying. "Henri did not."

He lifted his hand and in a heartbeat two servants stood at his side. A low conference ensued. Gwyn's only participation in it was as the recipient of a number of significant looks. When the servants retreated, she glared at him.

"They come quicker to you than they have to me in ten years," she admitted grudgingly.

He shrugged.

"Mayhap I ought to have been sterner," she reflected.

"You think I have been stern with your kitchen staff?"

"God's truth, Pagan, you've scared them witless."

He looked at the screens separating the corridor to the kitchens from the great hall. "They do not appear witless to me. They seem obedient."

"Quite. That is my point. I should have used more of your tactics," she mused. He looked at her. "You know, unsheathe a sword about supper time and bellow '*This is my castle!*'"

And bellow she did. The hall ground to a halt. It was nothing compared to the silence before. This was a full-on, drop-dead stoppage of all breath and movement throughout the cavernous hall. Every stricken eye flashed to the dais. The music faltered.

"Careful, Gwyn," he murmured by her ear.

If he had curled his fingers around her throat and begun squeezing, she couldn't have been more frightened. Indeed, this low restraint set her teeth clattering. He lifted his hand and ran his thumb along the underside of her jaw. Her swallow had to edge by his threatening caress, and he surely felt it.

"Had only I known, my lord," she whispered. "Your tactics are far superior."

"You did that, Gwyn, not I." His thigh brushed against hers, a slight contact that sent an entirely different kind of chill through her body. "Go upstairs. Now."

He lifted his hand and three servants appeared at his side, one with a tray of aromatic spices designed—she could tell by her nose—to have a sobering effect. She rose unsteadily.

"Show Lady Guinevere to our chambers," he instructed the servant at his side, who nodded briskly.

Then he raised his cup, occasioning a likewise and immediate response in every castle dweller in sight. She sent a dagger-like look around the hall in general, but no one was watching her anyway. All eyes were on Sauvage. "To the Lady Guinevere, my betrothed."

A hum of "Huzzah's" and the thumping of fists followed her out of the hall, accompanied by three servants who hadn't taken so much care with her since she'd been swaddled in cloths and burped on her mother's chest.

"I'm not a child, John," she snapped to one, a man she'd known for fifteen years.

"But he's said to treat you like you were, my lady."

She stopped so quickly the servants carried on a few steps before realising their cargo was left behind. John hurried back to her side. "He said to treat me like a child?" Her voice was high-pitched, incredulous, and aghast.

"Nay, nay, my lady," he stammered, realising his error. The last thing he needed was *two* nobles angry with him. "He only said to treat you as we would a precious jewel and we decided, didn't we?" he asked, sending an imploring look at his compatriots, who all nodded like sheep being led to slaughter. "We decided that meant like a child."

"Well," she snapped, picking up her skirts and walking

again. "I am not a child, nor witless, nor *drunk*," she added emphatically, then tripped on her skirt hem.

"Oh, no, milady," he huffed, helping her regain her footing, then wiping a sheen of sweat from his brow. "Not a child." Oh Lord, to truckle with two such fiercesome masters was too much to bear. Mayhap Wales held an easier lifestyle, with its bloody wars of succession and stern-eyed princes.

Chapter Eleven

She stood in the lord's chambers with her arms wrapped around her waist, her eyes full of wonder. All traces of drunkenness had left; it must have been Pagan who was intoxicating her.

He had been wandering for many years by his own admission, but the sight before her did not bespeak the lifestyle of a nomadic warrior. The candles flickered, blown by small gusts of breeze through the open window as she walked around the perimeter of the room. A life of campaigns in the service of an itinerant lord was not the way to create what she saw in front of her. For that, one needed a home. He'd said that was Everoot. And it looked as though he'd been coming home for a long, long time.

She suddenly and quite unwillingly understood why he had come to the Nest with a sword in his hand and revolt on his mind.

A glance at the window ledge made her smile. Crossing over, she ran her hand over the orange-eared cat, ferociously-furred and purring, and continued her examination of a room that had been hers only a day ago.

It had been transformed from the cold, military-like chamber—which she'd had neither the time nor money to change—to a place of indulgence and refinement. Well-wrought iron sconces were affixed to the wall and beeswax—beeswax!—candles burned from them, leaving none of the smokey mess tallow did. Pelts of fur were scattered across the floor, the extravagance staggering. She bent over and touched one, then straightened.

A series of finely stitched tapestries rippled like floating velvet against the walls, coaxing the dreary room to practically undulate with warmth. A finely carved wooden table abutted the doorframe and burned with more fat, squat candles.

Against the opposite walls stood a pair of oak wardrobes, polished to a reflecting shine. The one Gwyn shyly edged open held such a tumbleful of silk and fine fabrics her mouth dropped open. Why, this was silk and samite and . . . Her hands delved greedily into the luxurious pile. Here was velvet . . . and . . .

"Merciful heavens," she exclaimed aloud, backing up, *"those are women's clothes!"*

He had brought her clothes.

Some were her own, she realised, moving forward again. Here was a samite overtunic, so worn and old it could barely hold stiff against her body, but most of them were not hers. She had no silk, not anymore, and had never so much as touched velvet. But here were textile riches, some already cut and sewn. She held one up to her body—it would fit—then hurriedly shoved them all back inside, grimacing as she wrinkled the lush fabric. Griffyn had been planning for her.

The notion was very disturbing.

A reflecting mirror rested on the large table set against a third wall. Backing away from the wardrobe, she wandered over, confused by the clarity of the reflection bouncing back to her. Polished metal never shone like that.

She stretched out her hand hesitantly and ran her fingertips over the smoothest, coolest piece of alloy she had ever touched. What was it? She bent closer, until her nose touched the surface and her eyes stared back at her.

A sound outside the door her made her jerk back and spin, but no one was there. The rumble of masculine voices and footsteps faded away. All was quiet again. Some miscreants from the feast, no doubt, stumbling around for a privy. She turned back to the glistening surface. What on earth would motivate a warrior in the midst of a war to lug all these treasures to a far-flung northern province?

Gwyn stared back at her unmarred reflection. Was that what she looked like? Two eyes, a freckled nose, and a crooked mouth? Simple enough, she thought, turning away. Thank goodness she hadn't looked into a still pond of water since she was twelve.

Griffyn Sauvage may have estates in Normandy, but 'twas Everoot that had held his heart all these years, by the evidence of her eyes. And by that same stick, she measured his intent: he had been planning to make the Nest home for some long time.

The luxurious masculinity of the room was hypnotic. For a moment she could pretend there was no more pressing task than to relax, that no one wanted her to do anything, that she could stretch out on the bed and gaze at the ceiling and . . . what on earth was that?

A shelf had been bracketed to the wall. On it, flush with the wood, lay a pile of vellum and parchment manuscripts. Her head began to spin as she approached. She put out a finger and brushed it down the side of the bindings, then abruptly lifted one from its resting place.

Sitting on the bed with her feet tucked beneath her, she opened the massive volume of pages that was *Historia Regum Britanniae*. She recognised it; it was like the one at the abbey the de l'Amis patronised, where as a child she'd convinced the monks to at least *tell* her the tales, if not incur her father's wrath by actually teaching her to read them herself.

She traced her fingers over the beautifully etched lines on the pages. The blues and reds and greens were so brilliant they still looked wet. She touched an illustration that ran along the margin of one page, a bemused-looking monk holding a stylus, drawing a line to insert a missing A in its proper place in one of the words. Such whimsy and talent. She smiled and carefully turned another page.

"What do you think?"

She jerked her head up. Griffyn stood in front of the brazier, warming his hands. She hadn't heard him come in. He tossed her a casual glance before turning back to the flames. She got to her feet, book in hand.

"I think I am surprised," she admitted.

"By Monmouth?"

"By you." She indicated the shelves with a pointed finger.

He looked over his shoulder and smiled. "And what do you think of Geoffrey Monmouth's *History of the Kings of Britain*?"

It was impossible not to return the grin. "I daresay I don't know, but have heard 'tis pure invention."

"Ah, but well for we Welsh, who came out of it with King Arthur."

She peered at him curiously. "And where in your blood are you Welsh? 'Twas certainly not your father. 'Sauvage' is Norman through and through."

He nodded. "My father was many things. He liked to be thought of as Norman to the bone, and he surely did not disdain the title and lands he had here in England. But 'twas my mother who was a Welsh princess."

She lifted her brows and depressed the corners of her mouth briefly, playfully impressed. "What else is there?" she asked, nodding towards the shelves.

"The *Ecclesiastical History of England and Normandy*, Vitalis's work, of course. And Bebe's *Lives of the Abbots*," he went on, warming his hands over the brazier thoughtfully. "Let's see, there is the *Gesta Pontificum Anglorum* that Malmesbury wrote, which is more of an informal chronicle of the lives of the bishops than a full history. But 'tis sound. And useful."

She stared with a dropped jaw. Warrior, aye, she knew that. Seductor, fine, she could struggle against that. But well-read nobleman with a library to rival that of an affluent monastery? What defence had she there? She sat back down on the bed, its plump mattress giving under her weight.

"What do you think of the others, Guinevere?" he prompted.

"I can't read." Her words poked out from her mouth like they were lashed on sticks: stiff, clipped.

"A situation we'll see remedied, if you wish."

"Papa did not think much of reading, as it were," she informed him, eyeing her fingernails.

"But you did."

"I still do."

Griffyn watched her examine her fingertips so carefully, her slim shoulders rounded. It reminded him of that night a year ago, riding through the forest, when they'd shared a raging kiss, and after, she'd braced herself against a tree like an abandoned marionette, in all her brave, delicate beauty. Totally unexpected.

He set down the poker and crossed the room. Taking up her hand, he inspected the ragged nubs of her nails, the work-hardened edges of her slender fingers. "You've been working hard."

"As have we all." She tried to pull her hand away but he held tight. "'Tis nothing. Some of the chores I like."

He shifted just his eyes up. "You like cleaning privies?"

That made her smile. It was brief, though, and he wanted more of it. "I don't clean privies, actually," she said. "You find it hard to believe, that I would enjoy the work?"

"For certes. Most high-born women wish to do as little of it as possible."

The smile faded. "I am not most women," she murmured.

He watched the strange quiet descend on her, and had a sudden image of the weight of her burden over the past year. Alone, in the middle of a war, governing a vast estate with too little money and too much need. In their interviews of the household, everyone had a praiseful word to say of the lady, words given more force by the affection clinging to them.

"Have you ever seen my flowers?"

He looked up. A smile nudged at the faint dimple beside her mouth. Her *flowers*? He shook his head.

She smiled wider and it felt like the room expanded, like the breeze blew fresher through the shutters. "As I said, I like some of the chores I do."

Comprehension dawned. "Your *flowers*."

She nodded happily. Her black curls bobbed over her shoulders.

"Well then," he mused, looking at the small fingers held in his grasp. He stroked each between two of his own, feeling the slender, fragile bone within, delicately arching into his. "You must keep on doing the things you like. The rest, we'll find others to manage."

Her expansive face suddenly closed up again. When she pulled on her hand this time, he released her. She walked to the window and pushed the shutters open. The night was inky black and windy. A scent of rain was in the air.

"We so desperately need rain," she murmured, as if they were in idle chat about the weather. "I can't stop doing any of them," she went on, in the same neutral tone. "The fields still need to be ploughed, even when the men have staged a war. When my Welsh stewards run off or die, I must find someone to take their place, even when there is no one."

"Powys," he murmured, the sudden recollection shocking in its clarity. He could almost smell the leather of their damp saddles as they rode over the wild Welsh hills, almost hear his father complaining of the problem of keeping stewards alive in the Welsh marcher lands. Such a swift, clear memory.

She seemed to not have heard him. She was running her hand over the silken tapestry hanging beside the window. "When men and boys die in battle, their women are left to tend those fields, which leaves the castle short-staffed, and weeds know nothing of wars, laundry nothing of defeat." Her voice had grown hard and swift and bitter, and she turned her back to him. "They just need to be taken care of."

By me. Alone.

The words fairly thrust themselves into the suddenly quiet between them, but she did not speak them, and he did not ask. The silence grew longer.

A feeling of kinship swept through him. He felt his heart shift, which he definitely did not want. Dominance, lordship, lust: these things were known and acceptable. Affection and understanding: they were distinctly unwelcome.

So why was he walking across the room to stand at her curving back? And bending his head by her ear to speak in a gentle murmur?

"You need not take care of it all alone anymore, my lady." He began unlacing the silk wrap that coiled her hair in a thick rope down her back. He combed his fingers through the unbound tresses, his callouses catching. Her breathing quickened ever so slightly, so he bent nearer her ear and murmured, "You've a husband now, who can help with whatever needs to be taken care of."

"The laundry?"

He heard the catch in her voice, and decided this was why he'd crossed the room. To make her resistance crumble, to weaken her will. To get her into his bed, a willing, wanton partner as she'd been an autumn ago. She turned her head the slightest bit. Her words were incredulous. "You'll help with the laundry?"

"I will, if 'tis needed in some way." He pressed his lips to the nape of her neck. Her breath trembled out in a rush. "Although I cannot believe there isn't someone other than myself to plunge linens into that foul-smelling concoction that bubbles and burps in vast cauldrons."

Her body leaned backwards into him, just the slightest bit.

"'Tis indeed a most wretched reek, my lord," she admitted, a smile in her voice. "And they *are* ever-large tubs."

"Did I ever tell you?" he mused, inhaling the faint scent of rose clinging to her hair. "I once was in Scotland when a small pony found its unfortunate way into such a vat." He could feel her listening; her cheek was almost pressed against his jaw, her hair tickled his nose as she inched her head towards his voice ever so slightly.

"And?"

"Gone. Never to be seen again." His ran his hands down the outside of her arms. "He was a fat little pony too. Utterly vanished." He clucked his tongue.

She chuckled, faint and girlish. Her head notched up another inch. "And what about the weeds?"

"Well, now," he murmured. "Let's not lose our heads, Guinevere. I thought you said you *liked* doing that."

She laughed freely this time, a very fine sound. "And so, what now?" She turned around to face him, so his hands now rested in the curve of her spine. "I've lost my head, Griffyn, and you're scared of the laundry."

He smiled. "We'll have to find a way through. You can tend your roses and mix the cauldrons."

She laughed again. "And you can rescue the ponies and help me find a seneschal for the Everoot town of Ipsile-upon-Tyne. I'll have to tell you about it."

His hands fell away from her waist. Something sharp-edged clicked its teeth together inside his heart. A little gnashing. "I know about Ipsile-upon-Tyne," he said tightly. "On the Welsh Marches."

"How do you know about Ipsile?" she asked, smiling faintly. "Or that it borders Wales? Did William mention it?"

And like that, full-blown and dangerous, anger snapped back into the forefront, thick and undeniable. How could it ride up on him so swiftly, without warning or wishing it to be?

How did he know? How did he know about Ipsile or Wales, an entire borderland along the frontiers of his birthright?

He bent close to her ear, his breath a caress, his words a threat.

"Now, Guinevere, listen close, for this is the last time I will say it." He pitched his voice low, and he could feel her body edge closer to listen. "I rode o'er this turf before you were born. I know these lands from York to the Welsh Marches, their every hummock and hillside. I have dreamt of them for eighteen years, a dream which has grown in my soul like a bracken weed, which was once a fair bloom. I could walk them in the dark, map them in my sleep, and I swear by God I know them better than I know how to breathe.

"Do not ever ask me again how I know something *about my home*."

Their eyes locked, green on grey. One breath, two, and her pretty face was a study in shifting emotions, confusion and fear and sadness and . . . hate, for all he knew.

She drew herself up, straight as she could. "Then, my lord, I hope you think I have done well by them."

Griffyn's fingers tightened into the fisted rage that had been his only expression of thwarted desire for eighteen years. Done well? *Done well?* She had lived on his lands, ridden her horses o'er his hills, sniffed the breezes of his moors, while he'd been cast adrift in the world of politics and bloodshed, aching for home, and she had this placid, polite nothing to offer in return?

Rage poured through him so hot and rabid he suddenly couldn't see in front of his eyes.

Done well by them?

Gwyn stared in horrified fascination. From forehead to jaw, Griffyn's face was taut, whiplashed with pain. All colour was washed away save for that in his hooded eyes, where a fever burned and blackened the smokey grey to opaque soot. A muscle thudded by his jaw, strained by teeth set so solidly against themselves Gwen thought she could hear enamel chip.

And they were to make a marriage work?

St. Jude, what had she said? That she hoped she had done well by his lands? She'd spoken in the hope of placating him, but all she'd done was send him tripping into a fit of rage. She could do nothing right in his eyes. They were doomed.

Like a petrified rabbit, she held her ground, too scared to flee, too terrified to stay.

He lifted his head—God in Heaven, why make such a comely thing so tortured?—and passed a frigid glance over her face, freezing her blood to ice.

"How old were you when you came to the Nest, Gwyn?" he asked in a low voice. He ran the tip of his finger across the bare skin of her collarbone.

He could have swung a battle-axe at her head and Gwyn would have been less terrified. The dangerous, controlled pitch of his words was blood-chilling. There was nothing more unnerving than this denied restraint. That he could rein in such a fury and bring it to heel bespoke a will so disciplined it sent another shiver down her spine. But most of her focus was on the thick forefinger he was now sliding up the back of her neck.

"I was two, Griffyn," she said in a choked voice.

His hand finished its journey and cupped the back of her head, holding her in a gentle, inescapable capture. "I was eight when I left, Guinevere. And I have ne'er forgotten a thing about it. Or you." His fingers slipped away. "Leave."

"What?"

"Go. Go to your room."

"I have no roo—"

"The solar. *Go*."

"What in perdi—"

"Don't say it," he warned, his eyes glittering danger. He pointed to the door. "Go. Now. While it's safe."

She backed up in tripping steps. Her hands felt behind her for the cool iron of the door handle and wrenched it open. The door swung out so swiftly she tumbled a few steps before righting herself. What had happened? What *was* happening, to him, to her, to both of them together?

Before she turned and ran, she caught one last glimpse of Griffyn. He was standing with his head down, dark hair plastered to his neck, staring at the ground while his hands curled into fists that opened and closed in silent, unknowable depths of anguish.

Chapter Twelve

The storm didn't come, but the winds did. They lashed against the castle and bent huge trees into submission. Small woodland creatures scurried for safety. The night had a curious luminescence, a greenish-black hue, with stark white clouds scuttling against the hectic colouring as if racing for a safe haven. But there was none. The storm looked to stretch for miles, across into Scotland, and they all, clouds and creatures and men, would do best to hunker down and weather it.

Despite the gusting wind, Gwyn didn't close the shutters. A low fire burned in the brazier. She ought go walk on the ramparts. That's what she always did when restless and awake, when she should be well far into sleep.

Having decided, she stood curiously still, breathing in slow, measured breaths. She stared out at the storm, her view restricted by the narrow window frame and the tears threatening under her eyelids.

"Come."

The word rode like low thunder across the room. The sting of tears grew hot. How could his voice hold so much heat, when she was assured what awaited her if she turned around? Cold, frigid recriminations, benumbed rage.

She turned, sending her skirts into a billowing flute around her ankles before settling back to docility. His eyes burned a path through the darkened room.

"My lord?"

"Come back."

She crossed to him without argument, stepping slowly and deliberately, and stopped when she reached his shadowy figure.

"We are nothing but trouble together." Her prediction was soft and tremulous.

His dark head bent into a nod. "Nothing but."

"And yet you would have me with you?"

"I would."

She stepped in front of him and felt his heat at her back all the way down the curving staircase, past the guttering torchlamps, through the cold stone corridors, and into the lord's chambers, silent all the way.

He closed the door behind them, its solid thud forbidding. But Griffyn didn't spare her a look. He turned away and began undressing, not speaking to her at all.

Gwyn wandered to the window and swung open the shutters in time to see a jagged spear of lightning cut across the stormy sky before leaving it to darkness again. A strangely cold wind sneaked through the window. The world smelled close to hand. The odour of the bailey and barns rode up to her nose, and the sweeter, subtle smell of dying grass on the meadows came calm beneath it.

She turned. He was naked, his body a solid swipe of muscle and skin. Only one candle burned. Its flame leapt wildly in the wind.

"Come to bed." When she didn't move, he spoke again, his words heavy. "I will not touch you." He lay down without another word. The only sound was the moaning of the wind.

Maybe it was an hour later, maybe less, when she finally curled into the bed beside him and fell into a dreamless sleep.

* * *

It was still dark when Griffyn awoke. Still lying down, he scanned the bedchamber in his mind. He was home. Everything was as he'd dreamed. And it was hollow, like a gourd scraped and mashed. It was baffling. And infuriating. And he had the vague sense that Guinevere was both part of the reason and most of the cure.

It was almost as if she sensed his thoughts, for she stirred beside him in the bed. She mumbled something, then quieted again.

He looked over at her, tumbled beneath the furs, still clothed, her dress bunched up around her hips, her hair still in pins. A few strands had pulled free and were curled above her head on the pillow, like dark winding roads spied from a hilltop. She shifted again, flinging her hand out. It made contact with his chest but she didn't wake. The back of her hand stayed on his chest for a moment, then slid down to the furs.

What was he to do? Home with a mission denied and a wife who hated him, and he was starting to lose control. Guinevere was far too much woman for this marriage to be tranquil or predictable, but that was not the problem. The problem was, could he keep making the leap between the ledges of passion and respect, humour and hatred, when such dizzying chasms echoed below?

And if not, then what?

More to the point, the problem was, she was de l'Ami's daughter, and he did not know if he could ever forgive her for that.

But he wanted to. Enough cold remove, enough of wanting and never finding. Guinevere was everything he'd never known to wish for.

He rolled to his feet and pulled on his chausses. The air was cold. He placed another piece of wood on the fire and walked to the window. The shutters were swung wide, and he stepped into the stream of chalky light triangulated on the floor, leaning his shoulder against the wall. He stared out. The winds had passed, giving no rain, but leaving the world reverent and hushed in their wake.

He must have stood there for half an hour. Only twice did he move, both times to glance at the bed. A candle flame flared up, crackling fiercely before settling into a steady burn. The stream of white moonlight moved slowly across the floor.

"Griffyn?"

He didn't turn.

"My lord?"

He angled his head slightly in her direction.

"Is all well?"

The question was so sweeping, the realm of possible answers so vast, he had a sudden urge to laugh. Instead, he nodded.

"Sometimes when I cannot sleep, I walk the walls."

Her voice was quiet but her words had none of the indolence of sleep. He looked over his shoulder. "How often do you find the need to disturb the sentries?"

"Often."

He turned the rest of his body and crossed his arms over his chest.

"Oft enough that they have told me I must bring them something from the kitchen each time I do," she said softly. "Thus I pay for my disturbance."

He flicked his eyes to the window again. "The storm does not come."

He heard the soft rustle of furs. "Will you walk with me, my lord?"

She was standing in her rumpled green gown, her hair in utter disarray and falling down her back. He pushed off from the wall.

Wordlessly he picked up his shirt and tunic and threw them over his head, then sat on the edge of the bed and began pulling on his boots. Gwyn was sitting on the other side, putting on her own shoes. He could feel the bed dip and shift in small movements each time she bent over. His side of the mattress lowered more significantly when she rose, and he glanced over his shoulder.

Her back was to him. The loose sleeves of her tunic fell up around her shoulders when she bent her arms and fumbled with her hair to reassemble the mess of curls and knots.

"Don't."

Her hair spilled down over her shoulders as she simply dropped her hands and walked to the door. It was a brief climb to the doorway that led to the rooftop. The night was chilled, crisp and clear and full. Griffyn held the door for her, his arm stretched over her head as she ducked beneath him and stepped out onto the northern ramparts.

"God's in His Heaven when I am up here," she murmured, pulling her cape around her shoulders.

Griffyn ran his palm along the wall as they walked, feeling its cold solidness against his skin. It was a good castle, a good home. He let his gaze drift across the open plains. Curving in a smooth arc from west to east was a darkness that heralded the forests. But the trees were far ahead, and closer to hand stretched open fields and meadows, brown and russet in the darkness.

Further down, below the crest his army camped on, he could see the darkened humps of village buildings. He thought he could make out the farthest one, the apothecary shop. It was one of two places he had most loved as a boy. The stables and the leech, he mused. Horses and herbs.

A sudden memory leapt to mind. He'd been young, wandering on horseback on a lazy autumn evening after a hard day's ride, his beloved pony Rebel under him, his dog Tor at his side. The smells of heather, dying evergreen needles, and the distant sea had been pungent, making him linger in the woods even when the sky began to turn purple. His father would be furious, his mother worried, but Griffyn didn't turn his pony back yet. He was eight years old and set free upon the world. His father might have spawned him, his mother might have borned him, but 'twas this land that pulsed through his blood.

He'd paused his pony in the river. He could still feel the bones of Rebel's withers between his legs, the flat, firm feel of equine shoulder blades under his knees as the pony bent his muzzle into the cold water. Tor did the same, lunging into the water and splashing his reluctant playmate, barking and leaping in circles around the snow-white pony. Angling a dark, liquid brown eye at the nuisance, the pony swept her hoof through the burbling creek, drowning the puppy in an unexpected wave of water. The dog squeaked in amazement and sat down in the middle of the stream, puppy face dripping with water, utterly brought to heel. Griffyn had laughed aloud. He remembered knowing, even as a child, his life, at that moment, was as perfect as it might ever be.

"I used to feel that way too," he finally said.

The longing in his words drew Gwyn's gaze, but she didn't speak. They walked across the ramparts from west to east, silent. The sentries they passed nodded wordlessly, and the only sound was the wind sighing at the stones and an owl winging down from a tree branch to chase a hare racing across the field.

By unspoken agreement, they stopped near a merlon and let the wind pull at their capes. The moon was close to setting. Potent energy crouched both in the night and in the man beside her. Gwyn looked out over the distant hills, hills that she'd always thought of as her own.

Upon a time, there had been no question of what had gone before her, of how many other eyes had once passed over the lands and seen what she saw, felt what she felt. There had been no past, no connection to anything larger or other. What was had always been. But now everything was changed.

Griffyn had haunted these ramparts too, perhaps balanced on the stones in a perilous display of courageous idiocy as she had at seven years old, until her mother had pulled her down, holding Gwyn with one hand, her heart with the other.

Griffyn had walked these ramparts long before she had, ridden across the moors and felt the breeze at his back, just like she had.

Griffyn had surely watched sunrises from here, and laughed at thunderstorms, feeling secure in the bulwark of solid stone that lay underfoot. Just like she had.

What a sad place the world was, spinning itself out while people played at God. If she were taken from this place, her heart would break into a hundred jagged pieces, sharp edges of sorrow that would poke at her forever. This was her home.

And it was his too.

"I am sorry," she said dully.

The dark head beside her lifted. He'd been resting his chin on his outstretched arms and staring across the plains, but at the sound of her voice, he turned.

"Sorry for what?"

"For all of this." She swept her hand in a wide arc, indicating the world around them.

He paused. "For the nighttime, or just the fields?"

His gentle jest confused her. "For the wars, for the taking and losing." She waved her hand. "For what was done to you, because you had to leave this beautiful place."

A tear spilled over and sped down her face.

"Why, lady," he said in surprise, stepping closer. "'Tisn't your fault. I mayn't act it at times, but I do know that much."

"But if ever *I* was forced to leave," she explained through the tears that were now tumbling down her cheeks, "I would be so heartsick I think I might die."

He looked at the tears, then back into her eyes. "Indeed, I thought I might. But I didn't, and I am home again."

"And I am *glad*," she said almost viciously, gritting her teeth. To snatch one small moment of happiness amid all the sorrow of the world was but a small victory, but good, and she felt possessive of it as she had towards Jerv earlier, only this was more primal.

"You are glad?"

"I am glad," she vowed in a harsh whisper. "In all this wreck of a world, that one man can return to his home, 'tis a thing goodly beyond imagining, and I am *glad*."

Grey eyes roamed her tear-stained face. "Well, lady, you have astonished me once again."

"Again?"

"Again. As you did outside London, as you did in the bailey, as you did at dinner. I have known you for the length of two days, and you have already given me more to think about than a year of campaigns."

She gave a watery laugh. "Mayhap that is because there is not much to think about in a battle. Strike here, trample there. Let me see," she pretended to muse, resting her chin on her curled fingers, "would it be better to cut his heart out, or stick his head on a spike?" She dropped her hand. "These are not the kinds of things I would think would greatly tax one with a mind."

"But you," he said, reaching out to run the pad of his thumb along her jaw, "will tax me greatly, I suppose."

"I will try not to."

"Don't."

"Don't?"

He shook his head, a dark swing in the night air. "Just be what you are. I think I will enjoy getting to know you."

Whoever I am is changing swiftly, she decided, *for I have never felt like this before. Except when I was with you.*

His beautiful, chiseled features were dark and dangerous, the scar slashed across his cheek even more so. Whenever he moved the slightest bit, a ripple of rock-hewn flesh disturbed the soft material of his tunic. But this she had steeled herself against when he first arrived, his raw masculinity. It could never have turned her heart. It was his eyes that were her undoing. His battered, beautiful eyes.

"Griffyn. I did not . . ."

"Did not what?"

She stared out over the battlement wall. "Did not mean for them to capture you."

He absorbed this in silence. Then, "What?"

"I did not send them after you, Marcus and his men. 'Twas a terrible accident. I did not tell them your name apurpose, nor where you were."

"You didn't?"

She shook her head, still looking over the wall. "I tried to . . ."

"You tried to what?"

"Stop them," she said in a voice so small he could not possibly have heard unless he was standing directly at her back. Which he was.

"You tried to stop them," he repeated softly. His fingertip brushed against the sensitive skin at the base of her neck.

She inhaled sharply.

"Why?"

She shook her head. "I don't know. I don't know anything anymore."

His mouth pressed against the nape of her neck. Hot shivers danced out across her skin, like stars. "I know one thing, Raven."

"What?" she squeaked, because his fingers had slid around her waist.

"You're going to like what I'm about to do to you."

Chapter Thirteen

She turned to him just as a gust of wind blew through the embrasure they stood beside. Inside the billowing hood of de l'Ami green spun a sea of ebony curls, framing her upturned face, her cheeks beginning to blush pink from his words.

Griffyn slipped his hand into the warm nest of silk and flesh and cupped the nape of her neck. This intelligent, complicated woman who fairly pulsed with passion was going to be his wife. And suddenly, that did not seem so terrible a thing.

He laced his fingers through her hair, tipped her head back, and kissed her very gently. She shifted, leaned her head back, and opened for him.

There was nothing else to wait for. He deepened the kiss at once, no longer teasing or testing, but taking possession. His blood was charging, hot and slow. His tongue lashed at her, drawing out small whimpers and pants, inflaming him further.

His hands moved restlessly over her body, slipping into the curve of her waist, cupping her rounded bottom, pushing up her spine. And every move he made, Gwyn bent into it, her hands running over his shoulders and chest with equal fervor.

He crowded her against the wall, groaning as he nipped at her lips and neck. Her breath exploded out in a hot rush. Restrained power vibrated in the muscular thighs trapping her against the wall. A pulsing, wicked heat was pounding in her groin, her body aching for more. Slow and hot, the greedy little urges started pulsing between her thighs, making her push her hips forward into his.

"Not here," he said hoarsely, and grabbed her hand.

How long it took to get back to their room, Gwyn had no idea. If they passed sentries, she didn't know it. If the castle had caught fire and was burning, she wouldn't have felt it; her own body was ignited into flaming heat.

But when they entered the bedchamber, everything came into heightened awareness. The low burning fire, the faint scent of wood smoke, one candle still guttering in its holder. The way her skirts rustled against her thighs. The way he was looking at her.

"I am not in an easy way tonight, Guinevere," he rasped.

"We have ne'er had an easy way of it yet, Griffyn. Just let us be."

Still standing a foot away, he trailed his fingertips up one side of her body, from hip to arm. It was like a sudden gust of fire, the faint testing of a lion's claw, restrained and dangerous and only the start. He shifted his hand to the front of her body and did the same long, possessive sweep up, belly to breast. Her body unraveled as if it was uncoiling, her spine arching, her chin coming up, her head dropping to the side, her lips parting, her breath hot and slow.

Griffyn watched her, expressionless. But inside he was burning. His hardness pulsed and demanded release. In her. Slowly, as if he were offering communion, he pressed his thumb to her lips. She opened her lips a fraction wider and ran her teeth across his skin.

He clamped the back of her spine and jerked her to him. "Do you remember what I did to you before?" he asked roughly. His tongue flicked along the sensitive skin behind her earlobe, "At the inn?"

He felt her nod.

"I'm going to do it again." She sighed, a small, desperate sound. "And more."

He swiftly unlaced her gown, his fingers flying over the tattered silken ties, then pulled it over her head. Dropping his hand under the collar of the chemise, he scooped the cool weight of her breasts into his hands, pulling them over the top of the thin fabric. Her skin was cool under his hot hands, and he tore the flimsy fabric open from neck to knee, leaving the temptress's body exposed for his pleasure. Creamy skin, midnight silken hair, lush curves, ripe for a man's touch, and small red buds puckering, awaiting him.

He went down on his knees. He ran the flat of his hand across her straining belly and up to her breasts until she arched back, pushing out to him. Encasing her hips in his hands, he pushed her back into the wall, hard. One hand roamed her body freely, running down her leg, behind her knee, up her silky inner thigh. The other hand held her hips tight against the wall. She put her head back, her eyes closed. But he wanted her to watch. Watch what he was going to do to her.

"Look at me, Raven."

She dragged her face down. Dark hair streamed in rampant curls around her slender shoulders, down to her hips, and her heavy-lidded green eyes invited him to push her further. Her red lips were parted, her chest heaving, and her fingers slowly entwining in his hair.

With his elbow he nudged on her inner thigh, coaxing her to open for him. She did. She parted her legs with him kneeling at her feet. He slid a hand under to cup her buttocks. Leaning forward, he ran his tongue along the hot, wet seam of her womanhood.

Her body bucked into his deft hands. "Griffyn, no!"

He clamped his palm harder and pulled her forward. He licked again, pressing the tip of his tongue in a little further. Her fingers clenched in his hair. "Oh, no," she moaned, but this time her hips pressed forward, into his touch. His. Surrendered. Dizzy with victory, he slid his hand up and glided gently along the hot, pink seam, plied back her folds with his thumb and licked again, the smallest, fastest, tautest lick, right at the apex of her womanhood.

She erupted in a howl of such pleasure he almost spilled himself. He moved in again, sweeping his tongue against her in rhythmic strokes that made her writhe against the wall. His hands gripped her hips while he licked at her and whispered, asking her questions she couldn't answer, speaking forbidden words of desire against her flesh, driving her to a mindless state of craving, her body quivering beneath his touch. Small helpless whimpers and moans slipped out of her passion-torn body, hot, wet breathy things.

He spread her apart with his fingers and nuzzled deeper into the hot, slippery cave of pulsing pink flesh. Her strangled cries and pleadings grew louder. Licking and stroking, he let one, then two, fingers slip inside. Spreading her legs further, he stroked her with a third. She flung her head back so hard it hit the wall, her fingers restlessly tugging in his hair, a whimpering-wet goddess of passion.

Another slippery, pressured push came from his fingers deep inside, and Gwyn felt something start building in huge wakes. It shuddered in a slow wave through her womb, her legs, her head, her everything. It snaked in wicked ribbons up her back and down her legs and pushed at her, rolling her towards some cliff.

She arched her head back and wound her fingers more tightly in his hair. *"Oh, Griffyn."*

"Does it please you?"

Her gaze was locked in his as he ran his tongue across her again, and nudged his thick, wet fingers up inside her further, curling them at the tips.

"Ah, Griffyn, aye . . . *aye* . . ." she howled in a throaty cry as the pounding wave crashed and exploded and rocked her inside out. She fell and fell and tumbled into a river of such perfect pleasure she almost died. It was everywhere and everything, rampaging, wicked redemption.

Griffyn watched her come apart. Her head was thrown back, her face contorted in pleasure, her body shuddering against him in helpless spasms as she cried his name over and over, her wetness sliding against him, her fingers tugging helplessly at his hair, and she shuddered down the wall in a frenzied, moaning heap of kissing, panting, furious femininity. He could barely get his arms around her as she kissed him and sucked his lips and raked her nails along his back, wild and wanton and perfectly woman.

Somehow he dragged them to their feet and pushed her onto the closest object, which praise God was their bed, he thought dimly, because he'd have taken her in a water trough if that had been nearer.

He pushed her onto the mattress and knelt over her, ripping off his clothes. He lowered himself, stretched out over her, and ripped open the thin linen shift he hadn't got off before. Then he rested one elbow on either side of her head.

"You're mine," he whispered hoarsely, and closed her nipple between his teeth. Her breath exploded out of her as he flicked the nub with his tongue, still clenching it gently within his sharp teeth. He flicked again, harder and faster, his teeth an erotic danger just shy of pain, and she shuddered off the bed, up into his arms.

It was exquisite torture, holding her there, vibrating halfway into rapture. He released her breast and nipped a searing path down her belly and back up to the other, sucking her whole breast into his mouth while sliding his hand down her leg. He cupped her knee from the underside and bent it, pushing it out and down towards the mattress.

"Now the other one, Gwyn," he rumbled, licking a path of wet heat up her neck to her ear.

Her breath exploded out of her, around a heated whisper of his name.

"Spread your legs for me," the masculine growl came from beside her ear.

Her breath exploded out of her. She bent her other knee and let it fall down towards the mattress. Now she was nothing but open territory.

He positioned himself between her trembling thighs. "You are mine," he growled again, then thrust into her. It was a single, slow, determined onslaught. Her tight, slippery sex closed around the length of him, pulsing and pulling him in deeper. "Mine."

"Aye," she panted. "Yours."

He thrust again, another long, slow penetration.

"Griffyn," she moaned, her head twisting back and forth, her eyes half-closed in drugged lust. Her body rocked into his, her hips thrusting up and down, her nails bit into his forearm, returning his damaging passion measure for measure.

Their lovemaking was as fierce as anything Griffyn had ever known, battle or rage or fear. Occasionally their lips crossed one another, but mostly it was a hot, hard thing, their union more about possession and being possessed than tender affection. It was a damaging rhythm.

His head lowered, his forehead almost on her chest, he surged into her again and again, filling her, pushing her wide. Her panting became rhythmic, her thrusting hips more fierce. Release barreled down for him. He plunged deeper, pushing higher. Suddenly she froze.

"Oh my," she whispered.

He lifted his head. Her green eyes were locked on his. He smiled.

Inside of Gwyn, something shivered free. *Oh, thank-you-God, that fine, perilous half-smile. He is smiling at me again.*

He pushed in further, lifted his hips and tilted himself up. A shower of sparks sprayed across her back and belly. It surged up the back of her legs. Again he moved inside her, deeper, probing into something. . . .

"Oh, Jésu," she cried out.

His dark head was thrown back, the muscles in his neck taut, and when he moved this time, his palm was wrapped around her hip, holding her up as he pounded into her, and her body exploded. She shuddered upwards in stunning eruptions of fire, her womb clenching and releasing of its own accord, her muscles joined with his in an ancient dance. She howled her pleasure to the sky, to his ears, chanting his name. The earth shuddered beneath her, shaking her down to her bones, and Griffyn was above her, suddenly roaring her name too, driving her onwards further until the pleasure became an exquisite pain and she screamed and reveled in the shudders of her body as it exploded again and again, wasting her.

It felt like forever they lay there, reeling. Her head was awash, whirling and harmonized. The blood was roaring in her head and Griffyn's uneven breath was close by her ear. He was lying atop her, collapsed on her, but his weight was not oppressive, but comforting. He smelled musky and warm, and she knew a sudden, intense experience of belonging she'd never known before.

"Can you breathe?" His muffled voice drifted through her hair, warm against her neck.

She tightened her hands around his waist. He pressed his lips against her neck and said in a pleasant low rumble, "I think, mayhap, we can make this work."

She laughed sleepily.

"When do we start having babies?"

She chuckled again, and hugged him tighter. "Yesterday."

"Too long."

For a while they spoke in soft murmurs, speaking of simple things, small nothings, favourite places and childhood friends. Sleep crept in and they closed their eyes, bodies entangled in their sweaty embrace, and they fell asleep that way, never moving apart.

She woke up screaming.

Griffyn was rolling for his sword before his eyes were open, but he quickly realised the sounds came from Guinevere, who was sitting bolt upright in the bed. He reached over and pulled her to him.

"Hush," he murmured into her hair, right by her ear, a calm, intent sound to bring her back to consciousness. The screaming and flailing subsided, but her body stayed as rigid as a door post. "'Twas but a dream. Hush," he said over and over. Finally, she looked up.

"Oh, Griffyn," she whispered. "'Twas terrible. I dreamt of Papa."

Freeing one arm, he pushed a grip of pillows to the headboard. He tugged her over and onto his lap, so she sat between his thighs. She leaned against his chest.

"Tell me of them."

"The dreams?"

"Aye."

She peered up from between a few locks of her tousled black hair, her eyes saturated with fear and sadness. "Truly?"

"Truly."

"H-he came to me," she said, tears catching her voice. "He is always so pale, and without strength, lying there barely conscious. Like a wraith." Her voice was becoming flat and ephemeral, her words rote and dream-like. "His face is turned towards me, his eyes open as wide as they are able, staring at me. I keep seeing those images, at his last moment, clear as if they were before me now."

"But they are not, Raven," he said in a firm but gentle tone. He rubbed his hand across her shoulders and arms, pulling her back. "You are here now, with me, and 'tis over."

She looked at him blankly for a second, then nodded. "You are right. But, I keep hearing him."

"What does he say?" he asked, soothing her, trying to calm her fluttering heartbeat against his chest.

Her eyes were bright with tears in the moonlight. She swallowed. "'Wud guh,'" she repeated the eerie sounds. "'Wud. Guh. Saw.'"

She shook her head in confusion. "It was all so slow and laboured, I could not make the words out, just sounds. I have thought about it a hundred times, but they never mean anything." She balled her fist and hit it lightly against the bedcovers. "Then he said 'vayyy,' and carried the sound out." Her brow furrowed. "As if it were a chant or something. Then his voice trailed off, and that was the last thing he ever said to me: 'Vay. Sal.' Then he died."

Griffyn went still. She must have detected the change in him, because she looked over. "Do you know what it means?"

He shook his head, but his arms had tightened reflexively when he'd heard the last phrase. *Vay. Sal.*

Vessel.

"Was that all, Gwyn?" he asked carefully.

She nodded miserably. "That was it. Even the priest gave Extreme Unction while he was benumbed. For years he barely spoke to me, then, there at the last, that is what he came up with."

She straightened herself on his lap more comfortably, and he moved his arm unconsciously to support her. His head was spinning as he tried to focus on her fear and grief, rather than on the first hint he'd had of the treasure's existence at Everoot. So something *was* here. What chance Ionnes de l'Ami would speak of a 'Vessel' on his deathbed, if there was not something real to be spoken of?

He kissed the top of her head. "Can you sleep now?"

She nodded, but he tightened his arms when she would

have slipped off his lap. "Tell me of such dreams when you have them again."

She sighed. "I am sorry for the nighttime vigils you'll be forced to keep."

He kissed her forehead, then her nose. "I do not mind. Tell me if you recall anything else your father might have said."

Wary surprise filled her eyes. "You would hear what my father had to say?"

He shook his head. "The power of his words will go if you speak of them, that is all."

She nodded, but tears started filling her eyes again. "I do not think they will ever leave me. They have haunted me for so long already."

So, he pulled her down beside him and made her forget the whispered words of a dying man. Later, as she drifted off, she murmured in his ear, "I will tell you anything I remember, Griffyn."

He turned onto his back, hands behind his head, and lay awake for a long time, his mind turning. How likely was it that Ionnes de l'Ami had believed in legends too? How likely that he had shaped his life, then ended it, intent on a lie?

His heart started thudding a little faster as he stared at the ceiling. What harm could come from simply looking?

Chapter Fourteen

He began the next morning. It was not the only thing he did, nor even the first, but neither was it the last, and he was grimly aware of that.

Slowly, methodically, before the grey light of a mercifully damp dawn lightened the horizon, he was in the offices. A huge tumble of chests and coffers sat on the hard stone floor, rounded lids musty with dampness and pollen and dead bugs. Griffyn shoved several cone-handled torches into the iron rings hanging from the walls and started flinging them open. Each bang of wood against stone or metal bounced off the walls and came back at him, hollow and loud.

He pulled out a sheaf of documents from the first one. A sinking feeling rose inside his chest. Would this speak of the treasure? Would he even recognise it as such?

That is where he needed to rely on Alex. Trained and educated in the ancient mysteries, Alex was a Watcher, one of those who guarded the Guardian. He knew every nuance of Griffyn's unwanted heritage, every rumour, secret, or legend about Charlemagne and the legacy and what Griffyn was supposed to be. Griffyn carried the papers close to the torch and stood beneath its flickering light, reading.

A long time later, as the dim murmur of Prime bells

penetrated the stone walls of the office chamber, every chest had been open and searched. They'd dispensed nothing but old ledgers and deeds, signed with an *X* by men who'd regarded themselves as mighty, then died like everyone else.

Almost stunned, Griffyn sat back on the stone floor, spine against the wall. He planted the heel of one boot into an uneven edge of flagstone and stared across the icy, empty room. Coldness pressed through his woollen hose.

The rounded lids of the coffers were like flung open like yawning mouths, a dozen of them, baby birds waiting to be fed. Griffyn felt dirty. He'd have been better off as a fisherman. A blacksmythe. Anything but a nobleman.

He got to his feet and brushed himself off. He needed to talk to Alex.

They went up on the battlements in the misting rain just as the guard switched. From far down on the fields, and in the bailey below, rose the sounds of men as they began their daily labours, voices conversing, iron hitting stone, a cock crowing. Up here on the battlements, though, it was all muted, with only the light misting rain to sluice down around them. Tired men in damp hauberks lifted their hands in greeting as they passed inside.

Once they were alone, Griffyn said, "I've been looking around a bit."

Alex kept looking over the battlements. So did Griffyn. "And what did you find?"

"Nothing. But then, I suspect there will be locks my key will not open. Is that not so? I have a puzzle key, don't I?"

He could see Alex nod out of the corner of his eye. "There are three keys, each set inside the others. Yours is the iron one, the outer key."

"And inside?"

"A steel key, and a small gold one at the centre."

Griffyn turned his head slowly. "Why haven't you told me this before?"

Alex looked over too, and lifted his eyebrows. "I didn't know you were looking. You almost took my head off once, for even suggesting it." He paused. "Why didn't you get me?"

Griffyn shrugged. "I wanted to be alone."

"I see. Why, of a sudden?"

He shrugged again. "Lady Gwyn spoke of a dream, things her father said."

"You trust Ionnes de l'Ami and not your own father?"

Griffyn leaned his shoulder against a merlon and kicked one foot in front of the other, toe resting on the stone walkway. "I don't trust anyone, Alex, except you. For certes not either of the men who were ruined by it."

Alex was quiet for a minute. "Greed does motivate men, Griffyn," he said quietly. "But so do other things."

Griffyn looked out over the valley of the Nest. Mist was glistening off the russet and flaming gold leaves of the majestic oak tree that grew in the exact centre of the valley floor. Its leafy crown marked the hub of almost every castle event of the year. Hallmote, fairs, and summer courts were held there. Bonfires burned near its arching branches during the old pagan rituals his father had never seen fit to forbid. In the distance, men were trudging off to the fields. A faint scent of the sea slipped under the nearer smells of hay and wet stone and leather.

He rested his palms on the knobbly stone battlement wall. A wife could motivate a man, he supposed. Or a family.

"Stephen is going to sign a treaty with Henri," was what he said, though.

Alex paused, adjusting to the new course of their conversation. "I thought I saw another messenger come early this morn. So, Stephen will surrender."

"A few weeks at most."

"*Bien*. The war will end."

Griffyn ran his hand over his jaw. Stubble was already beginning to roughen the surface he'd shaved clean for the feast. "In most of England, maybe. I still have to tell Guinevere."

Alex gave an obligatory laugh, and Griffyn looked over.

"You needn't indulge me as regards Guinevere, Alex. I know you don't like her."

"'Tisn't that, Pagan. As far as I can see, she is brave and stalwart, commendable as a lady and a leader. 'Tisn't that I don't like her. I don't trust her."

Griffyn was quiet a moment, then gestured to the wall. "Aubrey the Mason is coming. He and his men will be here by the Sabbath."

Alex smiled. "The walls will be rebuilt by Yule—"

"—the castle by Easter," he finished with grim satisfaction, then looked over Alex's shoulder. Guinevere was coming through the misty morning. She was smiling. At him. The tight centre of his chest lightened a little. Still pleased, but not so savage or furious.

"Better than even my father had done."

Guinevere woke up and sat in the bed, taking a layer of furs with her. The room was empty, but a fire burned in the brazier. It was wonderfully chilly. It was also rather late in the morning, judging by the brightness of the pearly light. And yet, if so, why so grey? She shook her head, trying to clear it.

"My lady?"

Mary, her serving maid, was laying a bundle of wood by the brazier. Wood. They needed a fire. It was cool enough to need a fire. She smiled.

"Would you want help dressing?"

Gwyn shook her head.

"You'll be wanting to go to chapel, but Father Wessen is away at the village, seeing to Grania."

"She's ill again?" Gwyn asked distractedly.

"Aye. So, he said to tell you there won't be mass this morning—"

"Where is he?"

"Father Wessen?" She gave a confused look. "Forgive, my lady, but as I was saying—"

"Lord Griffyn."

"Oh." The young maid smiled as she reached to add another stick to the flames.

"Well?" Gwyn asked again, eyeing the maidservant dismally. Perhaps she *had* been a bit lax in her administration.

"He's about. He's been everywhere, my lady. The men are in the fields, and up on the walls."

"On the walls?"

"Aye. Repairs, my lady. They're fixing up the walls a'ready. They say a mason's coming, if ye can believe it."

Gwyn lay back in the bed and hugged the furs to her chest. Mary looked over with a smile.

"And it's raining."

They stared at each other for a moment, then Gwyn flew out of the bed, furs around her shoulders. *"Raining?"*

Mary's head bobbed. "Raining, a lovely sort of mist that'll soak deep into the ground, it will."

"Rain," Gwyn breathed, dragging the pelts behind as she went to the window. Indeed, rain. A solid sheet of light mist covered the world in a pearly shroud. Rain. The drought was over.

She dressed in under two minutes and ran down to the hall. Each step on the winding staircase was more excited than the last, although she didn't have to admit the reason until she reached the hall and Griffyn was not there.

He'd be outside. In the rain.

She took off so quickly an approaching servant blinked in surprise, then headed back to the kitchens with the tray of bread and ale.

She climbed to the battlements and found Griffyn ten minutes later, talking with Alex along one of the loneliest stretches of the endless curtain wall. He had a shoulder propped against one of the towering stone merlons, arms crossed over his chest, smiling. A flood of affection crowded into her heart.

He caught sight of her over Alex's shoulder. He continued talking, but now his eyes were on her. When she reached them, he stepped back a bit to allow her in.

"My lady."

"My lord," she murmured, then turned to respond to Alex's polite greeting.

"'Tis raining," she said softly and, if truth be told, a trifle stupidly. For her first words since their . . . last night, they were not terribly *absorbing* things.

Griffyn did not seem to mind. A corner of his mouth crooked up lazily and her world slipped into slow motion. She felt a blush begin in her cheeks.

The soft rain barely made a sound. Pungent scents were carried low on its back: wetness and worms and woodsmoke, and long, elusive trails of the sea. She leaned her face up and let the mist fall on it for a moment, then straightened, suddenly self-conscious. They were watching her.

"It smells good," she explained. The men sniffed obligingly.

"It smells different from Normandy," Alex allowed slowly.

Griffyn was still watching her. "Come," he said in a low-pitched voice that sent ripples of completely unnecessary desire pulsing through her blood. "Look at the walls."

She leaned over the wall. Forty soaring feet of ashlar stone lay in crumbles for half the length of the wall. Papa had had the money but not the time. Gwyn had possessed neither. The accompanying defensive tower was sixty feet of tumbling stone. Together they posed more danger to a passerby than a besieging army.

"The masons are coming," Griffyn said quietly, pointing. "The tower, the chapel, will be rebuilt."

She smiled.

"And over there," he swept his arm northwards. "We'll build the kitchens."

"We have kitchens, Griffyn."

"We have old kitchens. Wooden kitchens. I am talking about

stone. I've seen your cook. I've tasted her food. Her meals are awe-inspiring, her method is chaotic beyond reason."

"She's . . . enthusiastic," Gwyn allowed.

"She's terrifying."

She laughed.

"We'll have guests, Gwyn. Many. Your staff needs a new kitchen. We'll rebuild."

She nodded. The smile would not leave her face. "They do need that, you're right."

He leaned his forearms on the wall and clasped his hands together, looking out over the misty valley. "It will be strong again."

"It will be wonderful," she agreed in soft pride, then glanced at Alex. He was watching them, his eyes unreadable but certainly not friendly. She turned and gave a brief curtsey to Griffyn. "I will not disturb you any longer. My lord. Sir Alex."

She turned and continued walking to the southernmost turret, knowing, knowing, *knowing* he would follow.

She walked to the edge of the sixty-foot tower and tilted her face up to catch the moisture falling in gentle sheets over the land. She might never go back inside again. She would just stay here, in the misting rain, and wait for Griffyn, if she had to wait a hundred years.

Chapter Fifteen

Griffyn barely waited a full minute before he took off after her. When he reached the top, she was leaning back, arms behind her, palms resting on the top of the wall.

Beads of mist clung to her hair. A cloak was clasped at her neck. She wore a simple, demure dress and undertunic with long, tight sleeves, but the wetness of the day was moulding the white fabric tight against her skin. The round heaviness of her breasts was outlined, the small nubs straining against the material as she shivered and smiled.

A brisk breeze shot up the side of the walls, tossing her hair in airy strands of black silk. "Can you feel it? It's like silver in the air!" she called out.

Instead of replying, he turned and called to Alex. Gwyn watched as he went halfway down the stairs and crouched on them to speak with Alex, who had climbed midway to meet him. Griffyn rose, clapped Alex on his shoulder, and came back to the tower.

He walked towards her. Wordless, he caught her face between his hands, bent his head, and kissed her so she thought she would die from the tenderness. Like a breeze, he passed his lips over hers, two kisses, three, then slowly, painfully slow, he explored her mouth, her lips, her teeth, lighting fires in Gwyn's body everywhere she already ached to be touched.

She wrapped her hands around his waist, reveling in the feel of his body standing before her, hard and sturdy. His kiss deepened, and he walked her backwards, the front of his thighs pushing against the front of hers. Away from any prying eyes, he crowded her up against the curve of the stone tower, his hands hot and searching. Everywhere he touched burned, everywhere he had yet to touch ached.

"No," she gasped.

"Aye," he growled in her ear. Faster came the throbbing heat between her thighs, cords of wet, snapping lust that lashed at her and sent her body bucking against him.

"No," she protested weakly. "Not here."

"Alex is guarding the stairs."

"Pagan, no!"

He lifted his head. "Why, only last night 'twas 'Griffyn,'" he said with a twisted grin. "Have I lost so much in a day?"

She shook her head, fumbling for the skirt hem, trying to tug it down again. He pulled her up against him, his eyes holding hers with that strange absence of emotion. Intent and distant, it was a look that twined around her heart. He ran the back of his knuckle down her cheek. "You are so beautiful."

His hands closed over hers, his palms warm against the backs of her hands as he slowly made her curl her own fingers around the skirts and lift. The fabric bunched beneath their enjoined hands. With a gentle, irresistible pressure, he made her lift it higher. Cool air brushed over her knees. A hot tightening came between her thighs. His hands left hers and slid further up her leg to grip her hips, bare under the dress.

Moisture glittered in droplets on his dark hair as he lowered his head to her neck and grazed the sensitive skin with his teeth. Her breath shot out in a rush. Down her spine went a shiver, bolting across her breasts and belly.

"You want it too, Gwyn, don't you?" he asked in a husky rumble.

"God in Heaven," she whispered, feeling surrender reach for her, drag her under.

"Don't you?" he whispered, taunting her with her own raging need. "'Tis why you came looking for me, isn't it?"

He pressed her against the wall with his body, pushing her legs apart with his knee, bending her head back with his lips. In a smooth, practiced, breathtaking move, he lifted her up so she was astride his muscular thighs, her legs dangling on either side. He shifted and unlaced his codpiece. It fell away, leaving his arousal throbbing between them. Hot, like a velvet rod, he fell on her and she threw her head back. Her hands entwined around his neck and her body began moving, sliding against him as small explosions of heat sent her dizzy. His fingers searched along her folds and came away drenched.

With a smile damaging to her sanity, he looked at her. "Do not tell me no when your body says 'aye.'"

In a perfect move, he slid himself inside her with a satisfied growl. He pressed his palms against the stone above her head. She was supported by the wall and his powerful thighs, held between his arms. She ran her fingers down the wet fabric that clung to his torso, feeling muscles flexed with exertion. Her head dropped against the wall, dying in watching him. He was a magnificent beast in his sexual prime, all his impressive skill focused on her. His head was thrown back, eyes closed, neck straining as he moved deeper inside her, sending wave and after wave of wicked pleasure shuddering through her body.

Suddenly he looked down, fixing her in his unfathomable eyes. He leaned his torso back slightly, lifted his hips in a long, slow slide, tilting her pelvis out from the wall. Locking their gazes, he lifted his throbbing erection into her higher.

"Would you like a fair?"

"What?"

"A market, a fair. Here at the castle."

She tried to focus, but he was keeping up a slow, steady rhythm of thrusts and the way she straddled him, his length never left her much. He was a constant, perfect pressure deep inside her, nudging her up into the second circle of sexual bliss. Tormenting her by making her talk.

"No fairs here for years," she managed to gasp.

"I know there's been none, Gwyn. I'm asking if you would like one."

Another slow penetration. The shudders passed down to her thighs before could she respond. "Very much."

He bent by her face and lapped a path of hot desire from her shoulder to her ear. "They'll be here for the wedding."

"Who?"

"The merchants. And artisans. A fair, a celebration, to fill the week after our wedding."

"Griffyn, there's no one—"

"There are many. And they're coming to line the Nest. For you. Would you like that?"

In years past there had been fairs and markets at the Nest, great, rambling, festive affairs that brought merchants and peasants from miles around. Weekly markets, special markets, and a great annual fair come Yuletide, when no one could get anything fresh and the luster of summer was but a faint memory, and the whole world, it seemed, crowded into the Nest and, for a time, there'd be peace in the world.

But that had all stopped years ago. The wars had been too long, the money too short. Then Papa died. And for too many seasons the booths had been empty, the fields that once rang with the hawking of wares and the laughter of children were silent.

Could he bring that back too?

He was transforming her world. Everything was different. Every part of her, body, mind, soul was being touched, stilling old aches and stoking new fires.

She dropped her forehead onto his shoulder. "Aye," she murmured. "I would like it very much."

"Bien," he said into her hair, then lifted his hips again. Deep inside her, he touched something, pushed into some deranged region of erotic pleasure that sent her bucking between him and the wall.

"Griffyn, please," she moaned.

"Tell me what you want," he whispered in her ear. "Say it."

"Please," she was crying now, her body trembling at the edge of a sheer cliff, begging to jump. He slowed his pace.

"Say it," he growled in her ear, his voice low and husky as he thrust into her again, burrowing into the sensitive, pulsing flesh high inside. Waves of pleasure rippled down her back, shot through her spine, charged along the backs of her legs.

Clinging to his shoulders, her head fell back as her body bounced with the cadence of his penetration. His hands were tight on her hips as he immersed himself in her, fierce and possessive, thrusting and hard.

"Griffyn." It was a pant, begging for release.

"Tell me, Gwyn."

She whispered the words he taught her last night, "Make me come," and then she tumbled over the cliff, crying out his name.

When she opened her eyes a few moments later, he was watching her. He tightened his hold, and nuzzled into the warmth of her neck.

"For me?" she asked. It was a winsome, fragile thing, her question. He held her tighter.

"Just yourself, love."

Chapter Sixteen

They walked back to their chambers while mist fell like a single wet kiss on the world, his arm slung over her shoulder. Gwyn was certain she was experiencing the first peace she'd had for twelve years. It lasted five minutes.

They were drawing near one of the rooftop doorways that opened from ramparts to the keep. He dragged open the heavy door and held it. She slipped beneath his outstretched arm, just as he said, "Gwyn, there's been news."

It may have been his tone, or some other way of communicating beyond words, but Gwyn knew immediately the peaceful respite had been just that, a small, short break.

She pasted a false smile on her lips. "What news?" She aimed her brittle smile in his direction. His face grew watchful.

"Perhaps we should talk in our chambers," he said warily.

"Of course."

She swung away, her spine hitched straight as a spoke on a wagon wheel. She did not wait for him, and upon reaching their room, began immediately straightening the manuscripts and cups and other items left out last night. Last night, when he'd reminded her heart it was not yet dead. Too bad.

She heard his footstep at the door. She pushed the edge of a manuscript so it was even with the others on the shelf.

"Gwyn."

She began tidying already tidy clothes sitting on the shelves.

"Gwyn, there's news."

She picked up one of his tunics and smoothed it. "What sort of news?"

"News of Stephen."

A small sound of terror escaped her mouth. He looked at her oddly. She pulled the tunic in her hands taut and folded it in a rigid line down the middle, making a crease so tight it would never come out. "What of him?"

He laid one of his hands atop hers. His touch was warm. "He is signing a treaty with Henri. Early November, in Winchester."

She slipped her hands free and walked to the window. "What sort of treaty?"

"The sort that makes Stephen king in name only. He will yield the country shire by shire, and seek Henri's counsel on all matters of state. All adulterine castles built during his reign will be razed."

She nodded, as if he'd told her they needed fresh rushes in the hall. "So Henri will be king."

"Aye."

She looked out the window. The roofs of the buildings below were slick and bright with wetness. A boy in tattered breeches was rounding up an escaped chicken.

Her head felt immense, as if all the notions in the world could not fill it up. Every thought she had floated up and she couldn't catch hold of it again.

"'Tis for the best, Gwyn."

Someone came to help the boy. They herded the animal out of sight. "But how do you know that, for certes?"

His deep, resonant voice rumbled across the room. "Because it has to be."

She nodded dully, not looking around.

She heard his boots start across the room in her direction,

then stop. After a moment, they retreated and the door closed behind him.

A few minutes later came the sound of running footsteps. Shouting. Someone calling for Griffyn. Muted voices. Another messenger had arrived.

Gwyn stared out the window for perhaps half an hour. The misting rain slackened, then stopped.

King Stephen knew his son was not dead. Any agreement or treaty would simply be a ruse, a strategy to buy time, time for Guinevere to heal the prince and set him loose, to save her king and kingdom.

She'd made a promise. She'd given her word. What was different now? Nothing. Her duty remained, unchanged by sentiment. Unchanged by having a heart.

She felt it rising up inside her like a scream. To ward it off, she lifted her chin delicately, as if it were a glass phial.

She needed help. She must visit Marcus.

Slanting, sparkling sunlight began bursting through the clouds. It was going to be a beautiful day.

Griffyn loped down the stairs, Alex on his heels. William of the Five Strands hurried over as they entered the hall.

"A messenger, my lord. I took the liberty of putting him in your office." He gestured to the long corridor of offices that ran along the first-floor level of the castle.

Griffyn started forward, Alex directly behind. William brought up the rear, the sleeves of his overtunic wafting back in the breeze. They drew up at the door. William leaned forward and murmured, "He said 'twas exceedingly private, my lord. I hope I did not overstep?"

"You did well," Griffyn said, and touched him on the shoulder. He looked at Alex. "Wait here," he said, with a significant nod in William's direction. Alex's face tightened, but he nodded and took a step back, setting up by the wall outside the office chamber, with a suspicious eye on a nervous, flustered William.

It was dim and windowless inside the office chamber, lit only by several candles on the walls and tabletops. The young messenger had perched the edge of his rump on a bench beside the table, as if afraid his full weight would collapse the four-inch-thick oaken legs. He was begrimed and haggard, and looked like he hadn't eaten in days. He leapt to his feet as soon as Griffyn entered.

"My lord Everoot!"

"Your name, son?" Griffyn asked, striding forward.

"Richard, sir!"

"Sit, Richard." He picked up the jug of ale William had put in the room, and splashed some into a wooden mug. He thrust it at the boy, who took it and gulped down half.

"What news?" Griffyn asked when the boy's throat stopped moving.

Young Richard yanked the mug from his mouth in a frenzy of obedience. A wave of brown ale splashed over the rim, onto his tunic. "I carry a message from a knight in the north, my lord," he said briskly, pausing neither to wipe his mouth nor his drenched tunic.

"Who?"

"I'm given leave to say only that you do not know him."

"The message?"

Richard flung himself at the pouch hanging by his side and wrestled it free. He yanked the flap over, and drew out a crumpled roll of parchment. "My master asked only that if you did not wish to hear more after reading his missive, you would not hold it against me. Not," he gulped, trying to be inconspicuous, so it actually looked like he swallowed a bug, "make me eat the message."

Griffyn glanced up from the parchment. "That would taste awful."

"Aye, sir," Richard agreed with solemnity.

Griffyn checked the blotted seal, then broke the heavy red wax and rolled the scroll open.

> *My lord Everoot,*
> *I hear you have ridden north to take the Nest, and all that lies within. I have come upon something you may want. Or need. 'Tis a small thing, small enough to fit inside a keyhole. Young Richard has orders to await your victory, then deliver this message. Hold any arrogance perceived herewith to my self, not his.*
>
> > *Thankfully and in God, yours,*
> > *Someone with something you want*

The humming started inside Griffyn's chest, strong and whirling. As if he'd held this very possibility in the back of his mind, and now it was unfolding before him.

It could be a trick, of course. By someone who knew too much.

He looked up. "Where is this master of yours?"

Richard had small beads of sweat on his forehead. "Ipsile-upon-Tyne, my lord," he stammered. "The Red Cock Tavern. Awaiting your reply."

"Awaiting me."

"Aye, my lord, if you saw fit to—"

Griffyn was already halfway out the door. "Look alive, Richard. We ride."

He swung under the office doorway and ran smack into Alex. "I have to see to something," he said, and clapped Alex on the back.

Alex looked wildly between Griffyn and Richard, who was buzzing like an adolescent bee in his wake.

"Ready my guard," Griffyn said. "I'm going to Ipsile-upon-Tyne."

Alex looked at him in shock. "Pagan? Ispile? But what—"

He was already striding down the corridor, issuing orders

over his shoulder. "We leave in an hour. Rations for forty on the packs. Thirty men off the fields, on the walls, full armour. Pull the Everoot men." He loped across the great hall. William and Alex followed in his wake. "Feed young Richard a shovelful of food and give him a new mount. He rides back with us. Tell Fulk I want him too. Alex, I need you to stay here."

Alex pulled up like someone had yanked on his reins. Griffyn stopped beside him.

"Pagan," Alex said, his voice low and urgent. "I should be with you. If this is related in any way to—" He glanced at William, who had stopped just behind them. "Everoot's *cache*, I need to know of it. 'Tis of the utmost importance."

"So is having someone at the Nest whom I trust, Alex. We arrived here two days ago and required an army to get in. I cannot leave it unprotected. The men must be arranged, orders given and followed. The Sauvage presence must be felt. Shall I trust that to anyone but you?"

Alex's throat worked. He stared at the ground and shook his head. "No, my lord. I will see to it."

Griffyn clapped him on the shoulder and took the steps to the outer door three at a time. He kicked open the door. Sunlight streamed in.

"Must you go?"

Griffyn had come up to their bedchamber to say good-bye. He came without his squire Edmund, the boy being engaged in swift preparation of Noir, and so Griffyn was tugging on his tunic himself.

"I must," he replied, his words muffled by the fabric. Gwyn hurried up and unraveled the hem so he could pull it over his head, her fingers trembling with tension.

"But, now?" she persisted, thinking herself mad. Was this not a godsent answer to her prayers? Griffyn was leaving. She could visit Marcus. So why was she trying to convince him to stay? "'Tis just that it is so close . . . close to . . ."

He sat down on the bed and began tugging a boot on. "Close to what?"

She waved her hands in the air. "'Tis just a bad time to leave me!"

He buckled his spur on and dropped his foot. "Why?"

"Our wedding, I suppose," she explained shrilly.

He rose, gave her a kiss, and sat back down to wrangle on the other knee-high leather boot. "Your yearning is lessened?"

"No!"

He looked up slowly, several tendrils of dark hair curling just past his temples and cheekbones. She suddenly realised she had to cut his hair. That was her job now.

"Good," he said slowly. "Are you well, Gwyn? You're not—" His face suddenly lit up. He reached out and touched her wrist. "You don't think you're with child a'ready, do you?"

"No!" she almost shouted.

He drew back, peering at her as if she'd sprouted a growth on her forehead. "Well, Gwyn. I cannot fathom the mood possessing you. I must go. If you're worried about me and the fair maidens of Ipsile-upon-Tyne—"

"No!"

He looked over flatly. "'Twas but a jest. Would you please stop shouting at me?"

She nodded and fingered the tapestry, then snatched her hand away. "'Tis just, it's so soon," she finished lamely.

"I will be back." He got his spur buckled on and rose. "We will be wed, and we shall go to Ipsile-upon-Tyne and any other northern town you develop a sudden interest in. We've over two weeks until the wedding, Gwyn. I will be back in two days." He planted a swift kiss on her lips.

"Please don't go," she said again, in a whisper, but it wouldn't have mattered if she'd shouted, because he'd already left the room.

Chapter Seventeen

The wooden sign swinging in the darkness outside the tavern had a red cock on it, or at least a cock, rutted, chipped, and pockmarked such that it might have once been red.

Fulk snorted. "I doubt anyone ever went to the effort of painting it, my lord. Mayhap 'tis blood, and they just stuck it up there anyhow."

"That I'd believe," said Griffyn in fervent agreement.

They stood outside the Red Cock Tavern, pondering not only the wisdom of entering, but the wisdom of the man who would direct them there. Its thin walls listed precariously to the right. It was huddled between two other establishments of much the same ilk, and boasting much the same clientele. Fulk and he stood in an ice-encrusted puddle and stared at the slime-encrusted door.

"I've been in worse," Fulk announced.

"So have I," Griffyn said, just as firmly.

And they had, both of them, much worse. But neither wanted to go in here.

The night was cold and dark, and the mists were building. White ribboned ghosts swirled about their ankles like cats. The alleyway was narrow, and above them, the three-storey buildings lurched inwards, like old women over a cauldron. From between the shuttered windows of the tavern, small bright candles shone. A loud shout of laughter burst out, then someone opened the door and stumbled out. The door slammed shut. Griffyn looked at Fulk.

"At least they're laughin'," said Fulk grimly.

"Aye, but about what?"

They went inside. The tavern was mostly open space, filled with men in various stages of drunkenness. Seven or eight tables sat at odd angles across the crowded floor, and a long counter stretched along the length of the back wall. It was manned by two bartenders and strewn with drunk men, mugs of ale, and women covered in rouge and dilapatory pastes.

"Now *there's* paint," Fulk said, gazing reverently and solemnly at the buxom women.

Griffyn snorted. "Aye."

It was an unruly, festive crowd. They were packed together like cows, loud like cows, and stinking like cows.

"And cow piss," muttered Fulk as they crossed the threshold.

The men closest turned to regard them sullenly. In response to eighteen years of a civil war on the border between two hostile nations, the men of Ipsile had developed a fierce sense of community. They looked out for their own. Griffyn and Fulk were unknown quantities, and as such, treated with a polite regard that bordered just north of hostility. Griffyn did not care to enlighten them on the fact he was actually now their lord.

Fulk and he exchanged glances, then Griffyn shouldered his way towards an empty table he'd spotted, hoping Fulk was following behind. He glanced over his shoulder.

He wasn't. Fulk had detoured to the bar, and was staring open-mouthed at the cleavage of one of the prostitutes, ignoring the bartender standing in front of him. Griffyn sighed and pushed onwards to the table.

He got waylaid by an argument between a few drunken townsmen. When the shouting escalated and he heard the

words "Bloody fricking bastard," shouted near his right ear,
he stepped back just as a man's body was flung through the
air and landed with a sickening thud on a tabletop. The table
shimmied convulsively, then its four legs folded. The table,
with occupant, crashed to the ground. Griffyn stepped over
the wreckage and continued on.

The table he'd spied was still open. He edged onto the bench
behind it, back to the begrimed wall, and waited for Fulk, the
mysterious message-sender, or Satan to approach him. He was
making bets with himself on which would show first.

It was Fulk.

He plunked his armoured body down onto the bench next to
Griffyn, two pints in his fists. "Truth be told, my lord," he said,
shoving one pint at Griffyn so hard a portion of it splashed onto
the table, "those Scottish women are good to behold."

Griffyn reached for the mug. "How can you tell, behind the
cosmetics?" he asked, truly curious.

"Och," Fulk said with a confident air, sitting back and
pushing his belly out. "Ye can tell." He took a long pull from
his mug.

"Umm."

A figure pushed through the bodies filling the room and
approached their table. "My lord," the man said in a low
voice. "You came."

"Call me Pagan," Griffyn said swiftly, then his eyes focused and his breath jammed back into his throat.

De Louth. It was de Louth, Marcus's henchman, the one
who'd tried to kidnap Guinevere on the London highway, the
one who almost killed Griffyn.

Griffyn pushed to his feet, his breathing slow and controlled. His hand moved to his sword. Fulk rose beside him.
Tension pushed out of them like waves into the air, ready for
a fight.

"De Louth," Griffyn said, then flicked his gaze around the
pub. It was crowded and smokey. Men stood in small herds

everywhere, leaning over each other's shoulders, guffawing, clicking dice across the tabletops. No one seemed interested in this little corner of the room. He shifted his gaze back.

"You've nothing to fear from me," de Louth said quietly. "I give you my word." He stood a few paces back from the table, his hands near his hips, but palms turned forward, splayed. He had no weapon. At least not in his hands.

Griffyn's eyes ratcheted back up to de Louth's. "You sent me a message?"

"I did."

"Why?"

"That's what I'm here to tell you."

"You, or *him*?"

De Louth shook his head. "Not him. Just me."

"He doesn't know you're here?"

"If he knew I was here, he'd cut off my tongue. And my prick."

Griffyn smiled thinly. "So, your lord cannot trust you, but I should?"

De Louth dropped his hands. "Sir, you'll either believe me or you won't. But what will it hurt to listen?"

Fulk crossed his arms over his chest. "It might hurt the backs of our heads, if we were to get smacked upside them with a club while we were listening."

"I've come with no tricks, or men." He looked to Griffyn. "So, aye or nay? Do you want to hear what I've got to say?"

Griffyn felt the hilt of his sword butting up against his wrist, a comforting pressure. De Louth might be dirty, or not. There was no way to know except to listen.

He slid his gaze deliberately down to de Louth's thigh, where he'd punched through the flesh and bone with an arrow on the king's highway. De Louth was waiting for him when he looked up again.

A twisted smile lifted a corner of the knight's mouth. "It still hurts, if that'll make you happy."

"Some."

Griffyn looked around the room one last time, then gestured them to sit. Fulk took a deep drink from his mug. Griffyn sat back and said, "So? What do you have for me?"

De Louth reached inside a pouch hanging at his waist and held something aloft in the air between them. It was a chain. At the end swung a key.

Griffyn's heartbeat slowed. Thick and ponderous, it knocked out a beat that made his blood churn and head spin. A key. It looked lighter than the one around his neck, and he saw it was silver. *Steel.* And it would fit. He knew it would fit. It was as if the knowledge flowed through his blood, as if the key were already in his hand. This little steel key would fit inside his larger iron one, and the puzzle key, the one that would open the chest of the Hallows, would be one step closer to being complete.

"How did you come by this?" he asked hoarsely.

De Louth lowered the chain to the table. "I took it."

"From whom?"

"Endshire."

"*Marcus?* How in God's name did Marcus come by it?"

"He stole it. From the countess. Last year. I watched him."

"He took it from her?" Griffyn repeated in a low voice.

"Not off her person. She was gone by the time we got there. But it was lying on the floor of her bedchamber. Looked like it'd been left behind in a hurry. An accident."

"And Marcus found it," Griffyn said slowly, trying to picture the moment when Marcus realised what he had. "He must have been pleased."

De Louth snorted. "He looked like he was sucking on ice in Palestine. It mattered, to him." He sat back in his seat. "To you. To whoever tried to buy it from me last week."

Griffyn went still. "What?"

"Someone tried to buy it from me about a week ago." "*Who?*"

De Louth shook his head. The firelight from candles

glinted off a few grey hairs speckling his beard. He glanced at the mugs of ale. "I don't know. We met in a dark alleyway. He didn't speak much. I wouldn't know if he was sitting at the next table. There was one thing, though. I saw it when he was reaching for the bag under his tunic." De Louth's eyes met his from across the oaken tabletop. "He had a tattoo. A bright soaring eagle, inked right over his heart."

Griffyn and Fulk looked at one another.

"He was willing to pay a lot for that." De Louth nodded towards the chain and key, laid like a spiraling, linked snake on the table. A fat candle burned beside it, slowly spreading yellow wax like a sluggish volcano. "An awful lot."

"So why didn't you give it to him?"

De Louth shrugged. "I didn't trust him."

"You've developed quite a conscience over the past year," Griffyn observed coldly.

De Louth shrugged again. "A conscience? I dunno. I needed the money. And it wasn't Marcus's to begin with."

"So why didn't you sell it when you could?"

De Louth's gaze wandered back to the mugs of ale, then he poked his finger into the yellowish wax. More hot wax came chugging down into the recess, covering de Louth's thick, calloused finger. He pulled it free. "I don't think my answers will suit, my lord, but they're the only ones I've got. I didn't trust him."

Griffyn's face stayed hard. "Why are you doing this?"

"He took it from the countess. It's hers. Not his."

Griffyn's eyebrows inched up. "Truly, now: why?"

De Louth scowled. "I said you'd believe me or no. So, 'tis no. I don't much care. That belongs to the countess. Or," he added, sitting back, "you. But it sure as hell isn't Endshire's."

"And you're just so tired of all the stealing, is that it?" Griffyn's words were mocking, but his tone wasn't. Nor was it kindly. He was impassive. Blank. Pushing. Appraising.

"I'm tired of people getting shit on, my lord," de Louth replied. "I'm tired of watching it."

"Why?"

His face went red and he flung out his hand. "I don't know! I had a child. My wife died. I don't know. Just take the damn thing, will you?"

Griffyn swept up the key. Fulk slid his mug of ale across table to de Louth, who nodded and drank deeply.

"And why did you contact me?" Griffyn asked. He slid his thumb over the smooth, cool steel.

"I told you, I saw him take it from the countess. I knew where it belonged. From Everoot 'twas stolen, to Everoot 'tis returned."

"But you didn't send a messenger to the countess, you sent one to me."

De Louth looked at him in confusion. "You *are* Everoot, my lord."

"Call me Pagan," he said shortly, although no one could or would be listening in. It was loud and tumultuous, getting more crowded, and the room was practically tilting sideways with all the drunken revelry. Soon the fights would break out. Time to go.

"I knew your father."

Griffyn came out of his thoughts with a start. "What did you say?" he asked coldly.

"Your father," de Louth said. "I knew him. He didn't like Endshire much."

"No. He did not. How much? For the key."

De Louth set down the mug and wiped the back of his hand across his mouth. "I was going to name a price that would have beggared you. At least, one that would buy me a corody with the Templars for my old age. Since I'll likely go lame before my time." He patted his thigh, the one Griffyn had shot through with the arrow. "But I think I'll leave it at this: Take my daughter when she's of fostering age. As one of the countess's ladies. Raise her up right, and safe. I surely cannot do it." He smiled bitterly. "I cannot even choose a good master."

"You could choose another one, now."

De Louth got to his feet and shook his head. "No. I made a pledge."

"You *stole* this from him," Griffyn pointed out.

De Louth scowled at his incredulous tone. "Who's to say getting this thing out of his hands is not a way of honouring him? I saw the way he wanted it. The way the tattooed man wanted it." He glanced at the key. "'Twasn't a restful thing. So, we've a deal?"

Griffyn nodded. "Safe haven for your daughter when she's ready to be fostered."

"Aye. In seven years."

Griffyn looked up in surprise. "How old is she?"

De Louth pulled his cloak over his shoulders. Someone jostled him from behind, walking by with a fistful of mugs. He stepped closer to the table. "She was just born. Two weeks ago. I've got to go."

He turned and disappeared into the throng, just another pair of cloaked shoulders, then not even that.

Fulk and he walked side by side back to their inn. Griffyn had lodged his men at the monastery's guest hall just outside the town walls, but he and Fulk had needed to stay inside, to attend this meeting that occurred long after the gates were closed and locked for the night.

Their bootheels clacked loudly over the wet cobbles. The moonlight glistened on the streets and lit the alleyways in an eerie silver glow. The scent of wet hay mixed with damp leather and the faint odour of blood: Tanners Row was three blocks over, but its stench carried much further. A cat slunk out from a shadow.

Griffyn said quietly, "Where is yours, Fulk?"

The Scotsman nodded, as if he'd been waiting for the question. He stopped walking, reached up and unbuckled his gambeson. The corner of the heavy quilted doublet flapped down. Expressionless, he yanked on the collar of the tunic beneath and held the lantern in his left hand aloft. There, in the soft crevice where his collarbones met, just below this throat, was a small, brightly inked, soaring eagle.

Griffyn nodded. Fulk buckled up and they walked on. After a moment, Fulk said, "We get ruined every so often too, my lord, just like everyone else."

"Do all Watchers have the tattoo?" Griffyn asked grimly.

"Aye. But not in the same place."

Griffyn looked his query, in the form of a sidewise, raised-eyebrow glance. Fulk elaborated.

"We choose. We didna choose the duty, but we choose how it marks us. Or we're supposed to. Our power over the power of the thing."

Griffyn's gaze dropped to Fulk's chest, where the tattoo now lay hidden beneath his armour. "Why there?"

"It lies halfway between my head and my heart. Exactly where it's supposed to," he added dourly.

They walked in silence for another few moments and turned down a small, crooked alleyway. It was dark in the buildings overhanging the street, all candles extinguished by command, the *couvre-feu*, to prevent fire. In a few buildings, on the third floors, a rogue flame still burned here and there, but mostly they made their way by the lantern in Fulk's hand and the wet ground reflecting moonlight.

"And you're certain Gwyn knows nothing of it?" Griffyn asked.

Fulk shook his head. "Lady Gwynnie knows nothing."

"I suspect I owe you for that."

Fulk stopped walking, his gaze sharp beneath his bushy, grey-flecked eyebrows. "Ye owe nothing, my lord. I'm paying off old debts myself. Ye may not want to hear this, but if I could have, I'd have told Lady Gwyn everything. I think she's a right to know."

"I think that would be unbelievably dangerous."

Fulk nodded. "Aye. Every way ye turn, there's danger. Ye're the Heir. That's the way of it."

Danger was the least of it, Griffyn thought. It was the unveiled *craving* he recoiled from. He could already feel it building inside him. He ran his finger over the serrated edge of the steel key, still cupped in his hand. That made two. Two of the puzzle keys.

"There's three, Fulk?" he asked suddenly. "Three puzzle keys."

Fulk grunted. "Aye. Three keys that, when fitted together, open the gate to the resting place of the Hallows."

So why had his father given away two of them? Why make Griffyn hunt down his destiny?

He ran the key between his fingertips thoughtfully. "What do you remember of my father, Fulk?"

"Well, now, I recall he changed. He grew . . . hard." Fulk looked over briefly through the reflected moonlight. "I know ye think ye know yer father well, Pagan, and I'm sure ye do, but ye only know *that* part of him."

"Which part?"

"The part after the Crusades. He was different upon a time. Before."

"How?"

"Well, now, he and your mother, they sure did love each other. 'Twas as clear as anything."

Griffyn's mouth fell open. *"What?"*

"Dearer than that twice-blooming rose she was to him, and that's saying something. And you and he were inseparable upon a time, that ye were." Fulk pinched his eyes half-shut and peered at Griffyn's shocked face. "About two weeks before the coup that put Stephen on the throne, your father up and left for Normandy. The only thing he took with 'em was ye and yer mother. Now why would he have done that?" His eyes never left Griffyn's. "Take yer wee self, and leave everything else behind."

The rhetorical question hung in the air between them.

A familiar surge of anger flooded Griffyn's limbs. Indeed, his father had taken him, and his mother, and had left behind such a brutal legacy that his name was still remembered among the Norman tenants and noble neighbours as an accursed thing, *Mal Amour*: "Bad Love."

"And recall this," Fulk was saying. "Ye were thirteen when your father died. And he did not want ye Trained. I dunno what ye make of that, but there it is. And who knows, mayhap he was right. For centuries these things have laid quiet. Perhaps for a thousand more. This is ancient treasure. There's no rush."

"Not for my father, surely," Griffyn said bitterly. "He wanted to keep it all for himself. Thought he'd live forever." He paused. "Could he? Could something about the Hallows make him live forever?"

Fulk glanced around. It was dark and silent and empty. The lantern swung back and forth in his gloved hand. "There's a powerful lot o' rumours, aren't there, Pagan? The most I can tell ye is what ye already know: 'tis pure power."

They finished their frosty walk, passing darkened storefronts. The wooden platforms that served as shelves during the day were drawn up tight. As they passed one narrow building, Fulk muttered, "Agardly, the goldsmythe. That's where Lady Gwyn's harps were taken."

Griffyn pulled his mind to the present. "Harps?"

"Her mamma's little harps. Sold for seed. Probably gone now."

They reached their inn. Fulk swung the door wide, peered inside, sword in hand, then stepped back to let Griffyn enter. They trudged up the stairs to a small room at the back of the house, a luxury to have a single room, with two beds all to themselves.

"'Tis shivering cold these nights," Fulk grumbled as he sat down on one of the narrow, straw-filled cots that lined opposite walls. Griffyn unbuckled his belt with its array of weapons and threw himself on the other. There was enough space to sit and heave off your boots, if you didn't mind your nose touching the other bed when you bent forward to do so.

Fulk extinguished the single candle flame with a squeeze between his calloused finger and thumb. He punched his tunic around beneath his head and lowered his head with a grunt. "'Twill be good to be home again."

"Aye," Griffyn said distractedly. "I need but to stop at that Agardly's shop tomorrow, and we can be off."

Fulk's grizzled head came back up. He was grinning. "Ye'll make her real happy with that, my lord."

"That's the plan."

Griffyn lay, arms folded behind his head. A sliver of the crescent moon was visible through the window. It was indeed getting colder. The mornings were bringing frost. Soon the snows would come, and Griffyn meant to spend Yule at the Nest this year. Henri fitzEmpress would have to summon him with an armed escort to make it otherwise. This year, he would be home. With Guinevere.

She had not betrayed him. He could believe that, or spend the rest of his life suspecting everyone of everything. Half the time he'd be right. But half would be wrong, and if he was going to have Gwyn to wife, then have her he must. Wholeheartedly. He was in or he was out.

And may God forgive me for being the fool a second time, he thought, *but I believe she is honourable.*

Chapter Eighteen

It was barely two hours after Griffyn had left, but Gwyn was already in the stables, tightening the cinch around Windstalker's belly. Puffs of smoke appeared in front of her mouth with each exhale. Autumn had come with a vengeance.

It was three hours to Endly Hall, three back again. She would be home before Sext tomorrow. Long before Griffyn returned.

She must be quick, and no one could notice, not even for a moment, that she was gone.

A summons to Jerv had brought him on the run. She'd posted him in the landing outside her bedchamber, admonishing him to ensure she wasn't disturbed while she suffered a sudden, raging 'headache.' Jerv was instructed not to disturb her either. Her childhood friend was the only one she could trust to follow her instructions without question, and it was vitally important he ward off any potential visitors. Especially with Alexander about.

"What are you doing?" said a voice at her back.

She stifled a scream and spun. Jerv was standing there, not following her instructions whatsoever, looking confused and angry.

"What are you doing?" he asked again, looking rather stubborn.

"What are *you* doing?" she retorted, gathering her wits. "You're supposed to be posted outside my chambers."

"For your . . . headache?"

She started to retort with a haughty "aye," then stopped herself. That would be ridiculous and insulting. She turned to Wind and grabbed his reins. "I am going for a ride."

"Alone?"

"Aye."

"Have you lost your mind?"

"I have ridden these woods for fifteen years, Jerv. I know them. I will be safe."

"I will come with you."

"No."

She started to push past him, but he laid a hand on her arm, which he had not done since they were children, playing childhood games of tag and castles. This felt nothing like a game. She yanked on her arm. He didn't release.

"Gwyn, what are you doing?"

"Keeping an oath," she snapped. "Unlike you, who cannot follow simple instructions."

He let go her arm. "What kind of oath?" he asked slowly.

"The kingly kind."

Jerv's eyes narrowed. "Gwyn, what is going on? What are you doing?"

Tension had already squeezed the muscles in her neck and chest and back tight. Much more and she'd begin to collapse in on herself. Fear was working hard to make her back out of this oath. Jerv must not be allowed to assist.

"I am keeping faith," she whispered through gritted teeth. "I have no choice. Leave me to it." She pointed. "Go back inside. Guard my door."

He reached for her again. "*You* come back inside and—"

"And what?" She jerked away and fought to keep her voice at a whisper. "Forswear my oath? Prove faithless to my lord king?"

"Faithless? To Stephen? What are you doing in Stephen's name?"

"Making good on old promises."

Jerv stared. "God's bones," he said in a low voice. "What are you doing, Gwynnie?"

"Don't call me that!" They called her Gwynnie in tenderness, when they loved her. That would ruin everything. "But 'twas a deed done before Griffyn ever came," she added, hoping that would matter to him. To her.

"When?" he asked swiftly.

"August."

"August." Jerv's gaze shot ceiling-ward. "That was after Stephen was thrown from his horse. After the siege and truce at Wallingford . . . The truce." His words started running together. "Ipswich was taken in August, then Eustace died, and . . ." His words trailed off. He looked down slowly. "Gwynnie, what are you caught up in?"

"I cannot say."

"Will not."

"Fine. Will not." She looked up at the tumbled-down battlement walls, the ones Griffyn had given to Jerv to restore to greatness. Jerv had his path, his life's love. She gave a slightly bitter smile. "'Tis simple for you, Jerv. You have what you want. 'Tis a simple matter to think everything bad is over now."

He'd been her friend since childhood, but he was looking at her now like she was a stranger. One who'd spit in his tankard of ale. "I am not a child, Gwyn," he said coldly.

"Nor am I. I am holding to an oath, and 'tis eating me up."

Jerv raked his fingers through his hair. "If your oath is about keeping Stephen in power, prolonging this god-awful war, then it has nothing to do with the world we live in anymore. Nothing of goodness, or right. The war is over, Gwyn. Let it go."

"You think I want more *war*? You think I want more people to die, more lives to end?"

"You want something, else you wouldn't be doing whatever you're doing now."

"I want—. I want—." He looked disgusted. She started shaking with anger. "I do not recall being offered a choice, Jerv: 'Would you like to keep to your vow?'" she said in a sing-song, querying tone. "'Is it quite convenient to honour your oaths?' 'Has it grown in the least bit *inconvenient*? Do you regret anything you said or did, for we can surely forget the whole matter.'" She leaned forward and said in a furious, desperate whisper, her voice breaking, "I regret nigh on *everything*, Jerv. What matters that? Being sorry is never enough."

He stared a moment, then turned on his heel. He paused at the stable door and looked back. "Your father was wrong, Gwyn."

Her hand fluttered to her heart. "Papa? Wh-what are you talking about?"

"It was an accident. He should have forgiven you. But *this*? Whatever you're about to do? It will not make that right." He turned and stalked off.

Gwyn stood for a long time, staring at the stable door, hand at her chest. Jerv was wrong, completely wrong.

This had nothing to do with the guilt that crushed her spirit. Nothing whatsoever to do with the fact that her father had never forgiven her for killing his son and then his wife. It was completely unrelated to her desperate search for a way to prove herself worthy, to absolve herself of the sins of the past, and she, with no new penances to perform.

It was this or her heart would die.

She was still half a mile from Endly Hall when she was met by three gap-toothed Endshire scouts. They recognised

her on sight, of course, but they still rode close by, as if suspicious of her motives, trotting so close to Windstalker he
rolled his eyes. But Gwyn knew it was simply an excuse to let
their greedy eyes linger on her body, or their thighs to brush
against hers.

*Would that I could loose Griffyn on these wretches. He
would learn them their error*, she thought grimly, not realising she was already thinking of Griffyn as her protector.

They drew near Endly Hall. It was a square, embattled
affair, with a crenellated curtain wall patchworked in an ap-
proximate oval around its bailey. The squat, square keep hunkered at its centre. Two watch towers stood sentry, one facing
east, one south, each rising another twenty or so feet above
the wall, both slit with dark arrow loops.

On this bright sunny morning, small pricks of light moved
along the curtain walls, marking the helms of armed sentries.
Sable-black Endshire pennants snapped in the brisk autumn
breeze, hung at intervals along the wall's length, and double-
hung on either side of the east-tower gatehouse. Gwyn swallowed a lump as they passed under its jagged shadows.

Rusty iron winches screamed as the chains were lowered,
dropping the draw to allow entry. It fell with a thundering
blast. Mud splattered everywhere. Gwyn simmered as she
wiped clods of muck from her cloak and, snapping her wrist,
flicked them back to the ground. Ever was Marcus the purveyor of filth.

She was escorted to him at once. He was engaged in sword
practice with one of his men. Around them grouped ten or
so other soldiers, who shouted and hooted in obvious glee.
Marcus and his knight circled one another with wooden
blades, shields slung on their left forearms. The knight made
a sudden thrusting motion. Marcus spun, continued around
and swiped his sword in a low, slashing sweep. The blunted
wooden edge smashed into the side of his opponent's right
knee. The knight crumpled to the ground, hands clamped

around his leg, head thrown back and eyes screwed shut in silent, obvious pain.

Marcus shoved off the mail hood covering his head and tossed his blade at the man's feet. "Everywhere, Richard. You've got to be looking *everywhere*."

Eyes still squeezed tight, the knight nodded. The others helped him to his feet. Someone caught sight of Guinevere, and gestured to Marcus. He turned.

His eyebrows went up a fraction of an inch. Then he started forward, leaving faint bootprints in the damp dirt, tugging off his gloves as he came.

"Guinevere, what an unexpected pleasure. I faintly recall you saying something about, what was it? Something about 'never darkening your fetid door . . .'" He smiled apologetically. "I forget the rest."

"'*Again*.'"

"That was it." Cupping both thick leather gloves in one hand, he used them to wipe the sweat off his forehead. "So, is my door not so fetid, or has some other change been wrought?"

"Griffyn Sauvage has taken the Nest."

"I know." He lowered his gloves slowly. "And you?"

"We're betrothed."

He seemed to digest this, gaze on the dirt. She lowered her voice. "May we speak somewhere?"

His hawk-like eyes ratcheted back up. Despite the autumn chill, a trickle of sweat dripped into the gully between Gwyn's breasts. No matter how long they trained, his knights could *never* compete with their lord in the ability to perceive, compute, and adjust. Marcus was like an abacus, swiftly adding and subtracting the merits and weaknesses of his opponents, then crushing them beneath his deadly calculations.

He watched her a moment, then gestured to the keep. Servants eyed them as they passed, but kept their faces averted. The thump of their footsteps over cobbles and through rushes seemed to tap out the thundering of her heart. What sort of pact was she about to make?

They sat in a darkened corner of the great hall, the room being filled with nothing *but* darkened corners and cobwebs and sharp-ribbed canines. Marcus ordered a plate of food, then sent the servants from the room.

"What news have you of the south, Marcus?" she asked as soon as the room was empty. "I know nothing these last days. How do we stand?"

Marcus paused in chewing on a crust of bread. "You came all this way for a spot of news?" He smiled briefly. "Tell me, Gwynnie, by 'we,' do you mean Stephen?"

"I mean we who have pledged ourselves to the king," she snapped.

"Well, here is how 'we' stand, Gwyn: 'tis only a matter of time before Henri fitzEmpress sits on the throne. All the barons are turning to him."

"You mean *you* are turning," she retorted bitterly.

"I haven't. Yet."

"No. Not yet." Up in the north, men like Marcus had time to test the winds before committing themselves.

He shrugged. "'Tis but a matter of time until the country is Henri's."

"Only if men like you give it to him."

He sent her a level glance, then carved off a slice of cheese with a paring knife. "Your fealty is, as ever, in bold display, Gwyn, but it serves no purpose."

She clenched her jaw. "It serves some small purpose," she said through gritted teeth, "in that I can live with myself when I awake each morn."

"Meaning I am not able to? Or should not be?" He popped the cheese into his mouth.

She glared. "Loyalty is not a commodity to be bought and sold."

"Of course it is." Set deep within the lean face, his glittering eyes regarded her coolly. "If there is no price on it, my loyalty would be poorly regarded, indeed. I should be a fool."

"And we cannot have that."

A flicker of anger sparked in his eyes. "You are a child, Gwyn. Those who receive the kind of loyalty you describe are the only beneficiaries. The cherished *loyalists* are used, discarded, and the stench of their sacrifice blows away quickly. Should I be one of them, then? Truly, you surprise me. I thought you intelligent."

"And I thought you decent. Of a sort."

"Ah, Gwyn," he said, chuckling. "You thought no such thing." He leaned back in his chair. "But we would have made quite a union, you and I."

She looked at him sourly. "What, with your lack of loyalty and my excess?"

"Nay. With your fire and my ambition."

"Oh, that." She took a deep breath. Now or never. "You must come pledge your fealty for the lands you hold of Everoot, Marcus."

Marcus looked over like she'd lost her mind. "Did Sauvage send you here to tell me that?"

"Of course not. You're lucky Griffyn didn't ride here himself and burn all of Endshire to the ground."

"Griffyn?" he echoed her use of his Christian name, rather than a surname or other, less intimate appellation.

She brushed an invisible piece of dirt off her skirts. "He doesn't like you."

"He *owes* me," Marcus hissed.

She drew back slightly. "For what?"

"We go back."

Gwyn searched her memory. "Your fathers had a history."

Marcus ripped his gaze away. "My father was fond of Sauvage."

"Christian Sauvage, the father?"

Marcus gave a bark of bitter laughter. "Not a bit of that. At least, not in the end. But he was fond of your Griffyn."

Gwyn sat with this a moment. "More so than of you?"

Quick as a snake, Marcus's hand swung out. He stopped it barely a grass blade's length from her cheek. Gwyn's mouth dropped open, her face drained of colour. They stared at each other, shocked.

Marcus flung his hand down, as if it were a separate object he could let go free. "I am sorry, Gwyn. What I have with your *betrothed*"—he spit the word out—"is not yours to worry on."

"It might be," she said, her words shaky. Whatever old wounds lay here, they were potentially as fatal as a dry river-bed after a storm. People walking through were likely to get swept away. And again, she had no choice.

"You must come. Pledge fealty," she continued, trying to even out the tremble in her voice. "All the other barons are coming. Two weeks from now, our wedding. The night after, the ceremony of homage. You must be there."

Marcus shook his head. "You're asking an awful lot, Gwyn, with nothing to offer in return."

"Oh, I have paid, Marcus. You've taken."

He looked surprised. "Me?" He shook his head. "Not so much as your Griffyn."

"You took Papa's box."

He looked truly confused. "What box?"

"Oh, please, Marcus. My heirloom box. The one you took from Griffyn when your men captured him outside of London."

"Ah."

His complacency sent her tripping into a sudden fit of anger. "Does it please you to read the letters between my parents?" she snapped. "To read their private thoughts?"

He drew back slightly. "We're all very upset about our parents today, aren't we?" He brushed his hands together, wiping off crumbs. "I'll not pledge to Sauvage."

"Then you'll lose your lands."

He rested his hand on the rim of his mug and glanced at the crimson Endshire tapestry hanging on the wall behind the dais. "Let us not be fools, Gwyn. Stephen will fold by Yuletide. There's news of a treaty to come in just a few weeks. Stephen has no choice, now that Eustace is dead."

She closed her eyes. "Eustace is not dead. He's with me."

Marcus's expression did not change for a moment, but he did straighten his fingers and deliberately edge his mug off the table. It smashed to the ground, spilling ale all over the floor.

"Like that, Gwyn," he said in a calm, explanatory tone. "That is how quickly things change. What was, is no longer. Which is why I do not commit myself without cause. And considerable gain." He smiled. "Tell me about Eustace."

"He was brought to the Nest mid-August, and has been lying in illness ever since."

He looked at her sharply. "Ill? How bad?"

"Bad enough," she admitted. "He's been sweating out a fever for weeks now, and it doesn't break."

He drummed his fingers on the table. "I would speak with him."

"So would I. He is beyond talk, sweating and pitching his head about is all he can manage, that with effort."

Marcus rose and began pacing, his boots marking a tight circuit around the table. Then he stopped and looked at her. "Why are you here, Gwyn?" he asked, each word like a taste he was rolling over his tongue.

There it was again, that incisive mind, turned now towards her as the sudden object of his ambition. Gwyn took a deep breath. "I need help."

He let her words settle back into silence. "From me?"

She nodded.

"Say that again, Gwyn."

She swallowed thickly. It tasted bad. "I need your help."

A smile inched up his mouth. "I would be honoured."

She looked away. "I have to get Eustace out of the Nest."

He plucked at his lower lip thoughtfully. "Have you a plan?"

She offered the only one she'd been able to come up with. Its value was in its simplicity, which might also be its downfall. "When the other barons come to pledge fealty, you come as well. You're in the castle, you pledge fealty, you leave the next morning. With Eustace."

His smile kept getting bigger. "When is the ceremony of homage?"

"The fair begins the day before the wedding. The ceremony is the night after."

He sat down and seemed to consider this longer than was necessary. He had to agree. If he didn't . . .

She leaned forward and hissed, *"Just get him out of the Nest."*

He leaned back in his chair and looked at her. "Why, Gwyn. That doesn't sound like your usual devoted self."

She stared the wall behind Marcus's head, but could still feel his gaze on her.

"You don't want Sauvage to be hurt," he said, his voice filled with wonder and something else. "You are trying to be loyal to the king and in love with his enemy at the same time." He shook his head, his smile mocking. "It will never work, Gwynnie. You'll have to choose. One day."

"Can you do it?" she asked from between gritted teeth.

"Two weeks?"

She nodded tightly.

His smile returned. "I can do much more than that, Gwyn. 'Tis a simple matter."

His reply recalled to her Griffyn's words upon his arrival: *You think me a simple matter*. Which wasn't true at all. She thought him perilous and perfect, and had fallen so deeply into love they would never be able to drag her up again. But one did not follow one's heart. One did one's duty.

What mattered the heart? What had it ever done but kill, murder, destroy?

Following the heart made a person foolish, reckless. Other people got hurt. Brothers, mothers. Gwyn had made a vow, taken an oath. She had reparations to make. There was no room for feelings.

And Marcus was dead wrong. She could honour both Griffyn and the king. God would not be so cruel as to force her to choose between them. Or her father. And her promises. To leave her in his world with no way to redeem herself.

But Marcus had been right about one thing: getting Eustace out of the Nest was no longer an exercise in loyalty. It was a way to rid the Nest of treachery before Griffyn got killed by it.

Chapter Nineteen

She rode hard to be home by Sext. The mid-day meal should be starting soon. Make a showing in the hall, headache vanquished, and no one would be the wiser.

She reined the gelding into the northern woods and followed a barely marked path to the entrance of a hidden cave set within the face of a jagged rock ledge. Wind followed her faithfully inside.

She edged by the spring in the centre of the cave, its milky colour and sour smell unappetizing. But within its lightly burbling centre was a hot, sulfur spring that had eased her muscles on many a night. At the rear of the cave, Gwyn reached into a small hole. Her fingers touched the edge of the line of lanterns laid here. She pulled one out, lit it, and descended into a cool, earthen tunnel.

Hurrying now, she guided them to the end and poked her head out another door, on the northwest side of the inner bailey, just across from the secret door she'd brought Eustace through. No one was about. She rushed Wind through and jogged the gelding around to the front of the castle.

She began to encounter more people, servants and household staff who smiled and nodded. Did she notice a lot of strange looks in those smiles? A sickly trail of fear rippled through her stomach. Slowing to a walk, she loosened Wind's cinch and blew a curl off her face.

"Lady Guinevere?"

She jumped. The young page had materialised from nowhere. "Aye, Peter?"

"Sir Alex said to find you, for my lord Griffyn is returning," he piped cheerfully.

"Returning? Today?"

"Well, tonight," he clarified. The sun was soon to set.

She reached out and gripped his shoulders. *"When?"*

"Soon," he shouted back, utterly confused.

"Soon." She dropped her hands.

"Aye, my lady. And Sir Alex said to find you—"

Another thread of fear unravelled. "He said . . . he said to *find* me?"

"Well, my lady," explained the seven-year-old, confused as to why he was receiving such attention from the beautiful countess, but perfectly happy to be the object of her interest, "*we* all knew you were in your chambers, but Sir Alex said to find you. But I had to deliver a message first to Albert, the smythe. He's been having problems with the forge, and—"

"Thank you," she breathed and began towards the stables. Alex knew.

She hurried to the stables, passing Griffyn's squire Edmund along the way. At his heels tagged Renny, Griffyn's ancient hound.

"My lady!" shouted Edmund.

Her heart slammed against her chest as the boy hurried over.

"I saw in your cellars"—Edmund said, and Gwyn almost fainted—"the dulcimer you used to keep. Would it be possible for me to learn, do you think?"

Her hand fluttered over her chest, her face hot. "Why, yes, Edmund," she agreed shakily, trying to focus on the mundane matter. She had entirely forgotten the instrument, else she'd have sold it already. "I-I am certain we could find someone to teach you. My scribe used to play, just a bit, but he might still know a few lines to teach you."

Edmund's face lit up. "Thank you, my lady!"

"You're welcome," she replied, and bent to pat Renny on the head before going on for the stables.

The dog growled.

Gwyn ripped her hand back. She looked at Edmund, who appeared as shocked as she. She turned to the hound again and another low-pitched snarl rumbled out of his whitened muzzle.

"Why, my lady," Edmund exclaimed, tugging on the dog's collar. "I do not know what's into him! He was at your heels only yester—I mean the day before." He looked at her in swift concern. "How is your headache, my lady? I should have asked from the first."

"It's fine," she said slowly, looking warily at Renny as Edmund tugged the dog away. "'Tis fine now," she finished for no one, and headed shakily across the bailey to unsaddle Wind.

She hadn't made it forty paces before a Sauvage knight approached her.

"My lady Guinevere?"

Saints above, was every soul in the castle intent on her? She turned with a stiff smile.

"My lord is looking for you."

Dread curled up her spine. Good God, he was back already? "I will just cool down my horse," she said weakly, trying not to sound desperate. "Where is Lord Griffyn?"

"He's in the hall now, my lady, but said he'd see you in his chambers."

His chambers.

She took quite a bit longer than was necessary to walk Wind, rub his sweaty fur with straw to encourage circulation and massage the weary muscles, fill his water bucket, and thump the saddle over a horizontal post hammered into the wall, for cleaning later. For how long had he been back? What of Jerv? Had Griffyn come upon him, been told she was inside resting, then found the room empty? How in God's name would Jerv explain that? How would she?

The chilling notion made her wipe her hands on her skirts and march up the stairs to the keep. No Jerv. She passed the great hall, where tables were being laid for the meal. No Jerv. She passed a narrow window set in a recessed landing on the stairwell and peered out; no Jerv swinging from a post anywhere. That was a good sign.

Squaring her shoulders, she pushed open the door to the lord's chamber.

Griffyn was sitting on the bench, rummaging through a sack. He looked around at the sound of the door opening. A lock of dark hair fell over his forehead. "Guinevere! I've been looking for you. Where were you?"

"Riding," she said in a weak voice, about to fall into a dead faint. "My lord, truth, I am surprised to see you back so soon."

"As were the men. But I rode them hard." He ran his eyes over her body. "I wanted to get home."

Gwyn sat down on the mattress. She wasn't to be thrown in the cellars? Cursed? Beheaded? Did he even *know*?

"First, this," he said, and, reaching into his pocket, pulled out the ring of keys to the castle. Even from beneath his tunic, his rock-hard body radiated masculinity, but it was that damaging, sweet smile that made her heart start fluttering. He handed the household keys to her. "You'll want these. I should have returned them sooner."

She squeezed her eyes shut for a brief second, nodding her thanks.

"Come, now." He touched the tips of her fingers, helping her rise. "See what I've got." Excitement tinged his words as he rummaged around in a sack beside him. "See what I've got for you."

He pulled out one of her mother's small, chestnut-red harps, the one she'd sold to buy wheat. The other, black-dark, sat, tipped on its side, half hidden amid the linen folds.

Fierce, the memories pressed in close.

"These were your mother's?" she heard him asking dimly, as if from a distance.

She ran her hand across the smooth, carved wood. "They were."

"Good."

She brushed her fingers over the strings. Familiar, melodic whispers filled the room. She did it again, her eyes swimming.

"Good?" he said again, tentatively.

Her breath shot out in a weak, watery laugh. "More than good," and the tears spilled over.

"Bien." He ran the back of his fingers down her wet cheeks. "I know you miss her."

"Every day." Her voice caught. She smiled and touched the polished, red wood. "This will help."

Their eyes were inches apart, she standing, he sitting. He cupped the sides of her head and, pulling her down, kissed one cheek, then the other. Then he smiled, that lopsided, ferociously sensual grin, and she began heating up again. All he had to do was look at her and she was ready for him.

"Griffyn," she protested as he straightened, shaking her head but smiling nonetheless. "You should tell me about your trip—"

"I should lay you out on the bed."

She laughed. "Griffyn."

"Gwyn."

"Truly—"

He grabbed her hand. "Truly. I don't want to wait. My trip went fine. I—" His words stumbled for a moment. "I got your mother's harps, and am home again, hungry for you."

She raised an eyebrow. "'Twas news of my mother's harps

that sent you running to Ipsile? Nothing else?" she teased, but he stiffened. His fingers squeezed uncomfortably around hers.

"What do you mean?"

Her smile faltered. "I meant nothing, Griffyn. I was in jest."

His hand relaxed. "I am sorry. I am tired, 'tis hot, and 'twas a long ride. But this is a truth: I thought of *barely* nothing but you."

She laughed. "That suits well enough."

Reaching behind her, he tugged at the yellow laces that held her shorter, outer tunic. With each gentle tug, the material tightened around her breasts. The tunic slipped to the ground. He pushed aside the collar of the undertunic and pressed his lips to her bare shoulder.

"And you, Raven?" he murmured. "Did you think of me?"

"Every moment," she said in a voice barely whispered.

And just as he'd promised, he laid her out on the bed and took her to orgasm with such swift, stunning confidence she almost died from the pleasure.

And the pain. What had started as fierce loyalty to her king was turning into pure desperation. Griffyn must not be hurt by this. Yet she was depending on a most foul saviour in that regard, in Marcus fitzMiles.

Marcus sat whittling wood on a low bench in his herb garden. The mint was coming up fine, but the onions looked like vermin had got them. So be it. The cycle of life.

He shaved off another thin slice of wood. What Gwyn had given him was far too good to pass up. Far too juicy to do as she'd asked. Ride into the Nest, then out again, with only one ailing, dethroned prince to show for it? What then? Was he to prop Eustace on a saddle and shove him out before Henri fitzEmpress's armies? While Griffyn Sauvage got to nuzzle his Guinevere?

Gwynnie was fine and funny and sharp, but none too bright about these kinds of things.

And for all that Griffyn Sauvage was her betrothed, whom had she come to in her hour of need? Him. Marcus. A hot wash of pride filled his chest. She'd run from him a year ago, now she'd ridden straight to his keep, head bent, begging for help.

Of course, he'd have given succor if her head had been staked on a pike or screaming in his face. There was nothing he could refuse Guinevere. 'Twas her own fault she didn't know it. She never asked for anything.

She could have told him to support Stephen or Henri or Nur al-Din, the Muslim leader who was about to crush the Crusaders in Outremer. He would have done anything. Politics did not matter. Guinevere mattered. Her fierce fortitude, her lush body, her sharp, sharp mind. Marcus knew a jewel when he saw one, and every one he'd ever wanted lay within the Nest.

Sauvage would come out of the Nest, though. Marcus would ensure it. He would lure him out, close enough to parley, then give his ultimatum, without even the pretense of submission. Because he would never submit. Not to a Sauvage. He would submit to Lucifer before Griffyn Sauvage.

And if Gwyn thought Marcus had the Hallows chest, so much the better. The confusion would prove very useful in about two weeks.

The chest must have been tied to Sauvage's horse, which was rescued, Marcus later learned, by two of Sauvage's retinue. One of them was a Watcher, Alexander. Best to stay away from them; they had a habit of killing people who interfered with the Heirs. Had Marcus's father not been acquainted with that fact? Damned Scots.

Marcus's fingers twitched and a large chunk of wood fell to the ground. The small wooden figurine horse was now missing a leg. Marcus kicked it away.

But the chest had apparently *not* been recovered. It must be still sitting in the mud somewhere near where they'd apprehended Sauvage. Marcus would have to send a few discreet men to those woods, to kick aside every fern and find the thing.

And from there, his men could continue on to Henri fitzEmpress's camp, with some very interesting news.

At present, Marcus had only one of the puzzle keys. But by craft or cunning or cold hard steel, he intended to confiscate every single thing that mattered to the Heir.

He felt for the chilled weight of the steel key. It hung from his neck on a craftily-wrought steel strand he'd ordered and had de Louth secure for him on a recent trip to the city of Ipsile-upon-Tyne.

The key was just the beginning.

He whittled off another sliver of wood, then cursed as he sliced a gash through his thumb. Cupping his wrist, he held his hand out between his knees and let the blood drip onto the dirt, a bright red pool between the yellow leaves from the oak tree.

A time for everything and everything in its time. He straightened and dragged his knife along the wood figurine again. It sliced effortlessly. The time had come for Endshire to rise, and Sauvage to fall very, very far.

Griffyn met Alex in the hall the next morning. Griffyn was whistling. Alex looked over, eyebrows raised.

"Pagan? Are you well?"

Griffyn smiled and kept walking.

"You're whistling," Alex pointed out.

Griffyn looked over. "I am glad to be home, and to have her to wife is not so bad."

That was an understatement, thought Alexander as they strode towards the stables to meet a saddlemaker who was here to show off his wares. Alex glanced up at the keep windows and saw a flash of black move past one of them. It was strange, really. Griffyn had been looking for Lady Guinevere for an hour before she showed up yester eve, sweaty and out of breath, yet no one announced she'd ridden through the gates and returned.

The stables were cool after the afternoon sun, and the men spent an hour admiring the leatherwork of the exquisitely stitched saddles. When they made to leave, Alex glanced in at Gwyn's horse.

He was a fiery chestnut, with withers that grazed the underside of Alexander's nostrils and hooves large enough to crush a small child. For all that, though, he seemed good-natured, snuffing politely when presented a hand and nickering before they left. In truth, this was a Windstalker who couldn't be missed, really.

But a'missing he had been when Alex looked in an hour before Griffyn had arrived home yesterday. And missing, too, the night before, when Alex poked his nose into the stables on a whim, on a somewhat aimless search for anything amiss.

And the horse had not been there.

Chapter Twenty

Kneeling in the kitchen gardens, helping prepare the soils for winter, Gwyn tried to forget the mess she was now entangled in. There was nothing to be done about it. All she could do was wait. And hope.

The thought was almost laughable. Hope what? Hope that King Stephen would be conquered, or that Griffyn's lord would be crushed? Either way spelt ruin for someone she loved.

Truth be told, there was no guarantee Eustace would even live. He just might die.

Gwyn jerked her head up at the treacherous thought. Or rather, treacherous emotion. The thought was but a reality. The way relief swept through her was the villainy.

Her blood pounded as she stared at the clear blue sky. Wispy white sweeps of cloud dimmed the blinding blue brightness of the autumn sky. Cold dirt clumped under her fingernails. The inside of her nostrils burned hot and freezing cold with each breath.

She couldn't turn dirt another moment. She was too restless. She needed to walk the walls.

She scrambled to her feet, tugged on her skirts, and started for the battlements. She was moving at a rapid clip, head down, when she slammed into something hard.

"Uugghh!" exclaimed a voice. Alex staggered back a few steps, gripping his stomach and grimacing.

"Sir Alex," she gasped, and hurried forward. "Are you all right?"

He backed up a few more steps, holding out his hand, warding her off. "Fine, my lady."

She drew back and straightened her skirts, swirling them about her ankles. "What a nice evening." She said the polite nothing with her eyes averted. She did not want to see Alex, not with her suspicions about *his* suspicions floating through her mind.

"'Tis," he replied tonelessly.

"Yes, 'tis." She bent her head and started forward again.

"Been on any rides lately?"

She turned around slowly. "No."

"Ah. I just wondered if your horse had come up lame."

"No," she said more slowly than she had turned. "Why?"

Alex shrugged. "No, I didn't think so. I saw him gone from the stables, that is all."

Faint dread spread in a cold flood through her stomach. "I like to ride, sir. Has my lord some problem with that?"

He shook his head, his eyes never leaving hers. "Nay."

"Then I cannot see where it should concern you." She lifted her head in an icy pose and started walking away.

"If you hurt him, you will be sorry, Guinevere."

She stopped but did not turn. He didn't say anything more, and she started walking again, fighting not to clutch her chest, to hide her hammering heart.

"I have heard riding clears the head," he said to her back. "Especially when it aches."

It took all her reserves not to pick up her skirts and run.

Griffyn set his men loose on the Nest and its environs like worker bees of restoration and repair. A few began preparatory work on the crumbling stone of the castle's defensive walls, but most were sent to the fields.

October was for ploughing, the last of the year. Fighting men tended to fight, unless otherwise occupied. Practice with lance, falchion, and sword was a frequent device Griffyn used to stave off boredom and keep their fighting skills honed to a razor's edge, but ploughing was even better. It was more demanding, and more importantly, it was a joint effort. A common purpose tended to blur the divisions that led to bloodshed. His men were going to live here. They were going to build families together. Best to start now.

As he was trying to do.

He was aware of Gwyn wherever she went, in the kitchen gardens with Cook, talking with Raashid and William of the Five Strands—she'd insisted he stay on—about marling the fields of a distant manor, greeting a messenger or, most often, walking and talking with one of the multitude of women who inhabited the Nest.

Where did they all come from? he wondered as he helped haul stone on the walls the next afternoon.

"A bevy of breasts and giggles," Fulk gruffed when Griffyn brought it up. But Griffyn had seen him stop sweat-inducing labour to help one of those bright lights traverse a set of stairs, so he was not a reliable gruff.

Then again, it did appear Gwyn had adopted every orphaned or dispossessed waif from the River Clyde to the Ouse. They were everywhere, their bright gowns and winsome smiles making his men drop hammers and scatter handfuls of nails. And always, there was Guinevere, her voice carrying over the bailey, indistinct in words but bright in tone, her red or yellow or emerald green skirts floating over the cobbles as she hurried here and there.

He threw another wet shovelful of mortar onto a stone, aggravated with himself. Everything he'd been fighting for his whole life was here in front of him. But instead of reveling in it, he spent hours each day searching through dark, cobwebbed rooms.

He'd explored every chamber in the castle, from kitchen to chicken roost, upturned every chest, unlocked every box, examined every parchment of de l'Ami's. Nowhere was there a hint of anything more holy than tithes to monasteries and mission houses. Nothing whatsoever about safeguarding treasures coming out of the dark ages of Christendom.

It was as if every hint of it had been swept away by time. Or Ionnes de l'Ami, who'd wanted the Hallows above all things.

And now, Griffyn was starting to want them too.

He paused in his shoveling and wiped the back of his arm across his sweaty forehead, listening to the sounds of his men working. He stared over the battlement wall at the green expanse of the Nest's fertile fields and hills. No. He might be home again, but a life's mission realised was not enough anymore.

Not since he'd heard the dying words of Ionnes de l'Ami. Not since he'd been given a key that might unlock a treasure.

Gwyn was changing. Over the course of the weeks, she felt it, deep inside. Shifting like sheets of ice atop a melting river, rushing towards the falls, she was lost in Griffyn.

She even almost forgot. There were days where hours passed without her recalling the loyal treachery in her cellars. At times, it was as if Prince Eustace didn't exist. Until the night the messenger came.

The afternoon had tilted away in long slanting shadows when Gwyn climbed up on the battlement walls and let the wind blow her skirts back. She smiled at the bustling around her, which was slowing now as suppertime drew near. But even during the lull, there was a verve, a pulse, that had been absent for years.

The castle had come alive again.

The architect had arrived days ago, and every male over the age of ten was now up on the walls or down in the forests. Huge trees had been felled to make the scaffolding, and now wooden skeletons danced beside the tumbled-down ramparts, their steps and platforms filled with sweating men in chausses and boots, buckets of cement, and pages running hither and back again.

The valley resounded with the shouts of men and the ring of hammers, the slow squeal of cranes lifting the huge stone blocks into place on the castle walls. Cartwheels clattered over cobblestone, horses whinnied, children shouted and laughed, racing to pick up nails that had fallen or to carry water to the men.

But what moved Gwyn most of all was that the women were laughing again. Their dead husbands and fathers became more distant ghosts each time a Sauvage warrior smiled at them or their children.

She doubled rations for every soldier who had made one of her women laugh.

Out on the fields, too, came renewed life. Griffyn's men augmented her agricultural force considerably. The effects were immediate and obvious. Fast and furious the fields were ploughed now, ridge and furrow, ridge and furrow. For the first time in two years, Gwyn's heart lifted.

Griffyn seemed happy too, turning towards her with the half-smile that dimpled his cheeks and made her belly flip over. Of course, there were the days when no one knew where he was for hours, but she was far too busy to monitor him, and not inclined whatsoever. Unless he came upon her mid-day (which he had twice now, once in the landing outside their chambers, once in the orchards, both times bringing her to such a swift, stunning climax she was dizzy for half an hour afterwards) she might not see him from dawn until dinner.

Her job was to direct the children, tend the wounded, manage merchants and orders and servants, and ensure food and a steady stream of sweetened water made it up to the workers throughout the crisp autumn days. And throughout all the chaotic, loud commotion, Gwyn smiled.

Which is why as evening darkened the sky into a dusky twilight that evening, she knew very well why she climbed to the ramparts and let the wind blow back her skirts. Because she wanted to be near Griffyn, purveyor of miracles.

The air was wondrously chilled tonight, and the men were purple outlines along the ramparts, clustered in groups of twos and threes. Some leaned against stone merlons, some sat on the stairs, others perched on the walls themselves, legs dangling as the sweat dried on their tired faces. Every second man was one of Griffyn's, but their allegiance was indistinguishable under the cover of darkness, sweat, and the leather flasks being passed round.

Griffyn stood with a small group of men—Alex, Jerv, Fulk, a few others—the russet sunset flaming behind their outlines.

Guinevere approached. "My lord?"

He turned and smiled at her, that slow, lopsided grin. Even now, even after all they'd . . . *done*, the blood still rushed to her face. He held out his hand. "Come, Gwyn, see what we've done."

What they'd done was astonishing. They had almost completed repair along this section of the west battlement wall. Forty soaring feet of ashlar restored to its glory. Even the gap in the accompanying defensive tower had been repaired, up to twenty feet or so.

This is what Papa had dreamed of doing. Rebuilding, restoring the Nest to its glory.

"I know you don't care if he thought you a demon, Griffyn," she said softly, "but you should know that my father would have been proud of this. Of you."

Griffyn pursed his lips. "'Tis simply stone and strong men, Guinevere. Had your father wanted to, he could have done it."

Gwyn smiled sadly. "Perhaps. But I think, if he could have,

he would have. There was very little that mattered to him after, after—" She swallowed through the tightness in her throat. Behind them, men drifted back to their conversations. She could hear Alex say something soft but abrupt, then he fell silent.

"After Mamma died," Gwyn continued, "the only things that moved Papa were my mother's letters to him on Crusade. I remember watching him, after supper. He would sit on a bench in front of the fire trough, night after night, reading those letters til the flames burned out."

Griffyn caught up her hand in his. "Your mother was lettered?"

"Oh, certes. Papa ensured she could read and write before he left on Crusade. That little chest I gave you, back at Saint Alban's? All their letters were in there. Not that I could read them," she added. "But one day, I had hoped—"

She broke off as Griffyn's fingers tightened almost painfully around hers. His face looked odd.

"What is it?"

He didn't answer, but swung away to look at Alex, who was suddenly hurrying down the stairs, his boots clattering. Gwyn watched too, a knot of unease forming in the pit of her belly. Griffyn was still squeezing her fingers much too tightly.

She tugged on her hand.

He looked down slowly, with that odd, blank expression.

"Griffyn? What is it?" The small knot of uneasiness rethreaded itself into something prickly. But before she could name it 'fear,' it was gone, because Griffyn's gaze cleared, and his smile returned.

"My apologies, Gwyn. You were speaking of your father. Your mother, in fact, being able to read. And you, not."

She nodded, feeling very much like a missing conversation had just scurried away, much like Alex had down the stairs.

"You need not fear, Gwyn," Griffyn said, and this time, his fingers tightened just enough to lift her knuckles to his lips.

He pressed a kiss to each. "Your father is gone, as are his strictures. I will teach you to read."

She couldn't summon the will to speak the truth on the matter, to say she'd feared neither Papa nor his infrequent 'strictures.' What she feared then is what she suddenly realised she might need to fear again: the strange distancing of the Lord of Everoot. This going-away, when his body was still present.

She rested the side of her cheek against his long, hard body as he turned and responded to one of the men. He was sweaty, with a strong musky odour. She inhaled, feeling safe and protected and, well, that was sufficient.

This was all she wanted. Just to be near him, watch him turn his thoughtful grey gaze on whoever was speaking, occasionally asking questions or adding comments, but mostly listening. And people expanded under his attention. He was like a draught. They drank him in, grew brighter. His knights *and* hers. Jerv. Fulk.

Griffyn was making good what was once soiled, bringing life to what had been dead or dying. Papa hadn't possessed the heart to create what Griffyn was doing so effortlessly, in fifteen days, in enemy territory. Griffyn had simply swept in and made it good.

And she was going to betray him.

Madness.

She stared at the rock-strewn walkway underfoot, as a very novel, very reckless thought occurred to her: *Need she?*

There'd been no word from King Stephen. He could have had a messenger to Everoot within days if he'd wanted, even if he'd been standing on the cliffs of Dover. Why no news, then? No succor? No instructions for her?

Perhaps King Stephen *was* going to sign the treaty. Her heart fluttered. Perhaps there was no ruse. Mayhap 'twas over, and her king knew it. *She'd* concocted the notion that it was a lie. Her heart started rattling around in the wide, open space the dawning realisation created.

And on this flimsy foundation, she was to betray the most decent man she'd ever known?

Her mouth opened, without any real decision on her part. "Griffyn?"

It was like those mornings when she wanted just another moment of lying abed, warm under the furs, but her body would start moving on its own, climbing out into the cold morning air, doing what needed to be done, without her ever deciding anything.

Relief washed through her like sparkling rain. It was over. She was going to tell him about the prince.

"Griffyn?"

He looked down. "Aye?"

Her heart was hammering, her fingertips cold. "There's something I have to tell you."

Alex appeared just then, racing up the stairway. He stopped, one boot on the top step, panting slightly. His tunic was soiled from the day's work, half caught up in the waist of his hose, his blond head disheveled. He looked flushed, harried. Or excited.

"Pagan, you need to come. Now."

"What is it?"

Alex leaned forward. *"I found something."*

Before the words were fully out, Griffyn had dropped his arm off Gwyn's shoulder and was striding away. She stared after them, shocked. At the top of the stairs Griffyn suddenly turned, as if he'd just remembered her. "What did you want, Gwyn? Can it wait?"

She nodded stiffly. "Of course."

Alex glanced at her. "My lady," he said coldly, and turned away.

She let her wobbly legs lower her down to rest against the embrasure as Griffyn and Alex hurried down the stairs, wondering whether she ought to feel abandoned, or rescued.

And wondering what they had found. That they did not want her to see.

* * *

They stared at the small chest almost reverently.

"You found it among your things?"

"Among yours, Pagan," Alex replied. They were speaking very quietly. "Hervé took it from Noir when you were captured last September, after you dropped Guinevere at the Abbey. Hervé carried it to Normandy, gave it to Edmund your squire to pack with your other things. I did not think about it even once. But when Lady Guinevere just mentioned her father's letter, and a chest. . . ."

Griffyn did not need him to finish. 'Twas clear what he'd thought: this was the chest of the Hallows. For certes it would hold the third and final puzzle key. Where else would Ionnes de l'Ami have laid such a precious thing but in the revered chest itself?

Griffyn stared at it hard. For weeks now he'd been making his rounds of the castle, looking without knowing what he was looking for. Each day the search took more hours than the day before, and more of his attention. It was bordering, if he admitted it, on obsession.

And now, here was this little chest. It sat on the centre of the table. Small, easily hidden, highly alluring. Like a siren on the rocks. It may as well have had a heartbeat.

This must be it.

He and Alex looked at each other over the top of it. Then Griffyn pulled it to him. He ran his fingers over the iron latch. It fell open.

"It's not locked," he said in a flat voice. "Wouldn't such a thing be locked?"

His sight seemed clarified, making everything rich and vibrant, with sharp edges. The rest of the room, anything outside his direct line of attention, faded to white nothingness. The world was channeled through a parchment-thin funnel, the chest sitting at its vortex.

His heart beat strong in his chest, fast and loud as he lifted the curving lid. Alex sighed. It rode up on well-oiled hinges, no sign of age. Griffyn peered inside.

Papers. What looked to be yards of scrolled parchments, some with wax seals still half-attached, like teeth hanging by a sinew, about to fall out. Otherwise, there was not much: a tarnished ring, a scrap of linen, what looked like a short knife hilt, a handful of coins, a few other trinkets. But mostly, letters.

Just a box of letters. Like Guinevere had said.

No third key.

This wasn't the Hallows chest.

Something akin to rage welled up in him. It felt like all the emotions he'd ever eaten were pouring back up again. He took a deep breath to push them back down. More proof that, when it came to the treasure, men could not trust themselves. What they wanted overrode every other thing, including the truth. Griffyn had been certain this was the Hallows chest. But it wasn't.

Alex reached past him and pushed the letters roughly aside, jettisoning all the items in the chest onto the table. No keys came out, though, and Alex flung himself away from the table with a curse.

"God*dammit!*"

Griffyn took another breath to slow the hammering of his heart. His palms rested deceptively still on his thighs while Alex stalked to the window and cursed again, more quietly. Then he turned.

"That isn't it," he said in a thick voice. "That isn't the chest."

Griffyn didn't know what to feel. Thwarted, relieved, enraged: they all were swimming too close to the surface. His heart was still beating too fast, the awful hope had brushed too close.

"You've never seen the Hallows chest, have you, Alex?" he asked.

Alex shook his head. "Nay. The Heirs receive it at their

initiation, when they become true Guardians. Each has a Watcher witness to the ceremony."

Griffyn glanced over then. Purple-grey light streamed in through the unshuttered window. So did cold evening air. Alex stood by an unlit brazier, his arms crossed over his chest, glaring at the table where the chest sat.

"So I've kept that from you as well, Alex?" Griffyn said. "By my refusing my destiny all these years, you've never seen the Hallows chest."

Something flashed in the gaze Alex lifted to his, but Alex only shook his head. "Your father would not let you be Trained, Griffyn. 'Twasn't your doing. You would have been given the chest, but he stopped you from receiving the Training, just after we left England."

Griffyn nodded, his mind turning. "So this could be the Hallows chest," he said after a moment of reflection, "and you wouldn't even know it?"

"I thought it *was* the chest," Alex admitted ruefully.

They stared at it for long minutes. Shreds of thoughts and emotion still bobbed through Griffyn's mind, flotsam after the storm. Confusion. Determination. Fear, for he'd rushed here so quickly, left Guinevere behind.

Anger. The most potent thing left behind was anger, he realised. At his father.

It wasn't the anger that surprised him. He'd spent years doing that. It was the *why* of it that shocked him: he was angry because his father had not let him be Trained.

"And now, Alex?" he said dully. "What am I supposed to do now?"

"Why don't you read the letters?"

Griffyn started laughing, and that felt good. This is how it used to be, between Alex and him. Comraderie, laughter, friendship. But now, since the treasure was being spoken of, everything had changed. "Is that your guidance? I suspect I'd have thought of that myself."

Alex smiled. "I never said I was the wisest Watcher, but—"

"I'm stuck with you." Griffyn completed their long-standing jest. Alex smiled. They sobered, and Alex gestured to the parchment scrolls.

"So, what do they say?"

Griffyn picked one up. "Guinevere said these were letters between her parents, while de l'Ami was on Crusade." He unrolled it, the roughness of his fingers scraping against the parchment.

Dearest mine, I did not wed you to speak of you to others. I wed you to be something wondrous together. Without, I am fairly muddling through. Come to me. Why do we wait? I want your hair in my hands. I'll send Miles for you. Few can stand against him, and he thinks the world of you. You will be safe with him. Damietta will fall soon, and I think Jerusalem is next. My destiny lies in that City, and in you. Come to me.

The next were much the same, only further along.

Dearest mine, I was wrong to send for you. I cannot call Miles back, but if you have not yet left, do not. Do not come to this hell. The sands never stop shifting, the winds never stop blowing, and the fighting never ceases. If you come, I cannot think. Stay to home, build us one. I will come to it. I want a son, and however many daughters you demand from me. Keep yourself safe above all other things.

My love, 'tisn't going well. Not for us, nor our Dear Lord, not here in the Levant. I have prayed to God these missives reach you, that you did not leave the Nest. We've only enough food for days. The water is rancid, the horses are dying under us. Please God let you be to

*home. I want only to come home, to be with you in our
beloved Nest. The one light in this darkness is our dear
Ionnes. We must make him something special when we
return. Can you not ask your father for some of those
prickly Welsh hills? Ionnes would love their wildness, as
I love him. He is the reason I am able to hold on long
enough to see you again.*

> *Ellie, my love,*
> We've got it.

Griffyn lifted his head slowly. These letters were from *his*
father. To his mother. Christian Sauvage to his wife Alienor,
known to all as Ellie.

So Guinevere's father had been sitting in front of the fire
reading *these* letters, night after night. Love letters, from Christian Sauvage to his beloved wife, about his love for de l'Ami.
Before everything was wrecked.

Had de l'Ami repented, after all those years? Had torment
wracked his soul, in the dark, by the fire?

Griffyn's fingers tightened around the edges of the scrolls.
He forced himself to relax them. How fitting, that the last of
the letters spoke only of the treasure. All the love stopped
then. They'd found the treasure. Or been given it. But however it had happened, the Heir of Charlemagne, in the form
of his father, had laid his hands on some part of the treasure
in the Holy Lands. And that same blood now pounded
through Griffyn's body, making him want the thing with
something bordering on desperation.

Just like his father. Just like hers.

He jerked to his feet.

"Where are you going?" Alex exclaimed, shocked.

"To Guinevere." He flung the door open and walked out.

* * *

Gywn was down in her rose garden, walking between the rows of clipped thorny branches. Evening was purple and cold around her, but she did not care. She needed to soothe the restless energy out of her, until Griffyn came back and she could tell him the truth. It made her giddy with relief and fear.

The gates would soon close for the night. She heard the shouts of the guards, alerting those still down in the village or on the fields. *To home*, they called. *The gates are closing. Couvre-feu to hand. To home.*

She knelt beside the long bed of roses and gently mounded the dirt up around one plant's base with the edge of her hand. Soon, the twice-blooming buds would burst forth again, in time for Yule. Such beauty to look forward to, when everything else was always so dark and cold.

A shadow fell over the garden. Gwyn looked up. A lean, mailed figure stood over her. A messenger. No device, no insignia, no identifying design.

"Lady Guinevere?"

Her heart tapped out a faster beat. She nodded.

"I have something for you." His low-pitched voice carried no further than Gwyn's ears and the roses.

She got to her feet. "What is it? Who sent you?"

"I was instructed to give you this." He thrust out his hand. The mail armour encasing his arm stopped short of his hand, and there, balanced on his palm, rested a small leather pouch.

She put her hands behind her back. "What is that?"

"I do not know, my lady." He glanced around. "I must go."

She stared at the pouch. Only one person would be sending her secret messages. She snatched it off his palm. "What if my husband had been about?" she asked curtly, filled with anger and confusion.

His somber eyes met hers. "I was told you had not yet wed."

Her face flushed hot.

"If Lord Griffyn had been about, my lady, I would have given you this, instead." Another pouch, black leather, emerged

from the bag at his hip. He handed it to her, then flipped the
flap shut and bowed.

"My lady."

He was gone. The whole encounter had taken not a minute.
Gwyn stared at the two pouches, then opened the black
one first.

> *Guinevere,*
> *Many wishes for your approaching nuptials, dear*
> *friend! I unfortunately cannot come. Dear Stephenson*
> *has turned ill, and could never make the ride. But you*
> *know him—always so sickly! It has been so long since*
> *we last spoke, though. I miss our little chats, and will*
> *never forget our long talks in your rose garden. I recall*
> *your words so clearly. I trust you do not let them fade*
> *in your memory, either.*
>
> > *Best and warmest affection, old friend!*
> > *Ellspereth*

Gwyn had never met anyone named Ellspereth.

Trembling now, she lifted the flap on the other pouch and
shook out a light, cloth-covered bundle. She flung the fabric
open and out tumbled dozens of dead, dried rose petals, all
around her feet.

Chapter Twenty-One

Gwyn was standing by the window when Griffyn walked into their bedchamber. She swung around. He halted just inside the doorway, looking surprised to see her.

"I thought you'd be asleep."

And yet, they'd both come to the one place they knew the other would be.

She stood a minute, watching him, the look in her eyes too complicated to put a sound to, then she walked towards him with long strides, her skirts whispering over the rushes. Without a word, she stood on her toes, pulled his face down to hers, and kissed him.

He responded in kind, pulling her into an embrace, lifting her off her feet, holding her against him hard. Their mouths searched one another's with a sudden, desperate passion. Finally he lowered her back to the ground, but she kept her arms around him, hugging him tight.

"What is it, Gwyn?" he asked softly.

"Nothing," she murmured, then shook her head. "Nothing."

He pressed his lips into the silky warmth of the top of her head. "What did you want to tell me, earlier? I'm sorry I had to leave so suddenly."

She burrowed into his chest deeper. "I don't want to talk."

Neither did he. Whatever intensity was in him, it was in her too. And all it wanted was more passion, more fuel to the fire of his deep and intense desire for her. Not just her body. Her being, her heart, whatever moved her and animated her.

He wrapped her long dark, silk-entwined braid around his palm and dragged her head backwards.

"What do you want to do, Guinevere?" he asked in a low voice. Her face was tipped up to his, her breath hot.

"Whatever you want," she whispered back.

He descended, plying her mouth wide beneath him. She wrapped her arms around his neck and clung to him, her tongue meeting his every almost violent lash with one of her own, kissing so hard their teeth clicked together. Mouths still locked, his hand still wound amid her braid, he made her walk backwards until her legs hit the mattress and she sat.

Then he stood in front of her, wordless, their eyes locked, swiftly unwrapping her braid with one hand. He pushed the other, without warning or permission, down the front of her dress.

"Like that," he said almost roughly, as her hair came spilling out. "That is how I like it."

"Then that is how you shall have it," she said, her whispered words as rough-edged as his own. She reached forward and moulded her slender fingers around his erection. He dropped his head and closed his eyes, one hand resting gently on her head, the other still down the front of her dress. Her hand slid up and down the length of him, hard.

"Lean into me," he ordered hoarsely.

She did, until her forehead rested against his stomach. This gave him more space to push his hand down her bodice and trace the puckered areola of her nipple. Then he pinched it gently.

Her breath exploded out of her in a deep moan. He closed his fist around her hair and pressed his hips forward, into her mouth. Her warm, moist breath pressed into the material of his hose, at odds with the sharp edges of her teeth. Her tongue flicked out against him, a pushing wet pressure, doing to him what he'd done to her so many times, coaxing her into desire through her clothes.

"Jésu, woman," he growled, and gently pushed her back onto the bed. He tore at his clothes, flinging each item away. She was tearing at hers just as wildly, and he knelt on the bed beside her, helping her cast away her gown and chemise, his fingers fumbling where they were usually so sure.

"I love you, Gwyn," he said hoarsely, and swung one leg over her body, a knee on either side of her now trembling body. A tear spilled from the corner of her eye. It made him angry. He dashed it away with the back of a knuckle and bent his full attention to her body, stretched out on the furs for him to take.

Lowering his head, he sucked her breast into his mouth and sent his tongue flicking hotly over the taut red bud thrust up for him. She cried out as his teeth tightened around it, just enough to make her gasp. Her body arched with a moan and she reached for him, but he caught her wrists together and pressed them to the pillow above her head. With his other hand, he pressed a long, thick finger to her wetness, just one, swift stroke.

Her body bucked into the air, her head back.

Slippery, hot and wet, he sent his fingers plunging into her again. Her knees fell apart and her spine arched up, pushing her body up to him. He rolled to his side, his chest pressing against her sweaty ribs, one hand holding her wrists, the other driving his fingers in and out of her wet heat. He nipped at her breast, a sharp bite followed by a smooth, hot lap of his wicked tongue, taut and tight. Her breath came out hot and fast and ragged. She tugged sharply on her hands, to free them. He tightened his hold. Evidence of his desire pressed velvety and hard against her hip, and she shifted towards it.

"Please," she moaned, her mouth against his shoulder.

He reveled in watching her body writhe and buck at his command, in her long black hair tossed and knotted about on the pillow above, in hearing the small, breathy sounds shudder out of her. Her whimpers were growing more rhythmic, more gasping, less controlled.

He rose up between her legs and in one swift, rocking movement, sheathed himself within her, thrusting to the hilt. She flung her head back and reached for him, crying out.

"Wrap your legs around me," he ordered hoarsely. She did, holding him between her slippery, trembling thighs. Then, ankles locked behind his back, she pushed up onto her elbows and dropped her head back, her hips high in the air, meeting each pounding thrust of his.

Wet and tight, her flesh was hot, swelling, sweet womanly depths. He felt release barreling down on him. He plunged deeply into her again, then held, pushing steadily high inside her.

"Oh, *aye*," she cried. Her body was slicked with sweat, and she pleaded for him to move again, more. He could feel it coming for her, tightening her body, making her cries more reckless and rhythmic.

"Please, Griffyn, please, aye, please," she was moaning.

He rolled them over, holding her torso and hips close to him, until she was straddling him, stretched out over his belly and legs.

"Come on, my love," he whispered, his eyes locked on hers, his wide hands on her hips. "Now."

"You," she panted. "You too."

A passion-wasted laugh came out of him. "Oh, I will."

She sat up, straddling him, knees bent on either side of his body. She closed her eyes and dropped her head back, her hips rocking on him. He felt the tickle of her long hair drift across his bent knees and down his shins. He slid his hand down between them, pushed his thumb in to caress the swirling, wet nub. Her movements sped up, driving him deeper inside her pulsing, hot body. The room was silent, the only sound was pounding flesh, his grunts of pleasure, her gasps and mewlings. She lifted her arms and crossed them at the wrists, rested them on the top of her head, then arched back, her breasts jutting out, her lush mouth open and panting, and drove herself into him hard, whimpering with each thrust. Goddess.

He reached for the back of her neck and pulled her down to him, locking their mouths together in a deep, endless kiss. When he released her, she stayed bent low over his body, her chin up, eyes closed, hands splayed on the mattress, intent now on only one thing. He lifted his hips in rhythmic sweeps, watching her face, aiming for that spot high and deep inside her with every carnal thrust.

"Oh, Griffyn," she whispered. "Oh please."

He touched her face, she opened her eyes, and then her body exploded in shuddering undulations up and down the length of him as she howled out his name in gasping whimpers and spiraling moans.

The sheer force of his orgasm knocked Griffyn dizzy as he roared in release, her body quaking and shuddering around him. He wanted to engulf her, pull her inside of him and keep her safe from whatever had made that tear slide down her cheek, from whatever sorrow he was going to cause her, to hold her and just love her, and that would never be enough anymore, not with the lies already begun.

They lay, sprawled on the bed, catching their breath. Griffyn played with a lock of Gwyn's hair, lifting it, letting it run through his fingertips, then fall. After a moment, she rolled onto her belly and looked at him.

"Well. We succeeded in not talking."

He smiled faintly. "We should not talk more often."

Her body rippled with a small laugh. "I think we don't talk quite often enough."

"I don't." She smiled and ran her fingers along his jaw. He caught them up and kissed them. "That's all I want, Gwyn."

She rolled her eyes and gestured to the mattress. "*That?* All you want is to . . . not talk?"

He smiled. "I want small things. Family, harvest, children. *Bien?*"

She kissed his neck, dropping her eyes out of sight. He nestled his finger into the warm space under her chin and lifted. Her head came up, her eyes bright with tears. She smiled a watery smile. "I've been wanting children since I was only a child myself. I just never knew . . ."

"Never knew what?"

She shook her head.

The brazier was burning dimly. The moon was rising, and neither he nor Gwyn ever wished the shutters closed unless the weather demanded it. He pulled the furs up over her slim shoulders.

She rested a hand lightly on his chest and stroked her fingers idly. "And you, Griffyn? What of your dreams, as a child?"

He crossed his arms beneath his head. "I had a dream, as a child."

"Just the one? It must have been important."

He dropped his arm onto her shoulder and pulled her close and after all these years, he talked. "We left the Nest when I was eight. I used to lie in my bed, in Normandy, and all I wanted was to have it stop. I thought that meant coming home, as if that could fix everything. Hold everything at bay. But of course, that's a child's wish. Our past is like our shadow. It follows us everywhere. All any of us have is what we've been, and what we mean to become."

She watched him through the dark, flickering candlelight.

"I've decided," he continued, shifting his gaze down to hers, "what we intend to become matters more."

She pushed up to kiss his chin. "That's right. That has to be right."

"Or else we're doomed."

A moment later, she asked the question he'd practically begged her to ask, "What was 'it,' Griffyn? What did you want to have stop? What was coming home supposed to end?"

He stared up at the cobalt-blue linen weave stretched between the posts of the bedframe. "Nothing. My father. He was known as *Mal Amour*, bad love. In Normandy, he was a curse. Mothers used the threat of *Mal Amour* to make their children behave, or he would ride through their villages and take off the heads of their fathers, rape their mothers."

"Good God."

"My mother had the worst of it, I believe."

Griffyn did not think of his mother with any regularity. She'd been a quiet soul, barely verbal, and could do little to protect either herself or her son. Over the years, Griffyn's love for her had been as real and contorted as a wire wrapped around a supple willow trunk: devoted affection distended between the whetted filament of unwanted contempt.

All of which was the deep past. None of which mattered now. His father was dead almost thirteen years now, thank God, his mother, bless her soul, was too. And now he lay in his own home, in his own bed, with his own, astonishing woman, who was soon to be his wife. Things could be different now, could they not?

"Do you think she tried her best, Griffyn?"

The sound of her voice pulled him back. He looked down.

"Your mother." Her green eyes held his, intent, concerned. "Did she try her best?"

Well, that was a novel thought. "Yes," he said slowly. "I'm sure she did."

"And sometimes," she added after a moment, "it is just not enough, is it?"

"And sometimes," he pulled her close, "it is."

She nodded against his shoulder. That felt nice. This whole thing felt . . . unexpected. And what he'd been hoping for.

He'd been about to get submerged beneath wanting the thing, but came to Gwyn instead. Came to her, for her, for whatever lay inside her. And she'd lifted him out of it. Pulled him back from the muck and the pit.

"Tell me of yours, Gwyn," he said a moment later.

Her head shifted up a little. "My what?"

"Your anything."

She gave a little laugh and propped herself on an elbow to peer at him. "I'm quite sure I told you all about myself, a year ago, on horseback. You'll either be tired of hearing it, or have forgotten it entirely, which means it doesn't bear repeating."

He plucked a stray strand of hair from the corner of her mouth. "Marinated mushrooms and stained glass. And a bolt of a certain blue fabric, the shade of which you've never found."

"Oh, Jésu, Griffyn," she whispered.

He rolled her onto her side and tugged her backwards into him, so they formed a small, heated curve on the bed. "You remember wanting children when you were only a child, Gwyn, but I recall wanting you when I was barely a man."

She snuggled into him more deeply. "You didn't know me when you were a boy."

"I dreamt of you."

They lay so still for so long after that, she probably thought he was asleep when she finally whispered, "I wish I'd known to dream of someone like you, Griffyn. I've muddled through with such lesser dreams."

Chapter Twenty-Two

Griffyn was up on the walls with Harman, his architect and master mason, the next morning. The energetic Frenchman was gesturing to the nearest flanking tower.

"The problem, my lord, is that 'tis square. You see? No good!" He cut his hand through the air. "Round is better; no blind spots for your archers. And these walls," he continued in his confident, gravelly voice. His bulbous nose shone red in the afternoon sun as he pointed to the parchment plans fluttering on the battlement wall before them. A rock positioned at each corner kept it from fluttering off. "You see, my lord? 'Tis a simple matter, *non*? To build another tower, just so, opposite." He pointed again.

Griffyn nodded. A shot of cool air gusted over the walls. He brushed his hair back. "Another barbican."

Harman nodded. "Another killing zone, *non*? The arrow slits, too, I will make them crosslets, so more flexible. Flare them out, here on the inner sides, such that your archers can sit within. Happy boys they will be. We build a walkway overtop, and *voilà*." He turned his masonic squint to Griffyn and grinned. "A simple matter, *non*?"

"An expensive matter, *non*?"

Harman spread his hands and grinned. "*Mais, bien sûr,* my lord."

"But, of course," Griffyn echoed. He looked over the wall. A line of wagons was arriving, just cresting the hill and starting down the long, winding road from the south. A whole trainload of wagons. Just as he'd ordered. He smiled. Gwyn would want to know about this shipment immediately. He looked at the architect.

"Build it," he ordered, and clattered down the stairs.

He found her in their outer chamber, sitting with a few of her ladies-in-waiting. He wasn't surprised. She had women to spin and women to embroider, women to cook and women to fetch, women to distract his men and women to fall in the well, or at least stumble very near it, which might best be considered a particularly dramatic example of the former.

"My lady?" he said quietly, drawing near. The three fair maidens looked up, their faces flushed, then they giggled. Gwyn waved them off with a smile and started gathering the embroidery needles scattered across the table. "What can I do for you, Griffyn?"

"Why do you have so many?"

She looked at the needles, startled. "For embroidery, my lord. They break."

"Women. Servants. Ladies-in-waiting." He sat down beside her and plucked at the small patch of sewing Gwyn had been working on. "Why are there so many?"

"I would not worry too much, my lord," she said, gently removing the linen cloth from between his calloused, and dirty, fingertips. "Some of the men coming to pledge fealty to you are their fathers."

He picked up a needle and twirled until she plucked it free and put it with the others, punched through a thick, boiled stretch of stiff leather, which she then deposited in a small brown pouch. "Everyone is pleased the war is over, Gwyn, except you," he observed. "Glad to have a peaceful transition."

"'Tis true," she agreed pleasantly. "But I wager these ones are more grateful than most, because their daughters are here, safe and sound."

He lifted his eyebrows. "So the girls are about politics."

She laughed. "Hardly. Especially as most of them are not noble."

"Ah, and we turn to another timely topic: the servants one cannot turn around but for tripping over. Why are they here?"

She paused in folding up the small square of fabric. "Their husbands have died, or their fathers and brothers, fighting for my father and the king. They have no homes, no place in the world. We need washerwomen and milk maids."

"And almoners," he added wryly. "I noticed our almoner is a woman."

She smiled brightly. "She's quite good."

He reached for her hand. "We don't need *eighteen* washer-women, nor twelve dairy maids, Gwyn."

"Of course we do," she said placidly, and entwined her fingers in his. "You'll see. Your linens will be cleaner than anyone's in Northumbria."

"Even the Archbishop's?" he asked with mock astonishment, pulling her to her feet.

"Especially his."

He kissed the tip of her nose. "Come, I have something for you to see."

He walked her outside the chamber to the landing. Three slitted windows were cut deep in the six-foot rounded walls of the keep tower, which formed the landing and stairwell.

"Look," he ordered. "Out the window."

She walked to the northeastern window. Outside, a curl of smoke and a hub of activity bustled just inside the line of trees marking the eastern woods. She tipped her chin over her slim shoulder and smiled at him. "You're assarting some land."

She poked her head into the deep stone opening as far as she could. "'Tis wonderful," she said, her voice an excited muffle. "Really, wonderful." She pulled out, not smiling anymore. "For next year, of course. We shan't have seed enough for the fields that are already marled and ready for planting come spring."

He turned her by the shoulders and pointed towards the southern-facing window. She peered through. "Wagons?"

"How many?"

She looked again. "Four, five."

"There are more coming, Gwyn. Look."

She did. "What are they bringing?"

"What do you think?"

She leaned back and peered at him, arms crossed lightly, one eye narrowed. "Luxury or staple?"

He smiled. "Both. Something we need, but having it will make us feel rich indeed."

She laughed and rested her cool, slim fingertips on his forearm. *"Babies."*

He laughed, slung his arm around her shoulders, and pointed out the window again. "They don't come in wagons, Gwyn. Your mother should be ashamed. Now, what do you think is inside the wagons?"

"I haven't the foggiest notion." She snuggled into his chest. "You could have ordered us herbs from the Holy Lands or harps for the hall."

"Grain."

He felt her go still. "What?"

"Grain. For milling now, and seed for planting. Wheat, and rye, and barley."

She was still another moment, then her shoulders began to shake. He held her tighter and pressed his cheek against the top of her head while she cried.

* * *

She woke up in the night screaming again. Griffyn held her to his chest until she calmed, then said softly, "Your father?"

She stared straight ahead, her eyes glassy and red-rimmed. "Aye."

"Why do you dream of him so much, Gwyn? Why are they so awful?"

He didn't think she was going to answer, but finally she said, in a rote voice, "He never forgave me."

He ran his hand over her hair. "For what?"

"For killing my brother. And then my mother."

He tucked the furs up around her shoulders and pulled her closer. "What happened?"

She was silent a moment, then started talking in short, monotonal sentences. "I was ten. Out riding. I shouldn't have been. There'd been so many raids down from the north that spring. I was not allowed to leave the castle by myself. Not even to the village. I knew that. But I'd heard Mamma say she needed more elderflowers. Papa's bones were aching in the spring damp."

She stared across the room at the far wall. "I knew just where they were—I'd found a new cluster of them the summer before, by the river. I went to get them. I heard them. Mamma and Roger, calling me. At first, I heard them. I just didn't want to go. I—I rode away. I found the herbs. I was kneeling on the ground, then—"

She swallowed. "Riders. A raiding party. Half a dozen *routiers,* straight down from Scotland."

Her pace picked up, her words running together at times. "I got on Wind and tried to ride away, but they saw me. I hear them whopping and screaming, kicking their horses up behind me. I'm screaming too. Then, then—oh, *Roger.*" She was gulping and sobbing, the tears pouring out. "He and a few of his best men, galloping flat out. They're calling to me, I'm flying on Wind straight to the centre of them, they're closing in behind me. They're fighting. It's so *loud.* Godwillneverforgiveme

Roger's dead. I am alive, and Roger's bleeding to death on the grass," she whispered, pointing, as if he was before her now. "Oh God, please let me die."

Great, wrenching sobs shook her body. Griffyn stopped hushing her and just held her, rocking away the relived horror that had lifted the hair on the back of his neck.

Later, much later, when she calmed, he brushed back the hair from her wet, stricken face.

"And your mother never forgave you?"

"Of course she did. Then she died. Three months later. Her heart broke one night."

Griffyn took a deep, silent breath and let it out. "And your father, Gywn? He never forgave you?"

"No. Why should he?"

"It was an accident."

"I knew what I was doing," she answered in that flat, dead voice. She started shivering. "I knew I was doing wrong."

He held her until she fell asleep, maybe an hour later. He lay awake for a long time, though, watching her. She'd thrown the furs off her body, and was a shadow of rose and silk in the flickering firelight. One satiny forearm was flung above her head, the other dangled off the edge of the bed, delicate fingers curled in sleep. Her hair streamed out as if she was underwater, all except one ebony curl which had fallen across her face and rustled gently as she breathed. The room was quiet.

With one finger, he pulled the strand of hair away from her face and ran its softness between his fingers. A flicker of self-disgust made him look away. He did not like deceiving her. But even less did he like the idea of involving Guinevere in whatever unholy mess had destroyed their fathers. She would be protected from that if it were in his power at all. The one noble act left in him.

His hand went to the keys hanging around his neck, the black iron one and the little steel one de Louth had given him.

He'd had hope, for a while. Hope he and Gwyn were touching one another. Hope that things could be different. That their marriage could be different, that *he* could be different. But she'd never returned his declarations of love, just as his father had not, and inside of Griffyn, the desire for the treasure was building.

And so, it was all to be the same, awful story again. Destiny. He could no more reject it than he could cut off his legs and keep walking. Wanting had crept in at the first crack in his resistance. Skewered in and spread out, like a cobweb over his soul. And now he dreamed at night of it, of a treasure that would lift him up. Power him. Ennoble him.

And he *knew* it to be trash. If a thing could so corrupt a man's intentions, it was trash. Refuse. Carrion.

And still he wanted it. Not completely, not yet. But it was coming. He could see it like a great black bird, winging in from far away.

Chapter Twenty-Three

He stood in the cellars of the Nest early the next morning, a torch slammed into the cresset on the wall, angling the lighted end out into the air. In front of him was a door. An essentially hidden door, tucked here in the darkest recesses of the cellars.

He had stopped short at this crossroads in the tunnels and, half by touch, half by memory, found the door. The shadows danced in ghostly leaps, attesting to the presence of fresh, or at least moving, air that Griffyn could not detect.

He raked his fingers through his hair. "I've forgotten for all these years, and now I remember it so well." He leaned forward and peered down the long, dark expanse of the tunnel running to his right. It went on and on. "That goes to a cave in the wood, if I recall," he murmured, more to himself than Alex, who stood at his side, eyebrow lifted.

"You played down here?"

Griffyn smiled faintly. "All the time."

Alex shuddered. "And Guinevere? She was a child here too. Did she play down here?"

"I do not know," he murmured. The leather of his hauberk creaked in the narrow space; they'd come straight from work with the men in the practice fields at dawn. The hunt was going out this morning, but Griffyn sent Jerv at its head, claiming too much work, promising to join them the following day.

But Griffyn knew what was really happening. The infection was spreading. He was Christian Sauvage's son. It was in the blood.

Still, he considered, Gwyn did not seem to be stricken with the sickness that had destroyed their fathers. She was different. Different from anyone he'd ever known.

"But I would like to know," he said aloud. "I would like to know if she played down here." It was dank, close, dark, and would have been dense with cobwebs if spiders ever dared venture down here. They didn't, but an imaginative child certainly would. "I think she did."

"You're both mad, then," Alex muttered with conviction. He pointed the tip of his short blade at the door before them. A monstrous padlock hung off it like a fang, carved in the shape of a dragon's head. "Are you going to open it?"

"Are you going to ever start Watching?" Griffyn muttered in reply. Then he shoved the iron key around his neck into the lock. He hit a barrier. The key didn't fit.

Alex cursed.

He tried again, pushed harder. Nothing.

"Hack it off," Alex urged, his words swift and low.

"That's ludicrous," Griffyn said sharply, but in his mind it seemed more sacrilegious. "I think not."

Alex lifted his brows. "So, what now?"

"We wait."

Alex's eyes snapped to his. "In God's name, Griffyn, wait *for what*? How long can you wait?"

Griffyn drew back at the unprecedented fury. "Longer than you apparently."

Alex's granite gaze hardened even further. "Griffyn. I have been a Watcher for more years than you've been alive. I have been waiting for you my whole life. And now, all you *do* is wait. The world is at your command, if you do but reach out and take it."

"You have no idea," Griffyn replied in a low, barely controlled voice. "I never wanted this thing, your whole mission has been to have me reach out and take it, and now you've succeeded, and I want it, I am seeking it, and I hate it. So, I wait, a few days, a year: what matters that? In the end, I will be like all the others. Twisted, warped, missing from my own life."

Alex was quiet a moment. "Not all of them, Griffyn."

"I do not care!" he roared. The thunder bounced off the walls and kicked down the dirt tunnels. "I cannot say it any more clearly than this: *I despise it.* And now, all I can do is seek it. I leave my woman to follow the mere hint of it. I dream of it at night."

Alex paused. "What kind of dreams?"

Griffyn dropped down on a huge block of stone, jutting out a few feet from the rest of the close-set stones, almost as a seat for someone like him, sitting and pondering how to get into the inner chamber. He put his elbows on his knees, his forehead in his hands. "Leave."

"Griffyn, my every move has been to serve you. If—"

"Leave me."

Alex stood a moment, then turned and strode away. The torch flame stretched and swayed in the breeze of his retreat, then grew still and steady again. Griffyn pressed his face into his palms. He could smell the cold metal of the keys on them. Again, he was here, in a cellar, while the whole world was waiting in the fresh air above him.

Inside the padlocked cellar door, Duncan stood at the ready, short sword in hand, sweat trickling down his temples, prepared to be killed in the service of his lady. Prince Eustace lay dying behind him, but this had never been about a young prince he barely knew. 'Twas always about good lady Gwyn and her radiant smile.

Truth, she'd saved him and his little sister when the rebels tried to burn all of England to the ground. Papa and Mamma had roasted like cinders, but he'd hied it straight to Everoot, tugging Alice alongside, tripping and crying under the cover of a tattered cloak, pinched from a solider too drunk to realise. Papa had mentioned good Lady Gwyn, and right he'd been. She'd taken them in without a second word, given them food and a place, from now until they died, she'd promised, and she would, too.

The sounds of muted voices drifted away, and Duncan lowered his sword, his heart hammering. He sat down next to his charge, hoping Lady Gwyn would come soon and tell him what was happening abovestairs. Truth, he'd never expected to have a long life, but not until he came to Lady Gwyn had he expected to have such an exciting one.

Griffyn came upstairs from the cellars into the great hall and was met immediately by William of York, as dour and nervous as ever. "My lord. Another messenger."

Griffyn looked over. A middle-aged, muscular messenger sat at a table, but rose quickly at Griffyn's arrival.

"My lord," he said, smiling.

Griffyn returned the grin. "Ralph," he said warmly, grasping the arm of one of Henri's trusted messengers. Griffyn had used him himself a few times, with Henri's leave, on the most sensitive missions.

"What news?" he asked, releasing Ralph's arm. "Why are you two hundred miles north of Henri? Have you been fed?"

He glanced over Ralph's head and nodded to William of York, who nodded to a servant, who hurried to the passage of screens that comprised the hallway to the kitchens. Around the hall, off-duty knights and soldiers rested or talked or played games of dice. A few women, distaffs in hand, sat near the fire in a small, bright cluster, their chatter a low, pleasant hum.

Ralph pulled a document from the leather pouch at his hip. "The fitzEmpress is coming to Everoot."

"I know." Griffyn scanned the scrolled document. "A few weeks. Right after the treaty."

"No. Now. He'll be here in a day."

Griffyn looked up swiftly. "What? Why?"

Ralph's eyes met his. "He saw fit to come here first."

"Ahh." Griffyn nodded, utterly perplexed. He scanned the parchment again, then looked between the parchment and the scene outside of the window. It had grown colder. Billowing clouds were piling up on the horizon.

"Why?"

"Our lord Henri has ever done what he wanted to do."

"Indeed. But Ralph," Griffyn said quietly, *"why?"*

The messenger's eyes shifted away. "Henri's always been fond of you."

"Not that fond," Griffyn said grimly. "Not enough to post-pone a treaty that hands him the country." He glanced at the paper again.

"A messenger from fitzMiles did arrive two days ago," Ralph admitted reluctantly.

Griffyn nodded slowly, thoughtfully. "But what has that to do with me?"

"Fulk, what do you know of Eustace?" Gwyn asked as ca-sually as possible. The world was a blanket of grey, pearly mist this morning, bouncing their voices back like they were in a cave.

Fulk looked over in confusion. "Eustace?"

"The prince. As a man, I mean. His behaviours and such."

She stood next to her marshal, anxiety working to tighten her stomach into a churning, knotted mess below her hard, thundering heart. Ever since she'd risen this morning, there'd been the feel of impending doom. Perhaps it was simply the nightmares: they always made her feel sick to her stomach and bristly the following day.

But in her heart, she knew this was different. It *was* impending doom.

They stood near the tilting yards where the squires and knights trained. It was too early for many to be out at their jobs yet. Even Fulk, taskmaster that he was, did not require his men to train before they'd had a crust of bread and a mug of ale, so it was just Fulk and her, and one lone fourteen-year-old, desperate to be knighted, who whooped and hollered around the quintain, then spurred towards it with his lance. He speared the proper end, then got knocked violently in the back of the skull as it swung around before he'd galloped away. This was the third time that had happened in the five minutes Gwyn had been standing here.

Fulk, almost religiously dedicated to the meal she'd carried out for him, groaned and set the plate down on a round of wood.

"Excuse me, milady," he muttered, then turned and shouted, "Faster, Peter! Move yer weary self faster or ye'll be dumber than a stump by Yule. And ye've not so very many brains to give all away to a quintain," he added ominously.

Peter saluted. Fulk sighed and turned back. "Where did ye find this one, milady?"

"Where I found all the rest," she replied dully. "Dying somewhere."

Fulk grunted. "Well, that makes it worth somethin'. I'll give him this; he works harder than all the rest put together." He punched his knife tip through another hunk of meat. "Milady? Ye asked me a question."

Mist saturated everything. She brushed her wet hair back with a cold, damp fingertip. "Eustace. The prince. What kind of man is he?"

He considered her. "Ye mean, what kind of man *was* he?"

"Indeed. Was. What kind of man was he?"

Fulk's keen gaze scanned her face. "Ye've been in a war yer whole life, milady. What do ye think it does to men? Princes all the way down. It's got a *ruinin'* effect, it does."

"Not everyone. Not everyone gets ruined."

Fulk met her eye. "Ye're thinking of your Papa."

But she wasn't. She'd been thinking of Griffyn. Now, though, she was thinking of her father, thinking hard.

"He was no saint, Gwynnie. Ye've got to know that, after all this time. He was no better'n the rest in some ways."

"Was he worse?"

The question popped out before she could stop it, puffed up like a small white cloud in front of her lips. Fulk stopped chewing. His cropped head swiveled around.

"I suppose it's in how ye look at it, milady. Which side ye're on."

"And what if," she began. Her stomach churned sickeningly, as if she'd just ridden over a wave. "What if I were someone who already lived here at the Nest, when Papa came and captured it?"

Fulk looked away. "There was a fire."

Something sharp and wicked rose up in her throat. "What fire?" Fulk didn't answer. "What fire? Did Papa—"

She stopped short. *Leave it unfinished.* Her head floated light, dizzy. The mists kept bouncing their words back, cloaking them, so it felt like they were under a dock, whispering about piracy and shipwrecks and other, awful things.

Do not ask again.

The stiff, unwanted silence continued until Gwyn asked in crisp voice, "What about Eustace, Fulk? I asked about Eustace, the king's son."

Fulk cleared his throat, planted one beefy palm on the hilt of his knife, and cast a squinted eye at the ground. "Well, milady, he's meaner'n they come."

"What?"

"He'd a mind of his own, and not so's you'd respect it, but more like be disgusted by it."

"Well," she exclaimed, flabbergasted.

"And don't think yer brother thought any different, milady."

Her jaw fell open. "But they were friends."

Fulk shook his head. "None o' that. Eustace was goin' to be his king one day, that was all." He shoved a wedge of meat onto his knife tip. "Eustace was nothing but trouble, and bett'r for all of us that he's dead, forgive me Jésu," he finished, tossing a glance of half-hearted penance skyward.

"But Fulk?" she said in confusion. "Why did you support King Stephen, then, knowing Eustace would follow him to the throne?"

He gave her a surprised look, hunk of meat skewered and dangling, dripping, before his mouth. "Why, I wasn't supportin' him, milady. I was supportin' you."

And now it *was* piracy and shipwrecks and every other, awful thing.

Chapter Twenty-Four

Griffyn was sitting in the hall, alone, with a cup of ale, leaning over a sheaf of parchment, when Guinevere entered the room. He looked up and waved her closer.

"Gwyn. Good. I've just received word: Henri fitzEmpress is coming to the Nest sooner than expected. Should be here by the morrow. He'll be here for the wedding . . ."

His voice trailed off when he saw the way she stood in the archway. Dark, staring eyes under a halo of wild, spinning hair. Her cheeks were wet from tears, her fingers twisted in a tight ball in front of her stomach. He pushed to his feet. The chair toppled to the ground behind him.

"What is it?"

"When did your horse die, Griffyn?" she asked in a flat voice.

"What?"

"Your Rebel. The stables. When did they burn down?"

He paused. "When I was eight."

"I know. But when was that?"

"When we left England. When the wars began. When Stephen took the throne."

"When my father took Everoot?"

He was quiet a moment. "He burned it to the ground."

A single sob wracked her body. "That's what I thought."
She swallowed. "I have done something."

He went still. "What?"

"I did it before I knew you."

He watched her silently, coldness pouring through his limbs.

"But I kept doing it after, too, God save me."

"What?"

Her body seemed to suddenly wash away. She leaned her
shoulder against the stone archway. "I have the king's son in
the cellars."

His face screwed up in confusion. "Henri? He doesn't have
a son."

"Stephen does."

Gwyn watched as he stared, the implications settling like
bricks on mortar. Blazing eyes bored into hers, then he was up,
away from the table, striding to the door without another glance.

She called out after him with what breath was left in her
lungs. "There's another way."

He froze.

"There's a secret passageway to the cellars," she whispered
to his back. "In our chambers. Behind the tapestry."

His dark head swung back around with an animal fury,
slate grey eyes washed of colour.

"Did you think I didn't know?" he rasped, his voice harsh
like fire had scalded it. "Good God, Gwyn, *what were you
thinking?* All this time, you thought I didn't know, and you let
it be. With treason down below."

"I never meant it to be so," she whispered wretchedly, tears
streaming down her face.

"It is now."

He reached out, wrapped his fingers around her wrist, and
dragged her behind him up the stairs. She staggered as she
went, her heart hammering and breaking all at once.

"Alexander!" he shouted as they circled wildly up the

stairs. "Alexander! Jerv—" He spun around so fast she slammed into his chest. "Who else knows?"

His gaze lanced into her with a quiet ferocity that washed her knees clean of power. She touched the cold stony wall of the circular tower for support.

"Myself. Only myself. And Jerv—"

"Goddamn you," he whispered in a hoarse growl. "Goddamn you."

"Jerv doesn't know! Not about Eustace. He suspected something. And he," she gulped, "he told me to tell you, whatever it was. He told me to tell you."

His hand closed around her throat. His face was bare inches from hers. "He told you to tell me?"

A frantic nod.

"And you didn't?"

She shook her head, black hair tumbling. "I made a vow," she whispered in misery.

His face disfigured into a harsh, awful twisting of smile and grimace. "So? What good is your word, anything you say?"

He was gone, taking the stairs two at a time, disappearing up into the dim shadows of the stairwell. Gwyn stumbled behind, washed of tears, dying inside.

He kicked open the door to their bedchamber. Striding across the room, he ripped the tapestry from its mooring. It fluttered to the ground, a heap of bright dyes and tangled thread, revealing the oak door.

He yanked it open and bolted down the stairs into the darkness, bellowing as he went, "*Alexander!*"

A moment later, Alex appeared. His blond hair was rumpled, his eyes wild, one hand fumbling furiously to fasten his breeches. In the other, he held his sword belt. Gwyn pointed mutely to the wide-flung door.

Tossing her a confused, worried glance, Alex ran down into the darkness too, descending into the bowels of the castle. Gwyn followed, tripping over each step, her skin hot and cold all at once.

By the time her foot hit the bottom step, Griffyn and Alex were standing in front of the door. The huge dragon's-head padlock hung like a sullen guard, casting dour steel glints off the torchlight.

"You know about the door," she said in dull amazement.

"I don't have the key," he replied just as tonelessly.

Wordless, Gwyn stepped forward and, plucking the golden key from its pouch, shoved it into the dragon's mouth. It clicked, the mouth opened as if in a roar, and the lock sprang free. She stepped back. Griffyn stepped forward.

He pushed on the door and it swung open. He and Alex stood in front of her, huge hulking figures cast in sharp silhouettes by the single torch that burned inside.

Duncan leapt to his feet and blocked their path, his small sword drawn. Neither knight had eyes for him. They were staring into the cell, immobile.

"Down, Duncan," she ordered gently.

Griffyn and Alex disappeared into the chamber. She heard Alex say in a low voice, "Do you know what will happen if Henri fitzEmpress ever finds out about this?"

She fell back on the bottom step of the stairwell, her buttocks against the freezing stone, and stared numbly ahead.

Griffyn appeared in the doorway a moment later, his towering figure blocking all the light behind. But his eyes glittered with an illumination all their own, filled with quiet fury.

"He's dead."

Duncan appeared at Griffyn's side. "He went dead on his own some five minutes ago, milady. I kept him warm though. Just like you said to."

Her voice could barely reach a whisper. "I am sure you did, Duncan." She wrapped her arms around her sides and began to rock slowly. Nothing mattered anymore. She only had to do what needed to be done in the moment, and carry on to the next meaningless moment.

Griffyn put the heel of his hand on the side of his head and wiped upwards. "What have you done to us, Gwyn?" he said quietly.

His words brought the tears again. They swept in rivers down her face.

"What would you have had me do, Griffyn? You, who esteem oaths and vows so dearly they fairly *breathe* in the room with us, what would *you* have done? If your king, whom you love so well, gave you the most important thing he had, to keep safe? If you'd done so much damage to so many people, and had a chance to make it right? *If you'd given your word?* "

She looked away, unable to watch the anguish in his eyes. He was such a good man, and all he'd ever known was hurt, and betrayal, and loss. Good and awful God, she hadn't wanted to be one of them. She bent over as she continued speaking, tears streaming down her face.

"And then came the only man I could ever love, and to honour my vow meant I had to go against everything he'd been fighting for. Tell me, Griffyn, what would you have done?"

"I would have done what I wanted to," he said, his voice as cold and distant as a mountaintop. "That's what we all of us do."

A guard clattered down the main stairway at the other end of the hallway. He raced through the clammy stone corridor, shouting. "My lord! Praise God, I've found you. An army comes, riding hard and straight for the Nest."

Gwyn shot to her feet. "God save us all. *Marcus.*"

Griffyn gave her one long awful look. Then he and Alex and the soldier bolted back down the corridor, leaving a wake in the air that bobbed around Gwyn like a rising tide.

Chapter Twenty-Five

Griffyn stared over the battlements at the stream of soldiers washing down the hills. God Almighty, where had they all come from?

"Are the men ready?" He turned to Alex, whose squire was hurrying behind him, still buckling on his armour. Edmund was kneeling at Griffyn's feet, lashing his greaves into place over his shins.

All around them, chaos reigned. Men and boys shouted to one another. Armed soldiers spread out along the walls, still adjusting helms and arraying themselves every ten feet with crossbows and long bows. Women fled across the bailey, young children tripping before them. Chickens and goats ran kicking and clucking through the mayhem. A dog barked incessantly. It was a brilliantly sunlit world, made more so by the ominous clouds piling up like ashen mountains on the horizon.

Griffyn saw Gwyn coming. Skirts hitched above her knees, black curls streaming out behind her, she flew across the crowded expanse of the bailey. She skidded to a halt beside a cluster of terrified women, gave each a hug and pointed towards the castle, then was off again, coming towards them.

He looked back at Alex.

"At your command, my lord. The west side, Pagan."

Alex shoved his helm between his arm and his chest. "'Tis still weak."

Flicking his eyes across the riot around them, Griffyn nodded. "I know. Edmund?" He looked down at his fourteen-year-old squire. The boy's head jerked up. His face was bleached white. "Are we ready?"

"Aye, my lord," he stammered, getting to his feet.

Griffyn put his hand on the boy's shoulder. "We'll be fine. We've seen battle before, and I haven't let anyone take you from me yet."

Edmund blinked. "Aye, sir. I mean, *no sir.*"

Griffyn turned to Alex. "There's a passageway that leads underground. Behind the north side of the keep. The door is in the wall, under ivy. Light the lanterns. The way is long, but wide enough for two on foot, abreast. Take my personal guard and the left and right flanks and lead them through. It will bring you out there."

He pointed to a hill, maybe a hundred yards distant. The forest pushed right up to its edge and stopped. A clear, sloping green hillside swathed in yellow flowers spilled out below, straight to the valley floor.

He looked at Alex. "At my command, come down and kill whoever is left."

Alex's jaw tightened. "That means you're not joining us."

"I'll take the vanguard and ride out the front gates."

"But, Pagan. If I take the flanks and your guard . . ." He looked at Marcus's army again. There must be more than five hundred. "They'll slaughter you."

"We're the diversion, Alex. You're the force."

"Keep your guard with you," Alex insisted in an urgent, angry voice, his head down.

"They're the best fighters and riders. They'll be needed for your attack. Now go."

Alex stared at the ground and nodded curtly. "Aye."

"You too, Edmund."

The boy looked at him in horror. "I can't leave you, my lord! I won't!"

"You will. Go."

Edmund's earnest face crumpled. Alex clapped him on the shoulder and they started down the stairway just as Gwyn came up, running, holding a hand to her side.

"Griffyn," she called breathlessly. "Wait. There's something you must know."

"You've told me enough for one day."

She stopped midway up the stairs, just below him, and placed her hand on the leather cuff encasing his forearm. "Wait. There's a secret passageway, comes up in yonder woods—"

"I knew about that one too, Guinevere." He looked over her head. "At my command," he called to Alex, just as Alex peeled off to the right and began shouting to Griffyn's personal guard, gathering the force for the hillside attack.

His commands rang out loudly, and her face blanched. She looked down at the bailey, then back at him, comprehension dawning. "Griffyn. You cannot send your guard from your side. They would die for you." She lowered her voice. "You'll be killed."

"They're the best fighters—"

"They will be facing the weakest troops. Marcus's strongest will be waiting for *you*. Not Alex nor your guard nor Edmund—. You'll be killed."

He grabbed her by the shoulders and pulled her almost off her feet, until their faces were inches apart. "To save Everoot for you and ours, Guinevere, 'tis a thing I will do gladly. Do you not see that yet?"

"I do," she wept, wrapping her fingers around the mail armour. The rings pierced her skin.

He pulled away and gestured to a nearby knight. "Take her to the hall." He turned away. "She'll be needed there."

Gwyn felt her knees giving out. She was sliding to the

ground, holding her hand against the wall for support. The knight's hands were on her arms, pulling her up.

"My lady? Lady Gwyn, please come."

She dragged herself up by an act of will. Her back unbent along the curve of her spine until it was as straight as the sword Griffyn had just unsheathed as he walked to the front of his men. He spoke to them as he went, passing words of encouragement and victory, an order given briefly to a soldier here and there.

He never looked back.

"Please release me, Robert," she said with quiet dignity, turning to the knight. Time to do what was directly in front of her, no further, no more.

She started across the bailey, towards the main hall, where villagers and servants were coalescing in small, frightened bands of huddled humanity that she, simply, could not save.

Griffyn could, though.

Chapter Twenty-Six

Everoot's small army rode under the portcullis gates. Marcus sat at the top of the hill, watching and counting. He smiled. Rumours of Sauvage's numbers had been exaggerated. No surprise. The Sauvages had always received more than their fair share of everything: esteem, money, women.

His gaze swept over the troops again. But this was even better than he'd hoped. Even counting the men on the wall, he had him outnumbered five to one. The fitzEmpress's vaunted captain did not appear to be so unassailable after all.

The last of Everoot's mounted knights came through the gates. A few dozen foot soldiers marched behind, carrying battleaxes and pikes. Marcus leaned over and said to his herald, "Call for them all. We'll hold no one back. Everyone into the valley. This is going to be a rout."

The herald nodded and lifted the horn to his lips. He bugled different patterns. Along the front of the army, pennants of various styles shot into the air. First the horsemen rode forward in a line, the great destriers snorting and pawing, leather creaking. On their backs, the men were a row of anonymous, helmed faces. Behind clustered the foot soldiers, their armour hardly less sturdy for being made of layers of boiled leather.

Marcus wheeled his horse around. The knights were his

men, cleaved to him by vows of fealty, deeds of land, and a shared partiality for warring. Most of the foot soldiers were a different sort. They may share a certain *joie de guerre*, but they had few ties to bind. It was a ragtag army of unpaid mercenaries and debtors freed from Endshire holding cells.

Marcus knew he had to keep it simple, attempt nothing which required trust or skill to execute. And, above all, he must give them something to fight for.

"This is no siege, men!" he shouted. "To the death, now. No holding back. Foot follows the horses, no retreat. Whomever you kill, everything on him is yours. No plunder in the castle, only the village. But that, you may burn to the ground. And above all," he shoved his helm on his head and bellowed, *"Sauvage is mine."*

His horse reared up. Marcus lifted his arm and swept it down. The cavalry exploded like it was shot from a trebuchet, kicking heels and galloping hooves. The troops came running behind, thunder rolling into the valley.

They met in a violent clash of steel and flesh on the valley floor. Lances crashed into armoured chests, driving the men backwards off their saddles like sacks of bloody wheat. Their bodies hit the ground with dull thuds that rocked the earth. The cavalry made one determined, steady sweep through the ranks, then the swordplay began.

Long, polished blades swept at legs and heads, and men started screaming in pain and shouting to comrades. Horses reared up with red-rimmed noses, snorting foam. The foot soldiers rushed into the mix, slashing with pikes and swords. The sun glittered brightly on their wet, red blades.

Marcus spotted Sauvage from forty paces away. Sauvage had just clobbered one of the Endshire knights off a horse and spun his own huge, black destrier around when he caught Marcus's eye too. He sat back hard in the saddle and lifted his hands to his chest, pulling the reins tight, his eyes never leaving Marcus. The horse swung around, snorting in fury and pawing the air.

Marcus smiled. Griffyn glanced over Marcus's shoulder and smiled too.

Marcus jerked off his helm and spun to look over his shoulder. Bloody hell.

Hundreds of knights and horses, Sauvage pennants snapping in the wind, were hurtling down the hill towards his army. His entire army. It had been a trap.

The onrushing riders hit the wall of battle like a tidal wave, crashing up against its bloody shores with neighs and snorts and crashing steel. Marcus slammed his helm back on his head and spurred straight through the middle, towards Sauvage, who reined his stallion around in circles on a small rise of land, waiting for him.

"Well done," Marcus said, nodding towards the fresh wave of death to the right.

"I will kill every one of you."

"Call them off," he said shortly. "We have to talk."

Griffyn bent his elbow over the pommel of his saddle and leaned forward. "Every one of you."

"I mean it, Griffyn. Stand them down. I have something. For Guinevere."

Griffyn stared a moment, then stood in his stirrups and waved his arm in the air. His personal guard spurred towards him, Alex at their head. They moved with such triangulated force that the battle split open before them, like a sea parting. They skidded to a halt all around Griffyn. Twelve spears were lowered and aimed directly at Marcus's head. Griffyn spoke rapidly to Alex, then turned back to Marcus.

"You first."

Marcus cuffed his herald on the shoulder and the man bugled the retreat. Sauvage's pages waved flags in the air, and within one minute, the fighting ceased. Each army backed halfway up different sides of the gently sloping hills and stood, panting and sweating, weapons lowered, watching the small figures at the centre of the valley floor.

"Bring Guinevere to us," Griffyn ordered, his eyes never leaving Marcus.

Edmund spun and spurred his horse towards the castle, already hollering for Lady Gwyn.

Gwyn sat in the hall, helping to tear strips of linen into bandages. She only barely kept wrenching sobs at bay. Marcus's army looked strong. Griffyn hated her.

A huge pile of table linens sat on the dais table. Ten or so women were sitting at the table on either side of her, cutting and tearing, speaking in hushed whispers. Children were scattered all around the hall, not speaking, not playing.

A cluster of boys hovered near the door, feinting at one another with pretend swords, looking as though they wanted to run out and join the fray. Three older knights, far past the age of combat, kept them from doing so, primarily by telling stories of older combats, legends that entranced the young boys. Lancelot. Sir Gawain. The Irish god-king Cúchulainn.

Gwyn directed food and drink to be brought out in abundance, although no one was eating. But she had no intention of rationing stores. For what? This was no siege. They would win, and there'd be no need for rationing. Or they would lose, and Gwyn didn't plan on giving Marcus anything that was ripe or tasted good. Truth, she would poison the well herself if he rode under the gates.

A distant rattle drew her head up. It was outside, coming closer, getting louder. Soon, everyone in the great hall noticed it. People started looking around, murmuring.

Gwyn got to her feet. Her heart hammered. A loud crash reverberated through the hall. More clattering, loud, furious and fast, getting louder, coming closer. A shouted command:

"Open!" Another crash, then a horse's whinney that echoed to the rafters of the great hall.

"God in Heaven," she exhaled.

A snorting, sweaty horse appeared at the top of the stairs. Astride sat Edmund, Griffyn's squire. He'd ridden the animal straight up the outer stairwell, a suicidal act, rather than get off and waste the time to run inside.

"Oh no," she whispered. "Please God. Not Griffyn."

Edmund shouted, "Come, my lady! He calls for you."

She took one look at the line of women jamming up the narrow space behind the dais table, then scrambled atop and over the table. She fell to the ground on the other side, stumbled back to her feet, and took off running.

"Go, go, go!" she screamed. "Outside!"

Edmund spun and kicked the horse, who skidded and thumped wide-eyed to the outdoors and back down the stairs, leaping off the last four entirely. Edmund reined around just as Gwyn barreled out. She flung herself down the stairs two and three at a time, just shy of a headfirst plunge down the twenty-foot staircase, until she was only a few feet above Edmund's head. He caught her hand and yanked her off. She landed on the horse's back and they galloped hell-bent for the gates.

The gelding skidded almost sideways to take the turn just after the gates, which would lead them down to the valley. Edmund steadied him with his hands. Gwyn lay low and close to Edmund's back. The horse straightened and, with a kick and shout from Edmund, laid himself out flat for the final mad dash.

Dark clouds had scuttled over the sky. The storm on the horizon thundered ominously. A stab of lightning lit up the western horizon. Gwyn risked a glance over Edmund's shoulder. Would they make it in time? How bad was it? How long did they have? Would her beloved already be—

Standing next to Marcus?

She yelled above the rushing wind into Edmund's ear, "I thought he was dying!"

"Nay, lady," he shouted back, "but he's ready to kill."

She laid her cheek down on his back again and tried to stop from crying in reckless joy. He was alive. He wasn't dead, he wasn't dying. She could handle anything but that.

If she'd only known.

Chapter Twenty-Seven

She stood next to them, her chest still heaving. Marcus was looking at her. Griffyn was not. He stood without moving, staring at the horizon. In truth, he seemed lost in thought, as if this, none of it, mattered anymore.

Her red overtunic blew back in the breeze, revealing the bright yellow linen beneath. Wind tugged at her hair. The scent of the sea was strong today, and it rode under the smell of blood. Time to end this thing.

She pressed her fingertips to her temple, trapping the blowing hair beneath, and turned to Marcus. His eyes were calm, but something hectic lurked beneath their surface. He had sprouted an unkempt beard.

"What are you thinking, Marcus?" she demanded. "What is all this?" She waved at the soldiers. "Have you lost your mind?"

"Aye." He put his foot up on his helm, set on the ground beside him, and grinned quite like a madman. "How is Eustace?"

She shook her head. "You're too late to ruin me, Marcus. I did that myself. Griffyn knows. I told him."

"Oh, good." He glanced at Griffyn, who was still staring at some distant point on the horizon. "Then we can do business. Each of us has something the other wants."

"You have nothing I want," Gwyn snapped.

"Oh no? And only a fortnight ago I was your last hope. Tsk. Well, in any event, I have something Pagan might want."

"What are you talking about?" she asked, when it became clear Griffyn had no intention of opening his mouth. "Please, Marcus, stop. It's over, thank God. I was wrong."

"You *were* wrong, Gwyn, but 'tisn't over. Not yet. At the risk of repeating myself, I say again: I have something your Griffyn wants."

"You don't have anything I want, Marcus," Griffyn finally said without lowering his gaze. "You could kill me, if you dared. I do not care."

"But Guinevere does."

Something chill flowed down her back, and it had nothing to do with the roiling weather.

"You care very much, don't you, Gwyn, what happens to Griffyn? I can see it in your eyes. You'd do almost anything for him. Not *quite* anything, of course." He smiled. "The little treason in his cellars. I got that. But almost anything else. You don't want anything to happen to him, do you?"

"What are you talking about?" she whispered.

He shifted his crafty gaze back to Griffyn's profile. "Henri fitzEmpress is coming."

Gwyn waved this off. "We know that."

"He is riding for the north like the very devil is at his back. I'll wager you didn't know that. He should be here by day's end. Mayhap sooner. He's coming for Everoot."

"Why?" She couldn't even glance sidewise at Griffyn, her agony of self-loathing was so complete.

Marcus affected a baffled expression. "Who knows? Perhaps he got word of some perfidy here in the north."

She looked at him in growing horror. "Oh, Marcus, no. No."

"Did he know of your plan?" Marcus turned to look at Griffyn in mock appraisal. "Did she tell you how I was to hurry Eustace away, from under your nose?"

"Stop talking."

"But I chose a different route, Guinevere. It seemed wise to me to have a few manœvers that even you were not privy to. That, now," he gestured to the battlefield, "seems most wise."

She grabbed the thick mail of his hauberk sleeve. *What have you done?*

"Henri will know of your beloved's treachery, Gwynnie. Hiding the prince in his cellars?" Marcus clucked his tongue in mock dismay. "Henri is forgiving enough with those who've never claimed for him, but your betrothed? His right hand in the field, trusted councilor, esteemed diplomat? Première spy? *Friend*?" Marcus shook his head. "It always hurts most when those closest to us do the evil deeds. Treason is a terrible thing."

She was shaking her head, spilling hair from its case. "No, Marcus. No."

"Rather, I should say it hurts most when one is disemboweled while still alive, dismembered, parts flung to the four corners of the realm. That hurts a great deal."

The only reason Gwyn wasn't weeping was because she was about to scream. Her head was ready to explode with rage and self-hate and unadulterated fear.

Griffyn stood, arms crossed, staring out across the fields and distant forest. He shifted at this, angled his head in Gwyn's direction without actually looking at her. "This matters to you?"

"Of course," she exhaled the words, deep, hot sounds of agony.

Marcus clapped his hands together. "Then let us bargain. I am willing to do business. You want Griffyn safe."

"And what do you want?" she asked wretchedly.

"You."

Gwyn's mouth dropped open. Griffyn finally looked down. Marcus smiled.

"Glad to have your attention. Now," he continued in his

blithe tone, "maybe you"—he looked at Griffyn—"actually do *not* care if you're alive or dead. I do not know. Your father was a wild man, unpredictable, so perhaps it runs in the blood. But while you might not care so much about your living or dying, I have something you care about above all that."

An almost imperceptible shake of Griffyn's head. "You have nothing I want, fitzMiles."

"Oh, but I do. Something meant only for the heirs of Everoot. The one, true Heir."

This finally got a flicker in Griffyn's eye.

Marcus's voice dropped. "You know what I'm talking about, don't you? The thing you've been looking for? Oh, I've heard how you renounced the treasure, and your destiny. But I know you. I know this thing. You've been looking for it, haven't you? I have it, and I will give it to you. If you give me Guinevere."

The winds blew around them, pulling hair from helms and hair bands. Gwyn's skirts flattened against her legs, as if they'd tried to flee but got caught on her knees. She looked at Griffyn. His face was expressionless, but his eyes were furious, wrecked. The muscle beside his jaw ticked. She spun back to Marcus.

"What are you doing to him? What are you talking about? What is this thing?"

Marcus never looked at her. "Tell me, Griffyn: how much is she worth to you?"

Silence, again. It was as if Griffyn were doing battle inside himself, only barely aware of the words being said. Except that his eyes were locked on Marcus, his look murderous.

Gwyn's eyes filled up with hot tears. A year ago, she swore to kill herself before marrying Marcus. She and Griffyn had shared a laugh over it. Now it was Griffyn, not she, who would die if she did not submit. She bent her head.

"I will do it."

She said it so quietly neither man heard at first. For the

moment she was incidental, although she was the chip they were bargaining with, she who had incited this madness. Griffyn's face was impenetrable and hard as stone, but when Gwyn said it again, "I will marry you," he turned to her.

Marcus did too. Many emotions raced across his face, but all of them seemed to make him smile. "I've said it all along, Gwynnie: you're impetuous, but not stupid," he observed with real affection. Gwyn felt astonished at that. "So we have a deal."

"Yes."

"No."

They turned at the sound of Griffyn's voice. For he first time since he he'd learned of her betrayal, he was looking at her, and he didn't break his gaze, even when he said, "Leave us, fitzMiles. She's not marrying you."

Gwyn reached out. Her fingers brushed his arm. "Oh, but Griffyn, I must. They'll hang you if they find out about Eustace."

"There is nothing for you here, Marcus," he said, as if she hadn't spoken. "There's never been anything for you here. And fitzMiles," he added, shifting his gaze to Marcus's flushed face, "by this treason, you've forfeited the lands you hold of Everoot. I disseise thee."

Marcus laughed hoarsely, a little wildly. "Henri fitzEmpress will simply grant me others."

Griffyn's face hadn't changed during the entire interchange, but Gwyn saw the slightest ripple disturb it now. "That will not be my doing," he said softly. "And I answer for my deeds alone."

The mask settled back. His gaze swept to Alex. "If his men haven't left the hills in twenty minutes, kill them all."

He turned on his heel. Gwyn stared around her at the shocked, helmed faces, then took a step to follow him off the field.

But Marcus, master chef of intrigue, had one last sotelty to reveal, one last spectacular, complicated dish to add to this meal of madness Gwyn had helped him deliver to their doorstep.

"You'll never get it open, Sauvage," he called to Griffyn's back. "I have one of the keys."

Gwyn's heart dropped, if possible, another yard. It would be through the gates of Hell soon, where it belonged.

Griffin turned. Marcus lifted a chain from around his neck and held it in the air. On it hung a steel key. Gwyn gasped. She almost leapt forward to snatch it.

Just then, Griffyn lifted a chain from around his own neck. "You mean this?" he said, no inflection in his voice. And from his chain dangled a key, too.

Two keys in fact, one black like iron, the other silver like steel. Marcus's eyes flew wide, then narrowed. He whipped to his right, where de Louth stood, his captain. De Louth closed his eyes briefly.

"You bastard," spat Marcus, the truth dawning in a low, audible hiss. "You had a copy made, when you picked up the chain."

Griffyn met de Louth's eyes. "Your daughter: you should send her to me now. Come yourself, if you choose. You have a livery here for life."

Then he turned and walked off.

All around her, the huge Sauvage destriers started to move forward, pushing Marcus's forces back up the hill.

She shivered and hurried to Griffyn's side. "What is it? What does Marcus have?"

"A vessel," he said tonelessly.

"No," shouted Marcus to his back. "*Guinevere* is the Vessel. God's truth, didn't you know?" He gave a bark of mad laughter, and Griffyn drew to a halt. "At least my father taught me that much. The women who tend the roses are the Vessels. But that you don't know *that*?" He laughed again. "That means you haven't found the Hallows, yet, have you?"

Griffyn started walking.

Gwyn stared at Marcus's unfolding fury and madness. He stood, boot atop his helm, one arm crossed over his chest, the opposite elbow resting on his wrist, fingers pressed into his unkempt beard. Motionless. Smiling. "What Hallows?" she demanded.

He grinned. "Your father's little chest, Gwynnie? Remember that?"

Griffyn's step hitched.

"Your Griffyn wants it, Gwyn," Marcus called out, still grinning. *"Badly."*

"Please, Griffyn," she said, catching up to him again. "Let me go to him. 'Twill be madness if I stay. Every time you look at me, you'll remember. Every word I say will be suspect. Let me go."

He down looked at her from his cold, terrible heights. "No."

Tears burned at the back of her eyes, hot and painful. Her exhale came in a short, thrusting out-breath. "Saint Jude, Griffyn, let me go. *You'll be killed!* I can save you."

"No."

He did not wave her off, did not invite her closer. She was walking at his side and it was as if she was a thousand miles away.

Chapter Twenty-Eight

"So this *is* it," Griffyn said. He and Alex stood in the lord's chamber hours later, after the horses were rubbed down, the injured tended, the soldiers fed, and the children comforted. They were both staring at the small carved Guinevere chest, which is how he thought of it now, sitting square in the centre of the table.

Apparently; he *could* trust himself.

The sun was getting ready to set, not that one could tell from this side of the castle. On this northeastern side, the storm clouds were lowering, grey-edged and sullen, pumping across the sky. Griffyn walked away from the chest and threw another square of peat on the brazier. It flared into life, crackling.

"'I think I ne'er truly believed," he said.

Alex nodded. "Many thought your father waited too long to tell you about your destiny. The deathbed is no good place to lay such a burden on a young soul, for many reasons."

Griffyn pushed the coals and new fuel about, coaxing it into a hotter burn. "I once would have claimed my father did so because he wanted it all for himself. Trying to live forever."

"And now?"

"Now." He threw down the poker and sat back at the table. "Now I think he took me away from it. To protect me from the things it did to men. The things it did to him." He picked up the letters and trinkets scattered inside and laid them on the table. The tarnished ring, the scrap of reddish-purple linen, the blade hilt, the lock of hair, the coins.

"I know what you did, Alex," he said quietly.

There was a pause. "Pagan?" He could hear confusion and tension, spiraling together in Alex's voice.

"Did you know I have this?" Griffyn asked, and held up the steel key.

He heard Alex's breath suck in. "Where did you get it?"

"Same place you tried. De Louth."

Stillness descended behind him. If he wished to, Alex could simply whack him on the back of the head and be done with it.

"What did you plan to do with it, Alex, if you got hold of it?"

He heard Alex's boots thud as he came around. His face was bleached white. "I'd like to say, 'give it to you.'"

Griffyn leaned back, spine against the wall. "Yes. I'd like that too."

Alex grabbed a bench and dragged it near. He sat down, one leg on either side, leaning deeply forward. "There's so much I haven't told you, Pagan—"

"I know. Why not?"

Alex wiped his hand over the top of his head. "At first, 'twas simply that you did not want to know. Were rather *militant* in your wishing not to know, for many years."

"That I was. But you're supposed to be my protection, are you not, Alex? A Watcher?"

"Aye, we Watch, Griffyn. And protect. But we are protecting you, so you can protect the treasure. We are oath-bound to protect the treasure."

"Not me?" Griffyn said, but it wasn't a question.

Alex stood stiffly at the unspoken accusation of betrayal. "I am your friend, Pagan. I will always be your friend. I need no vow to make that so."

"And yet, you lied to me. Why did you not tell me you thought you had found one of the puzzle keys?"

"Because I couldn't be sure you were going to be a good Guardian," Alex burst out. "Good?" he added, then gave a short bark of laughter and began pacing the room. "I did not even know whether you would become one at all. You inherit the Blood, but the burden, as you said yourself, has to be chosen. No one can give it to you, or force it upon you. You must accept it." He stopped by the west-facing window and looked over. "I didn't know if you would."

Their eyes held. Griffyn nodded, accepting the indictment. "And?"

Alex's gaze flickered in confusion. "And what?"

"And why else didn't you tell me about the key?"

Alex flushed. He ran his hand over the wide window ledge, then over his mouth and chin, hard. "I don't know," he said. "'Twas a thing I liked, knowing, being the one who knew. The gatekeeper, I suppose."

"The power."

Alex nodded and looked over. "You didn't take me to Ipsile. You took Fulk instead. Why?"

Griffyn shrugged. "I suspected before then. De Louth just confirmed it."

"How did you know?"

He shrugged again. "You were too insistent, cared too much what I did with it. That's what it does. I don't need to be its scholar to know what it does. It makes men care about things that don't matter. It takes our souls."

The brazier fire had caught fully now, and its little flicking flames brightened the darkening room. Griffyn shifted. Took men's souls, indeed. How close he had come. Once the seed of desire had been watered the slightest bit, it sprouted like a weed. How long had he been at the Nest? Just shy of three weeks, and within two days he'd been chasing rumours of it halfway across the shire. Leaving Guinevere the space to do what she had done.

He smiled bitterly. "Perhaps our family isn't strong enough to guard this thing anymore. No one seems to have considered that."

The thick dye of Alex's blue surcoat absorbed the flickering brazier light as he shook his head firmly. "You are the proof that isn't so, Griffyn."

"Damning proof, methinks."

"You rejected it. On the battlefield, when given a choice, you let it go."

"I fail to see how that could keep it safe."

Alex sighed. "I fail to see any other way to do so."

Griffyn's eyebrows arched up. "So that's the test? To have it, you must reject it?"

"It depends on the choice each Guardian is given. That was yours." He swallowed. "No one else could do it, reject it. I couldn't."

Griffyn leaned forward, elbows on his knees. He stared at the small Guinevere chest. "My father thought there was something about the treasure that could make him live forever." He shifted his gaze to Alex. "Is there?"

"Maybe."

Griffyn nodded. He moved his elbow to the table and dropped his forearm across the tabletop. His fingers just barely touched the edge of the small, ornately carved chest. He let out a long breath.

"So, what now?" Alex said. "I mean, about me."

"What do you think?"

Alex stood still, his back rigid, his head down. Hoarsely, he said, "I think I made a mistake. I think I forgot you were my lord. My friend. I think I came too close. I know I am sorry."

Griffyn nodded. He interlaced his fingers and leaned forward, peering at the ground between his knees.

"I mean it, Pagan. It won't happen again."

He looked up. "I know. I won't let it."

Alex bowed his head. "My lord."

He reached out again to trace the worn wooden carvings on the small Guinevere chest with his fingertips. Abruptly, he sat back.

"So, I'm not to have a traitor's death?" Alex asked, quite seriously.

Griffyn smiled a little. "No."

"And you're not turning me out?" he asked, his voice cracking.

Griffyn shook his head.

"Nor Guinevere?"

He shook again.

Alex exhaled. "I would think you would want the two of us far away. You're keeping closest the ones who've betrayed you."

"I'm keeping closest the ones who've made mistakes, and know it." He looked at the chest. "I may need to be reminded of that from time to time."

Alex laughed bitterly. "Of what? That people are flawed?"

He shook his head and got to his feet. "That redemption is possible."

Gwyn was speaking with Fulk just outside the third-floor solar door. He'd been set as the guard outside her door, or rather he'd set himself there. The landing was dark, both from the late evening hour and the storm outside. Rain pelted the leaded windows.

"Lord Griffyn is not going to hurt me," Gwyn had protested, half laughing, the first glimmer of unburdened amusement in her life in a long time.

"I know, milady." Fulk straightened his tunic and cleared his throat. "'Tis just that, I'd rather stay close by."

Gwyn smiled. "Fulk, if I were a better woman, I'd marry you."

He hemmed and hawed and blushed. "Nothing to it, my lady. I've just been at protectin' ye for so long, t'would feel strange to stop now."

She leaned her shoulder against the doorway, unwilling to go inside and shut the door. And yet, she planned to stay up here until she heard from Griffyn, one way or another. Send her to a nunnery, to Marcus, to plead her case with Henri fitzEmpress. Whatever he wanted, she would do, if it meant being outlawed to Palestine. But for now, the storm outside was kicking up, things were dark, and she didn't want to close herself up in the room just yet.

"I think I know what Papa wanted, Fulk. I think he wanted Griffyn to have the chest."

"Well, sure he did."

She looked at him as if he'd just told her he was studying to be an alchemist. "Why, Fulk. Why didn't you tell me that before?"

"I had no idea ye were wondering about it," he retorted with an identical level of indignant surprise. "I had no idea ye thought 'twas anything but a chest."

"I didn't, really. Don't. And now Marcus has it. Whatever it is."

Fulk gruffed. "I wouldn't worry much, my lady. Pagan'll see everything he needs is brought home again."

She opened her mouth to say more, then shook her head. "Whatever was, doesn't matter anymore. We will simply wait and see what tomorrow brings."

"Aye, milady."

She leaned her shoulder against the doorframe, and Fulk leaned his back against the wall. They stared at the far window. The storm was crashing and kicking at the walls, much like that night a year back, when she'd fallen into love with Griffyn at the storm-tossed inn.

"Yes, don't you see?" she said thoughtfully. "'Wud. Guh. Saw.' I thought it meant something about 'giving.' Giving the

chest, of course. It must be. 'Griffyn Sauvage.' 'Give Sauvage.'"
She paused. "I don't quite understand the 'wud,' of course."

   "Wed."

   Gwyn's head turned slowly. "What?"

   "'Wed Griffyn Sauvage.'"

Chapter Twenty-Nine

She stood in the antechamber outside the lord's chamber. Edmund was looking at her beseechingly. Despite all the trauma and drama of the last days, his naïve earnestness was a light balm over her mood.

"Can you make it a'right, my lady?"

She laid a hand on his shoulder and smiled. "I will do my best." She glanced at the chamber door. "You go get some food, Edmund. And find my scribe. Have him teach you a few notes on the dulcimer." She smiled. "We need some music in this keep, Edmund. Do you not think?" He nodded vigorously. "Can you make me some?"

He puffed out his chest. "Rest assured, my lady," he promised, and hurried off.

She took a breath, turned, and rapped her knuckles lightly on the oaken door of the inner bedchamber. "My lord," she called, her voice raised slightly. "'Tis I."

There was a pause. The door swung open. Alex stood there, his body slightly to the side.

"Come in."

They stared at each other for half a moment, adversaries in some sudden truce, then she nodded and swept past him, into her bedroom. Griffyn looked up.

His hair was damp, sticking up in damp, dark spikes, and he was clad in chausses and a linsey-woolsey tunic. Its soft material draped against his hard stomach and over his powerful thighs, almost to the knee. He was sitting at the small table they'd played chess on so many nights, where he'd laid out manuscripts, where he once laid out her body.

From some reservoir she didn't know existed, more tears sprung up. She looked at the ceiling, pain pinching her nose. Hadn't she already wept herself dry?

"Come in, Guinevere." His deep masculine rumble drew her into the room more than his words. She took a few tentative steps forwards.

"My lord. I do not mean to disturb. I came only to—Why, you have Papa's chest!" she cried softly.

"Aye."

"When did you find it? Where? I thought Marcus had . . ."

Griffyn's chest expanded with a deep inward breath. "I found it a over a week ago."

She considered the various implications of this. "And you didn't tell me?"

"No." His eyes met hers. "I am sorry."

Her hand shot up, warding off the apology. "Please. Don't. Don't apologise to me. Whatever was, it matters naught anymore."

In the shadows behind him stood Alex. So be it. Everything was up to Griffyn now. She reached out and touched the box. "So beautiful," she murmured, then looked up. "Did you find Papa's letters inside?"

"I found *my* father's letters."

"What?"

He nodded.

She shook her head. "But why? Why would Papa have given it to me to protect if it wasn't—." She stopped herself and sat back with a thud. "Of course. The chest must be yours.

Your family's. Not mine. It belongs to Everoot, and we," she laughed bitterly, "were never Everoot."

"You are now."

Her eyes were filling up with tears. "Not yet," she said in a brittle, bright voice. "Our nuptials are not until the morn. And perhaps Henri will have off with my head before then."

"Henri will not have off with our head. You did no treachery. To him."

She stared at the table, her fingers closing around the edge of it. Splinters bit into the skin under her nails. "I will do whatever you wish me to, Griffyn. Nothing is as it was, and I know nothing anymore. Except," she added with certainty, "this is what Marcus was talking about. This chest. Whatever you needed, or wanted, 'tis in here." She tapped its lid.

"I know."

She looked at him, sitting there, his eyes unreadable, watching her. It brought a shiver down her spine. Not sexual, not fear. Just, shivery. "May I ask something, Griffyn?"

"Guinevere," he said in a low voice, "now is not the time to be timid. You may ask whatsoever you wish. As you say, what was, is no longer."

She was nodding in agreement, in support, in anything that would keep him talking to her and looking at her and being in any way remotely connected to her, but his next words brought her up short.

"The lies must stop. Yours. Mine."

She stopped mid-nod, her chin down. Her eyebrows went up. "You lied?"

He swept his hand in the air over the table, indicating the chest and assorted baubles. "I lied."

She exhaled a shaky laugh. "That hardly counts."

"Oh," he said grimly, "it counts."

Scattered across the table were things she'd picked up and held too many times to count, remnants of only God knew what, rings and scraps of fabric, a lock of hair, and the letters she could never read. Now, the leather thong Griffyn always wore around his neck was curled on the table too, its little iron key knotted at the end. Beside it sat the steel one.

She reached out to touch it. "The steel one. How?" She looked up. "How . . . ?"

"De Louth."

She almost laughed. *"What?"*

Griffyn glanced at Alex. "De Louth gave it to me."

"Marcus's most vile henchman gave you the key I lost a year ago in London?" she clarified in amazement.

"He did. He had a child. She'll be coming here, in a few years."

She did laugh now, a brief breath of amazement. "But of course. People come to you, Griffyn, with everything open. Of course he had a child and gave you a key. Of course."

She touched them briefly. "So, you have two keys."

"He *is* the key," said Alex from the shadows.

"I don't know what that means," she said shortly. She didn't care, either. Griffyn's grey gaze was on her. The planes of his face were lit by firelight and shadows. Somehow, without moving, he permeated a room, and she'd lost him. Given him away.

"There's a locked compartment beneath," she said in a shaky voice. "You cannot see it, but there, at the edge." She reached forward, pointing.

The room went completely silent. She looked up slowly into Griffyn's stunned eyes.

"What?" His voice was harsh and incredulous. She nodded.

"Have you seen inside, Guinevere?" Even more incredulity was in these words.

"Of course."

He sat forward sharply in his chair. "How did you ever do that?"

She shrugged. "Once, when I was young, I found this same

little chest and was playing with it. The bottom compartment just sprang open. Papa almost died of horror when he found me. He warned me off in no uncertain terms, and I never saw it again until the day he died."

She swallowed carefully. "After that, in those awful days, Marcus was ever underfoot, marauding about, hinting at treasures. And weddings. I tried everything I could to open this chest. I don't know, it just seemed important. And important that Marcus not even know it existed. I even tried holding a fiery hot poker stick to it, to burn it open. Nothing. You can see, it's not even scorched.

"Then, one night, I was exhausted, touching it—it is so beautiful," she said again, softly, "and suddenly I recalled what I'd done as a child. I put my hand just so," she splayed her fingers wide in demonstration, and placed them inside the chest, "and felt around, and pushed, and—"

The lid of the secret compartment sprang open.

Alex inhaled sharply. She looked up. Griffyn was watching her. "Disobedience has some small boons," she said ruefully.

Something like a smile lightened the measured remove on his face. "I must admit, I ne'er did view disobedience as quite the sin the Church does."

A small vestige of him came back in that moment. It was like fresh air moving through a sickroom. She smiled, close to tears. "No, Griffyn. You wouldn't."

He was brilliant to her. A bright, shining light. Excellent, without flaw, even amid his mistakes. Scarred face, sinful body, beautiful heart, he simply took her breath away.

And she had no right to it anymore.

"Is that what you needed, then?" she asked, keeping her voice carefully neutral. "To know what was underneath?"

The smile faded from his face. "Aye."

He slid his thumb under the flipped-up edge. All three of them leaned forward. For no reason she could explain,

Gwyn held her breath as he lifted the lid and revealed what was within.

"More documents," he said hoarsely, and closed his eyes. "It's not here."

Alex flung himself backwards against the wall, cursing. His boots cracked small stones underfoot as he turned and paced the room. Gwyn looked between them in amazement. "What? What is the matter?"

"The third key."

"A third key?"

"We need another key."

Bleak conviction dulled his words, but Gwyn's heart started beating faster. She leaned forward.

"I have a key. A little golden one."

Griffyn's grey eyes opened onto her, his gaze burning a path through the space between them like fire through a forest. She nodded, feeling giddy, and reached for the nondescript pouch sewn directly onto her skirts.

Every morning she performed this ritual, sewing the pouch to her skirts, ensuring the last thing her father had bequeathed to her stayed safe. Within its brown folds huddled the minuscule key her father placed in her hand on his deathbed. It was covered to both hide and protect its golden glow. For glow it did, as if burnished by the sun.

With trembling fingers, she ripped it from her skirts and dropped it into Griffyn's calloused palm.

His eyes held hers a moment, then his fingers closed around it. He swept up the two keys already on the table, one black, one silver, and pushed them together. They joined with a satisfying click. He fitted her little gold one into the centre of them, so it created a tri-colour puzzle key. The silver key sat inside the dark exterior of gnarled iron, looking like a silver lining on the inside of a storm cloud. Her key, gold at the centre of it all, glowed like the end of a rainbow.

"God above," Alex murmured.

"'Tis beautiful," breathed Gwyn.

Griffyn let out a long breath.

"And now?" Gwyn asked, looking up. "What now?"

Griffyn shook his head. "I have no idea."

She gestured to the chest, the scrolls still sitting in the hidden compartment. "What are those?"

Slowly they shifted their attention. Griffyn picked one up.

"Vellum," he said. Expensive. But the next one he lifted shocked her into a gasp.

"Is that copper?" she murmured, her mouth going dry. "What are they?"

Griffyn's face was a study in wonder. *"Maps."*

"Maps?"

He held up a handful of vellum sheets and a few in metal that looked like bronze.

She looked at them blankly. "What kind of maps?"

"Treasure maps," murmured Alex.

Gywn bent over the tabletop. She could indeed discern squiggly lines on some of the documents that might well mark the end of land masses or the beginning of waterways. She caught a brief glimpse of images of mythical animals, bright, vibrant colours, explosive lettering, and something that almost smelled of musty herbs and dew, ancient mystery.

She looked at Griffyn as he bent over the papers, his lips moving silently as he read the Latin script she'd recognized from the monks' manuscripts, unable to fathom the sense of destiny riding up her spine, filling her body with freshness and no small measure of fear.

"What is all this?" she whispered. "Who are you?"

"Charlemagne's heir." Alex's voice came from the shadows.

She looked over. "What does that mean?" she demanded. "What will it do to him?"

Griffyn's gaze lifted from the papers and held hers, but the look was unreadable. Another shiver brushed down her spine.

It was the sheer majesty of him, masked but palpable, that took her breath away.

Again, it was Alex who replied. "It means he has the burden and privilege of guarding treasures over a thousand years in the making," he said in a voice that would have carried to Henri's army, perched three leagues away, as if he'd waited Griffyn's whole life to say it aloud. "It means that while some claim to fight for God, what they truly claim is glory, and greed, while others, in secret, have the burden of protecting the true wealth of our collective souls. It means Griffyn's blood is the royal purple, in a way that cannot be bred anymore. It means he is noble and worthy. Guardian of the Hallows."

Gwyn looked at Griffyn, feeling desperate. "What Hallows? What hallowed things?"

"The Arc of the Covenant. The Amra Christi, Instruments of the Crucifixion. The Spear of Destiny. The Shroud of Turin."

It was Griffyn now who spoke, and his words came out like a chanted dirge, low and rhythmic, and made the hair on the back of Gwyn's neck stand up. "The Sudarium, the face cloth that covered Jesus's face. The Crown of Thorns."

Chills moved in shock waves down Gwyn's spine. Griffyn stopped, but Alex named one more, looking straight at Griffyn. "The Marian Chalice."

Gwyn's blood washed cold. *"The Holy Grail?"*

Alex almost shrugged. "He is Charlemagne's Heir. He is the Heir."

She stared at Griffyn, her lips parted as she tried to remember how to breathe. Yes, she could believe he was a child of kings. The hard, chiseled features of his face were anguished enough to hold such a burden. His eyes were complicated enough. Certainly his soul was wrecked enough, if that's what it took.

And she'd betrayed him.

The room, Griffyn's face, became difficult to see as the

tears filled up and flowed from her eyes. She bent her head and stretched her hand across the table. If he didn't want it, her, all he had to do was remain still. Or leave.

She waited. She heard bootsteps walking away. The door clicked shut. A single hard sob wracked her body.

Then Griffyn's hand closed on top of hers.

Her breath shot out in a jagged, gasping rush. Her forehead fell onto the length of her outstretched arm.

"I've no words, Griffyn," she cried, not trying to hide her sobs now. "My sorrow goes deeper than a well. I never meant for you to be hurt. It all went so wrong. Nothing matters to me but that you never get hurt again."

"'Twasn't only yourself."

She sniffled. "What are you talking about?"

"I lied, too."

She exhaled a short, sharp breath. It could have been a laugh, only there was nothing amusing. Probably never would be again. Then again, his hand was still lying atop hers, warm.

She lifted her head, her eyes puffy and hot. "That doesn't matter, Griffyn."

"I knew treasure was here," he continued, as if she hadn't spoken. "I knew the legends. I knew the truth. I knew people would hunt for it. I found a chest you thought was your father's, and I did not tell you. I rode for Ipsile-upon-Tyne to find a treasure, and I did not tell you. I knew all those things, and I didn't tell you, and that put us in danger."

"No! No, you didn't put me in danger—"

"*Us.* Us, in danger, and aye, you alone, too. I did it here, I did when I left you at the Saxon village, I did when I let you walk away from me into Saint Alban's Abbey, alone. I have put you in danger over and over again, when it has served my ends. I abandoned you, and I lied to you, and I am sorry."

She shook her head so vehemently hair fell all around her shoulders. "No, Griffyn. You cannot say you're sorry. Not to me."

"I am doing it. And I have more." He half-rose, reached across the table, cupped her face in one of his hands and whispered: "I forgive you. I forgive you. I forgive you."

Her breath exploded out in a gulping sob. She slid off the bench, to her knees, and laid her head in his lap, crying for the simple words she'd longed to hear her whole life, and to hear them now, from this good man, broke down all her barriers. She wept like a river. Wracking, hard sobs, quaking her body.

After a time, she became aware of his hand, gently stroking her head. She reached up blindly and touched his face. He held out his arms, for her to climb into his lap. She rose and swung one leg on each side, straddling him, her face a few inches above his. Her hair fell down around them like a cocoon. Griffyn rested his hands on her hips.

"And now, you tell me you forgive me too," he said hoarsely, like he needed to hear it. She shook her head.

"No matter what you say, there's nothing you've done that needs forgiving. But I will give you something I think you need more." She leaned close and whispered just above his lips, "I love you. I love you. I love you."

A corner of his mouth lifted and he leaned his forehead into hers. They sat that way for a long time, his hands on her hips, her forearms slung long over his shoulders, her hair falling like a dark curtain around them. His breath was unsteady for some of the time, hitching here and there, then it calmed and grew steady again. His thighs were powerful beneath her legs.

"Isn't there a bridge around here that needs defending?" she asked softly.

His hand tightened on her hips, then slid up her ribs. "Truth," he muttered, his words rough-edged. "We do know each other from the inside out."

"Let's be gentle."

"Indeed."

By now, the sun was starting to come up. The storm had spent itself. Bright, crisp, yellow light streamed though the eastern window. They were quiet for the longest time, their foreheads still touching.

"Henri will be here soon," she murmured. "I'll make sure you . . ." Her voice faded away. She had nothing left to finish the sentence with. She would what?

"Do not worry on Henri's account."

"I worry on *your* account," she replied with a shaky laugh.

"Henri and I have a long history, Gwyn. He knows me. I am not worried."

She blew out a breath of air.

"Tell me you love me again," he murmured against her neck.

"I love you again."

His fingertips stroked down her back.

"We'll be husband and wife in a few hours," she observed in a quiet voice.

He entwined their fingers and kissed them, one by one. "We already are."

Epilogue

Rain washed over the little church like a sparkling waterfall throughout the marriage ceremony. Henri fitzEmpress had arrived, his explosive Angevin temper in fine display, but, as Griffyn had known, his mind was sharper than his tongue, and he quickly stopped breathing fire when he heard the particulars.

And so they sat, afterwards, in the great hall, talking and drinking while the celebration unfurled around them. "She's smart," Henri observed. "And full of spirit. That's how I like them. But you'll have to watch her."

"No I won't." Griffyn lifted his wine cup towards Henri's, in toast. "But you'll surely have to watch Lady Eleanor."

Henri roared in laughter and smashed their cups together. "Indeed I shall. We've chosen women with strength of mind."

Griffyn grimaced good-naturedly. "That's one thing to call it."

He set down his cup and looked around the hall. People were everywhere, standing in small groups, talking and laughing. A minstrel sat beside the dais, strumming and singing softly to a small group. Later, he would sing to all, tales of fierce monsters and brave knights and newly wedded, warring Houses whose union would bring peace to the land.

Guinevere sat at the edge of the dais, encircled by children. She looked to be telling a story. He smiled faintly. The children sat, their little red lips parted in anticipation, rapt as they watched her bright face and slender hands move, spinning out a tale.

Henri's voice broke in. "You've made a good start here, Pagan. The people are happy, and well fed, and that will go a long way."

"That's been Guinevere's doing."

"Maybe. Everoot will be a good bulwark here in the north." Henri turned back and said bluntly, "There's rumours, Pagan."

Griffyn had known it would come. "About what?" he said.

Henri watched him over the rim of his pewter wine cup, reflecting ice-blue eyes on the metal. "Treasure."

Griffyn nodded slowly and met Henri's shrewd gaze. "My liege, know this: everything you need to know, you will know. Everything due you, you will have. Everoot stands true."

Henri considered him for a long minute, evidently weighing whether to allow the deflection, when treasure might be at stake. But something stayed him.

Perhaps a covert knowledge, passed down from a grandfather who had once given up rich Angevin lands to marry a witch and become King of Jerusalem. Perhaps a fringe sense of awareness, the sort that had him already talking about granting the Knights Templar rich lands throughout England.

Or perhaps it was the realisation that a treasure lying buried in the ground was not half as valuable as the treasure of a strong alliance. Whatever it was, Henri nodded.

"Aye. Everoot will stand true. I know that. Or at least," he lifted his cup again, "*you* will."

Griffyn bent his head. "My lord."

Later that night, he sat on the bed and watched Guinevere's sated, sleeping body stretched out on the furs beside him. No nightmares, no restless tossing. Just a faint smile crossing her face for a brief moment as she dreamed. If he had any part in giving her that, that was enough.

No, he admitted a moment later. Not quite enough. He

tugged the furs up by her shoulders and turned away. He had an obligation to at least read through the documents inside the Guinevere chest.

He gathered the scrolls together and sat on the edge of their bed, reading, while Gwyn slept by his side. He bent over them, scouring the Latin and Hebrew with his rusty memory, the candlelight flaming bright by his face. He quickly realised not all of the papers were maps. One, in fact, appeared to be instructions.

He bent further, his lips moving slowly, silently, for an hour or more. He was so intent on translation, in fact, that when the truth of the words sprang clear, he almost fell off the bed in amazement. Then he burst out laughing.

Gwyn lifted her head. "Griffyn?" she asked, her voice soft and sleepy.

"Do you know?"

"Know what?"

Griffyn gestured to the papers. "What I'm supposed to do with it?"

"The treasure?" She pushed herself onto her elbows. The sheets had pressed small pink creases onto her cheeks. "Alex said that only the Heirs know, the Guardians."

"I may be the Heir, but I haven't been a true Guardian. But now," he gestured again to the paper, "now, to know this? Yes. I choose the burden. I will become a Guardian."

Gwyn looked away. He could only see the top of her head. She lifted her hand to her chest, fingers still wrapped around the sheet.

"Gwyn?"

"You will be leaving, then. I'll see to your things first thing in the morning."

He looked at her in surprise. "Why?"

One long, slender finger loosed from the sheets to point at the documents and maps strewn across the bed. "You have to find those, is that it? You must find the Hallows."

He smiled faintly. "Not quite."

She squinted at him. He looked really quite pleased. He was reading those papers, and he looked pleased. She pushed herself up to sit. "What do you mean?"

"I don't have to find them. I know where they are."

Her eyes narrowed suspiciously. "Where?"

"Downstairs."

She felt the blood drain from her face.

"I'll show you."

She dressed hurriedly, dumbfounded, and followed him down the curving dark staircase, into the cellars. Their boots crushed small pebbles as they went, each holding a lantern aloft, Gwyn behind. The sounds of grit and tense breathing scraped against the stone-cased silence of the cellars, but Griffyn was surprised to find his heart was beating normally. Knowing what he knew now, he felt . . . free.

They stopped before the doorway where Eustace had been hidden. He pushed Gwyn's small little key into the dragon's mouth, and it dropped open. Swept clean of anything resembling straw or treachery, it looked like what it was meant to be: an antechamber.

He held up the lantern and pointed to the far wall. There, marked by a small rift in the stone, was a door. Another door carved out of the stone itself. Another huge door, towering above their heads. A door that would be completely hidden, if someone didn't already know it was there. Rock itself, it blended so well with the stone around it that it looked no different. It would stay concealed if Attila's armies came crashing through the gates of Everoot.

It must flow in the blood, he thought. He'd never seen it before, only read about it in the ancient texts upstairs, yet it was as familiar as his father's face. He felt with his fingers along the edges, sweeping away decades or more of dust and dirt and cobwebs, until the outline of a huge, stone carved door was clearly visible.

"I never knew it," Gwyn murmured behind him in a reverent tone.

He pressed the tri-colour puzzle key together again and slid it into a smooth, flat keyhole at the edge. Again, he'd never have known if he hadn't just read about it upstairs. And yet, it felt so familiar. Then he placed both palms against the cold rock and pushed.

Hung in these dark, damp cellars, the hinges should have been rusty and creak like old bones. But the door swung open soundlessly. A gust of cold, old air raced out from the echoing recesses, like a cloud of fluttering wings. Gwyn drew a sharp intake of air.

He turned and tipped his head to the side. "You've always liked adventures, Raven."

She laughed shakily. "You're wrong about that. I abhor adventure. It simply keeps finding me."

"No. *I* keep finding you."

She reached for his hand. "I love you."

Instead of taking her hand, he smiled and thrust a lantern in her palm. "Come." He turned and strode into the midnight darkness of the cavern, his own lantern held high in the air.

Gwyn took a steadying breath, pushed her foot over the rounded wooden threshold, and plunged into darkness.

It was like climbing into a silent, echoing catacomb. It surged straight through the underbelly of the earth, its rounded walls dripping with a wetness, coating the rock with moist slime. By torchlight, she could make out the etchings on the walls, strange and fantastical imagery that demanded awe and no little dose of fear.

She had a very dim memory just now; it flitted through her mind like a little bat. She'd been here once before. Very young. Her father had said something about these etchings. Said they had been painted long ago, the rock transported from far away. He never told her more than that, whether because he didn't know or didn't want *her* to know, Gwyn had no idea. But why would someone move *rock*?

A small spot of light coming from Griffyn's lantern flickered ahead in the distance, as he strode ahead, confident in the darkness. His face was lit up in relief, his cheekbones and nose, his determined, focused eyes. He paused, tipping his flame forward, until more pinpricks of light blazed forth here and there. He'd come into a chamber. She hurried forward as fast as she dared.

Torches hung on the wall and a lantern on a far table, set up almost like a monk's copyist desk. The tiny embers snapped to attention on cobwebbed wicks, then blazed into bright, confident flames that illuminated the entire room.

"Jésu wept," she said on an exhale.

Treasure.

A huge, long, broken sword hung on the wall. A pile of small vessels were lumped together on the desk, alongside a bejeweled belt and plain wooden goblet. Treasure. Not so many in number, but she felt like she was being blinded by the force of them, pushed against. To the wall, to the edge of the earth.

She put a shaking hand over her mouth. Griffyn's steady grey gaze was waiting when she looked his way.

"And what—" Her voice caught. "And what are you supposed to do with it all?"

Something like amusement flickered across his face. "I do believe I'm supposed to give it away."

Her hand dropped. "*What?* What about the maps? Aren't they . . . treasure maps?"

"Some. I'm supposed to return the treasures."

She stared. "To whom?"

"The world."

Gwyn nodded weakly and lowered herself into the copyist's seat before her knees gave out entirely. "I see. No, I don't. *When* are they to be returned?" She wiped her hand over her forehead. "Where? *Why?* I don't understand."

Griffyn's face was illuminated by the flickering light. "Charlemagne's Heir has reparations to make," he said simply. "Although I could never have guessed 'twould be this."

She stared at the ancient treasures. "It's so beautiful," she murmured, then looked at Griffyn. "A burden."

He shook his head. "No. Not anymore. Not if they're to be given away."

Gwyn closed her eyes. "When?"

He shook his head. "I don't know. At the right time, the right place. I have to read more, learn more. No, probably not now." He glanced at the treasures, then back to Gwyn. "I suspect our children will be Guardians for generations to come. But one day, when 'tis time, the treasures will be given back."

"How? How will you know? Who will decide where and when?"

"I don't know. It will, I assume, become clear to the ones who are living in the times. Should we be faced with a choice in our time, Guinevere, you and I will decide what to do, and how."

She backed up a step. "Us? I cannot intrude there, Griffyn. You are the Guardian."

"You were, too." He considered her pale face. "Would you leave it to me alone?"

Her eyes swam with tears. Her slim, cool fingers closed around his hand, like silver filigree on a crown. "Not if the whole world came riding for me would I leave your side," she whispered. "Not if you would have me there."

He pulled her to his chest, his arms wrapped around her body, a body so packed with good intent and strength and honour that she took his breath away, and Griffyn knew he had the greatest treasure of all.

He bent over her lips. "Before all others, Guinevere, I would have you. If I were offered a queen, I would choose you. If I were offered no pain, I would choose you. If every choice in the world were laid out before me, I would choose the you amid them all. I choose you above all other things."

Author's Note

There really *was* a Prince Eustace, the eldest son of King Stephen. And, according to the chroniclers, he really *was* brutal and in the end, when it became clear he would never be king, he became lethal. He led his own personal retinue on a murderous, burning, plundering spree, laying waste to the countryside for weeks, including the abbey at St. Edmunds, a saint known for his lack of humour and his fierce protectiveness.

Eustace seems to have suffered St. Edmund's wrath when, a few days later, he died 17 August 1153 due to a surfeit of lamprey eels. Or perhaps it was the rich food mixed with bitter anger. Whatever the recipe, it was perhaps a fitting end for a man who, for altogether different reasons, may have made as poor a king as his gallant father had.

Still, I always wondered . . . what would have happened if Eustace *hadn't* died that hot August day? If people only thought he died. If someone was made responsible for the care of this brutal prince, while the kingdom collapsed around her?

Regarding the betrothal . . . technically, if two people made *verba de furturo*, vows to be wed at some later point ('I *will* take thee' instead of 'I *do* take thee'), but followed that by consummation, they were, in the eyes of the Church, legally wed. I played rather loose with that in this story, as I needed Griffyn to be decisive in claiming what was his, but also needed Marcus to make one last stand for the thing that mattered most to him— or perhaps, the thing that mattered most and *that he had a chance of every securing*—because he would never have the Nest, and he would never be the Heir. And he would never have his father's love.

I love the sweeping, dangerous feel of the Middle Ages. If you do too, please come visit my Web site and let me know! *www.kriskennedy.net.*